The WAR of the WORLDS

Taking the Red Pill
Science, Philosophy and Religion in The Matrix

Seven Seasons of Buffy
Science Fiction and Fantasy Writers
Discuss Their Favorite Television Show

Five Seasons of Angel
Science Fiction and Fantasy Writers
Discuss Their Favorite Vampire

What Would Sipowicz Do?
Race, Rights and Redemption in NYPD Blue

The Anthology at the End of the Universe
Leading Science Fiction Authors on Douglas Adams'
The Hitchhiker's Guide to the Galaxy

Finding Serenity
Anti-Heroes, Lost Shepherds and Space Hookers
in Joss Whedon's Firefly

Fresh Perspectives On The
H. G. Wells Classic

The WAR of the WORLDS

H. G. Wells

ESSAYS EDITED BY
GLENN YEFFETH

BENBELLA BOOKS
DALLAS, TEXAS

BenBella Books, 6440 N. Central Expressway, Suite 617, Dallas, TX 75206
www.benbellabooks.com

Send feedback to feedback@benbellabooks.com

PUBLISHER: Glenn Yeffeth
EDITOR: Shanna Caughey
ASSOCIATE EDITOR: Leah Wilson
DIRECTOR OF MARKETING/PR: Laura Watkins

Printed in the United States of America
10 9 8 7 6 5 4 3 2 1

Library of Congress Cataloging-in-Publication Data

Wells, H. G. (Herbert George), 1866–1946.
War of the worlds : fresh perspectives on the H.G. Wells classic / edited by Glenn Yeffeth.
    p. cm.
    Contains the text of the novel plus new interpretations by others.
    ISBN 1-932100-55-5
    1. Imaginary wars and battles--Fiction. 2. Wells, H. G. (Herbert George), 1866-1946. War of the worlds. 3. Imaginary wars and battles in literature. 4. Mars (Planet)—Fiction. 5. Space warfare--Fiction. I. Yeffeth, Glenn, 1961- II. Title.

PR5774.W3 2005
823'.912—dc22

2005001050

Cover design by Mondolithic
Text design and composition by John Reinhardt Book Design

Distributed by Independent Publishers Group. To order call (800) 888-4741. www.ipgbook.com
For special sales contact Laura Watkins at laura@benbellabooks.com

Contents

ROBERT SILVERBERG

Introduction

A FEW YEARS BACK I wrote a novel in which the Earth is invaded by vastly superior alien beings, against whom we are unable to mount any significant defense. I would not, of course, make any pretense of having invented that theme, and in my dedication I let it be known that I was aware of who had:

FOR H. G. WELLS, THE FATHER OF US ALL

I meant it. Not only is _The War of the Worlds_ by H. G. Wells the first of all alien-invasion stories—a pathbreaking novel of stark originality by the finest mind that ever applied itself to the writing of science fiction—but it's possible to discern the hand of Wells behind almost every one of the major themes of modern science fiction. His achievement was dazzling and dizzying. He opened all the doors for us, a century ago, and we have been following in his myriad paths ever since.

Not that Wells can take credit for inventing science fiction itself. There were plenty of predecessors. We can trace the ancestry of that

1

sort of literary speculation back and back and back, through such figures of the middle and late nineteenth century as Jules Verne and Edgar
Allan Poe and H. Rider Haggard, and beyond them to Mary Shelley and
her *Frankenstein* of 1816, Jonathan Swift and *Gulliver's Travels* of 1727,
and on and on—Cyrano de Bergerac's *A Voyage to the Moon* of 1650, Sir
Thomas More's *Utopia* of 1516, and onward into Roman times, with the
second-century *True History* of Lucian of Samosata, and the Greek era,
with Plato's tales of lost Atlantis in *Timaeus* and *Critias*. Finally we get
to Homer's *The Odyssey* and the Sumerian epic of *Gilgamesh* before the
trail disappears into the mists of prehistory. I have no doubt that Cro-
Magnon storytellers were entertaining the tribe around those Ice Age
campfires with yarns about the wondrous unknown lands beyond the
rainbow.

It's a fine long pedigree, and I have recited it many times. Yet, somehow—Verne and Shelley and Swift notwithstanding—the immediate
ancestor of the particular kind of science fiction that has preoccupied
me for most of my life, the science fiction I found as a wonderstruck boy
in the pages of *Astounding Science Fiction*, the science fiction of Robert
A. Heinlein and Isaac Asimov and Jack Williamson and A. E. van Vogt,
the science fiction I myself have spent the last fifty years writing, was
H. G. Wells.

Sure, Plato invented a lost continent and told us wonderful tales
about it more than two thousand years ago, and Swift squeezed a lot
of satiric juice out of the imaginary lands and peoples he sent Gulliver
off to visit, and Cyrano spun a delightful yarn about getting himself to
the moon aboard a flying chariot powered by sky-rockets, and Mary
Shelley dreamed up a synthetic human being whose sad story has been
part of popular culture ever since. Those are legitimate science-fictional
themes, and their creators are legitimate progenitors of our field.

But for the origin of the specific *way* we write science fiction today,
the whole tone of it—for the characteristic mating of speculative plot
and scientifically informed thinking and realistic writing for the sake
of demonstrating in a rigorously logical manner the dramatic consequences of a single strikingly imaginative concept—we have to look to
Herbert George Wells.

Wells, who was born in Bromley, Kent, England, in 1866, managed
in his impoverished youth to obtain a scientific education that gave
him, he said, "an exceptionally clear and ordered view of the ostensibly
real universe." He had trouble with mathematics in his physics courses,
though, and he proved to have no gift at all for laboratory experiments,

and so he failed to get the first-class degree he needed for the career in science that he was hoping to have.

The only prospect that seemed open to him was the low-paying one of schoolteaching, a choice that he found uninspiring. He found the idea of teaching agreeable enough: he was nothing if not a teacher by inherent nature. But classroom teaching on the elementary-school level was not what Wells had in mind. He had no yearning to spend his days behind a desk trying to convey basic scientific information to restless young students concerned only with mastering enough data to pass their examinations. He bubbled with ideas of the most vivid and original sort, ideas that he longed to communicate to the whole world, and very quickly it occurred to him that he might be able to do it as a writer.

He turned to journalism first, setting forth his philosophical and scientific theories and beliefs in essays for newspapers and magazines. But gradually he glided into the more lucrative field of fiction, where, he realized, he could embody his ideas in books and stories that might win him a far larger audience than scientific essays ever could. And the kind of fiction that to the young Wells seemed most effective in conveying those ideas was what we would call science fiction today. He wrote his first science fiction stories in his early twenties at a time when the term "science fiction" was decades away from being invented, and, between *The Time Machine* (1895) and *In the Days of the Comet* (1906), poured forth such a torrent of imaginative novels and short stories that a vast legion of his successors, among whom I count myself, has spent an entire century running variations on the speculative themes that he was the first to employ.

The extent of Wells' conceptual originality during that fabulously prolific decade must inspire awe and humility in the soul of anyone who ventures to write science fiction in his wake. Certainly it does in me, and I know more than a little about what it is like to be a prolific writer.

Consider *The Time Machine*, an early draft of which dates from 1888 but which did not reach its present form until 1895. That was the first work of fiction to apply a technological solution to the classic human yearning to peer into the future. Earlier writers had employed such flimsy devices as dreams or trances or hypnosis, mere pretexts to set their narratives going, to give us their visions of things to come. A quintessential example is the biblical Book of Revelation, pure vision without any kind of rationalization. Washington Irving's Rip Van Winkle (1819) was a time traveler of sorts, simply falling asleep and waking up in the future. Edward Bellamy, in his 1887 novel *Looking Backward*, used suspended animation to send his nineteenth-century man into the year 2000.

But Wells, writing at a time when the automobile itself was still a fascinating novelty, came up with the startling and completely new notion of a *machine*, a solid, substantial, tangible machine, with quartz rods and nickel bars and glistening brass rails, in which to send his traveler zooming away to the ends of time. Thus he provided something that no writer of time-travel stories had thought of before: a time-traveling vehicle capable of being steered, and therefore under the volitional control of the voyager.

It hardly matters that a journey powered by such a device has no more scientific plausibility than one powered by the fumes of an opium pipe: by anchoring his fantastic fable to so tangible a mechanistic image, Wells made it *seem* plausible, at least long enough to get his time traveler on his way, and then could move that traveler through a variety of imagined futures for the sake of illustrating his fundamental narrative points. Through skillful writing he was able to give his gadget the texture and conviction of reality—an essential trick for attaining that willing suspension of disbelief that lies at the heart of all successful imaginative fiction. The time *machine* was a marvelous idea, which of course has been imitated countless times since. But Wells was the first to think of it.

Nor was he content to use his time machine as the vehicle for a mere sightseeing trip into the future, as earlier Victorian adventure-story writers might have chosen to do. Because he was a thinker and a social critic as well as a great storyteller, Wells embedded in his time-travel story his speculations on the future of industrial society, so that the novel is not just a recitation of wonders but also an expression of its author's insight into the workings of the rapidly changing society in which he lived. That kind of double vision has been the hallmark of the best science fiction ever since.

Wells followed that extraordinary work with *The Island of Dr. Moreau* (1896), the greatest of all scientific horror stories. In *The Odyssey* Circe transforms men into beasts, a sad business for her victims but not really all that difficult to achieve, as the somber and bloody events of the twentieth century so plainly demonstrated. But Wells' Dr. Moreau turns the much tougher trick of transforming beasts into men, and the result is not merely a novel of terrifying power but one that offers some profound and bleakly pessimistic thoughts about the nature of human nature. And hardly had *Moreau* reached the bookstalls but Wells was back with *The Invisible Man* (1897), another dark and brilliant thriller that showed, as Wells himself noted, "the danger of power without control, the development of the intelligence at the expense of human sympathy."

Still riding a great surge of creative energy, Wells produced book after book during the next few years, still focusing mainly on science fiction: *When the Sleeper Wakes* (1899), a nightmarish dystopian view of the twenty-second century; *The First Men in the Moon* (1901), a harsh satiric fantasy once more aimed at the difficult problem of maintaining individual identity within a huge totalitarian society; *The Food of the Gods* (1901), which examines the consequences of trying to create a race of supermen; and *In the Days of the Comet* (1906), in which human consciousness is radically transformed by a mysterious green gas emanating from the tail of a comet that sweeps past our world.

And then there were the short stories, published during the same years in every important British magazine—about sixty of them that constitute the finest single body of short science fiction ever produced by one writer: "The Star," "The Country of the Blind," "The Empire of the Ants," "In the Abyss," "The Door in the Wall," "The Crystal Egg," "The New Accelerator" and many more. They are captivating narratives packed with vivid imagery and provocative ideas, enough tales to fill a thousand closely printed pages when collected in one volume—an astonishing array of little masterpieces.

After that prodigious decade of science fiction writing Wells moved on to other things. His literary output remained enormous, but his greatest achievements in science fiction now were behind him, and his work in the years that followed consisted chiefly of mainstream novels portraying English life in the early twentieth century, books dealing with science, philosophy and history, and polemic nonfiction that explored many of the same issues of the effects of technological progress on human life that he had earlier looked into in his science fiction novels and stories. The titles of some of the many books tell the story: *The Outline of History* (1920), *The Salvaging of Civilization* (1921), *The Common Sense of World Peace* (1928), *The Science of Life* (1930) and so on through *The Fate of Homo Sapiens* (1939) and *Science and the World Mind* (1942), and seven more in a similar vein after that. He kept on writing right to the end of his long life, which came in 1946, just as the atomic bomb was transforming world history in a fashion that Wells himself, of course, had forecast many decades before.

His restlessly roving mind drove him again and again in those later years to venture also into novels of a science-fictional sort, though this later work, driven primarily by ideological issues, was usually didactic in tone, making little attempt to attain the sort of narrative power that he achieved in the earlier books. The philosopher within him was forever at war with the entertainer, but, with his literary reputation established, he rarely allowed the entertainer to gain the upper hand.

His visionary gifts never left him, though. In *The War in the Air* (1908) he seized on the recent invention of the airplane to portray the vast destruction that aerial bombardment would be wreaking less than a decade later. *The World Set Free* (1914) is famous for its prediction of atomic warfare, but, perhaps more notably, Wells also envisions the horrendous trench warfare that would characterize the great war about to break out. As late as 1933, with *The Shape of Things to Come*, this extraordinary man was still trying to tear away the veils that shroud the future and show us the dark and terrible wonders that he saw.

Of all the remarkable novels and stories that came pouring from him during the spectacular ten years when he essentially created modern science fiction, it is, I think, *The War of the Worlds* that has had the greatest impact on our culture.

It was published in magazine form in 1897 and as a book the next year, and thus was the fourth of the novels in that great early spate, following hard upon *The Time Machine*, *The Island of Dr. Moreau* and *The Invisible Man*. As we look back at *The War of the Worlds* now, our view of its originality of theme is obscured by the hundreds of later novels that also have told the tale of the invasion of Earth by terrifying alien beings: Philip Francis Nowlan's *Armageddon 2419* A.D. (1928), which gave us Buck Rogers; John Wyndham's *The Day of the Triffids* (1951); Robert A. Heinlein's *The Puppet Masters* (1951); Arthur C. Clarke's *Childhood's End* (1953); Jack Finney's *Invasion of the Body Snatchers* (1955); Theodore Sturgeon's *The Cosmic Rape* (1958); *Footfall* (1985) by Larry Niven and Jerry Pournelle; and my own books *Nightwings* (1969) and *The Alien Years* (1998), which is the one I dedicated to Wells. But Wells was the first. No writer before him had thought of the idea of an attack on Earth from beyond the atmosphere. And none of Wells' predecessors in the realm of speculative fiction, I suspect, would have been able to embody it so successfully in a novel.

The idea of alien life was itself a relatively recent one, at least in fiction, perhaps because of the risks involved in challenging established church teachings by postulating a creation other than the one described in the Book of Genesis. Such precursors of modern science fiction as Francis Godwin's *The Man in the Moon* (1638) and Voltaire's *Micromegas* (1752) depicted creatures native to other worlds, but they were basically human in design. Only in the late nineteenth century did a few writers begin to speculate about non-humanoid extraterrestrial life-forms, and it remained for Wells to carry the concept to its logical extreme by showing them descending upon our world on a mission of conquest.

With splendid economy Wells announces his theme, and even subtly foreshadows the ultimate resolution of his plot, in his very first sentence:

> No one would have believed, in the last years of the nineteenth century, that human affairs were being watched keenly and closely by intelligences greater than man's and yet as mortal as his own; that as men busied themselves about their affairs they were scrutinised and studied, perhaps almost as narrowly as a man with a microscope might scrutinise the transient creatures that swarm and multiply in a drop of water.

Intelligences greater than man's! What a subversive idea that would have been a few hundred years earlier, in that benighted era when our little world was thought to be the center of the universe! And, a few lines later, Wells expands the concept with this magnificently chilling passage:

> At most, terrestrial men fancied there might be other men upon Mars, perhaps inferior to themselves and ready to welcome a missionary enterprise. Yet, across the gulf of space, minds that are to our minds as ours are to the beasts that perish, intellects vast and cool and unsympathetic, regarded this earth with envious eyes and slowly and surely drew their plans against us.

Vast and cool and unsympathetic! In five words Wells creates for us the Alien Menace pure and simple, the dispassionate invulnerable enemy that his multitude of successors in science fiction have been examining and reexamining ever since. He gives us the full horror of the unknowability of the world beyond our planet's horizon in those five perfectly chosen words.

Note, too, the quick, sly reference to the possibility that we might have wanted, had we known of the existence of Mars' inhabitants, to send them "a missionary enterprise" to lift them from their mire of un-Christian ignorance. The darker corners of the world of 1897 were full of England's valiant missionaries, carrying the message of the Gospels to the savage heathens of far-off lands; but who would have dared suggest that we ourselves might seem to others every bit as savage and ignorant as those "natives" did to the missionaries of Queen Victoria's day?

And then the final introductory thematic thrust, in the second paragraph. What is the reason for those "plans against us" that the Martians are drawing up? Wells explains, in his best science-lecturer mode, that Mars is an older world than ours, dry and cold, with a steadily thinning atmosphere and shrinking oceans. It is a planet entering the "last stage of exhaustion." Its inhabitants, those creatures of vast, cool minds, are suffering. And so:

> The immediate pressure of necessity has brightened their intellects, enlarged their powers, and hardened their hearts. And looking across space, with instruments and intelligences such as we have scarcely dreamt of, they see, at its nearest distance, only 35,000,000 of miles sunward of them, a morning star of hope, our own warmer planet, green with vegetation and grey with water, with a cloudy atmosphere eloquent of fertility, with glimpses through its drifting cloud-wisps of broad stretches of populous country and narrow navy-crowded seas.

Whereupon, of course, they will descend upon our green and pleasant planet and take it from us, for they need it, and their need is great—they, whose minds are to ours "as ours are to those of the beasts that perish"—and we, who to the Martians are "as alien and lowly as are the monkeys and lemurs to us," simply don't matter at all, any more than the natives of the Congo or Mexico or the Spice Islands mattered to the European invaders who descended upon them to take their lands and their treasures from them during the great age of colonialism. Colonialism, imperialism, is one of Wells' targets here, just as the iniquities of industrial-age exploitation of labor were in *The Time Machine*.

But his primary task is to write a story, a fantastic story at that, not a sermon. That story unfolds in a quiet, matter-of-fact way, narrated for us by an anonymous eyewitness to the startling events. We are told very little about this narrator, because he is speaking to us in the first person, and what he is writing is not his autobiography but the account of a tremendous apocalyptic disaster. (Wells' model for *The War of the Worlds* may have been Daniel Defoe's *A Journal of the Plague Year* (1722), which in a similar way reports on a great disaster, though one of a non-fantastic kind.)

We know that Wells' narrator is an educated man, thoughtful, intelligent, a good observer. (He tells us himself that "at times I suffer from the strangest sense of detachment from myself and the world about me; I seem to watch it all from the outside, from somewhere inconceivably remote, out of time, out of space, out of the stress and tragedy of it all.") He is married; he lives in Woking, a suburb south of London, the same one where Wells lived; probably we are meant to think of him as Wells himself, since when he introduces himself to us, at the moment of the arrival of the first Martian spaceship, he is at home, writing in his study. We learn very little more about him than that. This is not a novel in which characterization is of central importance, one which deals primarily with the transformations of character that the events of the story bring about, as is the case in, say, *A Tale of Two Cities* or *Crime and Punishment*. Wells gives us, at every step, real and convincing human reactions to what is going on—the reactions of the narrator, and at one point the narrator's brother, and various others along the way. But what really matters is the succession of external events, and the reactions to those events that Wells seeks to depict are those of Londoners as a group, not the unique responses of the particular protagonists of a complex story.

It is not a complex story. The aliens land; they emerge from their spaceships; they demonstrate their invincibility at once, and from that point to the unexpected climax of the tale, there is no glimmer of hope that embattled humanity will be able to wage any sort of defense against them.

Wells' description of the Martians as they emerge from their cylindrical landing vehicles displays the mastery of a born storyteller, not the dryness of the lecture hall. "I think everyone expected to see a man emerge—possibly something a little unlike us terrestrial men, but in all essentials a man. I know I did," says our narrator.

But that is not what happens. Something resembling "a little gray snake"—a tentacle, the first alien tentacle in all of fiction—comes coiling up over the edge. The narrator feels a sudden chill. A woman screams. There is a general movement backward from the cylinder. And then:

A big greyish, rounded bulk, the size, perhaps, of a bear, was rising slowly and painfully out of the cylinder. As it budged up and caught the light, it glistened like wet leather. Two large dark-coloured eyes were regarding me steadfastly. It was rounded, and had, one might say, a face. There was a mouth under the eyes, the lipless brim of which quivered and panted, and dropped saliva. The body heaved and pulsated convulsively. A lank tentacular appendage gripped the edge of the cylinder, another swayed in the air.

Those who have never seen a living Martian can scarcely imagine the strange horror of their appearance.... Even at this first encounter, this first glimpse, I was overcome with disgust and dread.

There we have it. "[I]t glistened like wet leather.... I was overcome with disgust and dread." For the very first time, the aliens have landed, and Wells gives it to us with marvelous specificity and cunning evocation of dread. His intent is not, I think, to frighten us, despite that panting mouth and pulsating body, so much as it is to awaken us to the awesome possibilities that the universe holds. We are not alone. Nor are these Martians particularly evil. They are simply *other*. They have minds of their own, alien unemotional ones, and they have needs of their own too, which do not coincide with ours, anymore than the needs of Victorian-era imperialists coincided with the needs of the peoples whose lands they so cheerfully had taken control of.

And the Martians, whose intellects are so vast and cool and unsympathetic, swiftly proceed to take control of us. Their great ambulatory machines go marching unhurriedly through the countryside toward London, sweeping away all resistance with Heat-Rays and clouds of poison gas, creating a track of destruction as they advance, and consolidating their gains as they go. The core of the novel is an inexorable tale of steady retreat before the implacable enemy. One Martian is slain in its metallic fighting machine by cannon fire; retribution by the invaders is swift and terrible.

Wells now shifts the point of view from his suburban narrator to the narrator's younger brother, a medical student in London, in order to show us what is going on in the metropolis as word of the invasion begins to arrive. News traveled slowly in those days. The radio had not been invented yet; the telephone barely had a foothold in British life. And it is Sunday; "[T]he majority of people in London do not read Sunday papers," Wells tells us. The first reactions to the news from Woking are skeptical, even mocking, but then, as trustworthy accounts of the catastrophe continue to come in, uneasiness grows, a sense of danger is awakened, and the first signs of panic can be seen. Soon the people of London are in full flight northward. "And this was no disciplined march; it was a stampede—a stampede gigantic and terrible—without order and without a goal, six million people, unarmed and unprovisioned, driving headlong. It was the beginning of the rout of civilization, of the massacre of mankind."

It was also the beginning of insight, for Wells, into what the twentieth century, just ahead, might hold for Europe. His powerful chapter on the flight from London is a stunning prevision of the chaos of Europe in World War II, when long lines of bewildered civilians desperately fled this way and that in hope of escaping the fury of the clashing armies that were swarming through their cities and towns.

The evacuation of London introduces an apocalyptic tone into the book. Civilization collapses almost instantly. A kind of jungle savagery replaces the vaunted courtesy of the mild-mannered English as they struggle to escape the advance of the alien invaders and an appalling struggle for food and shelter commences.

In the midst of the madness Wells' narrator manages to stop the tale long enough for a discursion on the physiology and anatomy of the Martians: "Huge round bodies—or, rather, heads—about four feet in diameter, each body having in front of it a face.... The greater part of the structure was the brain, sending enormous nerves to the eyes, ear and tactile tentacles.... They did not eat, much less digest. Instead they took the fresh living blood of other creatures, and *injected* it into their own veins...." And so on, seven or eight pages on Martian physiology and even Martian sex life (they seemed not to have any, but reproduced by budding), until Wells gets his didactic side under control and returns to his account of the ongoing disaster, the continuing slide into total defeat and the return to barbarism.

Indeed it is a completely one-sided war, and the destruction of civilization is absolute. When the narrator, after several weeks, takes himself into London, he finds it all but deserted, dead and dying people everywhere, an eerie stillness prevailing. But then comes a strange, haunting cry, "great waves of sound sweeping down the broad, sunlit roadway," a sobbing wail, "Ulla, ulla, ulla, ulla." It is the death-cry of the Martians: Wells' harshly ironic resolution is at hand, and the world is saved after all.

There never had been a book of this sort before, and it was received by the readers of its day with astonishment and awe. One newspaper reviewer complained that certain sections were so brutal that "they caused insufferable distress to the feelings," but that was an exception to the general acclaim. Sales of the book were huge, and imitations followed almost instantly. (One, a hastily written novel by the American Garrett P. Serviss entitled *Edison's Conquest of Mars*, told of how Thomas Edison and a group of other scientists built a fleet of spaceships equipped with disintegrator rays and journeyed to Mars to pay the Martians back for the invasion.)

The book passed at once into popular mythology; "the Martians" became a shorthand term for all sorts of inimical alien being, and any sort of strange phenomenon was readily interpreted, sometimes jokingly, sometimes not, as the onset of an attack by "men from Mars." As late as 1938, when Orson Welles broadcast a brief dramatized version of the original novel on American radio that had the Martians landing in New Jersey, credulous listeners who had tuned in just too late to hear the opening announcement that the program was only a radio play told themselves that it was an eyewitness news report and were driven into a panic that has become legendary in media history.

More than a century after its first publication and despite all the imitators who have turned his concept into a cliché, Wells' fantastic novel still exerts its power. We respond to it because it digs into the profoundest archetypes of fear: in history, the coming of the Assyrian hordes, the descent upon the land of the armies of Genghis Khan, the onslaught of the Black Death, and, in fiction, the predecessor horrors of the giant squids that envelop the hull of Captain Nemo's submarine, the Frankenstein monster and the golem, the great white flukes of Moby Dick lashing the *Pequod*. A door opens, and something sinister and irresistible bursts forth, and we shiver in terror.

But Wells was not only a great storyteller; he was a supremely rational man. And so, as we are shown in those unforgettable final pages set in deserted London, the onslaught of the Martians was doomed from the start, and it is the very nature of their alienness that dooms them, not any effort on the part of humanity.

The novel can be seen as a tragedy of overreaching: an alien species, driven by the simple desire for our water, which they see as necessary to their own survival (i.e., by the dictates of colonial imperialism), the Martians come to us to seize our world, an act of hybris that brings their downfall, for they are biologically unfit to live here. From the Martian point of view the expedition is the mighty act of valor of a desperate race, and its failure is a tragedy akin to the tragedy of the Athenian expedition to Syracuse in the Peloponnesian War and the shattering of the Spanish Armada by the English in 1588. From the point of view of Wells' narrator and his fellow citizens, the invasion is a revelatory catastrophe illustrating not only the unexpected vulnerability of the proud human race but also the ease with which the lofty and self-admiring civilization of Victorian England could be toppled into the most brutal savagery. To Wells himself, the omniscient creator sitting high up above the battle, the book is, among many other things, a warning against overweening ambition, a sobering statement about the nonuniqueness of human life in a vast universe, and a clever display of the author's knowledge of the workings of biology. And for us *The War of the Worlds*, the prototype of all alien-invasion stories, is an imperishable part of our heritage of imaginative literature, a magnificent fantasy that glows forever in the mind of anyone who has read it.

Robert Silverberg is the author of dozens of science fiction novels and more than five hundred short stories. He is a many-time winner of the Hugo and Nebula awards and in 2004 was designated a Grand Master, one of twenty-one named so far, by the Science Fiction Writers of America.

H. G. WELLS

The War
of the Worlds

But who shall dwell in these worlds if they be inhabited? . . . Are we or they Lords of the World? . . . And how are all things made for man?

—KEPLER (quoted in *The Anatomy of Melancholy*)

BOOK ONE
The Coming of the Martians

. . .

CHAPTER ONE

The Eve of the War

NO ONE WOULD HAVE BELIEVED in the last years of the nineteenth century that this world was being watched keenly and closely by intelligences greater than man's and yet as mortal as his own; that as men busied themselves about their various concerns they were scrutinised and studied, perhaps almost as narrowly as a man with a microscope might scrutinise the transient creatures that swarm and multiply in a drop of water. With infinite complacency men went to and fro over this globe about their little affairs, serene in their assurance of their empire over matter. It is possible that the infusoria under the microscope do the same. No one gave a thought to the older worlds of space as sources of human danger, or thought of them only to dismiss the idea of life upon them as impossible or improbable. It is curious to recall some of the mental habits of those departed days. At most terrestrial men fancied there might be other men upon Mars, perhaps inferior to themselves and ready to welcome a missionary enterprise. Yet across the gulf of space, minds that are to our minds as ours are to those of the beasts that perish, intellects vast and cool and unsympathetic, regarded this earth with envious eyes, and slowly and surely drew their plans against us. And early in the twentieth century came the great disillusionment.

The planet Mars, I scarcely need remind the reader, revolves about the sun at a mean distance of 140,000,000 miles, and the light and heat it receives from the sun is barely half of that received by this world. It must be, if the nebular hypothesis has any truth, older than our world; and long before this earth ceased to be molten, life upon its surface must have begun its course. The fact that it is scarcely one seventh of the volume of the earth must have accelerated its cooling to the temperature at which life could begin. It has air and water and all that is necessary for the support of animated existence.

Yet so vain is man, and so blinded by his vanity, that no writer, up to the very end of the nineteenth century, expressed any idea that intelligent life might have developed there far, or indeed at all, beyond its earthly level. Nor was it generally understood that since Mars is older than our earth, with scarcely a quarter of the superficial area and remoter from the sun, it necessarily follows that it is not only more distant from time's beginning but nearer its end.

The secular cooling that must someday overtake our planet has already gone far indeed with our neighbour. Its physical condition is still largely a mystery, but we know now that even in its equatorial region the midday temperature barely approaches that of our coldest winter. Its air is much more attenuated than ours, its oceans have shrunk until they cover but a third of its surface, and as its slow seasons change huge snowcaps gather and melt about either pole and periodically inundate its temperate zones. That last stage of exhaustion, which to us is still incredibly remote, has become a present-day problem for the inhabitants of Mars. The immediate pressure of necessity has brightened their intellects, enlarged their powers, and hardened their hearts. And looking across space with instruments, and intelligences such as we have scarcely dreamed of, they see, at its nearest distance only 35,000,000 of miles sunward of them, a morning star of hope, our own warmer planet, green with vegetation and grey with water, with a cloudy atmosphere eloquent of fertility, with glimpses through its drifting cloud wisps of broad stretches of populous country and narrow, navy-crowded seas.

And we men, the creatures who inhabit this earth, must be to them at least as alien and lowly as are the monkeys and lemurs to us. The intellectual side of man already admits that life is an incessant struggle for existence, and it would seem that this too is the belief of the minds upon Mars. Their world is far gone in its cooling and this world is still crowded with life, but crowded only with what they regard as inferior animals. To carry warfare sunward is, indeed, their only escape from the destruction that, generation after generation, creeps upon them.

And before we judge of them too harshly we must remember what ruthless and utter destruction our own species has wrought, not only upon animals, such as the vanished bison and the dodo, but upon its inferior races. The Tasmanians, in spite of their human likeness, were entirely swept out of existence in a war of extermination waged by European immigrants, in the space of fifty years. Are we such apostles of mercy as to complain if the Martians warred in the same spirit?

The Martians seem to have calculated their descent with amazing subtlety—their mathematical learning is evidently far in excess of ours—and to have carried out their preparations with a well-nigh perfect unanimity. Had our instruments permitted it, we might have seen the gathering trouble far back in the nineteenth century. Men like Schiaparelli watched the red planet—it is odd, by-the-bye, that for countless centuries Mars has been the star of war—but failed to interpret the fluctuating appearances of the markings they mapped so well. All that time the Martians must have been getting ready.

During the opposition of 1894 a great light was seen on the illuminated part of the disk, first at the Lick Observatory, then by Perrotin of Nice, and then by other observers. English readers heard of it first in the issue of *Nature* dated August 2. I am inclined to think that this blaze may have been the casting of the huge gun, in the vast pit sunk into their planet, from which their shots were fired at us. Peculiar markings, as yet unexplained, were seen near the site of that outbreak during the next two oppositions.

The storm burst upon us six years ago now. As Mars approached opposition, Lavelle of Java set the wires of the astronomical exchange palpitating with the amazing intelligence of a huge outbreak of incandescent gas upon the planet. It had occurred towards midnight of the twelfth; and the spectroscope, to which he had at once resorted, indicated a mass of flaming gas, chiefly hydrogen, moving with an enormous velocity towards this earth. This jet of fire had become invisible about a quarter past twelve. He compared it to a colossal puff of flame suddenly and violently squirted out of the planet, "as flaming gases rushed out of a gun."

A singularly appropriate phrase it proved. Yet the next day there was nothing of this in the papers except a little note in the *Daily Telegraph*, and the world went in ignorance of one of the gravest dangers that ever threatened the human race. I might not have heard of the eruption at all had I not met Ogilvy, the well-known astronomer, at Ottershaw. He was immensely excited at the news, and in the excess of his feelings invited me up to take a turn with him that night in a scrutiny of the red planet.

In spite of all that has happened since, I still remember that vigil very distinctly: the black and silent observatory, the shadowed lantern throwing a feeble glow upon the floor in the corner, the steady ticking of the clockwork of the telescope, the little slit in the roof—an oblong profundity with the stardust streaked across it. Ogilvy moved about, invisible but audible. Looking through the telescope, one saw a circle of deep blue and the little round planet swimming in the field. It seemed such a little thing, so bright and small and still, faintly marked with transverse stripes, and slightly flattened from the perfect round. But so little it was, so silvery warm—a pin's-head of light! It was as if it quivered, but really this was the telescope vibrating with the activity of the clockwork that kept the planet in view.

As I watched, the planet seemed to grow larger and smaller and to advance and recede, but that was simply that my eye was tired. Forty millions of miles it was from us—more than forty millions of miles of void. Few people realise the immensity of vacancy in which the dust of the material universe swims.

Near it in the field, I remember, were three faint points of light, three telescopic stars infinitely remote, and all around it was the unfathomable darkness of empty space. You know how that blackness looks on a frosty starlight night. In a telescope it seems far profounder. And invisible to me because it was so remote and small, flying swiftly and steadily towards me across that incredible distance, drawing nearer every minute by so many thousands of miles, came the Thing they were sending us, the Thing that was to bring so much struggle and calamity and death to the earth. I never dreamed of it then as I watched; no one on earth dreamed of that unerring missile.

That night, too, there was another jetting out of gas from the distant planet. I saw it. A reddish flash at the edge, the slightest projection of the outline just as the chronometer struck midnight; and at that I told Ogilvy and he took my place. The night was warm and I was thirsty, and I went stretching my legs clumsily and feeling my way in the darkness, to the little table where the siphon stood, while Ogilvy exclaimed at the streamer of gas that came out towards us.

That night another invisible missile started on its way to the earth from Mars, just a second or so under twenty-four hours after the first one. I remember how I sat on the table there in the blackness, with patches of green and crimson swimming before my eyes. I wished I had a light to smoke by, little suspecting the meaning of the minute gleam I had seen and all that it would presently bring me. Ogilvy watched till one, and then gave it up; and we lit the lantern and walked over to his house. Down below in the darkness were Ottershaw and Chertsey and all their hundreds of people, sleeping in peace.

He was full of speculation that night about the condition of Mars, and scoffed at the vulgar idea of its having inhabitants who were signalling us. His idea was that meteorites might be falling in a heavy shower upon the planet, or that a huge volcanic explosion was in progress. He pointed out to me how unlikely it was that organic evolution had taken the same direction in the two adjacent planets.

"The chances against anything manlike on Mars are a million to one," he said.

Hundreds of observers saw the flame that night and the night after about midnight, and again the night after; and so for ten nights, a flame each night. Why the shots ceased after the tenth no one on earth has attempted to explain. It may be the gases of the firing caused the Martians inconvenience. Dense clouds of smoke or dust, visible through a powerful telescope on earth as little grey, fluctuating patches, spread through the clearness of the planet's atmosphere and obscured its more familiar features.

Even the daily papers woke up to the disturbances at last, and popular notes appeared here, there, and everywhere concerning the volcanoes upon Mars. The seriocomic periodical *Punch*, I remember, made a happy use of it in the political cartoon. And, all unsuspected, those missiles the Martians had fired at us drew earthward, rushing now at a pace of many miles a second through the empty gulf of space, hour by hour and day by day, nearer and nearer. It seems to me now almost incredibly wonderful that, with that swift fate hanging over us, men could go about their petty concerns as they did. I remember how jubilant Markham was at securing a new photograph of the planet for the illustrated paper he edited in those days. People in these latter times scarcely realise the abundance and enterprise of our nineteenth-century papers. For my own part, I was much occupied in learning to ride the bicycle, and busy upon a series of papers discussing the probable developments of moral ideas as civilisation progressed.

One night (the first missile then could scarcely have been 10,000,000 miles away) I went for a walk with my wife. It was starlight and I explained the Signs of the Zodiac to her, and pointed out Mars, a bright dot of light creeping zenithward, towards which so many telescopes were pointed. It was a warm night. Coming home, a party of excursionists from Chertsey or Isleworth passed us singing and playing music. There were lights in the upper windows of the houses as the people went to bed. From the railway station in the distance came the sound of shunting trains, ringing and rumbling, softened almost into melody by the distance. My wife pointed out to me the brightness of the red, green, and yellow signal lights hanging in a framework against the sky. It seemed so safe and tranquil.

. . .

CHAPTER TWO
The Falling Star

THEN CAME THE NIGHT of the first falling star. It was seen early in the morning, rushing over Winchester eastward, a line of flame high in the atmosphere. Hundreds must have seen it, and taken it for an ordinary falling star. Albin described it as leaving a greenish streak behind it that glowed for some seconds. Denning, our greatest authority on meteorites, stated that the height of its first appearance was about ninety or one hundred miles. It seemed to him that it fell to earth about one hundred miles east of him.

I was at home at that hour and writing in my study; and although my French windows face towards Ottershaw and the blind was up (for I loved in those days to look up at the night sky), I saw nothing of it. Yet this strangest of all things that ever came to earth from outer space must have fallen while I was sitting there, visible to me had I only looked up as it passed. Some of those who saw its flight say it travelled with a hissing sound. I myself heard nothing of that. Many people in Berkshire, Surrey, and Middlesex must have seen the fall of it, and, at most, have thought that another meteorite had descended.

No one seems to have troubled to look for the fallen mass that night.

But very early in the morning poor Ogilvy, who had seen the shooting star and who was persuaded that a meteorite lay somewhere on the common between Horsell, Ottershaw, and Woking, rose early with the idea of finding it. Find it he did, soon after dawn, and not far from the sand pits. An enormous hole had been made by the impact of the projectile, and the sand and gravel had been flung violently in every direction over the heath, forming heaps visible a mile and a half away. The heather was on fire eastward, and a thin blue smoke rose against the dawn.

The Thing itself lay almost entirely buried in sand, amidst the scattered splinters of a fir tree it had shivered to fragments in its descent. The uncovered part had the appearance of a huge cylinder, caked over and its outline softened by a thick scaly dun-coloured incrustation. It had a diameter of about thirty yards. He approached the mass, surprised at the size and more so at the shape, since most meteorites are rounded more or less completely. It was, however, still so hot from its flight through the air as to forbid his near approach. A stirring noise within its cylinder he ascribed to the unequal cooling of its surface; for at that time it had not occurred to him that it might be hollow.

He remained standing at the edge of the pit that the Thing had made for itself, staring at its strange appearance, astonished chiefly at its unusual shape and colour, and dimly perceiving even then some evidence of design in its arrival. The early morning was wonderfully still, and the sun, just clearing the pine trees towards Weybridge, was already warm. He did not remember hearing any birds that morning, there was certainly no breeze stirring, and the only sounds were the faint movements from within the cindery cylinder. He was all alone on the common.

Then suddenly he noticed with a start that some of the grey clinker, the ashy incrustation that covered the meteorite, was falling off the circular edge of the end. It was dropping off in flakes and raining down upon the sand. A large piece suddenly came off and fell with a sharp noise that brought his heart into his mouth.

For a minute he scarcely realised what this meant, and, although the heat was excessive, he clambered down into the pit close to the bulk to see the Thing more clearly. He fancied even then that the cooling of the body might account for this, but what disturbed that idea was the fact that the ash was falling only from the end of the cylinder.

And then he perceived that, very slowly, the circular top of the cylinder was rotating on its body. It was such a gradual movement that he discovered it only through noticing that a black mark that had been near him five minutes ago was now at the other side of the circumference. Even then he scarcely understood what this indicated, until he heard a muffled grating sound and saw the black mark jerk forward an inch or so. Then the thing came upon him in a flash. The cylinder was artificial—hollow—with an end that screwed out! Something within the cylinder was unscrewing the top!

"Good heavens!" said Ogilvy. "There's a man in it—men in it! Half roasted to death! Trying to escape!"

At once, with a quick mental leap, he linked the Thing with the flash upon Mars.

The thought of the confined creature was so dreadful to him that he forgot the heat and went forward to the cylinder to help turn. But luckily the dull radiation arrested him before he could burn his hands on the still-glowing metal. At that he stood irresolute for a moment, then turned, scrambled out of the pit, and set off running wildly into Woking. The time then must have been somewhere about six o'clock. He met a waggoner and tried to make him understand, but the tale he told and his appearance were so wild—his hat had fallen off in the pit—that the man simply drove on. He was equally unsuccessful with the pot-man who was just unlocking the doors of the public-house by Horsell Bridge. The fellow thought he was a lunatic at large and made an unsuccessful attempt to shut him into the taproom. That sobered him a little; and when he saw Henderson, the London journalist, in his garden, he called over the palings and made himself understood.

"Henderson," he called, "you saw that shooting star last night?"

"Well?" said Henderson.

"It's out on Horsell Common now."

"Good Lord!" said Henderson. "Fallen meteorite! That's good."

"But it's something more than a meteorite. It's a cylinder—an artificial cylinder, man! And there's something inside."

Henderson stood up with his spade in his hand.

"What's that?" he said. He was deaf in one ear.

Ogilvy told him all that he had seen. Henderson was a minute or so taking it in. Then he dropped his spade, snatched up his jacket, and came out into the road. The two men hurried back at once to the common, and found the cylinder still lying in the same position. But now the sounds inside had ceased, and a thin circle of bright metal showed between the top and the body of the cylinder. Air was either entering or escaping at the rim with a thin, sizzling sound.

They listened, rapped on the scaly burnt metal with a stick, and, meeting with no response, they both concluded the man or men inside must be insensible or dead.

Of course the two were quite unable to do anything. They shouted consolation and promises, and went off back to the town again to get help. One can imagine them, covered with sand, excited and disordered, running up the little street in the bright sunlight just as the shop folks were taking down their shutters and people were opening their bedroom windows. Henderson went into the railway station at once, in order to telegraph the news to London. The newspaper articles had prepared men's minds for the reception of the idea.

By eight o'clock a number of boys and unemployed men had already started for the common to see the "dead men from Mars." That was the form the story took. I heard of it first from my newspaper boy about a quarter to nine when I went out to get my *Daily Chronicle*. I was naturally startled, and lost no time in going out and across the Ottershaw bridge to the sand pits.

• • •

CHAPTER THREE

On Horsell Common

I FOUND A LITTLE CROWD of perhaps twenty people surrounding the huge hole in which the cylinder lay. I have already described the appearance of that colossal bulk, embedded in the ground. The turf and gravel about it seemed charred as if by a sudden explosion. No doubt its impact had caused a flash of fire. Henderson and Ogilvy were not there. I think they perceived that nothing was to be done for the present, and had gone away to breakfast at Henderson's house.

There were four or five boys sitting on the edge of the pit, with their feet dangling, and amusing themselves—until I stopped them—by throwing stones at the giant mass. After I had spoken to them about it, they began playing at "touch" in and out of the group of bystanders.

Among these were a couple of cyclists, a jobbing gardener I employed sometimes, a girl carrying a baby, Gregg the butcher and his little boy, and two or three loafers and golf caddies who were accustomed to hang about the railway station. There was very little talking. Few of the common people in England had anything but the vaguest astronomical ideas in those days. Most of them were staring quietly at the big tablelike end of the cylinder, which was still as Ogilvy and Henderson had left it. I fancy the popular expectation of a heap of charred corpses was disappointed at this inanimate bulk.

Some went away while I was there, and other people came. I clambered into the pit and fancied I heard a faint movement under my feet. The top had certainly ceased to rotate.

It was only when I got thus close to it that the strangeness of this object was at all evident to me. At the first glance it was really no more exciting than an overturned carriage or a tree blown across the road. Not so much so, indeed. It looked like a rusty gas float. It required a certain amount of scientific education to perceive that the grey scale of the Thing was no common oxide, that the yellowish-white metal that gleamed in the crack between the lid and the cylinder had an unfamiliar hue. "Extra-terrestrial" had no meaning for most of the onlookers.

At that time it was quite clear in my own mind that the Thing had come from the planet Mars, but I judged it improbable that it contained any living creature. I thought the unscrewing might be automatic. In spite of Ogilvy, I still believed that there were men in Mars. My mind ran fancifully on the possibilities of its containing manuscript, on the difficulties in translation that might arise, whether we should find coins and models in it, and so forth. Yet it was a little too large for assurance on this idea. I felt an impatience to see it opened. About eleven, as nothing seemed happening, I walked back, full of such thought, to my home in Maybury. But I found it difficult to get to work upon my abstract investigations.

In the afternoon the appearance of the common had altered very much. The early editions of the evening papers had startled London with enormous headlines:

"A MESSAGE RECEIVED FROM MARS."

"REMARKABLE STORY FROM WOKING,"

and so forth. In addition, Ogilvy's wire to the Astronomical Exchange had roused every observatory in the three kingdoms.

There were half a dozen flies or more from the Woking station standing in the road by the sand pits, a basket-chaise from Chobham, and a rather lordly carriage. Besides that, there was quite a heap of bicycles. In addition, a large number of people must have walked, in spite of the heat of the day, from Woking and Chertsey, so that there was altogether quite a considerable crowd—one or two gaily dressed ladies among the others.

It was glaringly hot, not a cloud in the sky nor a breath of wind, and the only shadow was that of the few scattered pine trees. The burning heather had been extinguished, but the level ground towards Ottershaw was blackened as far as one could see, and still giving off vertical streamers of smoke. An enterprising sweet-stuff dealer in the Chobham Road had sent up his son with a barrow-load of green apples and ginger beer.

Going to the edge of the pit, I found it occupied by a group of about half a dozen men—Henderson, Ogilvy, and a tall, fair-haired man that I afterwards learned was Stent, the Astronomer Royal, with several workmen wielding spades and pickaxes. Stent was giving directions in a clear, high-pitched voice. He was standing on the cylinder, which was now evidently much cooler; his face was crimson and streaming with perspiration, and something seemed to have irritated him.

A large portion of the cylinder had been uncovered, though its lower end was still embedded. As soon as Ogilvy saw me among the staring crowd on the edge of the pit he called to me to come down, and asked me if I would mind going over to see Lord Hilton, the lord of the manor.

The growing crowd, he said, was becoming a serious impediment to their excavations, especially the boys. They wanted a light railing put up, and help to keep the people back. He told me that a faint stirring was occasionally still audible within the case, but that the workmen had failed to unscrew the top, as it afforded no grip to them. The case appeared to be enormously thick, and it was possible that the faint sounds we heard represented a noisy tumult in the interior.

I was very glad to do as he asked, and so become one of the privileged spectators within the contemplated enclosure. I failed to find Lord Hilton at his house, but I was told he was expected from London by the six o'clock train from Waterloo; and as it was then about a quarter past five, I went home, had some tea, and walked up to the station to waylay him.

●　●　●

CHAPTER FOUR

The Cylinder Opens

WHEN I RETURNED TO THE COMMON the sun was setting. Scattered groups were hurrying from the direction of Woking, and one or two persons were returning. The crowd about the pit had increased, and stood out black against the lemon yellow of the sky—a couple of hundred people, perhaps. There were raised voices, and some sort of struggle appeared to be going on about the pit. Strange imaginings passed through my mind. As I drew nearer I heard Stent's voice:

"Keep back! Keep back!"

A boy came running towards me.

"It's a-movin'," he said to me as he passed; "a-screwin' and a-screwin' out. I don't like it. I'm a-goin' 'ome, I am."

I went on to the crowd. There were really, I should think, two or three hundred people elbowing and jostling one another, the one or two ladies there being by no means the least active.

"He's fallen in the pit!" cried some one.

"Keep back!" said several.

The crowd swayed a little, and I elbowed my way through. Every one seemed greatly excited. I heard a peculiar humming sound from the pit.

"I say!" said Ogilvy; "help keep these idiots back. We don't know what's in the confounded thing, you know!"

I saw a young man, a shop assistant in Woking I believe he was, standing on the cylinder and trying to scramble out of the hole again. The crowd had pushed him in.

The end of the cylinder was being screwed out from within. Nearly two feet of shining screw projected. Somebody blundered against me, and I narrowly missed being pitched onto the top of the screw. I turned, and as I did so the screw must have come out, for the lid of the cylinder fell upon the gravel with a ringing concussion. I stuck my elbow into the person behind me, and turned my head towards the Thing again. For a moment that circular cavity seemed perfectly black. I had the sunset in my eyes.

I think everyone expected to see a man emerge—possibly something a little unlike us terrestrial men, but in all essentials a man. I know I did. But, looking, I presently saw something stirring within the shadow: greyish billowy movements, one above another, and then two luminous disks—like eyes. Then something resembling a little grey snake, about the thickness of a walking stick, coiled up out of the writhing middle, and wriggled in the air towards me—and then another.

A sudden chill came over me. There was a loud shriek from a woman behind. I half turned, keeping my eyes fixed upon the cylinder still, from which other tentacles were now projecting, and began pushing my way back from the edge of the pit. I saw astonishment giving place to horror on the faces of the people about me. I heard inarticulate exclamations on all sides. There was a general movement backwards. I saw the shopman struggling still on the edge of the pit. I found myself alone, and saw the people on the other side of the pit running off, Stent among them. I looked again at the cylinder, and ungovernable terror gripped me. I stood petrified and staring.

A big greyish rounded bulk, the size, perhaps, of a bear, was rising slowly and painfully out of the cylinder. As it bulged up and caught the light, it glistened like wet leather.

Two large dark-coloured eyes were regarding me steadfastly. The mass that framed them, the head of the thing, was rounded, and had, one might say, a face. There was a mouth under the eyes, the lipless brim of which quivered and panted, and dropped saliva. The whole creature heaved and pulsated convulsively. A lank tentacular appendage gripped the edge of the cylinder, another swayed in the air.

Those who have never seen a living Martian can scarcely imagine the strange horror of its appearance. The peculiar V-shaped mouth with its pointed upper lip, the absence of brow ridges, the absence of a chin beneath the wedgelike lower lip, the incessant quivering of this mouth, the Gorgon groups of tentacles, the tumultuous breathing of the lungs in a strange atmosphere, the evident heaviness and painfulness of movement due to the greater gravitational energy of the earth—above all, the extraordinary intensity of the immense eyes—were at once vital, intense, inhuman, crippled, and monstrous. There was something fungoid in the oily brown skin, something in the clumsy deliberation of the tedious movements unspeakably nasty. Even at this first encounter, this first glimpse, I was overcome with disgust and dread.

Suddenly the monster vanished. It had toppled over the brim of the cylinder and fallen into the pit, with a thud like the fall of a great mass of leather. I heard it give a peculiar thick cry, and forthwith another of these creatures appeared darkly in the deep shadow of the aperture.

I turned and, running madly, made for the first group of trees, perhaps a hundred yards away; but I ran slantingly and stumbling, for I could not avert my face from these things.

There, among some young pine trees and furze bushes, I stopped, panting, and waited further developments. The common round the sand pits was dotted with people, standing like myself in a half-fascinated terror, staring at these creatures, or rather at the heaped gravel at the edge of the pit in which they lay. And then, with a renewed horror, I saw a round, black object bobbing up and down on the edge of the pit. It was the head of the shopman who had fallen in, but showing as a little black object against the hot western sun. Now he got his shoulder and knee up, and again he seemed to slip back until only his head was visible. Suddenly he vanished, and I could have fancied a faint shriek had reached me. I had a momentary impulse to go back and help him that my fears overruled.

Everything was then quite invisible, hidden by the deep pit and the heap of sand that the fall of the cylinder had made. Anyone coming along the road from Chobham or Woking would have been amazed at the sight—a dwindling multitude of perhaps a hundred people or more standing in a great irregular circle, in ditches, behind bushes, behind gates and hedges, saying little to one another and that in short, excited shouts, and staring, staring hard at a few heaps of sand. The barrow of ginger beer stood, a queer derelict, black against the burning sky, and in the sand pits was a row of deserted vehicles with their horses feeding out of nosebags or pawing the ground.

· ● ·

CHAPTER FIVE

The Heat-Ray

AFTER THE GLIMPSE I had had of the Martians emerging from the cylinder in which they had come to the earth from their planet, a kind of fascination paralysed my actions. I remained standing knee-deep in the heather, staring at the mound that hid them. I was a battleground of fear and curiosity.

I did not dare to go back towards the pit, but I felt a passionate longing to peer into it. I began walking, therefore, in a big curve, seeking some point of vantage and continually looking at the sand heaps that hid these new-comers to our earth. Once a leash of thin black whips, like the arms of an octopus, flashed across the sunset and was immediately withdrawn, and afterwards a thin rod rose up, joint by joint, bearing at its apex a circular disk that spun with a wobbling motion. What could be going on there?

Most of the spectators had gathered in one or two groups—one a little crowd towards Woking, the other a knot of people in the direction of Chobham. Evidently they shared my mental conflict. There were few near me. One man I approached—he was, I perceived, a neighbour of mine, though I did not know his name—and accosted. But it was scarcely a time for articulate conversation.

"What ugly brutes!" he said. "Good God! What ugly brutes!" He repeated this over and over again.

"Did you see a man in the pit?" I said; but he made no answer to that. We became silent, and stood watching for a time side by side, deriving, I fancy, a certain comfort in one another's company. Then I shifted my position to a little knoll that gave me the advantage of a yard or more of elevation and when I looked for him presently he was walking towards Woking.

The sunset faded to twilight before anything further happened. The crowd far away on the left, towards Woking, seemed to grow, and I heard now a faint murmur from it. The little knot of people towards Chobham dispersed. There was scarcely an intimation of movement from the pit.

It was this, as much as anything, that gave people courage, and I suppose the new arrivals from Woking also helped to restore confidence. At any rate, as the dusk came on a slow, intermittent movement upon the sand pits began, a movement that seemed to gather force as the stillness of the evening about the cylinder remained unbroken. Vertical black figures in twos and threes would advance, stop, watch, and advance again, spreading out as they did so in a thin irregular crescent that promised to enclose the pit in its attenuated horns. I, too, on my side began to move towards the pit.

Then I saw some cabmen and others had walked boldly into the sand pits, and heard the clatter of hoofs and the gride of wheels. I saw a lad trundling off the barrow of apples. And then, within thirty yards of the pit, advancing from the direction of Horsell, I noted a little black knot of men, the foremost of whom was waving a white flag.

This was the Deputation. There had been a hasty consultation, and since the Martians were evidently, in spite of their repulsive forms, intelligent creatures, it had been resolved to show them, by approaching them with signals, that we too were intelligent.

Flutter, flutter, went the flag, first to the right, then to the left. It was too far for me to recognise anyone there, but afterwards I learned that Ogilvy, Stent, and Henderson were with others in this attempt at communication. This little group had in its advance dragged inward, so to speak, the circumference of the now almost complete circle of people, and a number of dim black figures followed it at discreet distances.

Suddenly there was a flash of light, and a quantity of luminous greenish smoke came out of the pit in three distinct puffs, which drove up, one after the other, straight into the still air.

This smoke (or flame, perhaps, would be the better word for it) was so bright that the deep blue sky overhead and the hazy stretches of brown common towards Chertsey, set with black pine trees, seemed to darken abruptly as these puffs arose, and to remain the darker after their dispersal. At the same time a faint hissing sound became audible.

Beyond the pit stood the little wedge of people with the white flag at its apex, arrested by these phenomena, a little knot of small vertical black shapes upon the black ground. As the green smoke arose, their faces flashed out pallid green, and faded again as it vanished. Then slowly the hissing passed into a humming, into a long, loud, droning noise. Slowly a humped shape rose out of the pit, and the ghost of a beam of light seemed to flicker out from it.

Forthwith flashes of actual flame, a bright glare leaping from one to another, sprang from the scattered group of men. It was as if some invisible jet impinged upon them and flashed into white flame. It was as if each man were suddenly and momentarily turned to fire.

Then, by the light of their own destruction, I saw them staggering and falling, and their supporters turning to run.

I stood staring, not as yet realising that this was death leaping from man to man in that little distant crowd. All I felt was that it was something very strange. An almost noiseless and blinding flash of light, and a man fell headlong and lay still; and as the unseen shaft of heat passed over them, pine trees burst into fire, and every dry furze bush became with one dull thud a mass of flames. And far away towards Knaphill I saw the flashes of trees and hedges and wooden buildings suddenly set alight.

It was sweeping round swiftly and steadily, this flaming death, this invisible, inevitable sword of heat. I perceived it coming towards me by the flashing bushes it touched, and was too astounded and stupefied to stir. I heard the crackle of fire in the sand pits and the sudden squeal of a horse that was as suddenly stilled. Then it was as if an invisible yet intensely heated finger were drawn through the heather between me and the Martians, and all along a curving line beyond the sand pits the dark ground smoked and crackled.

Something fell with a crash far away to the left where the road from Woking station opens out on the common. Forthwith the hissing and humming ceased, and the black, dome-like object sank slowly out of sight into the pit.

All this had happened with such swiftness that I had stood motionless, dumbfounded and dazzled by the flashes of light. Had that death swept through a full circle, it must inevitably have slain me in my surprise. But it passed and spared me, and left the night about me suddenly dark and unfamiliar.

The undulating common seemed now dark almost to blackness, except where its roadways lay grey and pale under the deep blue sky of the early night. It was dark, and suddenly void of men. Overhead the stars were mustering, and in the west the sky was still a pale, bright, almost greenish blue. The tops of the pine trees and the roofs of Horsell came out sharp and black against the western afterglow. The Martians and their appliances were altogether invisible, save for that thin mast upon which their restless mirror wobbled. Patches of bush and isolated trees here and there smoked and glowed still, and the houses towards Woking station were sending up spires of flame into the stillness of the evening air.

Nothing was changed save for that and a terrible astonishment. The little group of black specks with the flag of white had been swept out of existence, and the stillness of the evening, so it seemed to me, had scarcely been broken.

It came to me that I was upon this dark common, helpless, unprotected, and alone. Suddenly, like a thing falling upon me from without, came—fear.

With an effort I turned and began a stumbling run through the heather.

The fear I felt was no rational fear, but a panic terror not only of the Martians, but of the dusk and stillness all about me. Such an extraordinary effect in unmanning me it had that I ran weeping silently as a child might do. Once I had turned, I did not dare to look back.

I remember I felt an extraordinary persuasion that I was being played with, that presently, when I was upon the very verge of safety, this mysterious death—as swift as the passage of light—would leap after me from the pit about the cylinder and strike me down.

．　●　．

CHAPTER SIX

The Heat-Ray in the Chobham Road

IT IS STILL A MATTER OF WONDER how the Martians are able to slay men so swiftly and so silently. Many think that in some way they are able to generate an intense heat in a chamber of practically absolute non-conductivity. This intense heat they project in a parallel beam against any object they choose, by means of a polished parabolic mirror of unknown composition, much as the parabolic mirror of a lighthouse projects a beam of light. But no one has absolutely proved these details. However it is done, it is certain that a beam of heat is the essence of the matter. Heat, and invisible, instead of visible, light. Whatever is combustible flashes into flame at its touch, lead runs like water, it softens iron, cracks and melts glass, and when it falls upon water, incontinently that explodes into steam.

That night nearly forty people lay under the starlight about the pit, charred and distorted beyond recognition, and all night long the common from Horsell to Maybury was deserted and brightly ablaze.

The news of the massacre probably reached Chobham, Woking, and Ottershaw about the same time. In Woking the shops had closed when the tragedy happened, and a number of people, shop people and so forth, attracted by the stories they had heard, were walking over the Horsell Bridge and along the road between the hedges that runs out at last upon the common. You may imagine the young people brushed up after the labours of the day, and making this novelty, as they would make any novelty, the excuse for walking together and enjoying a trivial flirtation. You may figure to yourself the hum of voices along the road in the gloaming. . . .

As yet, of course, few people in Woking even knew that the cylinder had opened, though poor Henderson had sent a messenger on a bicycle to the post office with a special wire to an evening paper.

As these folks came out by twos and threes upon the open, they found little knots of people talking excitedly and peering at the spinning mirror over the sand pits, and the new-comers were, no doubt, soon infected by the excitement of the occasion.

By half past eight, when the Deputation was destroyed, there may have been a crowd of three hundred people or more at this place, besides those who had left the road to approach the Martians nearer. There were three policemen too, one of whom was mounted, doing their best, under instructions from Stent, to keep the people back and deter them from approaching the cylinder. There was some booing from those more thoughtless and excitable souls to whom a crowd is always an occasion for noise and horse-play.

Stent and Ogilvy, anticipating some possibilities of a collision, had telegraphed from Horsell to the barracks as soon as the Martians emerged, for the help of a company of soldiers to protect these strange creatures from violence. After that they returned to lead that ill-fated advance. The description of their death, as it was seen by the crowd, tallies very closely with my own impressions: the three puffs of green smoke, the deep humming note, and the flashes of flame.

But that crowd of people had a far narrower escape than mine. Only the fact that a hummock of heathery sand intercepted the lower part of the Heat-Ray saved them. Had the elevation of the parabolic mirror been a few yards higher, none could have lived to tell the tale. They saw the flashes and the men falling and an invisible hand, as it were, lit the bushes as it hurried towards them through the twilight. Then, with a whistling note that rose above the droning of the pit, the beam swung close over their heads, lighting the tops of the beech trees that line the road, and splitting the bricks, smashing the windows, firing the window frames, and bringing down in crumbling ruin a portion of the gable of the house nearest the corner.

In the sudden thud, hiss, and glare of the igniting trees, the panic-stricken crowd seems to have swayed hesitatingly for some moments. Sparks and burning twigs began to fall into the road, and single leaves like puffs of flame. Hats and dresses caught fire. Then came a crying from the common. There were shrieks and shouts, and suddenly a mounted policeman came galloping through the confusion with his hands clasped over his head, screaming.

"They're coming!" a woman shrieked, and incontinently everyone was turning and pushing at those behind, in order to clear their way to Woking again. They must have bolted as blindly as a flock of sheep. Where the road grows narrow and black between the high banks the crowd jammed, and a desperate struggle occurred. All that crowd did not escape; three persons at least, two women and a little boy, were crushed and trampled there, and left to die amid the terror and the darkness.

· · ·

CHAPTER SEVEN
How I Reached Home

FOR MY OWN PART, I remember nothing of my flight except the stress of blundering against trees and stumbling through the heather. All about me gathered the invisible terrors of the Martians; that pitiless sword of heat seemed whirling to and fro, flourishing overhead before it descended and smote me out of life. I came into the road between the crossroads and Horsell, and ran along this to the crossroads.

At last I could go no further; I was exhausted with the violence of my emotion and of my flight, and I staggered and fell by the wayside. That was near the bridge that crosses the canal by the gasworks. I fell and lay still.

I must have remained there some time.

I sat up, strangely perplexed. For a moment, perhaps, I could not clearly understand how I came there. My terror had fallen from me like a garment. My hat had gone, and my collar had burst away from its fastener. A few minutes before, there had only been three real things before me—the immensity of the night and space and nature, my own feebleness and anguish, and the near approach of death. Now it was as if something turned over, and the point of view altered abruptly. There was no sensible transition from one state of mind to the other. I was immediately the self of every day again—a decent, ordinary citizen. The silent common, the impulse of my flight, the starting flames, were as if they had been in a dream. I asked myself had these latter things indeed happened? I could not credit it.

I rose and walked unsteadily up the steep incline of the bridge. My mind was blank wonder. My muscles and nerves seemed drained of their strength. I dare say I staggered drunkenly. A head rose over the arch, and the figure of a workman carrying a basket appeared. Beside him ran a little boy. He passed me, wishing me good night. I was minded to speak to him, but did not. I answered his greeting with a meaningless mumble and went on over the bridge.

Over the Maybury arch a train, a billowing tumult of white, firelit smoke, and a long caterpillar of lighted windows, went flying south— clatter, clatter, clap, rap, and it had gone. A dim group of people talked in the gate of one of the houses in the pretty little row of gables that was called Oriental Terrace. It was all so real and so familiar. And that behind me! It was frantic, fantastic! Such things, I told myself, could not be.

Perhaps I am a man of exceptional moods. I do not know how far my experience is common. At times I suffer from the strangest sense of detachment from myself and the world about me; I seem to watch it all from the outside, from somewhere inconceivably remote, out of time, out of space, out of the stress and tragedy of it all. This feeling was very strong upon me that night. Here was another side to my dream.

But the trouble was the blank incongruity of this serenity and the swift death flying yonder, not two miles away. There was a noise of business from the gasworks, and the electric lamps were all alight. I stopped at the group of people.

"What news from the common?" said I.

There were two men and a woman at the gate.

"Eh?" said one of the men, turning.

"What news from the common?" I said.

"Ain't yer just *been* there?" asked the men.

"People seem fair silly about the common," said the woman over the gate. "What's it all abart?"

"Haven't you heard of the men from Mars?" said I; "the creatures from Mars?"

"Quite enough," said the woman over the gate. "Thenks;" and all three of them laughed.

I felt foolish and angry. I tried and found I could not tell them what I had seen. They laughed again at my broken sentences.

"You'll hear more yet," I said, and went on to my home.

I startled my wife at the doorway, so haggard was I. I went into the dining room, sat down, drank some wine, and so soon as I could collect myself sufficiently I told her the things I had seen. The dinner, which was a cold one, had already been served, and remained neglected on the table while I told my story.

"There is one thing," I said, to allay the fears I had aroused; "they are the most sluggish things I ever saw crawl. They may keep the pit and kill people who come near them, but they cannot get out of it.... But the horror of them!"

"Don't, dear!" said my wife, knitting her brows and putting her hand on mine.

"Poor Ogilvy!" I said. "To think he may be lying dead there!"

My wife at least did not find my experience incredible. When I saw how deadly white her face was, I ceased abruptly.

"They may come here," she said again and again.

I pressed her to take wine, and tried to reassure her.

"They can scarcely move," I said.

I began to comfort her and myself by repeating all that Ogilvy had told me of the impossibility of the Martians establishing themselves on the earth. In particular I laid stress on the gravitational difficulty. On the surface of the earth the force of gravity is three times what it is on the surface of Mars. A Martian, therefore, would weigh three times more than on Mars, albeit his muscular strength would be the same. His own body would be a cope of lead to him. That, indeed, was the general opinion. Both *The Times* and the *Daily Telegraph*, for instance, insisted on it the next morning, and both overlooked, just as I did, two obvious modifying influences.

The atmosphere of the earth, we now know, contains far more oxygen or far less argon (whichever way one likes to put it) than does Mars. The invigorating influences of this excess of oxygen upon the Martians indisputably did much to counterbalance the increased weight of their bodies. And, in the second place, we all overlooked the fact that such mechanical intelligence as the Martian possessed was quite able to dispense with muscular exertion at a pinch.

But I did not consider these points at the time, and so my reasoning was dead against the chances of the invaders. With wine and food, the confidence of my own table, and the necessity of reassuring my wife, I grew by insensible degrees courageous and secure.

"They have done a foolish thing," said I, fingering my wineglass. "They are dangerous because, no doubt, they are mad with terror. Perhaps they expected to find no living things—certainly no intelligent living things.

"A shell in the pit," said I, "if the worst comes to the worst will kill them all."

The intense excitement of the events had no doubt left my perceptive powers in a state of erethism. I remember that dinner table with extraordinary vividness even now. My dear wife's sweet anxious face peering at me from under the pink lamp shade, the white cloth with its silver and glass table furniture—for in those days even philosophical writers had many little luxuries—the crimson-purple wine in my glass, are photographically distinct. At the end of it I sat, tempering nuts with a cigarette, regretting Ogilvy's rashness, and denouncing the shortsighted timidity of the Martians.

So some respectable dodo in the Mauritius might have lorded it in his nest, and discussed the arrival of that shipful of pitiless sailors in want of animal food. "We will peck them to death tomorrow, my dear."

I did not know it, but that was the last civilised dinner I was to eat for very many strange and terrible days.

· · ·

CHAPTER EIGHT
Friday Night

THE MOST EXTRAORDINARY THING to my mind, of all the strange and wonderful things that happened upon that Friday, was the dovetailing of the commonplace habits of our social order with the first beginnings of the series of events that was to topple that social order headlong. If on Friday night you had taken a pair of compasses and drawn a circle with a radius of five miles round the Woking sand pits,

I doubt if you would have had one human being outside it, unless it were some relation of Stent or of the three or four cyclists or London people lying dead on the common, whose emotions or habits were at all affected by the new-comers. Many people had heard of the cylinder, of course, and talked about it in their leisure, but it certainly did not make the sensation that an ultimatum to Germany would have done.

In London that night poor Henderson's telegram describing the gradual unscrewing of the shot was judged to be a canard, and his evening paper, after wiring for authentication from him and receiving no reply—the man was killed—decided not to print a special edition.

Even within the five-mile circle the great majority of people were inert. I have already described the behaviour of the men and women to whom I spoke. All over the district people were dining and supping; working men were gardening after the labours of the day, children were being put to bed, young people were wandering through the lanes love-making, students sat over their books.

Maybe there was a murmur in the village streets, a novel and dominant topic in the public-houses, and here and there a messenger, or even an eye-witness of the later occurrences, caused a whirl of excitement, a shouting, and a running to and fro; but for the most part the daily routine of working, eating, drinking, sleeping, went on as it had done for countless years—as though no planet Mars existed in the sky. Even at Woking station and Horsell and Chobham that was the case.

In Woking junction, until a late hour, trains were stopping and going on, others were shunting on the sidings, passengers were alighting and waiting, and everything was proceeding in the most ordinary way. A boy from the town, trenching on Smith's monopoly, was selling papers with the afternoon's news. The ringing impact of trucks, the sharp whistle of the engines from the junction, mingled with their shouts of "Men from Mars!" Excited men came into the station about nine o'clock with incredible tidings, and caused no more disturbance than drunkards might have done. People rattling Londonwards peered into the darkness outside the carriage windows, and saw only a rare, flickering, vanishing spark dance up from the direction of Horsell, a red glow and a thin veil of smoke driving across the stars, and thought that nothing more serious than a heath fire was happening. It was only round the edge of the common that any disturbance was perceptible. There were half a dozen villas burning on the Woking border. There were lights in all the houses on the common side of the three villages, and the people there kept awake till dawn.

A curious crowd lingered restlessly, people coming and going but the crowd remaining, both on the Chobham and Horsell bridges. One or two adventurous souls, it was afterwards found, went into the darkness and crawled quite near the Martians; but they never returned, for now and again a light-ray, like the beam of a warship's searchlight swept the common, and the Heat-Ray was ready to follow. Save for such, that big area of common was silent and desolate, and the charred bodies lay about on it all night under the stars, and all the next day. A noise of hammering from the pit was heard by many people.

So you have the state of things on Friday night. In the centre, sticking into the skin of our old planet Earth like a poisoned dart, was this cylinder. But the poison was scarcely working yet. Around it was a patch of silent common, smouldering in places, and with a few dark, dimly seen objects lying in contorted attitudes here and there. Here and there was a burning bush or tree. Beyond was a fringe of excitement, and farther than that fringe the inflammation had not crept as yet. In the rest of the world the stream of life still flowed as it had flowed for immemorial years. The fever of war that would presently clog vein and artery, deaden nerve and destroy brain, had still to develop.

All night long the Martians were hammering and stirring, sleepless, indefatigable, at work upon the machines they were making ready, and ever and again a puff of greenish-white smoke whirled up to the starlit sky.

About eleven a company of soldiers came through Horsell, and deployed along the edge of the common to form a cordon. Later a second company marched through Chobham to deploy on the north side of the common. Several officers from the Inkerman barracks had been on the common earlier in the day, and one, Major Eden, was reported to be missing. The colonel of the regiment came to the Chobham bridge and was busy questioning the crowd at midnight. The military authorities were certainly alive to the seriousness of the business. About eleven, the next morning's papers were able to say, a squadron of hussars, two Maxims, and about four hundred men of the Cardigan regiment started from Aldershot.

A few seconds after midnight the crowd in the Chertsey road, Woking, saw a star fall from heaven into the pine woods to the northwest. It had a greenish colour, and caused a silent brightness like summer lightning. This was the second cylinder.

• • •

CHAPTER NINE

The Fighting Begins

SATURDAY LIVES IN MY MEMORY as a day of suspense. It was a day of lassitude too, hot and close, with, I am told, a rapidly fluctuating barometer. I had slept but little, though my wife had succeeded in sleeping, and I rose early. I went into my garden before breakfast and stood listening, but towards the common there was nothing stirring but a lark.

The milkman came as usual. I heard the rattle of his chariot and I went round to the side gate to ask the latest news. He told me that during the night the Martians had been surrounded by troops, and that guns were expected. Then—a familiar, reassuring note—I heard a train running towards Woking.

"They aren't to be killed," said the milkman, "if that can possibly be avoided."

I saw my neighbour gardening, chatted with him for a time, and then strolled in to breakfast. It was a most unexceptional morning. My neighbour was of opinion that the troops would be able to capture or to destroy the Martians during the day.

"It's a pity they make themselves so unapproachable," he said. "It would be curious to know how they live on another planet; we might learn a thing or two."

He came up to the fence and extended a handful of strawberries, for his gardening was as generous as it was enthusiastic. At the same time he told me of the burning of the pine woods about the Byfleet Golf Links.

"They say," said he, "that there's another of those blessed things fallen there—number two. But one's enough, surely. This lot'll cost the insurance people a pretty penny before everything's settled." He laughed with an air of the greatest good humour as he said this. The woods, he said, were still burning, and pointed out a haze of smoke to me. "They will be hot under foot for days, on account of the thick soil of pine needles and turf," he said, and then grew serious over "poor Ogilvy."

After breakfast, instead of working, I decided to walk down towards the common. Under the railway bridge I found a group of soldiers— sappers, I think, men in small round caps, dirty red jackets unbuttoned, and showing their blue shirts, dark trousers, and boots coming to the calf. They told me no one was allowed over the canal, and, looking along the road towards the bridge, I saw one of the Cardigan men standing sentinel there. I talked with these soldiers for a time; I told them of my sight of the Martians on the previous evening. None of them had seen the Martians, and they had but the vaguest ideas of them, so that they plied me with questions. They said that they did not know who had authorised the movements of the troops; their idea was that a dispute had arisen at the Horse Guards. The ordinary sapper is a great deal better educated than the common soldier, and they discussed the peculiar conditions of the possible fight with some acuteness. I described the Heat-Ray to them, and they began to argue among themselves.

"Crawl up under cover and rush 'em, say I," said one.

"Get aht!" said another. "What's cover against this 'ere 'eat? Sticks to cook yer! What we got to do is to go as near as the ground'll let us, and then drive a trench."

"Blow yer trenches! You always want trenches; you ought to ha' been born a rabbit Snippy."

"Ain't they got any necks, then?" said a third, abruptly—a little, contemplative, dark man, smoking a pipe.

I repeated my description.

"Octopuses," said he, "that's what I calls 'em. Talk about fishers of men—fighters of fish it is this time!"

"It ain't no murder killing beasts like that," said the first speaker.

"Why not shell the darned things strite off and finish 'em?" said the little dark man. "You carn tell what they might do."

"Where's your shells?" said the first speaker. "There ain't no time. Do it in a rush, that's my tip, and do it at once."

So they discussed it. After a while I left them, and went on to the railway station to get as many morning papers as I could.

But I will not weary the reader with a description of that long morning and of the longer afternoon. I did not succeed in getting a glimpse of the common, for even Horsell and Chobham church towers were in the hands of the military authorities. The soldiers I addressed didn't know anything; the officers were mysterious as well as busy. I found people in the town quite secure again in the presence of the military, and I heard for the first time from Marshall, the tobacconist, that his son was among the dead on the common. The soldiers had made the people on the outskirts of Horsell lock up and leave their houses.

I got back to lunch about two, very tired for, as I have said, the day was extremely hot and dull; and in order to refresh myself I took a cold bath in the afternoon. About half past four I went up to the railway station to get an evening paper, for the morning papers had contained only a very inaccurate description of the killing of Stent, Henderson, Ogilvy, and the others. But there was little I didn't know. The Martians did not show an inch of themselves. They seemed busy in their pit, and there was a sound of hammering and an almost continuous streamer of smoke. Apparently they were busy getting ready for a struggle. "Fresh attempts have been made to signal, but without success," was the stereotyped formula of the papers. A sapper told me it was done by a man in a ditch with a flag on a long pole. The Martians took as much notice of such advances as we should of the lowing of a cow.

I must confess the sight of all this armament, all this preparation, greatly excited me. My imagination became belligerent, and defeated the invaders in a dozen striking ways; something of my schoolboy dreams of battle and heroism came back. It hardly seemed a fair fight to me at that time. They seemed very helpless in that pit of theirs.

About three o'clock there began the thud of a gun at measured intervals from Chertsey or Addlestone. I learned that the smouldering pine wood into which the second cylinder had fallen was being shelled, in the hope of destroying that object before it opened. It was only about five, however, that a field gun reached Chobham for use against the first body of Martians.

About six in the evening, as I sat at tea with my wife in the summerhouse talking vigorously about the battle that was lowering upon us, I heard a muffled detonation from the common, and immediately after a gust of firing. Close on the heels of that came a violent rattling crash, quite close to us, that shook the ground; and, starting out upon the lawn, I saw the tops of the trees about the Oriental College burst into smoky red flame, and the tower of the little church beside it slide down into ruin. The pinnacle of the mosque had vanished, and the roof line of the college itself looked as if a hundred-ton gun had been at work upon it. One of our chimneys cracked as if a shot had hit it, flew, and a piece of it came clattering down the tiles and made a heap of broken red fragments upon the flower bed by my study window.

I and my wife stood amazed. Then I realised that the crest of Maybury Hill must be within range of the Martians' Heat-Ray now that the college was cleared out of the way.

At that I gripped my wife's arm, and without ceremony ran her out into the road. Then I fetched out the servant, telling her I would go upstairs myself for the box she was clamouring for.

"We can't possibly stay here," I said; and as I spoke the firing re-opened for a moment upon the common.

"But where are we to go?" said my wife in terror.

I thought perplexed. Then I remembered her cousins at Leather-head.

"Leatherhead!" I shouted above the sudden noise.

She looked away from me downhill. The people were coming out of their houses, astonished.

"How are we to get to Leatherhead?" she said.

Down the hill I saw a bevy of hussars ride under the railway bridge; three galloped through the open gates of the Oriental College; two others dismounted, and began running from house to house. The sun, shining through the smoke that drove up from the tops of the trees, seemed blood red, and threw an unfamiliar lurid light upon everything.

"Stop here," said I; "you are safe here;" and I started off at once for the Spotted Dog, for I knew the landlord had a horse and dog cart. I ran, for I perceived that in a moment everyone upon this side of the hill would be moving. I found him in his bar, quite unaware of what was going on behind his house. A man stood with his back to me, talking to him.

"I must have a pound," said the landlord, "and I've no one to drive it."

"I'll give you two," said I, over the stranger's shoulder.

"What for?"

"And I'll bring it back by midnight," I said.

"Lord!" said the landlord; "what's the hurry? I'm selling my bit of a pig. Two pounds, and you bring it back? What's going on now?"

I explained hastily that I had to leave my home, and so secured the dog cart. At the time it did not seem to me nearly so urgent that the landlord should leave his. I took care to have the cart there and then, drove it off down the road, and, leaving it in charge of my wife and servant, rushed into my house and packed a few valuables, such plate as we had, and so forth. The beech trees below the house were burning while I did this, and the palings up the road glowed red. While I was occupied in this way, one of the dismounted hussars came running up. He was going from house to house, warning people to leave. He was going on as I came out of my front door, lugging my treasures, done up in a tablecloth. I shouted after him:

"What news?"

He turned, stared, bawled something about "crawling out in a thing like a dish cover," and ran on to the gate of the house at the crest. A sudden whirl of black smoke driving across the road hid him for a moment. I ran to my neighbour's door and rapped to satisfy myself of what I already knew, that his wife had gone to London with him and had locked up their house. I went in again, according to my promise, to get my servant's box, lugged it out, clapped it beside her on the tail of the dog cart, and then caught the reins and jumped up into the driver's seat beside my wife. In another moment we were clear of the smoke and noise, and spanking down the opposite slope of Maybury Hill towards Old Woking.

In front was a quiet sunny landscape, a wheat field ahead on either side of the road, and the Maybury Inn with its swinging sign. I saw the doctor's cart ahead of me. At the bottom of the hill I turned my head to look at the hillside I was leaving. Thick streamers of black smoke shot with threads of red fire were driving up into the still air, and throwing dark shadows upon the green treetops eastward. The smoke already extended far away to the east and west—to the Byfleet pine woods eastward, and to Woking on the west. The road was dotted with people running towards us. And very faint now, but very distinct through the hot, quiet air, one heard the whirr of a machine-gun that was presently stilled, and an intermittent cracking of rifles. Apparently the Martians were setting fire to everything within range of their Heat-Ray.

I am not an expert driver, and I had immediately to turn my attention to the horse. When I looked back again the second hill had hidden the black smoke. I slashed the horse with the whip, and gave him a loose rein until Woking and Send lay between us and that quivering tumult. I overtook and passed the doctor between Woking and Send.

. . .

CHAPTER TEN
In the Storm

LEATHERHEAD IS ABOUT TWELVE MILES from Maybury Hill. The scent of hay was in the air through the lush meadows beyond Pyrford, and the hedges on either side were sweet and gay with multitudes of dog-roses. The heavy firing that had broken out while we were driving down Maybury Hill ceased as abruptly as it began, leaving the evening very peaceful and still. We got to Leatherhead without misadventure about nine o'clock, and the horse had an hour's rest while I took supper with my cousins and commended my wife to their care.

My wife was curiously silent throughout the drive, and seemed oppressed with forebodings of evil. I talked to her reassuringly, pointing out that the Martians were tied to the pit by sheer heaviness, and at the utmost could but crawl a little out of it; but she answered only in monosyllables. Had it not been for my promise to the innkeeper, she would, I think, have urged me to stay in Leatherhead that night. Would that I had! Her face, I remember, was very white as we parted.

For my own part, I had been feverishly excited all day. Something very like the war fever that occasionally runs through a civilised community had got into my blood, and in my heart I was not so very sorry that I had to return to Maybury that night. I was even afraid that that last fusillade I had heard might mean the extermination of our invaders from Mars. I can best express my state of mind by saying that I wanted to be in at the death.

It was nearly eleven when I started to return. The night was unexpectedly dark; to me, walking out of the lighted passage of my cousins' house, it seemed indeed black, and it was as hot and close as the day. Overhead the clouds were driving fast, albeit not a breath stirred the shrubs about us. My cousins' man lit both lamps. Happily, I knew the road intimately. My wife stood in the light of the doorway, and watched me until I jumped up into the dog cart. Then abruptly she turned and went in, leaving my cousins side by side wishing me good hap.

I was a little depressed at first with the contagion of my wife's fears, but very soon my thoughts reverted to the Martians. At that time I was absolutely in the dark as to the course of the evening's fighting. I did not know even the circumstances that had precipitated the conflict. As I came through Ockham (for that was the way I returned, and not through Send and Old Woking) I saw along the western horizon a blood-red glow, which as I drew nearer, crept slowly up the sky. The driving clouds of the gathering thunderstorm mingled there with masses of black and red smoke.

Ripley Street was deserted, and except for a lighted window or so the village showed not a sign of life; but I narrowly escaped an accident at the corner of the road to Pyrford, where a knot of people stood with their backs to me. They said nothing to me as I passed. I do not know what they knew of the things happening beyond the hill, nor do I know if the silent houses I passed on my way were sleeping securely, or deserted and empty, or harassed and watching against the terror of the night.

From Ripley until I came through Pyrford I was in the valley of the Wey, and the red glare was hidden from me. As I ascended the little hill beyond Pyrford Church the glare came into view again, and the trees about me shivered with the first intimation of the storm that was upon me. Then I heard midnight pealing out from Pyrford Church behind me, and then came the silhouette of Maybury Hill, with its treetops and roofs black and sharp against the red.

Even as I beheld this a lurid green glare lit the road about me and showed the distant woods towards Addlestone. I felt a tug at the reins. I saw that the driving clouds had been pierced as it were by a thread of green fire, suddenly lighting their confusion and falling into the field to my left. It was the third falling star!

Close on its apparition, and blindingly violet by contrast, danced out the first lightning of the gathering storm, and the thunder burst like a rocket overhead. The horse took the bit between his teeth and bolted.

A moderate incline runs towards the foot of Maybury Hill, and down this we clattered. Once the lightning had begun, it went on in as rapid a succession of flashes as I have ever seen. The thunderclaps, treading one on the heels of another and with a strange crackling accompaniment, sounded more like the working of a gigantic electric machine than the usual detonating reverberations. The flickering light was blinding and confusing, and a thin hail smote gustily at my face as I drove down the slope.

At first I regarded little but the road before me, and then abruptly my attention was arrested by something that was moving rapidly down the opposite slope of Maybury Hill. At first I took it for the wet roof of a house, but one flash following another showed it to be in swift rolling movement. It was an elusive vision—a moment of bewildering darkness, and then, in a flash like daylight, the red masses of the Orphanage near the crest of the hill, the green tops of the pine trees, and this problematical object came out clear and sharp and bright.

And this Thing I saw! How can I describe it? A monstrous tripod, higher than many houses, striding over the young pine trees, and smashing them aside in its career; a walking engine of glittering metal, striding now across the heather; articulate ropes of steel dangling from it, and the clattering tumult of its passage mingling with the riot of the thunder. A flash, and it came out vividly, heeling over one way with two feet in the air, to vanish and reappear almost instantly as it seemed, with the next flash, a hundred yards nearer. Can you imagine a milking stool tilted and bowled violently along the ground? That was the impression those instant flashes gave. But instead of a milking stool imagine it a great body of machinery on a tripod stand.

Then suddenly the trees in the pine wood ahead of me were parted, as brittle reeds are parted by a man thrusting through them; they were snapped off and driven headlong, and a second huge tripod appeared, rushing, as it seemed, headlong towards me. And I was galloping hard to meet it! At the sight of the second monster my nerve went altogether. Not stopping to look again, I wrenched the horse's head hard round to the right and in another moment the dog cart had heeled over upon the horse; the shafts smashed noisily, and I was flung sideways and fell heavily into a shallow pool of water.

I crawled out almost immediately, and crouched, my feet still in the water, under a clump of furze. The horse lay motionless (his neck was broken, poor brute!) and by the lightning flashes I saw the black bulk of the overturned dog cart and the silhouette of the wheel still spinning slowly. In another moment the colossal mechanism went striding by me, and passed uphill towards Pyrford.

Seen nearer, the Thing was incredibly strange, for it was no mere insensate machine driving on its way. Machine it was, with a ringing metallic pace, and long, flexible, glittering tentacles (one of which gripped a young pine tree) swinging and rattling about its strange body. It picked its road as it went striding along, and the brazen hood that surmounted it moved to and fro with the inevitable suggestion of a head looking about. Behind the main body was a huge mass of white metal like a gigantic fisherman's basket, and puffs of green smoke squirted out from the joints of the limbs as the monster swept by me. And in an instant it was gone.

So much I saw then, all vaguely for the flickering of the lightning, in blinding highlights and dense black shadows.

As it passed it set up an exultant deafening howl that drowned the thunder—"Aloo! Aloo!"—and in another minute it was with its companion, half a mile away, stooping over something in the field. I have no doubt this Thing in the field was the third of the ten cylinders they had fired at us from Mars.

For some minutes I lay there in the rain and darkness watching, by the intermittent light, these monstrous beings of metal moving about in the distance over the hedge tops. A thin hail was now beginning, and as it came and went their figures grew misty and then flashed into clearness again. Now and then came a gap in the lightning, and the night swallowed them up.

I was soaked with hail above and puddle water below. It was some time before my blank astonishment would let me struggle up the bank to a drier position, or think at all of my imminent peril.

Not far from me was a little one-roomed squatter's hut of wood, surrounded by a patch of potato garden. I struggled to my feet at last, and, crouching and making use of every chance of cover, I made a run for this. I hammered at the door, but I could not make the people hear (if there were any people inside), and after a time I desisted, and, availing myself of a ditch for the greater part of the way, succeeded in crawling, unobserved by these monstrous machines, into the pine woods towards Maybury.

Under cover of this I pushed on, wet and shivering now, towards my own house. I walked among the trees trying to find the footpath. It was very dark indeed in the wood, for the lightning was now becoming infrequent, and the hail, which was pouring down in a torrent, fell in columns through the gaps in the heavy foliage.

If I had fully realised the meaning of all the things I had seen I should have immediately worked my way round through Byfleet to Street Cobham, and so gone back to rejoin my wife at Leatherhead. But that night the strangeness of things about me, and my physical wretchedness, prevented me, for I was bruised, weary, wet to the skin, deafened and blinded by the storm.

I had a vague idea of going on to my own house, and that was as much motive as I had. I staggered through the trees, fell into a ditch and bruised my knees against a plank, and finally splashed out into the lane that ran down from the College Arms. I say splashed, for the storm water was sweeping the sand down the hill in a muddy torrent. There in the darkness a man blundered into me and sent me reeling back.

He gave a cry of terror, sprang sideways, and rushed on before I could gather my wits sufficiently to speak to him. So heavy was the stress of the storm just at this place that I had the hardest task to win my way up the hill. I went close up to the fence on the left and worked my way along its palings.

Near the top I stumbled upon something soft, and, by a flash of lightning, saw between my feet a heap of black broadcloth and a pair of boots. Before I could distinguish clearly how the man lay, the flicker of light had passed. I stood over him waiting for the next flash. When it came, I saw that he was a sturdy man, cheaply but not shabbily dressed; his head was bent under his body, and he lay crumpled up close to the fence, as though he had been flung violently against it.

Overcoming the repugnance natural to one who had never before touched a dead body, I stooped and turned him over to feel for his heart. He was quite dead. Apparently his neck had been broken. The lightning flashed for a third time, and his face leaped upon me. I sprang to my feet. It was the landlord of the Spotted Dog, whose conveyance I had taken.

I stepped over him gingerly and pushed on up the hill. I made my way by the police station and the College Arms towards my own house. Nothing was burning on the hillside, though from the common there still came a red glare and a rolling tumult of ruddy smoke beating up against the drenching hail. So far as I could see by the flashes, the houses about me were mostly uninjured. By the College Arms a dark heap lay in the road.

Down the road towards Maybury Bridge there were voices and the sound of feet, but I had not the courage to shout or to go to them. I let myself in with my latchkey, closed, locked and bolted the door, staggered to the foot of the staircase, and sat down. My imagination was full of those striding metallic monsters, and of the dead body smashed against the fence.

I crouched at the foot of the staircase with my back to the wall, shivering violently.

• • •

CHAPTER ELEVEN
At the Window

I HAVE ALREADY SAID that my storms of emotion have a trick of exhausting themselves. After a time I discovered that I was cold and wet, and with little pools of water about me on the stair carpet. I got up almost mechanically, went into the dining room and drank some whiskey, and then I was moved to change my clothes.

After I had done that I went upstairs to my study, but why I did so I do not know. The window of my study looks over the trees and the railway towards Horsell Common. In the hurry of our departure this window had been left open. The passage was dark, and, by contrast with the picture the window frame enclosed, the side of the room seemed impenetrably dark. I stopped short in the doorway.

The thunderstorm had passed. The towers of the Oriental College and the pine trees about it had gone, and very far away, lit by a vivid red glare, the common about the sand pits was visible. Across the light huge black shapes, grotesque and strange, moved busily to and fro.

It seemed indeed as if the whole country in that direction was on fire—a broad hillside set with minute tongues of flame, swaying and writhing with the gusts of the dying storm, and throwing a red reflection upon the cloud scud above. Every now and then a haze of smoke from some nearer conflagration drove across the window and hid the Martian shapes. I could not see what they were doing, nor the clear form of them, nor recognise the black objects they were busied upon. Neither could I see the nearer fire, though the reflections of it danced on the wall and ceiling of the study. A sharp, resinous tang of burning was in the air.

I closed the door noiselessly and crept towards the window. As I did so, the view opened out until, on the one hand, it reached to the houses about Woking station, and on the other to the charred and blackened pine woods of Byfleet. There was a light down below the hill, on the railway, near the arch, and several of the houses along the Maybury road and the streets near the station were glowing ruins. The light upon the railway puzzled me at first; there were a black heap and a vivid glare, and to the right of that a row of yellow oblongs. Then I perceived this was a wrecked train, the fore part smashed and on fire, the hinder carriages still upon the rails.

Between these three main centres of light—the houses, the train, and the burning county towards Chobham—stretched irregular patches of dark country, broken here and there by intervals of dimly glowing and smoking ground. It was the strangest spectacle, that black expanse set with fire. It reminded me, more than anything else, of the Potteries at night. At first I could distinguish no people at all, though I peered intently for them. Later I saw against the light of Woking station a number of black figures hurrying one after the other across the line.

And this was the little world in which I had been living securely for years, this fiery chaos! What had happened in the last seven hours I still did not know; nor did I know, though I was beginning to guess, the relation between these mechanical colossi and the sluggish lumps I had seen disgorged from the cylinder. With a queer feeling of impersonal interest I turned my desk chair to the window, sat down, and stared at the blackened country, and particularly at the three gigantic black things that were going to and fro in the glare about the sand pits.

They seemed amazingly busy. I began to ask myself what they could be. Were they intelligent mechanisms? Such a thing I felt was impossible. Or did a Martian sit within each, ruling, directing, using, much as a man's brain sits and rules in his body? I began to compare the things to human machines, to ask myself for the first time in my life how an ironclad or a steam engine would seem to an intelligent lower animal.

The storm had left the sky clear, and over the smoke of the burning land the little fading pinpoint of Mars was dropping into the west, when a soldier came into my garden. I heard a slight scraping at the fence, and rousing myself from the lethargy that had fallen upon me, I looked down and saw him dimly, clambering over the palings. At the sight of another human being my torpor passed, and I leaned out of the window eagerly.

"Hist!" said I, in a whisper.

He stopped astride of the fence in doubt. Then he came over and across the lawn to the corner of the house. He bent down and stepped softly.

"Who's there?" he said, also whispering, standing under the window and peering up.

"Where are you going?" I asked.

"God knows."

"Are you trying to hide?"

"That's it."

"Come into the house," I said.

I went down, unfastened the door, and let him in, and locked the door again. I could not see his face. He was hatless, and his coat was unbuttoned.

"My God!" he said, as I drew him in.

"What has happened?" I asked.

"What hasn't?" In the obscurity I could see he made a gesture of despair. "They wiped us out—simply wiped us out," he repeated again and again.

He followed me, almost mechanically, into the dining room.

"Take some whiskey," I said, pouring out a stiff dose.

He drank it. Then abruptly he sat down before the table, put his head on his arms, and began to sob and weep like a little boy, in a perfect passion of emotion, while I, with a curious forgetfulness of my own recent despair, stood beside him, wondering.

It was a long time before he could steady his nerves to answer my questions, and then he answered perplexingly and brokenly. He was a driver in the artillery, and had only come into action about seven. At that time firing was going on across the common, and it was said the first party of Martians were crawling slowly towards their second cylinder under cover of a metal shield.

Later this shield staggered up on tripod legs and became the first of the fighting-machines I had seen. The gun he drove had been unlimbered near Horsell, in order to command the sand pits, and its arrival it was that had precipitated the action. As the limber gunners went to the rear, his horse trod in a rabbit hole and came down, throwing him into a depression of the ground. At the same moment the gun exploded behind him, the ammunition blew up, there was fire all about him, and he found himself lying under a heap of charred dead men and dead horses.

"I lay still," he said, "scared out of my wits, with the fore quarter of a horse atop of me. We'd been wiped out. And the smell—good God! Like burnt meat! I was hurt across the back by the fall of the horse, and there I had to lie until I felt better. Just like parade it had been a minute before—then stumble, bang, swish!"

"Wiped out!" he said.

He had hid under the dead horse for a long time, peeping out furtively across the common. The Cardigan men had tried a rush, in skirmishing order, at the pit, simply to be swept out of existence. Then the monster had risen to its feet and had begun to walk leisurely to and fro across the common among the few fugitives, with its headlike hood turning about exactly like the head of a cowled human being. A kind of arm carried a complicated metallic case, about which green flashes scintillated, and out of the funnel of this there smoked the Heat-Ray.

In a few minutes there was, so far as the soldier could see, not a living thing left upon the common, and every bush and tree upon it that was not already a blackened skeleton was burning. The hussars had been on the road beyond the curvature of the ground, and he saw nothing of them. He heard the Martians rattle for a time and then become still. The giant saved Woking station and its cluster of houses until the last; then in a moment the Heat-Ray was brought to bear, and the town became a heap of fiery ruins. Then the Thing shut off the Heat-Ray, and turning its back upon the artilleryman, began to waddle away towards the smouldering pine woods that sheltered the second cylinder. As it did so a second glittering Titan built itself up out of the pit.

The second monster followed the first, and at that the artilleryman began to crawl very cautiously across the hot heather ash towards Horsell. He managed to get alive into the ditch by the side of the road, and so escaped to Woking. There his story became ejaculatory. The place was impassable. It seems there were a few people alive there, frantic for the most part and many burned and scalded. He was turned aside by the fire, and hid among some almost scorching heaps of broken wall as one of the Martian giants returned. He saw this one pursue a man, catch him up in one of its steely tentacles, and knock his head against the trunk of a pine tree. At last, after nightfall, the artilleryman made a rush for it and got over the railway embankment.

Since then he had been skulking along towards Maybury, in the hope of getting out of danger Londonward. People were hiding in trenches and cellars, and many of the survivors had made off towards Woking village and Send. He had been consumed with thirst until he found one of the water mains near the railway arch smashed, and the water bubbling out like a spring upon the road.

That was the story I got from him, bit by bit. He grew calmer telling me and trying to make me see the things he had seen. He had eaten no food since midday, he told me early in his narrative, and I found some mutton and bread in the pantry and brought it into the room. We lit no lamp for fear of attracting the Martians, and ever and again our hands would touch upon bread or meat. As he talked, things about us came darkly out of the darkness, and the trampled bushes and broken rose trees outside the window grew distinct. It would seem that a number of men or animals had rushed across the lawn. I began to see his face, blackened and haggard, as no doubt mine was also.

When we had finished eating we went softly upstairs to my study, and I looked again out of the open window. In one night the valley had become a valley of ashes. The fires had dwindled now. Where flames had been there were now streamers of smoke; but the countless ruins of shattered and gutted houses and blasted and blackened trees that the night had hidden stood out now gaunt and terrible in the pitiless light of dawn. Yet here and there some object had had the luck to escape—a white railway signal here, the end of a greenhouse there, white and fresh amid the wreckage. Never before in the history of warfare had destruction been so indiscriminate and so universal. And shining with the growing light of the east, three of the metallic giants stood about the pit, their cowls rotating as though they were surveying the desolation they had made.

It seemed to me that the pit had been enlarged, and ever and again puffs of vivid green vapour streamed up and out of it towards the brightening dawn—streamed up, whirled, broke, and vanished.

Beyond were the pillars of fire about Chobham. They became pillars of bloodshot smoke at the first touch of day.

• • •

CHAPTER TWELVE

What I Saw
of the Destruction
# of Weybridge
and Shepperton

AS THE DAWN GREW BRIGHTER we withdrew from the window from which we had watched the Martians, and went very quietly down-stairs.

The artilleryman agreed with me that the house was no place to stay in. He proposed, he said, to make his way Londonward, and thence re-join his battery—No. 12, of the Horse Artillery. My plan was to return at once to Leatherhead; and so greatly had the strength of the Martians impressed me that I had determined to take my wife to Newhaven, and go with her out of the country forthwith. For I already perceived clearly that the country about London must inevitably be the scene of a disas-trous struggle before such creatures as these could be destroyed.

Between us and Leatherhead, however, lay the third cylinder, with its guarding giants. Had I been alone, I think I should have taken my chance and struck across country. But the artilleryman dissuaded me: "It's no kindness to the right sort of wife," he said, "to make her a wid-ow;" and in the end I agreed to go with him, under cover of the woods, northward as far as Street Cobham before I parted with him. Thence I would make a big detour by Epsom to reach Leatherhead.

I should have started at once, but my companion had been in active service and he knew better than that. He made me ransack the house for a flask, which he filled with whiskey; and we lined every available pocket with packets of biscuits and slices of meat. Then we crept out of the house, and ran as quickly as we could down the ill-made road by which I had come overnight. The houses seemed deserted. In the road lay a group of three charred bodies close together, struck dead by the Heat-Ray; and here and there were things that people had dropped—a clock, a slipper, a silver spoon, and the like poor valuables. At the corner turning up towards the post office a little cart, filled with boxes and furniture, and horseless, heeled over on a broken wheel. A cash box had been hastily smashed open and thrown under the debris.

Except the lodge at the Orphanage, which was still on fire, none of the houses had suffered very greatly here. The Heat-Ray had shaved the chimney tops and passed. Yet, save ourselves, there did not seem to be a living soul on Maybury Hill. The majority of the inhabitants had escaped, I suppose, by way of the Old Woking road—the road I had taken when I drove to Leatherhead—or they had hidden.

We went down the lane, by the body of the man in black, sodden now from the overnight hail, and broke into the woods at the foot of the hill. We pushed through these towards the railway without meeting a soul. The woods across the line were but the scarred and blackened ruins of woods; for the most part the trees had fallen, but a certain proportion still stood, dismal grey stems, with dark brown foliage instead of green.

On our side the fire had done no more than scorch the nearer trees; it had failed to secure its footing. In one place the woodmen had been at work on Saturday; trees, felled and freshly trimmed, lay in a clearing, with heaps of sawdust by the sawing-machine and its engine. Hard by was a temporary hut, deserted. There was not a breath of wind this morning, and everything was strangely still. Even the birds were hushed, and as we hurried along I and the artilleryman talked in whispers and looked now and again over our shoulders. Once or twice we stopped to listen.

After a time we drew near the road, and as we did so we heard the clatter of hoofs and saw through the tree stems three cavalry soldiers riding slowly towards Woking. We hailed them, and they halted while we hurried towards them. It was a lieutenant and a couple of privates of the 8th Hussars, with a stand like a theodolite, which the artilleryman told me was a heliograph.

"You are the first men I've seen coming this way this morning," said the lieutenant. "What's brewing?"

His voice and face were eager. The men behind him stared curiously. The artilleryman jumped down the bank into the road and saluted.

"Gun destroyed last night, sir. Have been hiding. Trying to rejoin battery, sir. You'll come in sight of the Martians, I expect, about half a mile along this road."

"What the dickens are they like?" asked the lieutenant.

"Giants in armour, sir. Hundred feet high. Three legs and a body like 'luminium, with a mighty great head in a hood, sir."

"Get out!" said the lieutenant. "What confounded nonsense!"

"You'll see, sir. They carry a kind of box, sir, that shoots fire and strikes you dead."

"What d'ye mean—a gun?"

"No, sir," and the artilleryman began a vivid account of the Heat-Ray. Halfway through, the lieutenant interrupted him and looked up at me. I was still standing on the bank by the side of the road.

"It's perfectly true," I said.

"Well," said the lieutenant, "I suppose it's my business to see it too. Look here"—to the artilleryman—"we're detailed here clearing people out of their houses. You'd better go along and report yourself to Brigadier-General Marvin, and tell him all you know. He's at Weybridge. Know the way?"

"I do," I said; and he turned his horse southward again.

"Half a mile, you say?" said he.

"At most," I answered, and pointed over the treetops southward. He thanked me and rode on, and we saw them no more.

Farther along we came upon a group of three women and two children in the road, busy clearing out a labourer's cottage. They had got hold of a little hand truck, and were piling it up with unclean-looking bundles and shabby furniture. They were all too assiduously engaged to talk to us as we passed.

By Byfleet station we emerged from the pine trees, and found the country calm and peaceful under the morning sunlight. We were far beyond the range of the Heat-Ray there, and had it not been for the silent desertion of some of the houses, the stirring movement of packing in others, and the knot of soldiers standing on the bridge over the railway and staring down the line towards Woking, the day would have seemed very like any other Sunday.

Several farm waggons and carts were moving creakily along the road to Addlestone, and suddenly through the gate of a field we saw, across a stretch of flat meadow, six twelve-pounders standing neatly at equal distances pointing towards Woking. The gunners stood by the guns waiting, and the ammunition waggons were at a business-like distance. The men stood almost as if under inspection.

"That's good!" said I. "They will get one fair shot, at any rate."

The artilleryman hesitated at the gate.

"I shall go on," he said.

Farther on towards Weybridge, just over the bridge, there were a number of men in white fatigue jackets throwing up a long rampart, and more guns behind.

"It's bows and arrows against the lightning, anyhow," said the artilleryman. "They 'aven't seen that fire-beam yet."

The officers who were not actively engaged stood and stared over the treetops southwestward, and the men digging would stop every now and again to stare in the same direction.

Byfleet was in a tumult; people packing, and a score of hussars, some of them dismounted, some on horseback, were hunting them about. Three or four black government waggons, with crosses in white circles, and an old omnibus, among other vehicles, were being loaded in the village street. There were scores of people, most of them sufficiently sabbatical to have assumed their best clothes. The soldiers were having the greatest difficulty in making them realise the gravity of their position. We saw one shrivelled old fellow with a huge box and a score or more of flower pots containing orchids, angrily expostulating with the corporal who would leave them behind. I stopped and gripped his arm.

"Do you know what's over there?" I said, pointing at the pine tops that hid the Martians.

"Eh?" said he, turning. "I was explainin' these is vallyble."

"Death!" I shouted. "Death is coming! Death!" and leaving him to digest that if he could, I hurried on after the artilleryman. At the corner I looked back. The soldier had left him, and he was still standing by his box, with the pots of orchids on the lid of it, and staring vaguely over the trees.

No one in Weybridge could tell us where the headquarters were established; the whole place was in such confusion as I had never seen in any town before. Carts, carriages everywhere, the most astonishing miscellany of conveyances and horseflesh. The respectable inhabitants of the place, men in golf and boating costumes, wives prettily dressed, were packing, river-side loafers energetically helping, children excited, and, for the most part, highly delighted at this astonishing variation of their Sunday experiences. In the midst of it all the worthy vicar was very pluckily holding an early celebration, and his bell was jangling out above the excitement.

I and the artilleryman, seated on the step of the drinking fountain, made a very passable meal upon what we had brought with us. Patrols of soldiers—here no longer hussars, but grenadiers in white—were warning people to move now or to take refuge in their cellars as soon as the firing began. We saw as we crossed the railway bridge that a growing crowd of people had assembled in and about the railway station, and the swarming platform was piled with boxes and packages. The ordinary traffic had been stopped, I believe, in order to allow of the passage of troops and guns to Chertsey, and I have heard since that a savage struggle occurred for places in the special trains that were put on at a later hour.

We remained at Weybridge until midday, and at that hour we found ourselves at the place near Shepperton Lock where the Wey and Thames join. Part of the time we spent helping two old women to pack a little cart. The Wey has a treble mouth, and at this point boats are to be hired, and there was a ferry across the river. On the Shepperton side was an inn with a lawn, and beyond that the tower of Shepperton Church—it has been replaced by a spire—rose above the trees.

Here we found an excited and noisy crowd of fugitives. As yet the flight had not grown to a panic, but there were already far more people than all the boats going to and fro could enable to cross. People came panting along under heavy burdens; one husband and wife were even carrying a small outhouse door between them, with some of their household goods piled thereon. One man told us he meant to try to get away from Shepperton station.

There was a lot of shouting, and one man was even jesting. The idea people seemed to have here was that the Martians were simply formidable human beings, who might attack and sack the town, to be certainly destroyed in the end. Every now and then people would glance nervously across the Wey, at the meadows towards Chertsey, but everything over there was still.

Across the Thames, except just where the boats landed, everything was quiet, in vivid contrast with the Surrey side. The people who landed there from the boats went tramping off down the lane. The big ferryboat had just made a journey. Three or four soldiers stood on the lawn of the inn, staring and jesting at the fugitives, without offering to help. The inn was closed, as it was now within prohibited hours.

"What's that?" cried a boatman, and "Shut up, you fool!" said a man near me to a yelping dog. Then the sound came again, this time from the direction of Chertsey, a muffled thud—the sound of a gun.

The fighting was beginning. Almost immediately unseen batteries across the river to our right, unseen because of the trees, took up the chorus, firing heavily one after the other. A woman screamed. Everyone stood arrested by the sudden stir of battle, near us and yet invisible to us. Nothing was to be seen save flat meadows, cows feeding unconcernedly for the most part, and silvery pollard willows motionless in the warm sunlight.

"The sojers'll stop 'em," said a woman beside me, doubtfully. A haziness rose over the treetops.

Then suddenly we saw a rush of smoke far away up the river, a puff of smoke that jerked up into the air and hung; and forthwith the ground heaved under foot and a heavy explosion shook the air, smashing two or three windows in the houses near, and leaving us astonished.

"Here they are!" shouted a man in a blue jersey. "Yonder! D'yer see them? Yonder!"

Quickly, one after the other, one, two, three, four of the armoured Martians appeared, far away over the little trees, across the flat meadows that stretched towards Chertsey, and striding hurriedly towards the river. Little cowled figures they seemed at first, going with a rolling motion and as fast as flying birds.

Then, advancing obliquely towards us, came a fifth. Their armoured bodies glittered in the sun as they swept swiftly forward upon the guns, growing rapidly larger as they drew nearer. One on the extreme left, the remotest that is, flourished a huge case high in the air, and the ghostly, terrible Heat-Ray I had already seen on Friday night smote towards Chertsey, and struck the town.

At sight of these strange, swift, and terrible creatures the crowd near the water's edge seemed to me to be for a moment horror-struck. There was no screaming or shouting, but a silence. Then a hoarse murmur and a movement of feet—a splashing from the water. A man, too frightened to drop the portmanteau he carried on his shoulder, swung ground and sent me staggering with a blow from the corner of his burden. A woman thrust at me with her hand and rushed past me. I turned with the rush of the people, but I was not too terrified for thought. The terrible Heat-Ray was in my mind. To get under water! That was it!

"Get under water!" I shouted, unheeded.

I faced about again, and rushed towards the approaching Martian, rushed right down the gravelly beach and headlong into the water. Others did the same. A boatload of people putting back came leaping out as I rushed past. The stones under my feet were muddy and slippery, and the river was so low that I ran perhaps twenty feet scarcely waist-deep. Then, as the Martian towered overhead scarcely a couple of hundred yards away, I flung myself forward under the surface. The splashes of the people in the boats leaping into the river sounded like thunderclaps in my ears. People were landing hastily on both sides of the river. But the Martian machine took no more notice for the moment of the people running this way and that than a man would of the confusion of ants in a nest against which his foot has kicked. When, half suffocated, I raised my head above water, the Martian's hood pointed at the batteries that were still firing across the river, and as it advanced it swung loose what must have been the generator of the Heat-Ray.

In another moment it was on the bank, and in a stride wading half-way across. The knees of its foremost legs bent at the farther bank, and in another moment it had raised itself to its full height again, close to the village of Shepperton. Forthwith the six guns which, unknown to anyone on the right bank, had been hidden behind the outskirts of that village, fired simultaneously. The sudden near concussion, the last close upon the first, made my heart jump. The monster was already raising the case generating the Heat-Ray as the first shell burst six yards above the hood.

I gave a cry of astonishment. I saw and thought nothing of the other four Martian monsters; my attention was riveted upon the nearer incident. Simultaneously two other shells burst in the air near the body as the hood twisted round in time to receive, but not in time to dodge, the fourth shell.

The shell burst clean in the face of the Thing. The hood bulged, flashed, was whirled off in a dozen tattered fragments of red flesh and glittering metal.

"Hit!" shouted I, with something between a scream and a cheer.

I heard answering shouts from the people in the water about me. I could have leaped out of the water with that momentary exultation.

The decapitated colossus reeled like a drunken giant; but it did not fall over. It recovered its balance by a miracle, and, no longer heeding its steps and with the camera that fired the Heat-Ray now rigidly upheld, it reeled swiftly upon Shepperton. The living intelligence, the Martian within the hood, was slain and splashed to the four winds of heaven, and the Thing was now but a mere intricate device of metal whirling to destruction. It drove along in a straight line, incapable of guidance. It struck the tower of Shepperton Church, smashing it down as the impact of a battering ram might have done, swerved aside, blundered on and collapsed with tremendous force into the river out of my sight.

A violent explosion shook the air, and a spout of water, steam, mud, and shattered metal shot far up into the sky. As the camera of the Heat-Ray hit the water, the latter had immediately flashed into steam. In another moment a huge wave, like a muddy tidal bore but almost scaldingly hot, came sweeping round the bend upstream. I saw people struggling shorewards, and heard their screaming and shouting faintly above the seething and roar of the Martian's collapse.

For a moment I heeded nothing of the heat, forgot the patent need of self-preservation. I splashed through the tumultuous water, push-ing aside a man in black to do so, until I could see round the bend. Half a dozen deserted boats pitched aimlessly upon the confusion of the waves. The fallen Martian came into sight downstream, lying across the river, and for the most part submerged.

Thick clouds of steam were pouring off the wreckage, and through the tumultuously whirling wisps I could see, intermittently and vaguely, the gigantic limbs churning the water and flinging a splash and spray of mud and froth into the air. The tentacles swayed and struck like living arms, and, save for the helpless purposelessness of these movements, it was as if some wounded thing were struggling for its life amid the waves. Enormous quantities of a ruddy-brown fluid were spurting up in noisy jets out of the machine.

My attention was diverted from this death flurry by a furious yelling, like that of the thing called a siren in our manufacturing towns. A man, knee-deep near the towing path, shouted inaudibly to me and pointed. Looking back, I saw the other Martians advancing with gigantic strides down the riverbank from the direction of Chertsey. The Shepperton guns spoke this time unavailingly.

At that I ducked at once under water, and, holding my breath until movement was an agony, blundered painfully ahead under the surface as long as I could. The water was in a tumult about me, and rapidly growing hotter.

When for a moment I raised my head to take breath and throw the hair and water from my eyes, the steam was rising in a whirling white fog that at first hid the Martians altogether. The noise was deafening. Then I saw them dimly, colossal figures of grey, magnified by the mist. They had passed by me, and two were stooping over the frothing, tu-multuous ruins of their comrade.

The third and fourth stood beside him in the water, one perhaps two hundred yards from me, the other towards Laleham. The generators of the Heat-Rays waved high, and the hissing beams smote down this way and that.

The air was full of sound, a deafening and confusing conflict of nois-es—the clangorous din of the Martians, the crash of falling houses, the thud of trees, fences, sheds flashing into flame, and the crackling and roaring of fire. Dense black smoke was leaping up to mingle with the steam from the river, and as the Heat-Ray went to and fro over Wey-bridge its impact was marked by flashes of incandescent white, that gave place at once to a smoky dance of lurid flames. The nearer houses still stood intact, awaiting their fate, shadowy, faint and pallid in the steam, with the fire behind them going to and fro.

For a moment perhaps I stood there, breast-high in the almost boiling water, dumbfounded at my position, hopeless of escape. Through the reek I could see the people who had been with me in the river scrambling out of the water through the reeds, like little frogs hurrying through grass from the advance of a man, or running to and fro in utter dismay on the towing path.

Then suddenly the white flashes of the Heat-Ray came leaping towards me. The houses caved in as they dissolved at its touch, and darted out flames; the trees changed to fire with a roar. The Ray flickered up and down the towing path, licking off the people who ran this way and that, and came down to the water's edge not fifty yards from where I stood. It swept across the river to Shepperton, and the water in its track rose in a boiling weal crested with steam. I turned shoreward.

In another moment the huge wave, well-nigh at the boiling-point had rushed upon me. I screamed aloud, and scalded, half blinded, agonised, I staggered through the leaping, hissing water towards the shore. Had my foot stumbled, it would have been the end. I fell helplessly, in full sight of the Martians, upon the broad, bare gravelly spit that runs down to mark the angle of the Wey and Thames. I expected nothing but death.

I have a dim memory of the foot of a Martian coming down within a score of yards of my head, driving straight into the loose gravel, whirling it this way and that and lifting again; of a long suspense, and then of the four carrying the debris of their comrade between them, now clear and then presently faint through a veil of smoke, receding interminably, as it seemed to me, across a vast space of river and meadow. And then, very slowly, I realised that by a miracle I had escaped.

● ● ●

CHAPTER THIRTEEN
How I Fell in with the Curate

AFTER GETTING THIS SUDDEN LESSON in the power of terrestrial weapons, the Martians retreated to their original position upon Horsell Common; and in their haste, and encumbered with the debris of their smashed companion, they no doubt overlooked many such a stray and negligible victim as myself. Had they left their comrade and pushed on forthwith, there was nothing at that time between them and London but batteries of twelve-pounder guns, and they would certainly have reached the capital in advance of the tidings of their approach; as sudden, dreadful, and destructive their advent would have been as the earthquake that destroyed Lisbon a century ago.

But they were in no hurry. Cylinder followed cylinder on its interplanetary flight; every twenty-four hours brought them reinforcement. And meanwhile the military and naval authorities, now fully alive to the tremendous power of their antagonists, worked with furious energy. Every minute a fresh gun came into position until, before twilight, every copse, every row of suburban villas on the hilly slopes about Kingston and Richmond, masked an expectant black muzzle. And through the charred and desolated area—perhaps twenty square miles altogether— that encircled the Martian encampment on Horsell Common, through charred and ruined villages among the green trees, through the blackened and smoking arcades that had been but a day ago pine spinneys, crawled the devoted scouts with the heliographs that were presently to warn the gunners of the Martian approach. But the Martians now understood our command of artillery and the danger of human proximity, and not a man ventured within a mile of either cylinder, save at the price of his life.

It would seem that these giants spent the earlier part of the afternoon in going to and fro, transferring everything from the second and third cylinders—the second in Addlestone Golf Links and the third at Pyrford—to their original pit on Horsell Common. Over that, above the blackened heather and ruined buildings that stretched far and wide, stood one as sentinel, while the rest abandoned their vast fighting-machines and descended into the pit. They were hard at work there far into the night, and the towering pillar of dense green smoke that rose therefrom could be seen from the hills about Merrow, and even, it is said, from Banstead and Epsom Downs.

And while the Martians behind me were thus preparing for their next sally, and in front of me humanity gathered for the battle, I made my way with infinite pains and labour from the fire and smoke of burning Weybridge towards London.

I saw an abandoned boat, very small and remote, drifting downstream; and throwing off the most of my sodden clothes, I went after it, gained it, and so escaped out of that destruction. There were no oars in the boat, but I contrived to paddle, as well as my parboiled hands would allow, down the river towards Halliford and Walton, going very tediously and continually looking behind me, as you may well understand. I followed the river, because I considered that the water gave me my best chance of escape should these giants return.

The hot water from the Martian's overthrow drifted downstream with me, so that for the best part of a mile I could see little of either bank. Once, however, I made out a string of black figures hurrying across the meadows from the direction of Weybridge. Halliford, it seemed, was deserted, and several of the houses facing the river were on fire. It was strange to see the place quite tranquil, quite desolate under the hot blue sky, with the smoke and little threads of flame going straight up into the heat of the afternoon. Never before had I seen houses burning without the accompaniment of an obstructive crowd. A little farther on the dry reeds up the bank were smoking and glowing, and a line of fire inland was marching steadily across a late field of hay.

For a long time I drifted, so painful and weary was I after the violence I had been through, and so intense the heat upon the water. Then my fears got the better of me again, and I resumed my paddling. The sun scorched my bare back. At last, as the bridge at Walton was coming into sight round the bend, my fever and faintness overcame my fears, and I landed on the Middlesex bank and lay down, deadly sick, amid the long grass. I suppose the time was then about four or five o'clock. I got up presently, walked perhaps half a mile without meeting a soul, and then lay down again in the shadow of a hedge. I seem to remember talking, wanderingly, to myself during that last spurt. I was also very thirsty, and bitterly regretful I had drunk no more water. It is a curious thing that I felt angry with my wife; I cannot account for it, but my impotent desire to reach Leatherhead worried me excessively.

I do not clearly remember the arrival of the curate, so that probably I dozed. I became aware of him as a seated figure in soot-smudged shirt sleeves, and with his upturned, clean-shaven face staring at a faint flickering that danced over the sky. The sky was what is called a mackerel sky—rows and rows of faint down-plumes of cloud, just tinted with the midsummer sunset.

I sat up, and at the rustle of my motion he looked at me quickly.

"Have you any water?" I asked abruptly.

He shook his head.

"You have been asking for water for the last hour," he said.

For a moment we were silent, taking stock of each other. I dare say he found me a strange enough figure, naked, save for my water-soaked trousers and socks, scalded, and my face and shoulders blackened by the smoke. His face was a fair weakness, his chin retreated, and his hair lay in crisp, almost flaxen curls on his low forehead; his eyes were rather large, pale blue, and blankly staring. He spoke abruptly, looking vacantly away from me.

"What does it mean?" he said. "What do these things mean?"

I stared at him and made no answer.

He extended a thin white hand and spoke in almost a complaining tone.

"Why are these things permitted? What sins have we done? The morning service was over, I was walking through the roads to clear my brain for the afternoon, and then—fire, earthquake, death! As if it were Sodom and Gomorrah! All our work undone, all the work— What are these Martians?"

"What are we?" I answered, clearing my throat.

He gripped his knees and turned to look at me again. For half a minute, perhaps, he stared silently.

"I was walking through the roads to clear my brain," he said. "And suddenly—fire, earthquake, death!"

He relapsed into silence, with his chin now sunken almost to his knees.

Presently he began waving his hand.

"All the work—all the Sunday schools— What have we done—what has Weybridge done? Everything gone—everything destroyed. The church! We rebuilt it only three years ago. Gone! Swept out of existence! Why?"

Another pause, and he broke out again like one demented.

"The smoke of her burning goeth up for ever and ever!" he shouted.

His eyes flamed, and he pointed a lean finger in the direction of Weybridge.

By this time I was beginning to take his measure. The tremendous tragedy in which he had been involved—it was evident he was a fugitive from Weybridge—had driven him to the very verge of his reason.

"Are we far from Sunbury?" I said, in a matter-of-fact tone.

"What are we to do?" he asked. "Are these creatures everywhere? Has the earth been given over to them?"

"Are we far from Sunbury?"

"Only this morning I officiated at early celebration—"

"Things have changed," I said, quietly. "You must keep your head. There is still hope."

"Hope!"

"Yes. Plentiful hope—for all this destruction!"

I began to explain my view of our position. He listened at first, but as I went on the interest dawning in his eyes gave place to their former stare, and his regard wandered from me.

"This must be the beginning of the end," he said, interrupting me. "The end! The great and terrible day of the Lord! When men shall call upon the mountains and the rocks to fall upon them and hide them— hide them from the face of Him that sitteth upon the throne!"

I began to understand the position. I ceased my laboured reasoning, struggled to my feet, and, standing over him, laid my hand on his shoulder.

"Be a man!" said I. "You are scared out of your wits! What good is religion if it collapses under calamity? Think of what earthquakes and floods, wars and volcanoes, have done before to men! Did you think God had exempted Weybridge? He is not an insurance agent."

For a time he sat in blank silence.

"But how can we escape?" he asked, suddenly. "They are invulnerable, they are pitiless."

"Neither the one nor, perhaps, the other," I answered. "And the mightier they are the more sane and wary should we be. One of them was killed yonder not three hours ago."

"Killed!" he said, staring about him. "How can God's ministers be killed?"

"I saw it happen." I proceeded to tell him. "We have chanced to come in for the thick of it," said I, "and that is all."

"What is that flicker in the sky?" he asked abruptly.

I told him it was the heliograph signalling—that it was the sign of human help and effort in the sky.

"We are in the midst of it," I said, "quiet as it is. That flicker in the sky tells of the gathering storm. Yonder, I take it are the Martians, and Londonward, where those hills rise about Richmond and Kingston and the trees give cover, earthworks are being thrown up and guns are being placed. Presently the Martians will be coming this way again."

And even as I spoke he sprang to his feet and stopped me by a gesture.

"Listen!" he said.

From beyond the low hills across the water came the dull resonance of distant guns and a remote weird crying. Then everything was still. A cockchafer came droning over the hedge and past us. High in the west the crescent moon hung faint and pale above the smoke of Weybridge and Shepperton and the hot, still splendour of the sunset.

"We had better follow this path," I said, "northward."

. . .

CHAPTER FOURTEEN

In London

MY YOUNGER BROTHER was in London when the Martians fell at Woking. He was a medical student working for an imminent examination, and he heard nothing of the arrival until Saturday morning. The morning papers on Saturday contained, in addition to lengthy special articles on the planet Mars, on life in the planets, and so forth, a brief and vaguely worded telegram, all the more striking for its brevity.

The Martians, alarmed by the approach of a crowd, had killed a number of people with a quick-firing gun, so the story ran. The telegram concluded with the words: "Formidable as they seem to be, the Martians have not moved from the pit into which they have fallen, and, indeed, seem incapable of doing so. Probably this is due to the relative strength of the earth's gravitational energy." On that last text their leader-writer expanded very comfortably.

Of course all the students in the crammer's biology class, to which my brother went that day, were intensely interested, but there were no signs of any unusual excitement in the streets. The afternoon papers puffed scraps of news under big headlines. They had nothing to tell beyond the movements of troops about the common, and the burning of the pine woods between Woking and Weybridge, until eight. Then the *St. James's Gazette*, in an extra-special edition, announced the bare fact of the interruption of telegraphic communication. This was thought to be due to the falling of burning pine trees across the line. Nothing more of the fighting was known that night, the night of my drive to Leatherhead and back.

My brother felt no anxiety about us, as he knew from the description in the papers that the cylinder was a good two miles from my house. He made up his mind to run down that night to me, in order, as he says, to see the Things before they were killed. He dispatched a telegram, which never reached me, about four o'clock, and spent the evening at a music hall.

In London, also, on Saturday night there was a thunderstorm, and my brother reached Waterloo in a cab. On the platform from which the midnight train usually starts he learned, after some waiting, that an accident prevented trains from reaching Woking that night. The nature of the accident he could not ascertain; indeed, the railway authorities did not clearly know at that time. There was very little excitement in the station, as the officials, failing to realise that anything further than a breakdown between Byfleet and Woking junction had occurred, were running the theatre trains which usually passed through Woking round by Virginia Water or Guildford. They were busy making the necessary arrangements to alter the route of the Southampton and Portsmouth Sunday League excursions. A nocturnal newspaper reporter, mistaking my brother for the traffic manager, to whom he bears a slight resemblance, waylaid and tried to interview him. Few people, excepting the railway officials, connected the breakdown with the Martians.

I have read, in another account of these events, that on Sunday morning "all London was electrified by the news from Woking." As a matter of fact, there was nothing to justify that very extravagant phrase. Plenty of Londoners did not hear of the Martians until the panic of Monday morning. Those who did took some time to realise all that the hastily worded telegrams in the Sunday papers conveyed. The majority of people in London do not read Sunday papers.

The habit of personal security, moreover, is so deeply fixed in the Londoner's mind, and startling intelligence so much a matter of course in the papers, that they could read without any personal tremors: "About seven o'clock last night the Martians came out of the cylinder, and, moving about under an armour of metallic shields, have completely wrecked Woking station with the adjacent houses, and massacred an entire battalion of the Cardigan Regiment. No details are known. Maxims have been absolutely useless against their armour; the field guns have been disabled by them. Flying hussars have been galloping into Chertsey. The Martians appear to be moving slowly towards Chertsey or Windsor. Great anxiety prevails in West Surrey, and earthworks are being thrown up to check the advance Londonward." That was how the Sunday *Sun* put it, and a clever and remarkably prompt "handbook" article in the *Referee* compared the affair to a menagerie suddenly let loose in a village.

No one in London knew positively of the nature of the armoured Martians, and there was still a fixed idea that these monsters must be sluggish: "crawling," "creeping painfully"—such expressions occurred in almost all the earlier reports. None of the telegrams could have been written by an eyewitness of their advance. The Sunday papers printed separate editions as further news came to hand, some even in default of it. But there was practically nothing more to tell people until late in the afternoon, when the authorities gave the press agencies the news in their possession. It was stated that the people of Walton and Weybridge, and all the district were pouring along the roads Londonward, and that was all.

My brother went to church at the Foundling Hospital in the morning, still in ignorance of what had happened on the previous night. There he heard allusions made to the invasion, and a special prayer for peace. Coming out, he bought a *Referee*. He became alarmed at the news in this, and went again to Waterloo station to find out if communication were restored. The omnibuses, carriages, cyclists, and innumerable people walking in their best clothes seemed scarcely affected by the strange intelligence that the news venders were disseminating. People were interested, or, if alarmed, alarmed only on account of the local residents. At the station he heard for the first time that the Windsor and Chertsey lines were now interrupted. The porters told him that several remarkable telegrams had been received in the morning from Byfleet and Chertsey stations, but that these had abruptly ceased. My brother could get very little precise detail out of them.

"There's fighting going on about Weybridge" was the extent of their information.

The train service was now very much disorganised. Quite a number of people who had been expecting friends from places on the South-Western network were standing about the station. One grey-headed old gentleman came and abused the South-Western Company bitterly to my brother. "It wants showing up," he said.

One or two trains came in from Richmond, Putney, and Kingston, containing people who had gone out for a day's boating and found the locks closed and a feeling of panic in the air. A man in a blue and white blazer addressed my brother, full of strange tidings.

"There's hosts of people driving into Kingston in traps and carts and things, with boxes of valuables and all that," he said. "They come from Molesey and Weybridge and Walton, and they say there's been guns heard at Chertsey, heavy firing, and that mounted soldiers have told them to get off at once because the Martians are coming. We heard guns firing at Hampton Court station, but we thought it was thunder. What the dickens does it all mean? The Martians can't get out of their pit, can they?"

My brother could not tell him.

Afterwards he found that the vague feeling of alarm had spread to the clients of the underground railway, and that the Sunday excursionists began to return from all over the South-Western "lung"—Barnes, Wimbledon, Richmond Park, Kew, and so forth—at unnaturally early hours; but not a soul had anything more than vague hearsay to tell of. Everyone connected with the terminus seemed ill-tempered.

About five o'clock the gathering crowd in the station was immensely excited by the opening of the line of communication, which is almost invariably closed, between the South-Eastern and the South-Western stations, and the passage of carriage trucks bearing huge guns and carriages crammed with soldiers. These were the guns that were brought up from Woolwich and Chatham to cover Kingston. There was an exchange of pleasantries: "You'll get eaten!" "We're the beast-tamers!" and so forth. A little while after that a squad of police came into the station and began to clear the public off the platforms, and my brother went out into the street again.

The church bells were ringing for evensong, and a squad of Salvation Army lassies came singing down Waterloo Road. On the bridge a number of loafers were watching a curious brown scum that came drifting down the stream in patches. The sun was just setting, and the Clock Tower and the Houses of Parliament rose against one of the most peaceful skies it is possible to imagine, a sky of gold, barred with long transverse stripes of reddish-purple cloud. There was talk of a floating body. One of the men there, a reservist he said he was, told my brother he had seen the heliograph flickering in the west.

In Wellington Street my brother met a couple of sturdy roughs who had just been rushed out of Fleet Street with still-wet newspapers and staring placards. "Dreadful catastrophe!" they bawled one to the other down Wellington Street. "Fighting at Weybridge! Full description! Repulse of the Martians! London in Danger!" He had to give threepence for a copy of that paper.

Then it was, and then only, that he realised something of the full power and terror of these monsters. He learned that they were not merely a handful of small sluggish creatures, but that they were minds swaying vast mechanical bodies; and that they could move swiftly and smite with such power that even the mightiest guns could not stand against them.

They were described as "vast spiderlike machines, nearly a hundred feet high, capable of the speed of an express train, and able to shoot out a beam of intense heat." Masked batteries, chiefly of field guns, had been planted in the country about Horsell Common, and especially between the Woking district and London. Five of the machines had been seen moving towards the Thames, and one, by a happy chance, had been destroyed. In the other cases the shells had missed, and the batteries had been at once annihilated by the Heat-Rays. Heavy losses of soldiers were mentioned, but the tone of the dispatch was optimistic.

The Martians had been repulsed; they were not invulnerable. They had retreated to their triangle of cylinders again, in the circle about Woking. Signallers with heliographs were pushing forward upon them from all sides. Guns were in rapid transit from Windsor, Portsmouth, Aldershot, Woolwich—even from the north; among others, long wire-guns of ninety-five tons from Woolwich. Altogether one hundred and sixteen were in position or being hastily placed, chiefly covering London. Never before in England had there been such a vast or rapid concentration of military material.

Any further cylinders that fell, it was hoped, could be destroyed at once by high explosives, which were being rapidly manufactured and distributed. No doubt, ran the report, the situation was of the strangest and gravest description, but the public was exhorted to avoid and discourage panic. No doubt the Martians were strange and terrible in the extreme, but at the outside there could not be more than twenty of them against our millions.

The authorities had reason to suppose, from the size of the cylinders, that at the outside there could not be more than five in each cylinder—fifteen altogether. And one at least was disposed of—perhaps more. The public would be fairly warned of the approach of danger, and elaborate measures were being taken for the protection of the people in the threatened southwestern suburbs. And so, with reiterated assurances of the safety of London and the ability of the authorities to cope with the difficulty, this quasi-proclamation closed.

This was printed in enormous type on paper so fresh that it was still wet, and there had been no time to add a word of comment. It was curious, my brother said, to see how ruthlessly the usual contents of the paper had been hacked and taken out to give this place.

All down Wellington Street people could be seen fluttering out the pink sheets and reading, and the Strand was suddenly noisy with the voices of an army of hawkers following these pioneers. Men came scrambling off buses to secure copies. Certainly this news excited people intensely, whatever their previous apathy. The shutters of a map shop in the Strand were being taken down, my brother said, and a man in his Sunday raiment, lemon-yellow gloves even, was visible inside the window hastily fastening maps of Surrey to the glass.

Going on along the Strand to Trafalgar Square, the paper in his hand, my brother saw some of the fugitives from West Surrey. There was a man with his wife and two boys and some articles of furniture in a cart such as greengrocers use. He was driving from the direction of Westminster Bridge; and close behind him came a hay waggon with five or six respectable-looking people in it, and some boxes and bundles. The faces of these people were haggard, and their entire appearance contrasted conspicuously with the Sabbath-best appearance of the people on the omnibuses. People in fashionable clothing peeped at them out of cabs. They stopped at the Square as if undecided which way to take, and finally turned eastward along the Strand. Some way behind these came a man in workday clothes, riding one of those old-fashioned tricycles with a small front wheel. He was dirty and white in the face.

My brother turned down towards Victoria, and met a number of such people. He had a vague idea that he might see something of me. He noticed an unusual number of police regulating the traffic. Some of the refugees were exchanging news with the people on the omnibuses. One was professing to have seen the Martians. "Boilers on stilts, I tell you, striding along like men." Most of them were excited and animated by their strange experience.

Beyond Victoria the public-houses were doing a lively trade with these arrivals. At all the street corners groups of people were reading papers, talking excitedly, or staring at these unusual Sunday visitors. They seemed to increase as night drew on, until at last the roads, my brother said, were like Epsom High Street on a Derby Day. My brother addressed several of these fugitives and got unsatisfactory answers from most.

None of them could tell him any news of Woking except one man, who assured him that Woking had been entirely destroyed on the previous night.

"I come from Byfleet," he said; "man on a bicycle came through the place in the early morning, and ran from door to door warning us to come away. Then came soldiers. We went out to look, and there were clouds of smoke to the south—nothing but smoke, and not a soul coming that way. Then we heard the guns at Chertsey, and folks coming from Weybridge. So I've locked up my house and come on."

At the time there was a strong feeling in the streets that the authorities were to blame for their incapacity to dispose of the invaders without all this inconvenience.

About eight o'clock a noise of heavy firing was distinctly audible all over the south of London. My brother could not hear it for the traffic in the main thoroughfares, but by striking through the quiet back streets to the river he was able to distinguish it quite plainly.

He walked from Westminster to his apartments near Regent's Park, about two. He was now very anxious on my account, and disturbed at the evident magnitude of the trouble. His mind was inclined to run, even as mine had run on Saturday, on military details. He thought of all those silent, expectant guns, of the suddenly nomadic countryside; he tried to imagine "boilers on stilts" a hundred feet high.

There were one or two cartloads of refugees passing along Oxford Street, and several in the Marylebone Road, but so slowly was the news spreading that Regent Street and Portland Place were full of their usual Sunday-night promenaders, albeit they talked in groups, and along the edge of Regent's Park there were as many silent couples "walking out" together under the scattered gas lamps as ever there had been. The night was warm and still, and a little oppressive; the sound of guns continued intermittently, and after midnight there seemed to be sheet lightning in the south.

He read and re-read the paper, fearing the worst had happened to me. He was restless, and after supper prowled out again aimlessly. He returned and tried in vain to divert his attention to his examination notes. He went to bed a little after midnight, and was awakened from lurid dreams in the small hours of Monday by the sound of door knockers, feet running in the street, distant drumming, and a clamour of bells. Red reflections danced on the ceiling. For a moment he lay astonished, wondering whether day had come or the world gone mad. Then he jumped out of bed and ran to the window.

His room was an attic and as he thrust his head out, up and down the street there were a dozen echoes to the noise of his window sash, and heads in every kind of night disarray appeared. Enquiries were being shouted. "They are coming!" bawled a policeman, hammering at the door; "the Martians are coming!" and hurried to the next door.

The sound of drumming and trumpeting came from the Albany Street Barracks, and every church within earshot was hard at work killing sleep with a vehement disorderly tocsin. There was a noise of doors opening, and window after window in the houses opposite flashed from darkness into yellow illumination.

Up the street came galloping a closed carriage, bursting abruptly into noise at the corner, rising to a clattering climax under the window, and dying away slowly in the distance. Close on the rear of this came a couple of cabs, the forerunners of a long procession of flying vehicles, going for the most part to Chalk Farm station, where the North-Western special trains were loading up, instead of coming down the gradient into Euston.

For a long time my brother stared out of the window in blank astonishment, watching the policemen hammering at door after door, and delivering their incomprehensible message. Then the door behind him opened, and the man who lodged across the landing came in, dressed only in shirt, trousers, and slippers, his braces loose about his waist, his hair disordered from his pillow.

"What the devil is it?" he asked. "A fire? What a devil of a row!"

They both craned their heads out of the window, straining to hear what the policemen were shouting. People were coming out of the side streets, and standing in groups at the corners talking.

"What the devil is it all about?" said my brother's fellow lodger.

My brother answered him vaguely and began to dress, running with each garment to the window in order to miss nothing of the growing excitement. And presently men selling unnaturally early newspapers came bawling into the street:

"London in danger of suffocation! The Kingston and Richmond defences forced! Fearful massacres in the Thames Valley!"

And all about him—in the rooms below, in the houses on each side and across the road, and behind in the Park Terraces and in the hundred other streets of that part of Marylebone, and the Westbourne Park district and St. Pancras, and westward and northward in Kilburn and St. John's Wood and Hampstead, and eastward in Shoreditch and Highbury and Haggerston and Hoxton, and, indeed, through all the vastness of London from Ealing to East Ham—people were rubbing their eyes, and opening windows to stare out and ask aimless questions, dressing hastily as the first breath of the coming storm of Fear blew through the streets. It was the dawn of the great panic. London, which had gone to bed on Sunday night oblivious and inert, was awakened, in the small hours of Monday morning, to a vivid sense of danger.

Unable from his window to learn what was happening, my brother went down and out into the street, just as the sky between the parapets of the houses grew pink with the early dawn. The flying people on foot and in vehicles grew more numerous every moment. "Black Smoke!" he heard people crying, and again "Black Smoke!" The contagion of such a unanimous fear was inevitable. As my brother hesitated on the door-step, he saw another news vender approaching, and got a paper forthwith. The man was running away with the rest, and selling his papers for a shilling each as he ran—a grotesque mingling of profit and panic.

And from this paper my brother read that catastrophic dispatch of the Commander-in-Chief:

"The Martians are able to discharge enormous clouds of a black and poisonous vapour by means of rockets. They have smothered our batteries, destroyed Richmond, Kingston, and Wimbledon, and are advancing slowly towards London, destroying everything on the way. It is impossible to stop them. There is no safety from the Black Smoke but in instant flight."

That was all, but it was enough. The whole population of the great six-million city was stirring, slipping, running; presently it would be pouring *en masse* northward.

"Black Smoke!" the voices cried. "Fire!"

The bells of the neighbouring church made a jangling tumult, a cart carelessly driven smashed, amid shrieks and curses, against the water trough up the street. Sickly yellow lights went to and fro in the houses, and some of the passing cabs flaunted unextinguished lamps. And overhead the dawn was growing brighter, clear and steady and calm.

He heard footsteps running to and fro in the rooms, and up and down stairs behind him. His landlady came to the door, loosely wrapped in dressing gown and shawl; her husband followed ejaculating.

As my brother began to realise the import of all these things, he turned hastily to his own room, put all his available money—some ten pounds altogether—into his pockets, and went out again into the streets.

. . .

CHAPTER FIFTEEN
What Had Happened in Surrey

IT WAS WHILE THE CURATE had sat and talked so wildly to me under the hedge in the flat meadows near Halliford, and while my brother was watching the fugitives stream over Westminster Bridge, that the Martians had resumed the offensive. So far as one can ascertain from the conflicting accounts that have been put forth, the majority of them remained busied with preparations in the Horsell pit until nine that night, hurrying on some operation that disengaged huge volumes of green smoke.

But three certainly came out about eight o'clock and, advancing slowly and cautiously, made their way through Byfleet and Pyrford towards Ripley and Weybridge, and so came in sight of the expectant batteries against the setting sun. These Martians did not advance in a body, but in a line, each perhaps a mile and a half from his nearest fellow. They communicated with one another by means of sirenlike howls, running up and down the scale from one note to another.

It was this howling and firing of the guns at Ripley and St. George's Hill that we had heard at Upper Halliford. The Ripley gunners, unseasoned artillery volunteers who ought never to have been placed in such a position, fired one wild, premature, ineffectual volley, and bolted on horse and foot through the deserted village, while the Martian, without using his Heat-Ray, walked serenely over their guns, stepped gingerly among them, passed in front of them, and so came unexpectedly upon the guns in Painshill Park, which he destroyed.

The St. George's Hill men, however, were better led or of a better mettle. Hidden by a pine wood as they were, they seem to have been quite unsuspected by the Martian nearest to them. They laid their guns as deliberately as if they had been on parade, and fired at about a thousand yards' range.

The shells flashed all round him, and he was seen to advance a few paces, stagger, and go down. Everybody yelled together, and the guns were reloaded in frantic haste. The overthrown Martian set up a prolonged ululation, and immediately a second glittering giant, answering him, appeared over the trees to the south. It would seem that a leg of the tripod had been smashed by one of the shells. The whole of the second volley flew wide of the Martian on the ground, and, simultaneously, both his companions brought their Heat-Rays to bear on the battery. The ammunition blew up, the pine trees all about the guns flashed into fire, and only one or two of the men who were already running over the crest of the hill escaped.

After this it would seem that the three took counsel together and halted, and the scouts who were watching them report that they remained absolutely stationary for the next half hour. The Martian who had been overthrown crawled tediously out of his hood, a small brown figure, oddly suggestive from that distance of a speck of blight, and apparently engaged in the repair of his support. About nine he had finished, for his cowl was then seen above the trees again.

It was a few minutes past nine that night when these three sentinels were joined by four other Martians, each carrying a thick black tube. A similar tube was handed to each of the three, and the seven proceeded to distribute themselves at equal distances along a curved line between St. George's Hill, Weybridge, and the village of Send, southwest of Ripley.

A dozen rockets sprang out of the hills before them so soon as they began to move, and warned the waiting batteries about Ditton and Esher. At the same time four of their fighting machines, similarly armed with tubes, crossed the river, and two of them, black against the western sky, came into sight of myself and the curate as we hurried wearily and painfully along the road that runs northward out of Halliford. They moved, as it seemed to us, upon a cloud, for a milky mist covered the fields and rose to a third of their height.

At this sight the curate cried faintly in his throat, and began running; but I knew it was no good running from a Martian, and I turned aside and crawled through dewy nettles and brambles into the broad ditch by the side of the road. He looked back, saw what I was doing, and turned to join me.

The two halted, the nearer to us standing and facing Sunbury, the remoter being a grey indistinctness towards the evening star, away towards Staines.

The occasional howling of the Martians had ceased; they took up their positions in the huge crescent about their cylinders in absolute silence. It was a crescent with twelve miles between its horns. Never since the devising of gunpowder was the beginning of a battle so still. To us and to an observer about Ripley it would have had precisely the same effect—the Martians seemed in solitary possession of the darkling night, lit only as it was by the slender moon, the stars, the afterglow of the daylight, and the ruddy glare from St. George's Hill and the woods of Painshill.

But facing that crescent everywhere—at Staines, Hounslow, Ditton, Esher, Ockham, behind hills and woods south of the river, and across the flat grass meadows to the north of it, wherever a cluster of trees or village houses gave sufficient cover—the guns were waiting. The signal rockets burst and rained their sparks through the night and vanished, and the spirit of all those watching batteries rose to a tense expectation. The Martians had but to advance into the line of fire, and instantly those motionless black forms of men, those guns glittering so darkly in the early night, would explode into a thunderous fury of battle.

No doubt the thought that was uppermost in a thousand of those vigilant minds, even as it was uppermost in mine, was the riddle—how much they understood of us. Did they grasp that we in our millions were organized, disciplined, working together? Or did they interpret our spurts of fire, the sudden stinging of our shells, our steady investment of their encampment, as we should the furious unanimity of onslaught in a disturbed hive of bees? Did they dream they might exterminate us? (At that time no one knew what food they needed.) A hundred such questions struggled together in my mind as I watched that vast sentinel shape. And in the back of my mind was the sense of all the huge unknown and hidden forces Londonward. Had they prepared pitfalls? Were the powder mills at Hounslow ready as a snare? Would the Londoners have the heart and courage to make a greater Moscow of their mighty province of houses?

Then, after an interminable time, as it seemed to us, crouching and peering through the hedge, came a sound like the distant concussion of a gun. Another nearer, and then another. And then the Martian beside us raised his tube on high and discharged it, gunwise, with a heavy report that made the ground heave. The one towards Staines answered him. There was no flash, no smoke, simply that loaded detonation.

I was so excited by these heavy minute-guns following one another that I so far forgot my personal safety and my scalded hands as to clamber up into the hedge and stare towards Sunbury. As I did so a second report followed, and a big projectile hurtled overhead towards Hounslow. I expected at least to see smoke or fire, or some such evidence of its work. But all I saw was the deep blue sky above, with one solitary star, and the white mist spreading wide and low beneath. And there had been no crash, no answering explosion. The silence was restored; the minute lengthened to three.

"What has happened?" said the curate, standing up beside me.

"Heaven knows!" said I.

A bat flickered by and vanished. A distant tumult of shouting began and ceased. I looked again at the Martian, and saw he was now moving eastward along the riverbank, with a swift, rolling motion.

Every moment I expected the fire of some hidden battery to spring upon him; but the evening calm was unbroken. The figure of the Martian grew smaller as he receded, and presently the mist and the gathering night had swallowed him up. By a common impulse we clambered higher. Towards Sunbury was a dark appearance, as though a conical hill had suddenly come into being there, hiding our view of the farther country; and then, remoter across the river, over Walton, we saw another such summit. These hill-like forms grew lower and broader even as we stared.

Moved by a sudden thought, I looked northward, and there I perceived a third of these cloudy black kopjes had risen.

Everything had suddenly become very still. Far away to the southeast, marking the quiet, we heard the Martians hooting to one another, and then the air quivered again with the distant thud of their guns. But the earthly artillery made no reply.

Now at the time we could not understand these things, but later I was to learn the meaning of these ominous kopjes that gathered in the twilight. Each of the Martians, standing in the great crescent I have described, had discharged, by means of the gunlike tube he carried, a huge canister over whatever hill, copse, cluster of houses, or other possible cover for guns, chanced to be in front of him. Some fired only one of these, some two—as in the case of the one we had seen; the one at Ripley is said to have discharged no fewer than five at that time. These canisters smashed on striking the ground—they did not explode—and incontinently disengaged an enormous volume of heavy, inky vapour, coiling and pouring upward in a huge and ebony cumulus cloud, a gaseous hill that sank and spread itself slowly over the surrounding country. And the touch of that vapour, the inhaling of its pungent wisps, was death to all that breathes.

It was heavy, this vapour, heavier than the densest smoke, so that, after the first tumultuous uprush and outflow of its impact, it sank down through the air and poured over the ground in a manner rather liquid than gaseous, abandoning the hills, and streaming into the valleys and ditches and watercourses even as I have heard the carbonic-acid gas that pours from volcanic clefts is wont to do. And where it came upon water some chemical action occurred, and the surface would be instantly covered with a powdery scum that sank slowly and made way for more. The scum was absolutely insoluble, and it is a strange thing, seeing the instant effect of the gas, that one could drink without hurt the water from which it had been strained. The vapour did not diffuse as a true gas would do. It hung together in banks, flowing sluggishly down the slope of the land and driving reluctantly before the wind, and very slowly it combined with the mist and moisture of the air, and sank to the earth in the form of dust. Save that an unknown element giving a group of four lines in the blue of the spectrum is concerned, we are still entirely ignorant of the nature of this substance.

Once the tumultuous upheaval of its dispersion was over, the black smoke clung so closely to the ground, even before its precipitation, that fifty feet up in the air, on the roofs and upper stories of high houses and on great trees, there was a chance of escaping its poison altogether, as was proved even that night at Street Cobham and Ditton.

The man who escaped at the former place tells a wonderful story of the strangeness of its coiling flow, and how he looked down from the church spire and saw the houses of the village rising like ghosts out of its inky nothingness. For a day and a half he remained there, weary, starving and sun-scorched, the earth under the blue sky and against the prospect of the distant hills a velvet-black expanse, with red roofs, green trees, and, later, black-veiled shrubs and gates, barns, outhouses, and walls, rising here and there into the sunlight.

But that was at Street Cobham, where the black vapour was allowed to remain until it sank of its own accord into the ground. As a rule the Martians, when it had served its purpose, cleared the air of it again by wading into it and directing a jet of steam upon it.

This they did with the vapour banks near us, as we saw in the star-light from the window of a deserted house at Upper Halliford, whither we had returned. From there we could see the searchlights on Rich-mond Hill and Kingston Hill going to and fro, and about eleven the win-dows rattled, and we heard the sound of the huge siege guns that had been put in position there. These continued intermittently for the space of a quarter of an hour, sending chance shots at the invisible Martians at Hampton and Ditton, and then the pale beams of the electric light vanished, and were replaced by a bright red glow.

Then the fourth cylinder fell—a brilliant green meteor—as I learned afterwards, in Bushey Park. Before the guns on the Richmond and Kingston line of hills began, there was a fitful cannonade far away in the southwest, due, I believe, to guns being fired haphazard before the black vapour could overwhelm the gunners.

So, setting about it as methodically as men might smoke out a wasps' nest, the Martians spread this strange stifling vapour over the London-ward country. The horns of the crescent slowly moved apart, until at last they formed a line from Hanwell to Coombe and Malden. All night through their destructive tubes advanced. Never once, after the Martian at St. George's Hill was brought down, did they give the artillery the ghost of a chance against them. Wherever there was a possibility of guns being laid for them unseen, a fresh canister of the black vapour was dis-charged, and where the guns were openly displayed the Heat-Ray was brought to bear.

By midnight the blazing trees along the slopes of Richmond Park and the glare of Kingston Hill threw their light upon a network of black smoke, blotting out the whole valley of the Thames and extending as far as the eye could reach. And through this two Martians slowly waded, and turned their hissing steam jets this way and that.

They were sparing of the Heat-Ray that night, either because they had but a limited supply of material for its production or because they did not wish to destroy the country but only to crush and overawe the opposition they had aroused. In the latter aim they certainly succeeded. Sunday night was the end of the organised opposition to their movements. After that no body of men would stand against them, so hopeless was the enterprise. Even the crews of the torpedo-boats and destroyers that had brought their quick-firers up the Thames refused to stop, mutinied, and went down again. The only offensive operation men ventured upon after that night was the preparation of mines and pitfalls, and even in that their energies were frantic and spasmodic.

One has to imagine, as well as one may, the fate of those batteries towards Esher, waiting so tensely in the twilight. Survivors there were none. One may picture the orderly expectation, the officers alert and watchful, the gunners ready, the ammunition piled to hand, the limber gunners with their horses and waggons, the groups of civilian spectators standing as near as they were permitted, the evening stillness, the ambulances and hospital tents with the burned and wounded from Weybridge; then the dull resonance of the shots the Martians fired, and the clumsy projectile whirling over the trees and houses and smashing amid the neighbouring fields.

One may picture, too, the sudden shifting of the attention, the swiftly spreading coils and bellyings of that blackness advancing headlong, towering heavenward, turning the twilight to a palpable darkness, a strange and horrible antagonist of vapour striding upon its victims, men and horses near it seen dimly, running, shrieking, falling headlong, shouts of dismay, the guns suddenly abandoned, men choking and writhing on the ground, and the swift broadening-out of the opaque cone of smoke. And then night and extinction—nothing but a silent mass of impenetrable vapour hiding its dead.

Before dawn the black vapour was pouring through the streets of Richmond, and the disintegrating organism of government was, with a last expiring effort, rousing the population of London to the necessity of flight.

• • •

CHAPTER SIXTEEN
The Exodus from London

SO YOU UNDERSTAND THE ROARING WAVE of fear that swept through the greatest city in the world just as Monday was dawning—the stream of flight rising swiftly to a torrent, lashing in a foaming tumult round the railway stations, banked up into a horrible struggle about the shipping in the Thames, and hurrying by every available channel northward and eastward. By ten o'clock the police organisation, and by midday even the railway organisations, were losing coherency, losing shape and efficiency, guttering, softening, running at last in that swift liquefaction of the social body.

All the railway lines north of the Thames and the South-Eastern people at Cannon Street had been warned by midnight on Sunday, and trains were being filled. People were fighting savagely for standing-room in the carriages even at two o'clock. By three, people were being trampled and crushed even in Bishopsgate Street, a couple of hundred yards or more from Liverpool Street station; revolvers were fired, people stabbed, and the policemen who had been sent to direct the traffic, exhausted and infuriated, were breaking the heads of the people they were called out to protect.

And as the day advanced and the engine drivers and stokers refused to return to London, the pressure of the flight drove the people in an ever-thickening multitude away from the stations and along the north-ward-running roads. By midday a Martian had been seen at Barnes, and a cloud of slowly sinking black vapour drove along the Thames and across the flats of Lambeth, cutting off all escape over the bridges in its sluggish advance. Another bank drove over Ealing, and surrounded a little island of survivors on Castle Hill, alive, but unable to escape.

After a fruitless struggle to get aboard a North-Western train at Chalk Farm—the engines of the trains that had loaded in the goods yard there ploughed through shrieking people, and a dozen stalwart men fought to keep the crowd from crushing the driver against his furnace—my brother emerged upon the Chalk Farm road, dodged across through a hurrying swarm of vehicles, and had the luck to be foremost in the sack of a cycle shop. The front tire of the machine he got was punctured in dragging it through the window, but he got up and off, notwithstanding, with no further injury than a cut wrist. The steep foot of Haverstock Hill was impassable owing to several overturned horses, and my brother struck into Belsize Road.

So he got out of the fury of the panic, and, skirting the Edgware Road, reached Edgware about seven, fasting and wearied, but well ahead of the crowd. Along the road people were standing in the roadway, curious, wondering. He was passed by a number of cyclists, some horsemen, and two motor cars. A mile from Edgware the rim of the wheel broke, and the machine became unridable. He left it by the roadside and trudged through the village. There were shops half opened in the main street of the place, and people crowded on the pavement and in the doorways and windows, staring astonished at this extraordinary procession of fugitives that was beginning. He succeeded in getting some food at an inn.

For a time he remained in Edgware not knowing what next to do. The flying people increased in number. Many of them, like my brother, seemed inclined to loiter in the place. There was no fresh news of the invaders from Mars.

At that time the road was crowded, but as yet far from congested. Most of the fugitives at that hour were mounted on cycles, but there were soon motor cars, hansom cabs, and carriages hurrying along, and the dust hung in heavy clouds along the road to St. Albans.

It was perhaps a vague idea of making his way to Chelmsford, where some friends of his lived, that at last induced my brother to strike into a quiet lane running eastward. Presently he came upon a stile, and, crossing it, followed a footpath northeastward. He passed near several farmhouses and some little places whose names he did not learn. He saw few fugitives until, in a grass lane towards High Barnet, he happened upon two ladies who became his fellow travellers. He came upon them just in time to save them.

He heard their screams, and, hurrying round the corner, saw a couple of men struggling to drag them out of the little pony-chaise in which they had been driving, while a third with difficulty held the frightened pony's head. One of the ladies, a short woman dressed in white, was simply screaming; the other, a dark, slender figure, slashed at the man who gripped her arm with a whip she held in her disengaged hand.

My brother immediately grasped the situation, shouted, and hurried towards the struggle. One of the men desisted and turned towards him, and my brother, realising from his antagonist's face that a fight was unavoidable, and being an expert boxer, went into him forthwith and sent him down against the wheel of the chaise.

It was no time for pugilistic chivalry and my brother laid him quiet with a kick, and gripped the collar of the man who pulled at the slender lady's arm. He heard the clatter of hoofs, the whip stung across his face, a third antagonist struck him between the eyes, and the man he held wrenched himself free and made off down the lane in the direction from which he had come.

Partly stunned, he found himself facing the man who had held the horse's head, and became aware of the chaise receding from him down the lane, swaying from side to side, and with the women in it looking back. The man before him, a burly rough, tried to close, and he stopped him with a blow in the face. Then, realising that he was deserted, he dodged round and made off down the lane after the chaise, with the sturdy man close behind him, and the fugitive, who had turned now, following remotely.

Suddenly he stumbled and fell; his immediate pursuer went head-long, and he rose to his feet to find himself with a couple of antagonists again. He would have had little chance against them had not the slender lady very pluckily pulled up and returned to his help. It seems she had had a revolver all this time, but it had been under the seat when she and her companion were attacked. She fired at six yards' distance, narrowly missing my brother. The less courageous of the robbers made off, and his companion followed him, cursing his cowardice. They both stopped in sight down the lane, where the third man lay insensible.

"Take this!" said the slender lady, and she gave my brother her revolver.

"Go back to the chaise," said my brother, wiping the blood from his split lip.

She turned without a word—they were both panting—and they went back to where the lady in white struggled to hold back the frightened pony.

The robbers had evidently had enough of it. When my brother looked again they were retreating.

"I'll sit here," said my brother, "if I may;" and he got upon the empty front seat. The lady looked over her shoulder.

"Give me the reins," she said, and laid the whip along the pony's side. In another moment a bend in the road hid the three men from my brother's eyes.

So, quite unexpectedly, my brother found himself, panting, with a cut mouth, a bruised jaw, and bloodstained knuckles, driving along an unknown lane with these two women.

He learned they were the wife and the younger sister of a surgeon living at Stanmore, who had come in the small hours from a dangerous case at Pinner, and heard at some railway station on his way of the Martian advance. He had hurried home, roused the women—their servant had left them two days before—packed some provisions, put his revolver under the seat—luckily for my brother—and told them to drive on to Edgware, with the idea of getting a train there. He stopped behind to tell the neighbours. He would overtake them, he said, at about half past four in the morning, and now it was nearly nine and they had seen nothing of him. They could not stop in Edgware because of the growing traffic through the place, and so they had come into this side lane.

That was the story they told my brother in fragments when presently they stopped again, nearer to New Barnet. He promised to stay with them, at least until they could determine what to do, or until the missing man arrived, and professed to be an expert shot with the revolver—a weapon strange to him—in order to give them confidence.

They made a sort of encampment by the wayside, and the pony became happy in the hedge. He told them of his own escape out of London, and all that he knew of these Martians and their ways. The sun crept higher in the sky, and after a time their talk died out and gave place to an uneasy state of anticipation. Several wayfarers came along the lane, and of these my brother gathered such news as he could. Every broken answer he had deepened his impression of the great disaster that had come on humanity, deepened his persuasion of the immediate necessity for prosecuting this flight. He urged the matter upon them.

"We have money," said the slender woman, and hesitated.

Her eyes met my brother's, and her hesitation ended.

"So have I," said my brother.

She explained that they had as much as thirty pounds in gold, besides a five-pound note, and suggested that with that they might get upon a train at St. Albans or New Barnet. My brother thought that was hopeless, seeing the fury of the Londoners to crowd upon the trains, and broached his own idea of striking across Essex towards Harwich and thence escaping from the country altogether.

Mrs. Elphinstone—that was the name of the woman in white—would listen to no reasoning, and kept calling upon "George"; but her sister-in-law was astonishingly quiet and deliberate, and at last agreed to my brother's suggestion. So, designing to cross the Great North Road, they went on towards Barnet, my brother leading the pony to save it as much as possible. As the sun crept up the sky the day became excessively hot, and under foot a thick, whitish sand grew burning and blinding, so that they travelled only very slowly. The hedges were grey with dust. And as they advanced towards Barnet a tumultuous murmuring grew stronger.

They began to meet more people. For the most part these were staring before them, murmuring indistinct questions, jaded, haggard, unclean. One man in evening dress passed them on foot, his eyes on the ground. They heard his voice, and, looking back at him, saw one hand clutched in his hair and the other beating invisible things. His paroxysm of rage over, he went on his way without once looking back.

As my brother's party went on towards the crossroads to the south of Barnet they saw a woman approaching the road across some fields on their left, carrying a child and with two other children; and then passed a man in dirty black, with a thick stick in one hand and a small portmanteau in the other. Then round the corner of the lane, from between the villas that guarded it at its confluence with the high road, came a little cart drawn by a sweating black pony and driven by a sallow youth in a bowler hat, grey with dust. There were three girls, East End factory girls, and a couple of little children crowded in the cart.

"This'll tike us rahnd Edgware?" asked the driver, wild-eyed, white-faced; and when my brother told him it would if he turned to the left, he whipped up at once without the formality of thanks.

My brother noticed a pale grey smoke or haze rising among the houses in front of them, and veiling the white facade of a terrace beyond the road that appeared between the backs of the villas. Mrs. Elphinstone suddenly cried out at a number of tongues of smoky red flame leaping up above the houses in front of them against the hot, blue sky. The tumultuous noise resolved itself now into the disorderly mingling of many voices, the gride of many wheels, the creaking of waggons, and the staccato of hoofs. The lane came round sharply not fifty yards from the crossroads.

"Good heavens!" cried Mrs. Elphinstone. "What is this you are driving us into?"

My brother stopped.

For the main road was a boiling stream of people, a torrent of human beings rushing northward, one pressing on another. A great bank of dust, white and luminous in the blaze of the sun, made everything within twenty feet of the ground grey and indistinct and was perpetually renewed by the hurrying feet of a dense crowd of horses and of men and women on foot, and by the wheels of vehicles of every description.

"Way!" my brother heard voices crying. "Make way!"

It was like riding into the smoke of a fire to approach the meeting point of the lane and road; the crowd roared like a fire, and the dust was hot and pungent. And, indeed, a little way up the road a villa was burning and sending rolling masses of black smoke across the road to add to the confusion.

Two men came past them. Then a dirty woman, carrying a heavy bundle and weeping. A lost retriever dog, with hanging tongue, circled dubiously round them, scared and wretched, and fled at my brother's threat.

So much as they could see of the road Londonward between the houses to the right was a tumultuous stream of dirty, hurrying people, pent in between the villas on either side; the black heads, the crowded forms, grew into distinctness as they rushed towards the corner, hurried past, and merged their individuality again in a receding multitude that was swallowed up at last in a cloud of dust.

"Go on! Go on!" cried the voices. "Way! Way!"

One man's hands pressed on the back of another. My brother stood at the pony's head. Irresistibly attracted, he advanced slowly, pace by pace, down the lane.

Edgware had been a scene of confusion, Chalk Farm a riotous tumult, but this was a whole population in movement. It is hard to imagine that host. It had no character of its own. The figures poured out past the corner, and receded with their backs to the group in the lane. Along the margin came those who were on foot threatened by the wheels, stumbling in the ditches, blundering into one another.

The carts and carriages crowded close upon one another, making little way for those swifter and more impatient vehicles that darted forward every now and then when an opportunity showed itself of doing so, sending the people scattering against the fences and gates of the villas.

"Push on!" was the cry. "Push on! They are coming!"

In one cart stood a blind man in the uniform of the Salvation Army, gesticulating with his crooked fingers and bawling, "Eternity! Eternity!" His voice was hoarse and very loud so that my brother could hear him long after he was lost to sight in the dust. Some of the people who crowded in the carts whipped stupidly at their horses and quarrelled with other drivers; some sat motionless, staring at nothing with miserable eyes; some gnawed their hands with thirst, or lay prostrate in the bottoms of their conveyances. The horses' bits were covered with foam, their eyes bloodshot.

There were cabs, carriages, shop cars, waggons, beyond counting; a mail cart, a road-cleaner's cart marked "Vestry of St. Pancras," a huge timber waggon crowded with roughs. A brewer's dray rumbled by with its two near wheels splashed with fresh blood.

"Clear the way!" cried the voices. "Clear the way!"

"Eter-nity! Eter-nity!" came echoing down the road.

There were sad, haggard women tramping by, well dressed, with children that cried and stumbled, their dainty clothes smothered in dust, their weary faces smeared with tears. With many of these came men, sometimes helpful, sometimes lowering and savage. Fighting side by side with them pushed some weary street outcast in faded black rags, wide-eyed, loud-voiced, and foul-mouthed. There were sturdy workmen thrusting their way along, wretched, unkempt men, clothed like clerks or shopmen, struggling spasmodically; a wounded soldier my brother noticed, men dressed in the clothes of railway porters, one wretched creature in a nightshirt with a coat thrown over it.

But varied as its composition was, certain things all that host had in common. There were fear and pain on their faces, and fear behind them. A tumult up the road, a quarrel for a place in a waggon, sent the whole host of them quickening their pace; even a man so scared and broken that his knees bent under him was galvanised for a moment into renewed activity. The heat and dust had already been at work upon this multitude. Their skins were dry, their lips black and cracked. They were all thirsty, weary, and footsore. And amid the various cries one heard disputes, reproaches, groans of weariness and fatigue; the voices of most of them were hoarse and weak. Through it all ran a refrain:

"Way! Way! The Martians are coming!"

Few stopped and came aside from that flood. The lane opened slantingly into the main road with a narrow opening, and had a delusive appearance of coming from the direction of London. Yet a kind of eddy of people drove into its mouth; weaklings elbowed out of the stream, who for the most part rested but a moment before plunging into it again. A little way down the lane, with two friends bending over him, lay a man with a bare leg, wrapped about with bloody rags. He was a lucky man to have friends.

A little old man, with a grey military moustache and a filthy black frock coat, limped out and sat down beside the trap, removed his boot—his sock was blood-stained—shook out a pebble, and hobbled on again; and then a little girl of eight or nine, all alone, threw herself under the hedge close by my brother, weeping.

"I can't go on! I can't go on!"

My brother woke from his torpor of astonishment and lifted her up, speaking gently to her, and carried her to Miss Elphinstone. So soon as my brother touched her she became quite still, as if frightened.

"Ellen!" shrieked a woman in the crowd, with tears in her voice— "Ellen!" And the child suddenly darted away from my brother, crying "Mother!"

"They are coming," said a man on horseback, riding past along the lane.

"Out of the way, there!" bawled a coachman, towering high; and my brother saw a closed carriage turning into the lane.

The people crushed back on one another to avoid the horse. My brother pushed the pony and chaise back into the hedge, and the man drove by and stopped at the turn of the way. It was a carriage, with a pole for a pair of horses, but only one was in the traces. My brother saw dimly through the dust that two men lifted out something on a white stretcher and put it gently on the grass beneath the privet hedge.

One of the men came running to my brother.

"Where is there any water?" he said. "He is dying fast, and very thirsty. It is Lord Garrick."

"Lord Garrick!" said my brother; "the Chief Justice?"

"The water?" he said.

"There may be a tap," said my brother, "in some of the houses. We have no water. I dare not leave my people."

The man pushed against the crowd towards the gate of the corner house.

"Go on!" said the people, thrusting at him. "They are coming! Go on!"

Then my brother's attention was distracted by a bearded, eagle-faced man lugging a small handbag, which split even as my brother's eyes rested on it and disgorged a mass of sovereigns that seemed to break up into separate coins as it struck the ground. They rolled hither and thither among the struggling feet of men and horses. The man stopped and looked stupidly at the heap, and the shaft of a cab struck his shoulder and sent him reeling. He gave a shriek and dodged back, and a cartwheel shaved him narrowly.

"Way!" cried the men all about him. "Make way!"

So soon as the cab had passed, he flung himself, with both hands open, upon the heap of coins, and began thrusting handfuls in his pocket. A horse rose close upon him, and in another moment, half rising, he had been borne down under the horse's hoofs.

"Stop!" screamed my brother, and pushing a woman out of his way, tried to clutch the bit of the horse.

Before he could get to it, he heard a scream under the wheels, and saw through the dust the rim passing over the poor wretch's back. The driver of the cart slashed his whip at my brother, who ran round behind the cart. The multitudinous shouting confused his ears. The man was writhing in the dust among his scattered money, unable to rise, for the wheel had broken his back, and his lower limbs lay limp and dead. My brother stood up and yelled at the next driver, and a man on a black horse came to his assistance.

"Get him out of the road," said he; and, clutching the man's collar with his free hand, my brother lugged him sideways. But he still clutched after his money, and regarded my brother fiercely, hammering at his arm with a handful of gold. "Go on! Go on!" shouted angry voices behind.

"Way! Way!"

There was a smash as the pole of a carriage crashed into the cart that the man on horseback stopped. My brother looked up, and the man with the gold twisted his head round and bit the wrist that held his collar. There was a concussion, and the black horse came staggering sideways, and the carthorse pushed beside it. A hoof missed my brother's foot by a hair's breadth. He released his grip on the fallen man and jumped back. He saw anger change to terror on the face of the poor wretch on the ground, and in a moment he was hidden and my brother was borne backward and carried past the entrance of the lane, and had to fight hard in the torrent to recover it.

He saw Miss Elphinstone covering her eyes, and a little child, with all a child's want of sympathetic imagination, staring with dilated eyes at a dusty something that lay black and still, ground and crushed under the rolling wheels. "Let us go back!" he shouted, and began turning the pony round. "We cannot cross this—hell," he said and they went back a hundred yards the way they had come, until the fighting crowd was hidden. As they passed the bend in the lane my brother saw the face of the dying man in the ditch under the privet, deadly white and drawn, and shining with perspiration. The two women sat silent, crouching in their seat and shivering.

Then beyond the bend my brother stopped again. Miss Elphinstone was white and pale, and her sister-in-law sat weeping, too wretched even to call upon "George." My brother was horrified and perplexed. So soon as they had retreated he realised how urgent and unavoidable it was to attempt this crossing. He turned to Miss Elphinstone, suddenly resolute.

"We must go that way," he said, and led the pony round again.

For the second time that day this girl proved her quality. To force their way into the torrent of people, my brother plunged into the traffic and held back a cab horse, while she drove the pony across its head. A waggon locked wheels for a moment and ripped a long splinter from the chaise. In another moment they were caught and swept forward by the stream. My brother, with the cabman's whip marks red across his face and hands, scrambled into the chaise and took the reins from her.

"Point the revolver at the man behind," he said, giving it to her, "if he presses us too hard. No!—point it at his horse."

Then he began to look out for a chance of edging to the right across the road. But once in the stream he seemed to lose volition, to become a part of that dusty rout. They swept through Chipping Barnet with the torrent; they were nearly a mile beyond the centre of the town before they had fought across to the opposite side of the way. It was din and confusion indescribable; but in and beyond the town the road forks repeatedly, and this to some extent relieved the stress.

They struck eastward through Hadley, and there on either side of the road, and at another place farther on they came upon a great multitude of people drinking at the stream, some fighting to come at the water. And farther on, from a lull near East Barnet, they saw two trains running slowly one after the other without signal or order—trains swarming with people, with men even among the coals behind the engines—going northward along the Great Northern Railway. My brother supposes they must have filled outside London, for at that time the furious terror of the people had rendered the central termini impossible.

Near this place they halted for the rest of the afternoon, for the violence of the day had already utterly exhausted all three of them. They began to suffer the beginnings of hunger; the night was cold, and none of them dared to sleep. And in the evening many people came hurrying along the road nearby their stopping place, fleeing from unknown dangers before them, and going in the direction from which my brother had come.

. . .

CHAPTER SEVENTEEN
The "Thunder Child"

HAD THE MARTIANS AIMED only at destruction, they might on Monday have annihilated the entire population of London, as it spread itself slowly through the home counties. Not only along the road through Barnet, but also through Edgware and Waltham Abbey, and along the roads eastward to Southend and Shoeburyness, and south of the Thames to Deal and Broadstairs, poured the same frantic rout. If one could have hung that June morning in a balloon in the blazing blue above London every northward and eastward road running out of the tangled maze of streets would have seemed stippled black with the streaming fugitives, each dot a human agony of terror and physical distress. I have set forth at length in the last chapter my brother's account of the road through Chipping Barnet, in order that my readers may realise how that swarming of black dots appeared to one of those concerned. Never before in the history of the world had such a mass of human beings moved and suffered together. The legendary hosts of Goths and Huns, the hugest armies Asia has ever seen, would have been but a drop in that current. And this was no disciplined march; it was a stampede—a stampede gigantic and terrible—without order and without a goal, six million people unarmed and unprovisioned, driving headlong. It was the beginning of the rout of civilisation, of the massacre of mankind.

Directly below him the balloonist would have seen the network of streets far and wide, houses, churches, squares, crescents, gardens—already derelict—spread out like a huge map, and in the southward BLOTTED. Over Ealing, Richmond, Wimbledon, it would have seemed as if some monstrous pen had flung ink upon the chart. Steadily, incessantly, each black splash grew and spread, shooting out ramifications this way and that, now banking itself against rising ground, now pouring swiftly over a crest into a new-found valley, exactly as a gout of ink would spread itself upon blotting paper.

And beyond, over the blue hills that rise southward of the river, the glittering Martians went to and fro, calmly and methodically spreading their poison cloud over this patch of country and then over that, laying it again with their steam jets when it had served its purpose, and taking possession of the conquered country. They do not seem to have aimed at extermination so much as at complete demoralisation and the destruction of any opposition. They exploded any stores of powder they came upon, cut every telegraph, and wrecked the railways here and there. They were hamstringing mankind. They seemed in no hurry to extend the field of their operations, and did not come beyond the central part of London all that day. It is possible that a very considerable number of people in London stuck to their houses through Monday morning. Certain it is that many died at home suffocated by the Black Smoke.

Until about midday the Pool of London was an astonishing scene. Steamboats and shipping of all sorts lay there, tempted by the enormous sums of money offered by fugitives, and it is said that many who swam out to these vessels were thrust off with boathooks and drowned. About one o'clock in the afternoon the thinning remnant of a cloud of the black vapour appeared between the arches of Blackfriars Bridge. At that the Pool became a scene of mad confusion, fighting, and collision, and for some time a multitude of boats and barges jammed in the northern arch of the Tower Bridge, and the sailors and lightermen had to fight savagely against the people who swarmed upon them from the riverfront. People were actually clambering down the piers of the bridge from above.

When, an hour later, a Martian appeared beyond the Clock Tower and waded down the river, nothing but wreckage floated above Limehouse.

Of the falling of the fifth cylinder I have presently to tell. The sixth star fell at Wimbledon. My brother, keeping watch beside the women in the chaise in a meadow, saw the green flash of it far beyond the hills. On Tuesday the little party, still set upon getting across the sea, made its way through the swarming country towards Colchester.

The news that the Martians were now in possession of the whole of London was confirmed. They had been seen at Highgate, and even, it was said, at Neasden. But they did not come into my brother's view until the morrow.

That day the scattered multitudes began to realise the urgent need of provisions. As they grew hungry the rights of property ceased to be regarded. Farmers were out to defend their cattle-sheds, granaries, and ripening root crops with arms in their hands. A number of people now, like my brother, had their faces eastward, and there were some desperate souls even going back towards London to get food. These were chiefly people from the northern suburbs, whose knowledge of the Black Smoke came by hearsay. He heard that about half the members of the government had gathered at Birmingham, and that enormous quantities of high explosives were being prepared to be used in automatic mines across the Midland counties.

He was also told that the Midland Railway Company had replaced the desertions of the first day's panic, had resumed traffic, and was running northward trains from St. Albans to relieve the congestion of the home counties. There was also a placard in Chipping Ongar announcing that large stores of flour were available in the northern towns and that within twenty-four hours bread would be distributed among the starving people in the neighbourhood. But this intelligence did not deter him from the plan of escape he had formed, and the three pressed eastward all day, and heard no more of the bread distribution than this promise. Nor, as a matter of fact, did anyone else hear more of it. That night fell the seventh star, falling upon Primrose Hill. It fell while Miss Elphinstone was watching, for she took that duty alternately with my brother. She saw it.

On Wednesday the three fugitives—they had passed the night in a field of unripe wheat—reached Chelmsford, and there a body of the inhabitants, calling itself the Committee of Public Supply, seized the pony as provisions, and would give nothing in exchange for it but the promise of a share in it the next day. Here there were rumours of Martians at Epping, and news of the destruction of Waltham Abbey Powder Mills in a vain attempt to blow up one of the invaders.

People were watching for Martians here from the church towers. My brother, very luckily for him as it chanced, preferred to push on at once to the coast rather than wait for food, although all three of them were very hungry. By midday they passed through Tillingham, which, strangely enough, seemed to be quite silent and deserted, save for a few furtive plunderers hunting for food. Near Tillingham they suddenly came in sight of the sea, and the most amazing crowd of shipping of all sorts that it is possible to imagine.

For after the sailors could no longer come up the Thames, they came on to the Essex coast, to Harwich and Walton and Clacton, and afterwards to Foulness and Shoebury, to bring off the people. They lay in a huge sickle-shaped curve that vanished into mist at last towards the Naze. Close inshore was a multitude of fishing smacks—English, Scotch, French, Dutch, and Swedish; steam launches from the Thames, yachts, electric boats; and beyond were ships of large burden, a multitude of filthy colliers, trim merchantmen, cattle ships, passenger boats, petroleum tanks, ocean tramps, an old white transport even, neat white and grey liners from Southampton and Hamburg; and along the blue coast across the Blackwater my brother could make out dimly a dense swarm of boats chaffering with the people on the beach, a swarm which also extended up the Blackwater almost to Maldon.

About a couple of miles out lay an ironclad, very low in the water, almost, to my brother's perception, like a water-logged ship. This was the ram *Thunder Child*. It was the only warship in sight, but far away to the right over the smooth surface of the sea—for that day there was a dead calm—lay a serpent of black smoke to mark the next ironclads of the Channel Fleet, which hovered in an extended line, steam up and ready for action, across the Thames estuary during the course of the Martian conquest, vigilant and yet powerless to prevent it.

At the sight of the sea, Mrs. Elphinstone, in spite of the assurances of her sister-in-law, gave way to panic. She had never been out of England before, she would rather die than trust herself friendless in a foreign country, and so forth. She seemed, poor woman, to imagine that the French and the Martians might prove very similar. She had been growing increasingly hysterical, fearful, and depressed during the two days' journeyings. Her great idea was to return to Stanmore. Things had been always well and safe at Stanmore. They would find George at Stanmore.

It was with the greatest difficulty they could get her down to the beach, where presently my brother succeeded in attracting the attention of some men on a paddle steamer from the Thames. They sent a boat and drove a bargain for thirty-six pounds for the three. The steamer was going, these men said, to Ostend.

It was about two o'clock when my brother, having paid their fares at the gangway, found himself safely aboard the steamboat with his charges. There was food aboard, albeit at exorbitant prices, and the three of them contrived to eat a meal on one of the seats forward.

There were already a couple of score of passengers aboard, some of whom had expended their last money in securing a passage, but the captain lay off the Blackwater until five in the afternoon, picking up passengers until the seated decks were even dangerously crowded. He would probably have remained longer had it not been for the sound of guns that began about that hour in the south. As if in answer, the ironclad seaward fired a small gun and hoisted a string of flags. A jet of smoke sprang out of her funnels.

Some of the passengers were of opinion that this firing came from Shoeburyness, until it was noticed that it was growing louder. At the same time, far away in the southeast the masts and upperworks of three ironclads rose one after the other out of the sea, beneath clouds of black smoke. But my brother's attention speedily reverted to the distant firing in the south. He fancied he saw a column of smoke rising out of the distant grey haze.

The little steamer was already flapping her way eastward of the big crescent of shipping, and the low Essex coast was growing blue and hazy, when a Martian appeared, small and faint in the remote distance, advancing along the muddy coast from the direction of Foulness. At that the captain on the bridge swore at the top of his voice with fear and anger at his own delay, and the paddles seemed infected with his terror. Every soul aboard stood at the bulwarks or on the seats of the steamer and stared at that distant shape, higher than the trees or church towers inland, and advancing with a leisurely parody of a human stride.

It was the first Martian my brother had seen, and he stood, more amazed than terrified, watching this Titan advancing deliberately towards the shipping, wading farther and farther into the water as the coast fell away. Then, far away beyond the Crouch, came another, striding over some stunted trees, and then yet another, still farther off, wading deeply through a shiny mudflat that seemed to hang halfway up between sea and sky. They were all stalking seaward, as if to intercept the escape of the multitudinous vessels that were crowded between Foulness and the Naze. In spite of the throbbing exertions of the engines of the little paddle-boat, and the pouring foam that her wheels flung behind her, she receded with terrifying slowness from this ominous advance.

Glancing northwestward, my brother saw the large crescent of shipping already writhing with the approaching terror; one ship passing behind another, another coming round from broadside to end on, steamships whistling and giving off volumes of steam, sails being let out, launches rushing hither and thither. He was so fascinated by this and by the creeping danger away to the left that he had no eyes for anything seaward. And then a swift movement of the steamboat (she had suddenly come round to avoid being run down) flung him headlong from the seat upon which he was standing. There was a shouting all about him, a trampling of feet, and a cheer that seemed to be answered faintly. The steamboat lurched and rolled him over upon his hands.

He sprang to his feet and saw to starboard, and not a hundred yards from their heeling, pitching boat, a vast iron bulk like the blade of a plough tearing through the water, tossing it on either side in huge waves of foam that leaped towards the steamer, flinging her paddles helplessly in the air, and then sucking her deck down almost to the waterline.

A douche of spray blinded my brother for a moment. When his eyes were clear again he saw the monster had passed and was rushing landward. Big iron upperworks rose out of this headlong structure, and from that twin funnels projected and spat a smoking blast shot with fire. It was the torpedo ram, *Thunder Child*, steaming headlong, coming to the rescue of the threatened shipping.

Keeping his footing on the heaving deck by clutching the bulwarks, my brother looked past this charging leviathan at the Martians again, and he saw the three of them now close together, and standing so far out to sea that their tripod supports were almost entirely submerged. Thus sunken, and seen in remote perspective, they appeared far less formidable than the huge iron bulk in whose wake the steamer was pitching so helplessly. It would seem they were regarding this new antagonist with astonishment. To their intelligence, it may be, the giant was even such another as themselves. The *Thunder Child* fired no gun, but simply drove full speed towards them. It was probably her not firing that enabled her to get so near the enemy as she did. They did not know what to make of her. One shell, and they would have sent her to the bottom forthwith with the Heat-Ray.

She was steaming at such a pace that in a minute she seemed halfway between the steamboat and the Martians—a diminishing black bulk against the receding horizontal expanse of the Essex coast.

Suddenly the foremost Martian lowered his tube and discharged a canister of the black gas at the ironclad. It hit her larboard side and glanced off in an inky jet that rolled away to seaward, an unfolding torrent of Black Smoke, from which the ironclad drove clear.

To the watchers from the steamer, low in the water and with the sun in their eyes, it seemed as though she were already among the Martians.

They saw the gaunt figures separating and rising out of the water as they retreated shoreward, and one of them raised the camera-like generator of the Heat-Ray. He held it pointing obliquely downward, and a bank of steam sprang from the water at its touch. It must have driven through the iron of the ship's side like a white-hot iron rod through paper.

A flicker of flame went up through the rising steam, and then the Martian reeled and staggered. In another moment he was cut down, and a great body of water and steam shot high in the air. The guns of the *Thunder Child* sounded through the reek, going off one after the other, and one shot splashed the water high close by the steamer, ricocheted towards the other flying ships to the north, and smashed a smack to matchwood.

But no one heeded that very much. At the sight of the Martian's collapse the captain on the bridge yelled inarticulately, and all the crowding passengers on the steamer's stern shouted together. And then they yelled again. For, surging out beyond the white tumult, drove something long and black, the flames streaming from its middle parts, its ventilators and funnels spouting fire.

She was alive still; the steering gear, it seems, was intact and her engines working. She headed straight for a second Martian, and was within a hundred yards of him when the Heat-Ray came to bear. Then with a violent thud, a blinding flash, her decks, her funnels, leaped upward. The Martian staggered with the violence of her explosion, and in another moment the flaming wreckage, still driving forward with the impetus of its pace, had struck him and crumpled him up like a thing of cardboard. My brother shouted involuntarily. A boiling tumult of steam hid everything again.

"Two!" yelled the captain.

Everyone was shouting. The whole steamer from end to end rang with frantic cheering that was taken up first by one and then by all in the crowding multitude of ships and boats that was driving out to sea.

The steam hung upon the water for many minutes, hiding the third Martian and the coast altogether. And all this time the boat was paddling steadily out to sea and away from the fight; and when at last the confusion cleared, the drifting bank of black vapour intervened, and nothing of the *Thunder Child* could be made out, nor could the third Martian be seen. But the ironclads to seaward were now quite close and standing in towards shore past the steamboat.

The little vessel continued to beat its way seaward, and the ironclads receded slowly towards the coast, which was hidden still by a marbled bank of vapour, part steam, part black gas, eddying and combining in the strangest way. The fleet of refugees was scattering to the northeast; several smacks were sailing between the ironclads and the steamboat. After a time, and before they reached the sinking cloud bank, the warships turned northward, and then abruptly went about and passed into the thickening haze of evening southward. The coast grew faint, and at last indistinguishable amid the low banks of clouds that were gathering about the sinking sun.

Then suddenly out of the golden haze of the sunset came the vibration of guns, and a form of black shadows moving. Everyone struggled to the rail of the steamer and peered into the blinding furnace of the west, but nothing was to be distinguished clearly. A mass of smoke rose slanting and barred the face of the sun. The steamboat throbbed on its way through an interminable suspense.

The sun sank into grey clouds, the sky flushed and darkened, the evening star trembled into sight. It was deep twilight when the captain cried out and pointed. My brother strained his eyes. Something rushed up into the sky out of the greyness—rushed slantingly upward and very swiftly into the luminous clearness above the clouds in the western sky; something flat and broad, and very large, that swept round in a vast curve, grew smaller, sank slowly, and vanished again into the grey mystery of the night. And as it flew it rained down darkness upon the land.

BOOK TWO
The Earth under the Martians

• • •

CHAPTER ONE
Under Foot

IN THE FIRST BOOK I have wandered so much from my own adventures to tell of the experiences of my brother that all through the last two chapters I and the curate have been lurking in the empty house at Halliford whither we fled to escape the Black Smoke. There I will resume. We stopped there all Sunday night and all the next day—the day of the panic—in a little island of daylight, cut off by the Black Smoke from the rest of the world. We could do nothing but wait in aching inactivity during those two weary days.

My mind was occupied by anxiety for my wife. I figured her at Leatherhead, terrified, in danger, mourning me already as a dead man. I paced the rooms and cried aloud when I thought of how I was cut off from her, of all that might happen to her in my absence. My cousin I knew was brave enough for any emergency, but he was not the sort of man to realise danger quickly, to rise promptly. What was needed now was not bravery, but circumspection. My only consolation was to believe that the Martians were moving Londonward and away from her. Such vague anxieties keep the mind sensitive and painful. I grew very weary and irritable with the curate's perpetual ejaculations; I tired of the sight of his selfish despair. After some ineffectual remonstrance I kept away from him, staying in a room—evidently a children's schoolroom—containing globes, forms, and copybooks. When he followed me thither, I went to a box room at the top of the house and, in order to be alone with my aching miseries, locked myself in.

We were hopelessly hemmed in by the Black Smoke all that day and the morning of the next. There were signs of people in the next house on Sunday evening—a face at a window and moving lights, and later the slamming of a door. But I do not know who these people were, nor what became of them. We saw nothing of them next day. The Black Smoke drifted slowly riverward all through Monday morning, creeping nearer and nearer to us, driving at last along the roadway outside the house that hid us.

A Martian came across the fields about midday, laying the stuff with a jet of superheated steam that hissed against the walls, smashed all the windows it touched, and scalded the curate's hand as he fled out of the front room. When at last we crept across the sodden rooms and looked out again, the country northward was as though a black snowstorm had passed over it. Looking towards the river, we were astonished to see an unaccountable redness mingling with the black of the scorched meadows.

For a time we did not see how this change affected our position, save that we were relieved of our fear of the Black Smoke. But later I perceived that we were no longer hemmed in, that now we might get away. So soon as I realised that the way of escape was open, my dream of action returned. But the curate was lethargic, unreasonable.

"We are safe here," he repeated; "safe here."

I resolved to leave him—would that I had! Wiser now for the artilleryman's teaching, I sought out food and drink. I had found oil and rags for my burns, and I also took a hat and a flannel shirt that I found in one of the bedrooms. When it was clear to him that I meant to go alone—had reconciled myself to going alone—he suddenly roused himself to come. And all being quiet throughout the afternoon, we started about five o'clock, as I should judge, along the blackened road to Sunbury.

In Sunbury, and at intervals along the road, were dead bodies lying in contorted attitudes, horses as well as men, overturned carts and luggage, all covered thickly with black dust. That pall of cindery powder made me think of what I had read of the destruction of Pompeii. We got to Hampton Court without misadventure, our minds full of strange and unfamiliar appearances, and at Hampton Court our eyes were relieved to find a patch of green that had escaped the suffocating drift. We went through Bushey Park, with its deer going to and fro under the chestnuts, and some men and women hurrying in the distance towards Hampton, and so we came to Twickenham. These were the first people we saw.

Away across the road the woods beyond Ham and Petersham were still afire. Twickenham was uninjured by either Heat-Ray or Black

Smoke, and there were more people about here, though none could give us news. For the most part they were like ourselves, taking advantage of a lull to shift their quarters. I have an impression that many of the houses here were still occupied by scared inhabitants, too frightened even for flight. Here too the evidence of a hasty rout was abundant along the road. I remember most vividly three smashed bicycles in a heap, pounded into the road by the wheels of subsequent carts. We crossed Richmond Bridge about half past eight. We hurried across the exposed bridge, of course, but I noticed floating down the stream a number of red masses, some many feet across. I did not know what these were— there was no time for scrutiny—and I put a more horrible interpretation on them than they deserved. Here again on the Surrey side were black dust that had once been smoke, and dead bodies—a heap near the approach to the station; but we had no glimpse of the Martians until we were some way towards Barnes.

We saw in the blackened distance a group of three people running down a side street towards the river, but otherwise it seemed deserted. Up the hill Richmond town was burning briskly; outside the town of Richmond there was no trace of the Black Smoke.

Then suddenly, as we approached Kew, came a number of people running, and the upperworks of a Martian fighting-machine loomed in sight over the housetops, not a hundred yards away from us. We stood aghast at our danger, and had the Martian looked down we must immediately have perished. We were so terrified that we dared not go on, but turned aside and hid in a shed in a garden. There the curate crouched, weeping silently, and refusing to stir again.

But my fixed idea of reaching Leatherhead would not let me rest, and in the twilight I ventured out again. I went through a shrubbery, and along a passage beside a big house standing in its own grounds, and so emerged upon the road towards Kew. The curate I left in the shed, but he came hurrying after me.

That second start was the most foolhardy thing I ever did. For it was manifest the Martians were about us. No sooner had the curate overtaken me than we saw either the fighting-machine we had seen before or another, far away across the meadows in the direction of Kew Lodge. Four or five little black figures hurried before it across the green-grey of the field, and in a moment it was evident this Martian pursued them. In three strides he was among them, and they ran radiating from his feet in all directions. He used no Heat-Ray to destroy them, but picked them up one by one. Apparently he tossed them into the great metallic carrier wnich projected behind him, much as a workman's basket hangs over his shoulder.

It was the first time I realised that the Martians might have any other purpose than destruction with defeated humanity. We stood for a moment petrified, then turned and fled through a gate behind us into a walled garden, fell into, rather than found, a fortunate ditch, and lay there, scarce daring to whisper to each other until the stars were out.

I suppose it was nearly eleven o'clock before we gathered courage to start again, no longer venturing into the road, but sneaking along hedgerows and through plantations, and watching keenly through the darkness, he on the right and I on the left, for the Martians, who seemed to be all about us. In one place we blundered upon a scorched and blackened area, now cooling and ashen, and a number of scattered dead bodies of men, burned horribly about the heads and trunks but with their legs and boots mostly intact; and of dead horses, fifty feet, perhaps, behind a line of four ripped guns and smashed gun carriages.

Sheen, it seemed, had escaped destruction, but the place was silent and deserted. Here we happened on no dead, though the night was too dark for us to see into the side roads of the place. In Sheen my companion suddenly complained of faintness and thirst, and we decided to try one of the houses.

The first house we entered, after a little difficulty with the window, was a small semi-detached villa, and I found nothing eatable left in the place but some mouldy cheese. There was, however, water to drink; and I took a hatchet, which promised to be useful in our next house-breaking.

We then crossed to a place where the road turns towards Mortlake. Here there stood a white house within a walled garden, and in the pantry of this domicile we found a store of food—two loaves of bread in a pan, an uncooked steak, and the half of a ham. I give this catalogue so precisely because, as it happened, we were destined to subsist upon this store for the next fortnight. Bottled beer stood under a shelf, and there were two bags of haricot beans and some limp lettuces. This pantry opened into a kind of wash-up kitchen, and in this was firewood; there was also a cupboard, in which we found nearly a dozen of burgundy, tinned soups and salmon, and two tins of biscuits.

We sat in the adjacent kitchen in the dark—for we dared not strike a light—and ate bread and ham, and drank beer out of the same bottle. The curate, who was still timorous and restless, was now, oddly enough, for pushing on, and I was urging him to keep up his strength by eating when the thing happened that was to imprison us.

"It can't be midnight yet," I said, and then came a blinding glare of vivid green light. Everything in the kitchen leaped out, clearly visible in green and black, and vanished again. And then followed such a concussion as I have never heard before or since. So close on the heels of this as to seem instantaneous came a thud behind me, a clash of glass, a crash and rattle of falling masonry all about us, and the plaster of the ceiling came down upon us, smashing into a multitude of fragments upon our heads. I was knocked headlong across the floor against the oven handle and stunned. I was insensible for a long time, the curate told me, and when I came to we were in darkness again, and he, with a face wet, as I found afterwards, with blood from a cut forehead, was dabbing water over me.

For some time I could not recollect what had happened. Then things came to me slowly. A bruise on my temple asserted itself.

"Are you better?" asked the curate in a whisper.

At last I answered him. I sat up.

"Don't move," he said. "The floor is covered with smashed crockery from the dresser. You can't possibly move without making a noise, and I fancy *they* are outside."

We both sat quite silent, so that we could scarcely hear each other breathing. Everything seemed deadly still, but once something near us, some plaster or broken brickwork, slid down with a rumbling sound. Outside and very near was an intermittent, metallic rattle.

"That!" said the curate, when presently it happened again.

"Yes," I said. "But what is it?"

"A Martian!" said the curate.

I listened again.

"It was not like the Heat-Ray," I said, and for a time I was inclined to think one of the great fighting-machines had stumbled against the house, as I had seen one stumble against the tower of Shepperton Church.

Our situation was so strange and incomprehensible that for three or four hours, until the dawn came, we scarcely moved. And then the light filtered in, not through the window, which remained black, but through a triangular aperture between a beam and a heap of broken bricks in the wall behind us. The interior of the kitchen we now saw greyly for the first time.

The window had been burst in by a mass of garden mould, which flowed over the table upon which we had been sitting and lay about our feet. Outside, the soil was banked high against the house. At the top of the window frame we could see an uprooted drainpipe. The floor was littered with smashed hardware; the end of the kitchen towards the house was broken into, and since the daylight shone in there, it was evident the greater part of the house had collapsed. Contrasting vividly with this ruin was the neat dresser, stained in the fashion, pale green, and with a number of copper and tin vessels below it, the wallpaper imitating blue and white tiles, and a couple of coloured supplements fluttering from the walls above the kitchen range.

As the dawn grew clearer, we saw through the gap in the wall the body of a Martian, standing sentinel, I suppose, over the still glowing cylinder. At the sight of that we crawled as circumspectly as possible out of the twilight of the kitchen into the darkness of the scullery.

Abruptly the right interpretation dawned upon my mind.

"The fifth cylinder," I whispered, "the fifth shot from Mars, has struck this house and buried us under the ruins!"

For a time the curate was silent, and then he whispered: "God have mercy upon us!"

I heard him presently whimpering to himself.

Save for that sound we lay quite still in the scullery; I for my part scarce dared breathe, and sat with my eyes fixed on the faint light of the kitchen door. I could just see the curate's face, a dim, oval shape, and his collar and cuffs. Outside there began a metallic hammering, then a violent hooting, and then again, after a quiet interval, a hissing like the hissing of an engine. These noises, for the most part problematical, continued intermittently, and seemed if anything to increase in number as time wore on. Presently a measured thudding and a vibration that made everything about us quiver and the vessels in the pantry ring and shift, began and continued. Once the light was eclipsed, and the ghostly kitchen doorway became absolutely dark. For many hours we must have crouched there, silent and shivering, until our tired attention failed. . . .

At last I found myself awake and very hungry. I am inclined to believe we must have spent the greater portion of a day before that awakening. My hunger was at a stride so insistent that it moved me to action. I told the curate I was going to seek food, and felt my way towards the pantry. He made me no answer, but so soon as I began eating the faint noise I made stirred him up and I heard him crawling after me.

• • •

CHAPTER TWO

What We Saw
from the Ruined House

AFTER EATING WE CREPT BACK to the scullery, and there I must have dozed again, for when presently I looked round I was alone. The thudding vibration continued with wearisome persistence. I whispered for the curate several times, and at last felt my way to the door of the kitchen. It was still daylight, and I perceived him across the room, lying against the triangular hole that looked out upon the Martians. His shoulders were hunched, so that his head was hidden from me.

I could hear a number of noises almost like those in an engine shed; and the place rocked with that beating thud. Through the aperture in the wall I could see the top of a tree touched with gold and the warm blue of a tranquil evening sky. For a minute or so I remained watching the curate, and then I advanced, crouching and stepping with extreme care amid the broken crockery that littered the floor.

I touched the curate's leg, and he started so violently that a mass of plaster went sliding down outside and fell with a loud impact. I gripped his arm, fearing he might cry out, and for a long time we crouched motionless. Then I turned to see how much of our rampart remained. The detachment of the plaster had left a vertical slit open in the debris, and by raising myself cautiously across a beam I was able to see out of this gap into what had been overnight a quiet suburban roadway. Vast, indeed, was the change that we beheld.

The fifth cylinder must have fallen right into the midst of the house we had first visited. The building had vanished, completely smashed, pulverised, and dispersed by the blow. The cylinder lay now far beneath the original foundations—deep in a hole, already vastly larger than the pit I had looked into at Woking. The earth all round it had splashed under that tremendous impact—"splashed" is the only word—and lay in heaped piles that hid the masses of the adjacent houses. It had behaved exactly like mud under the violent blow of a hammer. Our house had collapsed backward; the front portion, even on the ground floor, had been destroyed completely; by a chance the kitchen and scullery had escaped, and stood buried now under soil and ruins, closed in by tons of earth on every side save towards the cylinder. Over that aspect we hung now on the very edge of the great circular pit the Martians were engaged in making. The heavy beating sound was evidently just behind us, and ever and again a bright green vapour drove up like a veil across our peephole.

The cylinder was already opened in the centre of the pit, and on the farther edge of the pit, amid the smashed and gravel-heaped shrubbery, one of the great fighting-machines, deserted by its occupant, stood stiff and tall against the evening sky. At first I scarcely noticed the pit and the cylinder, although it has been convenient to describe them first, on account of the extraordinary glittering mechanism I saw busy in the excavation, and on account of the strange creatures that were crawling slowly and painfully across the heaped mould near it.

The mechanism it certainly was that held my attention first. It was one of those complicated fabrics that have since been called handling-machines, and the study of which has already given such an enormous impetus to terrestrial invention. As it dawned upon me first, it present-ed a sort of metallic spider with five jointed, agile legs, and with an extraordinary number of jointed levers, bars, and reaching and clutch-ing tentacles about its body. Most of its arms were retracted, but with three long tentacles it was fishing out a number of rods, plates, and bars which lined the covering and apparently strengthened the walls of the cylinder. These, as it extracted them, were lifted out and deposited upon a level surface of earth behind it.

Its motion was so swift, complex, and perfect that at first I did not see it as a machine, in spite of its metallic glitter. The fighting-machines were coordinated and animated to an extraordinary pitch, but nothing to compare with this. People who have never seen these structures, and have only the ill-imagined efforts of artists or the imperfect descriptions of such eye-witnesses as myself to go upon, scarcely realise that living quality.

I recall particularly the illustration of one of the first pamphlets to give a consecutive account of the war. The artist had evidently made a hasty study of one of the fighting-machines, and there his knowledge ended. He presented them as tilted, stiff tripods, without either flexibil-ity or subtlety, and with an altogether misleading monotony of effect. The pamphlet containing these renderings had a considerable vogue, and I mention them here simply to warn the reader against the impres-sion they may have created. They were no more like the Martians I saw in action than a Dutch doll is like a human being. To my mind, the pamphlet would have been much better without them.

At first, I say, the handling-machine did not impress me as a machine, but as a crablike creature with a glittering integument, the controlling Martian whose delicate tentacles actuated its movements seeming to be simply the equivalent of the crab's cerebral portion. But then I perceived the resemblance of its grey-brown, shiny, leathery integument to that of the other sprawling bodies beyond, and the true nature of this dexterous workman dawned upon me. With that realisation my interest shifted to those other creatures, the real Martians. Already I had had a transient impression of these, and the first nausea no longer obscured my observation. Moreover, I was concealed and motionless, and under no urgency of action.

They were, I now saw, the most unearthly creatures it is possible to conceive. They were huge round bodies—or, rather, heads—about four feet in diameter, each body having in front of it a face. This face had no nostrils—indeed, the Martians do not seem to have had any sense of smell, but it had a pair of very large dark-coloured eyes, and just beneath this a kind of fleshy beak. In the back of this head or body—I scarcely know how to speak of it—was the single tight tympanic surface, since known to be anatomically an ear, though it must have been almost useless in our dense air. In a group round the mouth were sixteen slender, almost whiplike tentacles, arranged in two bunches of eight each. These bunches have since been named rather aptly, by that distinguished anatomist, Professor Howes, the *hands*. Even as I saw these Martians for the first time they seemed to be endeavouring to raise themselves on these hands, but of course, with the increased weight of terrestrial conditions, this was impossible. There is reason to suppose that on Mars they may have progressed upon them with some facility.

The internal anatomy, I may remark here, as dissection has since shown, was almost equally simple. The greater part of the structure was the brain, sending enormous nerves to the eyes, ear, and tactile tentacles. Besides this were the bulky lungs, into which the mouth opened, and the heart and its vessels. The pulmonary distress caused by the denser atmosphere and greater gravitational attraction was only too evident in the convulsive movements of the outer skin.

And this was the sum of the Martian organs. Strange as it may seem to a human being, all the complex apparatus of digestion, which makes up the bulk of our bodies, did not exist in the Martians. They were heads—merely heads. Entrails they had none. They did not eat, much less digest. Instead, they took the fresh, living blood of other creatures, and *injected* it into their own veins. I have myself seen this being done, as I shall mention in its place. But, squeamish as I may seem, I cannot bring myself to describe what I could not endure even to continue watching. Let it suffice to say, blood obtained from a still living animal, in most cases from a human being, was run directly by means of a little pipette into the recipient canal. . . .

The bare idea of this is no doubt horribly repulsive to us but at the same time I think that we should remember how repulsive our carnivorous habits would seem to an intelligent rabbit.

The physiological advantages of the practice of injection are undeniable, if one thinks of the tremendous waste of human time and energy occasioned by eating and the digestive process. Our bodies are half made up of glands and tubes and organs, occupied in turning heterogeneous food into blood. The digestive processes and their reaction upon the nervous system sap our strength and colour our minds. Men go happy or miserable as they have healthy or unhealthy livers, or sound gastric glands. But the Martians were lifted above all these organic fluctuations of mood and emotion.

Their undeniable preference for men as their source of nourishment is partly explained by the nature of the remains of the victims they had brought with them as provisions from Mars. These creatures, to judge from the shrivelled remains that have fallen into human hands, were bipeds with flimsy, silicious skeletons (almost like those of the silicious sponges) and feeble musculature, standing about six feet high and having round, erect heads, and large eyes in flinty sockets. Two or three of these seem to have been brought in each cylinder, and all were killed before earth was reached. It was just as well for them, for the mere attempt to stand upright upon our planet would have broken every bone in their bodies.

And while I am engaged in this description, I may add in this place certain further details which, although they were not all evident to us at the time, will enable the reader who is unacquainted with them to form a clearer picture of these offensive creatures.

In three other points their physiology differed strangely from ours. Their organisms did not sleep, any more than the heart of man sleeps. Since they had no extensive muscular mechanism to recuperate, that periodical extinction was unknown to them. They had little or no sense of fatigue, it would seem. On earth they could never have moved without effort, yet even to the last they kept in action. In twenty-four hours

they did twenty-four hours of work, as even on earth is perhaps t
with the ants.

In the next place, wonderful as it seems in a sexual world, the Martians were absolutely without sex, and therefore without any of the tumultuous emotions that arise from that difference among men. A young Martian, there can now be no dispute, was really born upon earth during the war, and it was found attached to its parent, partially *budded* off, just as young lilybulbs bud off, or like the young animals in the freshwater polyp.

In man, in all the higher terrestrial animals, such a method of increase has disappeared; but even on this earth it was certainly the primitive method. Among the lower animals, up even to those first cousins of the vertebrated animals, the Tunicates, the two processes occur side by side, but finally the sexual method superseded its competitor altogether. On Mars, however, just the reverse has apparently been the case.

It is worthy of remark that a certain speculative writer of quasi-scientific repute, writing long before the Martian invasion, did forecast for man a final structure not unlike the actual Martian condition. His prophecy, I remember, appeared in November or December, 1893, in a long-defunct publication, the *Pall Mall Budget*, and I recall a caricature of it in a pre-Martian periodical called *Punch*. He pointed out—writing in a foolish, facetious tone—that the perfection of mechanical appliances must ultimately supersede limbs; the perfection of chemical devices, digestion; that such organs as hair, external nose, teeth, ears, and chin were no longer essential parts of the human being, and that the tendency of natural selection would lie in the direction of their steady diminution through the coming ages. The brain alone remained a cardinal necessity. Only one other part of the body had a strong case for survival, and that was the hand, "teacher and agent of the brain." While the rest of the body dwindled, the hands would grow larger.

There is many a true word written in jest, and here in the Martians we have beyond dispute the actual accomplishment of such a suppression of the animal side of the organism by the intelligence. To me it is quite credible that the Martians may be descended from beings not unlike ourselves, by a gradual development of brain and hands (the latter giving rise to the two bunches of delicate tentacles at last) at the expense of the rest of the body. Without the body the brain would, of course, become a mere selfish intelligence, without any of the emotional substratum of the human being.

The last salient point in which the systems of these creatures differed from ours was in what one might have thought a very trivial particular. Micro-organisms, which cause so much disease and pain on earth, have either never appeared upon Mars or Martian sanitary science eliminated them ages ago. A hundred diseases, all the fevers and contagions of human life, consumption, cancers, tumours and such morbidities, never enter the scheme of their life. And speaking of the differences between the life on Mars and terrestrial life, I may allude here to the curious suggestions of the red weed.

Apparently the vegetable kingdom in Mars, instead of having green for a dominant colour, is of a vivid blood-red tint. At any rate, the seeds which the Martians (intentionally or accidentally) brought with them gave rise in all cases to red-coloured growths. Only that known popularly as the red weed, however, gained any footing in competition with terrestrial forms. The red creeper was quite a transitory growth, and few people have seen it growing. For a time, however, the red weed grew with astonishing vigour and luxuriance. It spread up the sides of the pit by the third or fourth day of our imprisonment, and its cactus-like branches formed a carmine fringe to the edges of our triangular window. And afterwards I found it broadcast throughout the country, and especially wherever there was a stream of water.

The Martians had what appears to have been an auditory organ, a single round drum at the back of the head-body, and eyes with a visual range not very different from ours except that, according to Philips, blue and violet were as black to them. It is commonly supposed that they communicated by sounds and tentacular gesticulations; this is asserted, for instance, in the able but hastily compiled pamphlet (written evidently by someone not an eye-witness of Martian actions) to which I have already alluded, and which, so far, has been the chief source of information concerning them. Now no surviving human being saw so much of the Martians in action as I did. I take no credit to myself for an accident, but the fact is so. And I assert that I watched them closely time after time, and that I have seen four, five, and (once) six of them sluggishly performing the most elaborately complicated operations together without either sound or gesture. Their peculiar hooting invariably preceded feeding; it had no modulation, and was, I believe, in no sense a signal, but merely the expiration of air preparatory to the suctional operation. I have a certain claim to at least an elementary knowledge of psychology, and in this matter I am convinced—as firmly as I am convinced of anything—that the Martians interchanged thoughts without any physical intermediation. And I have been convinced of this in spite of strong preconceptions. Before the Martian invasion, as an occasional reader here or there may remember, I had written with some little vehemence against the telepathic theory.

The Martians wore no clothing. Their conceptions of ornament and decorum were necessarily different from ours; and not only were they evidently much less sensible of changes of temperature than we are, but changes of pressure do not seem to have affected their health at all seriously. Yet though they wore no clothing, it was in the other artificial additions to their bodily resources that their great superiority over man lay. We men, with our bicycles and road-skates, our Lilienthal soaring-machines, our guns and sticks and so forth, are just in the beginning of the evolution that the Martians have worked out. They have become practically mere brains, wearing different bodies according to their needs just as men wear suits of clothes and take a bicycle in a hurry or an umbrella in the wet. And of their appliances, perhaps nothing is more wonderful to a man than the curious fact that what is the dominant feature of almost all human devices in mechanism is absent—the *wheel* is absent; among all the things they brought to earth there is no trace or suggestion of their use of wheels. One would have at least expected it in locomotion. And in this connection it is curious to remark that even on this earth Nature has never hit upon the wheel, or has preferred other expedients to its development. And not only did the Martians either not know of (which is incredible), or abstain from, the wheel, but in their apparatus singularly little use is made of the fixed pivot or relatively fixed pivot, with circular motions thereabout confined to one plane. Almost all the joints of the machinery present a complicated system of sliding parts moving over small but beautifully curved friction bearings. And while upon this matter of detail, it is remarkable that the long leverages of their machines are in most cases actuated by a sort of sham musculature of the disks in an elastic sheath; these disks become polarised and drawn closely and powerfully together when traversed by a current of electricity. In this way the curious parallelism to animal motions, which was so striking and disturbing to the human beholder, was attained. Such quasi-muscles abounded in the crablike handling-machine which, on my first peeping out of the slit, I watched unpacking the cylinder. It seemed infinitely more alive than the actual Martians lying beyond it in the sunset light, panting, stirring ineffectual tentacles, and moving feebly after their vast journey across space.

While I was still watching their sluggish motions in the sunlight, and noting each strange detail of their form, the curate reminded me of his presence by pulling violently at my arm. I turned to a scowling face, and silent, eloquent lips. He wanted the slit, which permitted only one of us to peep through; and so I had to forego watching them for a time while he enjoyed that privilege.

When I looked again, the busy handling-machine had already put together several of the pieces of apparatus it had taken out of the cylinder into a shape having an unmistakable likeness to its own; and down on the left a busy little digging mechanism had come into view, emitting jets of green vapour and working its way round the pit, excavating and embanking in a methodical and discriminating manner. This it was which had caused the regular beating noise, and the rhythmic shocks that had kept our ruinous refuge quivering. It piped and whistled as it worked. So far as I could see, the thing was without a directing Martian at all.

* * *

CHAPTER THREE
The Days of Imprisonment

THE ARRIVAL OF A SECOND FIGHTING-MACHINE drove us from our peephole into the scullery, for we feared that from his elevation the Martian might see down upon us behind our barrier. At a later date we began to feel less in danger of their eyes, for to an eye in the dazzle of the sunlight outside our refuge must have been blank blackness, but at first the slightest suggestion of approach drove us into the scullery in heart-throbbing retreat. Yet terrible as was the danger we incurred, the attraction of peeping was for both of us irresistible. And I recall now with a sort of wonder that, in spite of the infinite danger in which we were between starvation and a still more terrible death, we could yet struggle bitterly for that horrible privilege of sight. We would race across the kitchen in a grotesque way between eagerness and the dread of making a noise, and strike each other, and thrust add kick, within a few inches of exposure.

The fact is that we had absolutely incompatible dispositions and habits of thought and action, and our danger and isolation only accentuated the incompatibility. At Halliford I had already come to hate the curate's trick of helpless exclamation, his stupid rigidity of mind. His endless muttering monologue vitiated every effort I made to think out a line of action, and drove me at times, thus pent up and intensified, almost to the verge of craziness. He was as lacking in restraint as a silly woman. He would weep for hours together, and I verily believe that to the very end this spoiled child of life thought his weak tears in some way efficacious. And I would sit in the darkness unable to keep my mind off him by reason of his importunities. He ate more than I did, and it was in vain I pointed out that our only chance of life was to stop in the house until the Martians had done with their pit, that in that long patience a time might presently come when we should need food. He ate and drank impulsively in heavy meals at long intervals. He slept little.

As the days wore on, his utter carelessness of any consideration so intensified our distress and danger that I had, much as I loathed doing it, to resort to threats, and at last to blows. That brought him to reason for a time. But he was one of those weak creatures, void of pride, timorous, anaemic, hateful souls, full of shifty cunning, who face neither God nor man, who face not even themselves.

It is disagreeable for me to recall and write these things, but I set them down that my story may lack nothing. Those who have escaped the dark and terrible aspects of life will find my brutality, my flash of rage in our final tragedy, easy enough to blame; for they know what is wrong as well as any, but not what is possible to tortured men. But those who have been under the shadow, who have gone down at last to elemental things, will have a wider charity.

And while within we fought out our dark, dim contest of whispers, snatched food and drink, and gripping hands and blows, without, in the pitiless sunlight of that terrible June, was the strange wonder, the unfamiliar routine of the Martians in the pit. Let me return to those first new experiences of mine. After a long time I ventured back to the peephole, to find that the new-comers had been reinforced by the occupants of no fewer than three of the fighting-machines. These last had brought with them certain fresh appliances that stood in an orderly manner about the cylinder. The second handling-machine was now completed, and was busied in serving one of the novel contrivances the big machine had brought. This was a body resembling a milk can in its general form, above which oscillated a pear-shaped receptacle, and from which a stream of white powder flowed into a circular basin below.

The oscillatory motion was imparted to this by one tentacle of the handling-machine. With two spatulate hands the handling-machine was digging out and flinging masses of clay into the pear-shaped receptacle above, while with another arm it periodically opened a door and removed rusty and blackened clinkers from the middle part of the machine. Another steely tentacle directed the powder from the basin along a ribbed channel towards some receiver that was hidden from me by the mound of bluish dust. From this unseen receiver a little thread of green smoke rose vertically into the quiet air. As I looked, the handling-machine, with a faint and musical clinking, extended, telescopic fashion, a tentacle that had been a moment before a mere blunt projection, until its end was hidden behind the mound of clay. In another second it had lifted a bar of white aluminium into sight, untarnished as yet, and shining dazzlingly, and deposited it in a growing stack of bars that stood at the side of the pit. Between sunset and starlight this dexterous machine must have made more than a hundred such bars out of the crude clay, and the mound of bluish dust rose steadily until it topped the side of the pit.

The contrast between the swift and complex movements of these contrivances and the inert panting clumsiness of their masters was acute, and for days I had to tell myself repeatedly that these latter were indeed the living of the two things.

The curate had possession of the slit when the first men were brought to the pit. I was sitting below, huddled up, listening with all my ears. He made a sudden movement backward, and I, fearful that we were observed, crouched in a spasm of terror. He came sliding down the rubbish and crept beside me in the darkness, inarticulate, gesticulating, and for a moment I shared his panic. His gesture suggested a resignation of the slit, and after a little while my curiosity gave me courage, and I rose up, stepped across him, and clambered up to it. At first I could see no reason for his frantic behaviour. The twilight had now come, the stars were little and faint, but the pit was illuminated by the flickering green fire that came from the aluminium-making. The whole picture was a flickering scheme of green gleams and shifting rusty black shadows, strangely trying to the eyes. Over and through it all went the bats, heeding it not at all. The sprawling Martians were no longer to be seen, the mound of blue-green powder had risen to cover them from sight, and a fighting-machine, with its legs contracted, crumpled, and abbreviated, stood across the corner of the pit. And then, amid the clangour of the machinery, came a drifting suspicion of human voices, that I entertained at first only to dismiss.

I crouched, watching this fighting-machine closely, satisfying myself now for the first time that the hood did indeed contain a Martian. As the green flames lifted I could see the oily gleam of his integument and the brightness of his eyes. And suddenly I heard a yell, and saw a long tentacle reaching over the shoulder of the machine to the little cage that hunched upon its back. Then something—something struggling violently—was lifted high against the sky, a black, vague enigma against the starlight; and as this black object came down again, I saw by the green brightness that it was a man. For an instant he was clearly visible. He was a stout, ruddy, middle-aged man, well dressed; three days before, he must have been walking the world, a man of considerable consequence. I could see his staring eyes and gleams of light on his studs and watch chain. He vanished behind the mound, and for a moment there was silence. And then began a shrieking and a sustained and cheerful hooting from the Martians.

I slid down the rubbish, struggled to my feet, clapped my hands over my ears, and bolted into the scullery. The curate, who had been crouching silently with his arms over his head, looked up as I passed, cried out quite loudly at my desertion of him, and came running after me.

That night, as we lurked in the scullery, balanced between our horror and the terrible fascination this peeping had, although I felt an urgent need of action I tried in vain to conceive some plan of escape; but afterwards, during the second day, I was able to consider our position with great clearness. The curate, I found, was quite incapable of discussion; this new and culminating atrocity had robbed him of all vestiges of reason or forethought. Practically he had already sunk to the level of an animal. But as the saying goes, I gripped myself with both hands. It grew upon my mind, once I could face the facts, that terrible as our position was, there was as yet no justification for absolute despair. Our chief chance lay in the possibility of the Martians making the pit nothing more than a temporary encampment. Or even if they kept it permanently, they might not consider it necessary to guard it, and a chance of escape might be afforded us. I also weighed very carefully the possibility of our digging a way out in a direction away from the pit, but the chances of our emerging within sight of some sentinel fighting-machine seemed at first too great. And I should have had to do all the digging myself. The curate would certainly have failed me.

It was on the third day, if my memory serves me right, that I saw the lad killed. It was the only occasion on which I actually saw the Martians feed. After that experience I avoided the hole in the wall for the better part of a day. I went into the scullery, removed the door, and spent some hours digging with my hatchet as silently as possible; but when I had made a hole about a couple of feet deep the loose earth collapsed noisily, and I did not dare continue. I lost heart, and lay down on the scullery floor for a long time, having no spirit even to move. And after that I abandoned altogether the idea of escaping by excavation.

It says much for the impression the Martians had made upon me that at first I entertained little or no hope of our escape being brought about by their overthrow through any human effort. But on the fourth or fifth night I heard a sound like heavy guns.

It was very late in the night, and the moon was shining brightly. The Martians had taken away the excavating-machine, and, save for a fighting-machine that stood in the remoter bank of the pit and a handling-machine that was buried out of my sight in a corner of the pit immediately beneath my peephole, the place was deserted by them. Except for the pale glow from the handling-machine and the bars and patches of white moonlight the pit was in darkness, and, except for the clinking of the handling-machine, quite still. That night was a beautiful serenity; save for one planet, the moon seemed to have the sky to herself. I heard a dog howling, and that familiar sound it was that made me listen. Then I heard quite distinctly a booming exactly like the sound of great guns. Six distinct reports I counted, and after a long interval six again. And that was all.

• • •

CHAPTER FOUR
The Death of the Curate

IT WAS ON THE SIXTH DAY of our imprisonment that I peeped for the last time, and presently found myself alone. Instead of keeping close to me and trying to oust me from the slit, the curate had gone back into the scullery. I was struck by a sudden thought. I went back quickly and quietly into the scullery. In the darkness I heard the curate drinking. I snatched in the darkness, and my fingers caught a bottle of burgundy.

For a few minutes there was a tussle. The bottle struck the floor and broke, and I desisted and rose. We stood panting and threatening each other. In the end I planted myself between him and the food, and told him of my determination to begin a discipline. I divided the food in the pantry, into rations to last us ten days. I would not let him eat any more that day. In the afternoon he made a feeble effort to get at the food. I had been dozing, but in an instant I was awake. All day and all night we sat face to face, I weary but resolute, and he weeping and complaining of his immediate hunger. It was, I know, a night and a day, but to me it seemed—it seems now—an interminable length of time.

And so our widened incompatibility ended at last in open conflict. For two vast days we struggled in undertones and wrestling contests. There were times when I beat and kicked him madly, times when I cajoled and persuaded him, and once I tried to bribe him with the last bottle of burgundy, for there was a rain-water pump from which I could get water. But neither force nor kindness availed; he was indeed beyond reason. He would neither desist from his attacks on the food nor from his noisy babbling to himself. The rudimentary precautions to keep our imprisonment endurable he would not observe. Slowly I began to realise the complete overthrow of his intelligence, to perceive that my sole companion in this close and sickly darkness was a man insane.

From certain vague memories I am inclined to think my own mind wandered at times. I had strange and hideous dreams whenever I slept. It sounds paradoxical, but I am inclined to think that the weakness and insanity of the curate warned me, braced me, and kept me a sane man.

On the eighth day he began to talk aloud instead of whispering, and nothing I could do would moderate his speech.

"It is just, O God!" he would say, over and over again. "It is just. On me and mine be the punishment laid. We have sinned, we have fallen short. There was poverty, sorrow; the poor were trodden in the dust, and I held my peace. I preached acceptable folly—my God, what folly!—when I should have stood up, though I died for it, and called upon them to repent-repent!...Oppressors of the poor and needy!... The wine press of God!"

Then he would suddenly revert to the matter of the food I withheld from him, praying, begging, weeping, at last threatening. He began to raise his voice—I prayed him not to. He perceived a hold on me—he threatened he would shout and bring the Martians upon us. For a time that scared me; but any concession would have shortened our chance of escape beyond estimating. I defied him, although I felt no assurance that he might not do this thing. But that day, at any rate, he did not. He talked with his voice rising slowly, through the greater part of the eighth and ninth days—threats, entreaties, mingled with a torrent of half-sane and always frothy repentance for his vacant sham of God's service, such as made me pity him. Then he slept awhile, and began again with renewed strength, so loudly that I must needs make him desist.

"Be still!" I implored.

He rose to his knees, for he had been sitting in the darkness near the copper.

"I have been still too long," he said, in a tone that must have reached the pit, "and now I must bear my witness. Woe unto this unfaithful city! Woe! Woe! Woe! Woe! Woe! To the inhabitants of the earth by reason of the other voices of the trumpet—"

"Shut up!" I said, rising to my feet, and in a terror lest the Martians should hear us. "For God's sake—"

"Nay," shouted the curate, at the top of his voice, standing likewise and extending his arms. "Speak! The word of the Lord is upon me!"

In three strides he was at the door leading into the kitchen.

"I must bear my witness! I go! It has already been too long delayed."

I put out my hand and felt the meat chopper hanging to the wall. In a flash I was after him. I was fierce with fear. Before he was halfway across the kitchen I had overtaken him. With one last touch of humanity I turned the blade back and struck him with the butt. He went headlong forward and lay stretched on the ground. I stumbled over him and stood panting. He lay still.

Suddenly I heard a noise without, the run and smash of slipping plaster, and the triangular aperture in the wall was darkened. I looked up and saw the lower surface of a handling-machine coming slowly across the hole. One of its gripping limbs curled amid the debris; another limb appeared, feeling its way over the fallen beams. I stood petrified, staring. Then I saw through a sort of glass plate near the edge of the body the face, as we may call it, and the large dark eyes of a Martian, peering, and then a long metallic snake of tentacle came feeling slowly through the hole.

I turned by an effort, stumbled over the curate, and stopped at the scullery door. The tentacle was now some way, two yards or more, in the room, and twisting and turning, with queer sudden movements, this way and that. For a while I stood fascinated by that slow, fitful advance. Then, with a faint, hoarse cry, I forced myself across the scullery. I trembled violently; I could scarcely stand upright. I opened the door of the coal cellar, and stood there in the darkness staring at the faintly lit doorway into the kitchen, and listening. Had the Martian seen me? What was it doing now?

Something was moving to and fro there, very quietly; every now and then it tapped against the wall, or started on its movements with a faint metallic ringing, like the movements of keys on a split-ring. Then a heavy body—I knew too well what—was dragged across the floor of the kitchen towards the opening. Irresistibly attracted, I crept to the door and peeped into the kitchen. In the triangle of bright outer sunlight I saw the Martian, in its Briareus of a handling-machine, scrutinizing the curate's head. I thought at once that it would infer my presence from the mark of the blow I had given him.

I crept back to the coal cellar, shut the door, and began to cover myself up as much as I could, and as noiselessly as possible in the darkness, among the firewood and coal therein. Every now and then I paused, rigid, to hear if the Martian had thrust its tentacles through the opening again.

Then the faint metallic jingle returned. I traced it slowly feeling over the kitchen. Presently I heard it nearer—in the scullery, as I judged. I thought that its length might be insufficient to reach me. I prayed copiously. It passed, scraping faintly across the cellar door. An age of almost intolerable suspense intervened; then I heard it fumbling at the latch! It had found the door! The Martians understood doors!

It worried at the catch for a minute, perhaps, and then the door opened.

In the darkness I could just see the thing—like an elephant's trunk more than anything else—waving towards me and touching and examining the wall, coals, wood and ceiling. It was like a black worm swaying its blind head to and fro.

Once, even, it touched the heel of my boot. I was on the verge of screaming; I bit my hand. For a time the tentacle was silent. I could have fancied it had been withdrawn. Presently, with an abrupt click, it gripped something—I thought it had me!—and seemed to go out of the cellar again. For a minute I was not sure. Apparently it had taken a lump of coal to examine.

I seized the opportunity of slightly shifting my position, which had become cramped, and then listened. I whispered passionate prayers for safety.

Then I heard the slow, deliberate sound creeping towards me again. Slowly, slowly it drew near, scratching against the walls and tapping the furniture.

While I was still doubtful, it rapped smartly against the cellar door and closed it. I heard it go into the pantry, and the biscuit-tins rattled and a bottle smashed, and then came a heavy bump against the cellar door. Then silence that passed into an infinity of suspense.

Had it gone?

At last I decided that it had.

It came into the scullery no more; but I lay all the tenth day in the close darkness, buried among coals and firewood, not daring even to crawl out for the drink for which I craved. It was the eleventh day before I ventured so far from my security.

· · ·

CHAPTER FIVE

The Stillness

MY FIRST ACT before I went into the pantry was to fasten the door between the kitchen and the scullery. But the pantry was empty; every scrap of food had gone. Apparently, the Martian had taken it all on the previous day. At that discovery I despaired for the first time. I took no food, or no drink either, on the eleventh or the twelfth day.

At first my mouth and throat were parched, and my strength ebbed sensibly. I sat about in the darkness of the scullery, in a state of despondent wretchedness. My mind ran on eating. I thought I had become deaf, for the noises of movement I had been accustomed to hear from the pit had ceased absolutely. I did not feel strong enough to crawl noiselessly to the peephole, or I would have gone there.

On the twelfth day my throat was so painful that, taking the chance of alarming the Martians, I attacked the creaking rain-water pump that stood by the sink, and got a couple of glassfuls of blackened and tainted rain water. I was greatly refreshed by this, and emboldened by the fact that no enquiring tentacle followed the noise of my pumping.

During these days, in a rambling, inconclusive way, I thought much of the curate and of the manner of his death.

On the thirteenth day I drank some more water, and dozed and thought disjointedly of eating and of vague impossible plans of escape. Whenever I dozed I dreamt of horrible phantasms, of the death of the curate, or of sumptuous dinners; but, asleep or awake, I felt a keen pain that urged me to drink again and again. The light that came into the scullery was no longer grey, but red. To my disordered imagination it seemed the colour of blood.

On the fourteenth day I went into the kitchen, and I was surprised to find that the fronds of the red weed had grown right across the hole in the wall, turning the half-light of the place into a crimson-coloured obscurity.

It was early on the fifteenth day that I heard a curious, familiar sequence of sounds in the kitchen, and, listening, identified it as the snuffing and scratching of a dog. Going into the kitchen, I saw a dog's nose peering in through a break among the ruddy fronds. This greatly surprised me. At the scent of me he barked shortly.

I thought if I could induce him to come into the place quietly I should be able, perhaps, to kill and eat him; and in any case, it would be advisable to kill him, lest his actions attracted the attention of the Martians.

I crept forward, saying "Good dog!" very softly; but he suddenly withdrew his head and disappeared.

I listened—I was not deaf—but certainly the pit was still. I heard a sound like the flutter of a bird's wings, and a hoarse croaking, but that was all.

For a long while I lay close to the peephole, but not daring to move aside the red plants that obscured it. Once or twice I heard a faint pitter-patter like the feet of the dog going hither and thither on the sand far below me, and there were more birdlike sounds, but that was all. At length, encouraged by the silence, I looked out.

Except in the corner, where a multitude of crows hopped and fought over the skeletons of the dead the Martians had consumed, there was not a living thing in the pit.

I stared about me, scarcely believing my eyes. All the machinery had gone. Save for the big mound of greyish-blue powder in one corner, certain bars of aluminium in another, the black birds, and the skeletons of the killed, the place was merely an empty circular pit in the sand.

Slowly I thrust myself out through the red weed, and stood upon the mound of rubble. I could see in any direction save behind me, to the north, and neither Martians nor sign of Martians were to be seen. The pit dropped sheerly from my feet, but a little way along the rubbish afforded a practicable slope to the summit of the ruins. My chance of escape had come. I began to tremble.

I hesitated for some time, and then, in a gust of desperate resolution, and with a heart that throbbed violently, I scrambled to the top of the mound in which I had been buried so long.

I looked about again. To the northward, too, no Martian was visible.

When I had last seen this part of Sheen in the daylight it had been a straggling street of comfortable white and red houses, interspersed with abundant shady trees. Now I stood on a mound of smashed brickwork, clay, and gravel, over which spread a multitude of red cactus-shaped plants, knee-high, without a solitary terrestrial growth to dispute their footing. The trees near me were dead and brown, but further a network of red thread scaled the still living stems.

The neighbouring houses had all been wrecked, but none had been burned; their walls stood, sometimes to the second story, with smashed windows and shattered doors. The red weed grew tumultuously in their roofless rooms. Below me was the great pit, with the crows struggling for its refuse. A number of other birds hopped about among the ruins. Far away I saw a gaunt cat slink crouchingly along a wall, but traces of men there were none.

The day seemed, by contrast with my recent confinement, dazzlingly bright, the sky a glowing blue. A gentle breeze kept the red weed that covered every scrap of unoccupied ground gently swaying. And oh! the sweetness of the air!

. • .

CHAPTER SIX
The Work of Fifteen Days

FOR SOME TIME I STOOD TOTTERING on the mound regardless of my safety. Within that noisome den from which I had emerged I had thought with a narrow intensity only of our immediate security. I had not realised what had been happening to the world, had not anticipated this startling vision of unfamiliar things. I had expected to see Sheen in ruins—I found about me the landscape, weird and lurid, of another planet.

For that moment I touched an emotion beyond the common range of men, yet one that the poor brutes we dominate know only too well. I felt as a rabbit might feel returning to his burrow and suddenly confronted by the work of a dozen busy navvies digging the foundations of a house. I felt the first inkling of a thing that presently grew quite clear in my mind, that oppressed me for many days, a sense of dethronement, a persuasion that I was no longer a master, but an animal among the animals, under the Martian heel. With us it would be as with them, to lurk and watch, to run and hide; the fear and empire of man had passed away.

But so soon as this strangeness had been realised it passed, and my dominant motive became the hunger of my long and dismal fast. In the direction away from the pit I saw, beyond a red-covered wall, a patch of garden ground unburied. This gave me a hint, and I went knee-deep, and sometimes neck-deep, in the red weed. The density of the weed gave me a reassuring sense of hiding. The wall was some six feet high, and when I attempted to clamber it I found I could not lift my feet to the crest. So I went along by the side of it, and came to a corner and a rockwork that enabled me to get to the top, and tumble into the garden I coveted. Here I found some young onions, a couple of gladiolus bulbs, and a quantity of immature carrots, all of which I secured, and, scrambling over a ruined wall, went on my way through scarlet and crimson trees towards Kew—it was like walking through an avenue of gigantic blood drops—possessed with two ideas: to get more food, and to limp, as soon and as far as my strength permitted, out of this accursed unearthly region of the pit.

Some way farther, in a grassy place, was a group of mushrooms which also I devoured, and then I came upon a brown sheet of flowing shallow water, where meadows used to be. These fragments of nourishment served only to whet my hunger. At first I was surprised at this flood in a hot, dry summer, but afterwards I discovered that it was caused by the tropical exuberance of the red weed. Directly this extraordinary growth encountered water it straightway became gigantic and of unparalleled fecundity. Its seeds were simply poured down into the water of the Wey and Thames, and its swiftly growing and Titanic water fronds speedily choked both those rivers.

At Putney, as I afterwards saw, the bridge was almost lost in a tangle of this weed, and at Richmond, too, the Thames water poured in a broad and shallow stream across the meadows of Hampton and Twickenham. As the water spread the weed followed them, until the ruined villas of the Thames valley were for a time lost in this red swamp, whose margin I explored, and much of the desolation the Martians had caused was concealed.

In the end the red weed succumbed almost as quickly as it had spread. A cankering disease, due, it is believed, to the action of certain bacteria, presently seized upon it. Now by the action of natural selection, all terrestrial plants have acquired a resisting power against bacterial diseases—they never succumb without a severe struggle, but the red weed rotted like a thing already dead. The fronds became bleached, and then shrivelled and brittle. They broke off at the least touch, and the waters that had stimulated their early growth carried their last vestiges out to sea.

My first act on coming to this water was, of course, to slake my thirst. I drank a great deal of it and, moved by an impulse, gnawed some fronds of red weed; but they were watery, and had a sickly, metallic taste. I found the water was sufficiently shallow for me to wade securely, although the red weed impeded my feet a little; but the flood evidently got deeper towards the river, and I turned back to Mortlake. I managed to make out the road by means of occasional ruins of its villas and fences and lamps, and so presently I got out of this spate and made my way to the hill going up towards Roehampton and came out on Putney Common.

Here the scenery changed from the strange and unfamiliar to the wreckage of the familiar: patches of ground exhibited the devastation of a cyclone, and in a few score yards I would come upon perfectly undisturbed spaces, houses with their blinds trimly drawn and doors closed, as if they had been left for a day by the owners, or as if their inhabitants slept within. The red weed was less abundant; the tall trees along the lane were free from the red creeper. I hunted for food among the trees, finding nothing, and I also raided a couple of silent houses, but they had already been broken into and ransacked. I rested for the remainder of the daylight in a shrubbery, being, in my enfeebled condition, too fatigued to push on.

All this time I saw no human beings, and no signs of the Martians. I encountered a couple of hungry-looking dogs, but both hurried circuitously away from the advances I made them. Near Roehampton I had seen two human skeletons—not bodies, but skeletons, picked clean— and in the wood by me I found the crushed and scattered bones of several cats and rabbits and the skull of a sheep. But though I gnawed parts of these in my mouth, there was nothing to be got from them.

After sunset I struggled on along the road towards Putney, where I think the Heat-Ray must have been used for some reason. And in the garden beyond Roehampton I got a quantity of immature potatoes, sufficient to stay my hunger. From this garden one looked down upon Putney and the river. The aspect of the place in the dusk was singularly desolate: blackened trees, blackened, desolate ruins, and down the hill the sheets of the flooded river, red-tinged with the weed. And over all—silence. It filled me with indescribable terror to think how swiftly that desolating change had come.

For a time I believed that mankind had been swept out of existence, and that I stood there alone, the last man left alive. Hard by the top of Putney Hill I came upon another skeleton, with the arms dislocated and removed several yards from the rest of the body. As I proceeded I became more and more convinced that the extermination of mankind was, save for such stragglers as myself, already accomplished in this part of the world. The Martians, I thought, had gone on and left the country desolated, seeking food elsewhere. Perhaps even now they were destroying Berlin or Paris, or it might be they had gone northward.

* ● *

CHAPTER SEVEN
The Man on Putney Hill

I SPENT THAT NIGHT IN THE INN that stands at the top of Putney Hill, sleeping in a made bed for the first time since my flight to Leatherhead. I will not tell the needless trouble I had breaking into that house—afterwards I found the front door was on the latch—nor how I ransacked every room for food, until just on the verge of despair, in what seemed to me to be a servant's bedroom, I found a rat-gnawed crust and two tins of pineapple. The place had been already searched and emptied. In the bar I afterwards found some biscuits and sandwiches that had been overlooked. The latter I could not eat, they were too rotten, but the former not only stayed my hunger, but filled my pockets. I lit no lamps, fearing some Martian might come beating that part of London for food in the night. Before I went to bed I had an interval of restlessness, and prowled from window to window, peering out for some sign of these monsters. I slept little. As I lay in bed I found myself thinking consecutively—a thing I do not remember to have done since my last argument with the curate. During all the intervening time my mental condition had been a hurrying succession of vague emotional states or a sort of stupid receptivity. But in the night my brain, reinforced, I suppose, by the food I had eaten, grew clear again, and I thought.

Three things struggled for possession of my mind: the killing of the curate, the whereabouts of the Martians, and the possible fate of my wife. The former gave me no sensation of horror or remorse to recall; I saw it simply as a thing done, a memory infinitely disagreeable but quite without the quality of remorse. I saw myself then as I see myself now, driven step by step towards that hasty blow, the creature of a sequence of accidents leading inevitably to that. I felt no condemnation; yet the memory, static, unprogressive, haunted me. In the silence of the night, with that sense of the nearness of God that sometimes comes into the stillness and the darkness, I stood my trial, my only trial, for that moment of wrath and fear. I retraced every step of our conversation from the moment when I had found him crouching beside me, heedless of my thirst, and pointing to the fire and smoke that streamed up from the ruins of Weybridge. We had been incapable of co-operation—grim chance had taken no heed of that. Had I foreseen, I should have left him at Halliford. But I did not foresee; and crime is to foresee and do. And I set this down as I have set all this story down, as it was. There were no witnesses—all these things I might have concealed. But I set it down, and the reader must form his judgment as he will.

And when, by an effort, I had set aside that picture of a prostrate body, I faced the problem of the Martians and the fate of my wife. For the former I had no data; I could imagine a hundred things, and so, unhappily, I could for the latter. And suddenly that night became terrible. I found myself sitting up in bed, staring at the dark. I found myself praying that the Heat-Ray might have suddenly and painlessly struck her out of being. Since the night of my return from Leatherhead I had not prayed. I had uttered prayers, fetish prayers, had prayed as heathens mutter charms when I was in extremity; but now I prayed indeed, pleading steadfastly and sanely, face to face with the darkness of God. Strange night! Strangest in this, that so soon as dawn had come, I, who had talked with God, crept out of the house like a rat leaving its hiding place—a creature scarcely larger, an inferior animal, a thing that for any passing whim of our masters might be hunted and killed. Perhaps they also prayed confidently to God. Surely, if we have learned nothing else, this war has taught us pity—pity for those witless souls that suffer our dominion.

The morning was bright and fine, and the eastern sky glowed pink, and was fretted with little golden clouds. In the road that runs from the top of Putney Hill to Wimbledon was a number of poor vestiges of the panic torrent that must have poured Londonward on the Sunday night after the fighting began. There was a little two-wheeled cart inscribed with the name of Thomas Lobb, Greengrocer, New Malden, with a smashed wheel and an abandoned tin trunk; there was a straw hat trampled into the now hardened mud, and at the top of West Hill a lot of blood-stained glass about the overturned water trough. My movements were languid, my plans of the vaguest. I had an idea of going to Leatherhead, though I knew that there I had the poorest chance of finding my wife. Certainly, unless death had overtaken them suddenly, my cousins and she would have fled thence; but it seemed to me I might find or learn there whither the Surrey people had fled. I knew I wanted to find my wife, that my heart ached for her and the world of men, but I had no clear idea how the finding might be done. I was also sharply aware now of my intense loneliness. From the corner I went, under cover of a thicket of trees and bushes, to the edge of Wimbledon Common, stretching wide and far.

That dark expanse was lit in patches by yellow gorse and broom; there was no red weed to be seen, and as I prowled, hesitating, on the verge of the open, the sun rose, flooding it all with light and vitality. I came upon a busy swarm of little frogs in a swampy place among the trees. I stopped to look at them, drawing a lesson from their stout resolve to live. And presently, turning suddenly, with an odd feeling of being watched, I beheld something crouching amid a clump of bushes. I stood regarding this. I made a step towards it, and it rose up and became a man armed with a cutlass. I approached him slowly. He stood silent and motionless, regarding me.

As I drew nearer I perceived he was dressed in clothes as dusty and filthy as my own; he looked, indeed, as though he had been dragged through a culvert. Nearer, I distinguished the green slime of ditches mixing with the pale drab of dried clay and shiny, coaly patches. His black hair fell over his eyes, and his face was dark and dirty and sunken, so that at first I did not recognise him. There was a red cut across the lower part of his face.

"Stop!" he cried, when I was within ten yards of him, and I stopped. His voice was hoarse. "Where do you come from?" he said.

I thought, surveying him.

"I come from Mortlake," I said. "I was buried near the pit the Martians made about their cylinder. I have worked my way out and escaped."

"There is no food about here," he said. "This is my country. All this hill down to the river, and back to Clapham, and up to the edge of the common. There is only food for one. Which way are you going?"

I answered slowly.

"I don't know," I said. "I have been buried in the ruins of a house thirteen or fourteen days. I don't know what has happened."

He looked at me doubtfully, then started, and looked with a changed expression.

"I've no wish to stop about here," said I. "I think I shall go to Leatherhead, for my wife was there."

He shot out a pointing finger.

"It is you," said he; "the man from Woking. And you weren't killed at Weybridge?"

I recognised him at the same moment.

"You are the artilleryman who came into my garden."

"Good luck!" he said. "We are lucky ones! Fancy *you*!" He put out a hand, and I took it. "I crawled up a drain," he said. "But they didn't kill everyone. And after they went away I got off towards Walton across the fields. But— It's not sixteen days altogether—and your hair is grey." He looked over his shoulder suddenly. "Only a rook," he said. "One gets to know that birds have shadows these days. This is a bit open. Let us crawl under those bushes and talk."

"Have you seen any Martians?" I said. "Since I crawled out—"

"They've gone away across London," he said. "I guess they've got a bigger camp there. Of a night, all over there, Hampstead way, the sky is alive with their lights. It's like a great city, and in the glare you can just see them moving. By daylight you can't. But nearer—I haven't seen them—" (he counted on his fingers) "five days. Then I saw a couple across Hammersmith way carrying something big. And the night before last"—he stopped and spoke impressively—"it was just a matter of lights, but it was something up in the air. I believe they've built a flying-machine, and are learning to fly."

I stopped, on hands and knees, for we had come to the bushes.

"Fly!"

"Yes," he said, "fly."

I went on into a little bower, and sat down.

"It is all over with humanity," I said. "If they can do that they will simply go round the world."

He nodded.

"They will. But— It will relieve things over here a bit. And besides—" He looked at me. "Aren't you satisfied it IS up with humanity? I am. We're down; we're beat."

I stared. Strange as it may seem, I had not arrived at this fact—a fact perfectly obvious so soon as he spoke. I had still held a vague hope; rather, I had kept a lifelong habit of mind. He repeated his words, "We're beat." They carried absolute conviction.

"It's all over," he said. "They've lost *one*—just *one*. And they've made their footing good and crippled the greatest power in the world. They've walked over us. The death of that one at Weybridge was an accident. And these are only pioneers. They kept on coming. These green stars—I've seen none these five or six days, but I've no doubt they're falling somewhere every night. Nothing's to be done. We're under! We're beat!"

I made him no answer. I sat staring before me, trying in vain to devise some countervailing thought.

"This isn't a war," said the artilleryman. "It never was a war, any more than there's war between man and ants."

Suddenly I recalled the night in the observatory.

"After the tenth shot they fired no more—at least, until the first cylinder came."

"How do you know?" said the artilleryman. I explained. He thought. "Something wrong with the gun," he said. "But what if there is? They'll get it right again. And even if there's a delay, how can it alter the end? It's just men and ants. There's the ants builds their cities, live their lives, have wars, revolutions, until the men want them out of the way, and then they go out of the way. That's what we are now—just ants. Only—"

"Yes," I said.

"We're eatable ants."

We sat looking at each other.

"And what will they do with us?" I said.

"That's what I've been thinking," he said; "that's what I've been thinking. After Weybridge I went south—thinking. I saw what was up. Most of the people were hard at it squealing and exciting themselves. But I'm not so fond of squealing. I've been in sight of death once or twice; I'm not an ornamental soldier, and at the best and worst, death—it's just death. And it's the man that keeps on thinking comes through. I saw everyone tracking away south. Says I, 'Food won't last this way,' and I turned right back. I went for the Martians like a sparrow goes for man. All round"—he waved a hand to the horizon—"they're starving in heaps, bolting, treading on each other...."

He saw my face, and halted awkwardly.

"No doubt lots who had money have gone away to France," he said. He seemed to hesitate whether to apologise, met my eyes, and went on: "There's food all about here. Canned things in shops; wines, spirits, mineral waters; and the water mains and drains are empty. Well, I was telling you what I was thinking. 'Here's intelligent things,' I said, 'and it seems they want us for food. First, they'll smash us up—ships, machines, guns, cities, all the order and organisation. All that will go. If we were the size of ants we might pull through. But we're not. It's all too bulky to stop. That's the first certainty.' Eh?"

I assented.

"It is; I've thought it out. Very well, then—next; at present we're caught as we're wanted. A Martian has only to go a few miles to get a crowd on the run. And I saw one, one day, out by Wandsworth, picking houses to pieces and routing among the wreckage. But they won't keep

ng that. So soon as they've settled all our guns and ships, and
ed our railways, and done all the things they are doing over there,
the‚ will begin catching us systematic, picking the best and storing us
in cages and things. That's what they will start doing in a bit. Lord! They
haven't begun on us yet. Don't you see that?"

"Not begun!" I exclaimed.

"Not begun. All that's happened so far is through our not having
the sense to keep quiet—worrying them with guns and such foolery.
And losing our heads, and rushing off in crowds to where there wasn't
any more safety than where we were. They don't want to bother us yet.
They're making their things—making all the things they couldn't bring
with them, getting things ready for the rest of their people. Very likely
that's why the cylinders have stopped for a bit, for fear of hitting those
who are here. And instead of our rushing about blind, on the howl, or
getting dynamite on the chance of busting them up, we've got to fix ourselves up according to the new state of affairs. That's how I figure it out.
It isn't quite according to what a man wants for his species, but it's about
what the facts point to. And that's the principle I acted upon. Cities, nations, civilisation, progress—it's all over. That game's up. We're beat."

"But if that is so, what is there to live for?"

The artilleryman looked at me for a moment.

"There won't be any more blessed concerts for a million years or so; there
won't be any Royal Academy of Arts, and no nice little feeds at restaurants.
If it's amusement you're after, I reckon the game is up. If you've got any
drawing-room manners or a dislike to eating peas with a knife or dropping
aitches, you'd better chuck 'em away. They ain't no further use."

"You mean—"

"I mean that men like me are going on living—for the sake of the
breed. I tell you, I'm grim set on living. And if I'm not mistaken, you'll
show what insides *you've* got, too, before long. We aren't going to be exterminated. And I don't mean to be caught either, and tamed and fattened
and bred like a thundering ox. Ugh! Fancy those brown creepers!"

"You don't mean to say—"

"I do. I'm going on, under their feet. I've got it planned; I've thought
it out. We men are beat. We don't know enough. We've got to learn
before we've got a chance. And we've got to live and keep independent
while we learn. See! That's what has to be done."

I stared, astonished, and stirred profoundly by the man's resolution.

"Great God!" cried I. "But you are a man indeed!" And suddenly I
gripped his hand.

"Eh!" he said, with his eyes shining. "I've thought it out, eh?"

"Go on," I said.

"Well, those who mean to escape their catching must get ready. I'm getting ready. Mind you, it isn't all of us that are made for wild beasts; and that's what it's got to be. That's why I watched you. I had my doubts. You're slender. I didn't know that it was you, you see, or just how you'd been buried. All these—the sort of people that lived in these houses, and all those damn little clerks that used to live down that way—they'd be no good. They haven't any spirit in them—no proud dreams and no proud lusts; and a man who hasn't one or the other—Lord! What is he but funk and precautions? They just used to skedaddle off to work—I've seen hundreds of 'em, bit of breakfast in hand, running wild and shining to catch their little season-ticket train, for fear they'd get dismissed if they didn't; working at businesses they were afraid to take the trouble to understand; skedaddling back for fear they wouldn't be in time for dinner; keeping indoors after dinner for fear of the back streets, and sleeping with the wives they married, not because they wanted them, but because they had a bit of money that would make for safety in their one little miserable skedaddle through the world. Lives insured and a bit invested for fear of accidents. And on Sundays—fear of the hereafter. As if hell was built for rabbits! Well, the Martians will just be a godsend to these. Nice roomy cages, fattening food, careful breeding, no worry. After a week or so chasing about the fields and lands on empty stomachs, they'll come and be caught cheerful. They'll be quite glad after a bit. They'll wonder what people did before there were Martians to take care of them. And the bar loafers, and mashers, and singers—I can imagine them. I can imagine them," he said, with a sort of sombre gratification. "There'll be any amount of sentiment and religion loose among them. There's hundreds of things I saw with my eyes that I've only begun to see clearly these last few days. There's lots will take things as they are—fat and stupid; and lots will be worried by a sort of feeling that it's all wrong, and that they ought to be doing something. Now whenever things are so that a lot of people feel they ought to be doing something, the weak, and those who go weak with a lot of complicated thinking, always make for a sort of do-nothing religion, very pious and superior, and submit to persecution and the will of the Lord. Very likely you've seen the same thing. It's energy in a gale of funk, and turned clean inside out. These cages will be full of psalms and hymns and piety. And those of a less simple sort will work in a bit of—what is it?—eroticism."

He paused.

"Very likely these Martians will make pets of some of them; train them to do tricks—who knows?—get sentimental over the pet boy who grew up and had to be killed. And some, maybe, they will train to hunt us."

"No," I cried, "that's impossible! No human being—"

"What's the good of going on with such lies?" said the artilleryman. "There's men who'd do it cheerful. What nonsense to pretend there isn't!"

And I succumbed to his conviction.

"If they come after me," he said; "Lord, if they come after me!" and subsided into a grim meditation.

I sat contemplating these things. I could find nothing to bring against this man's reasoning. In the days before the invasion no one would have questioned my intellectual superiority to his—I, a professed and recognised writer on philosophical themes, and he, a common soldier; and yet he had already formulated a situation that I had scarcely realised.

"What are you doing?" I said presently. "What plans have you made?"

He hesitated.

"Well, it's like this," he said. "What have we to do? We have to invent a sort of life where men can live and breed, and be sufficiently secure to bring the children up. Yes—wait a bit, and I'll make it clearer what I think ought to be done. The tame ones will go like all tame beasts; in a few generations they'll be big, beautiful, rich-blooded, stupid—rubbish! The risk is that we who keep wild will go savage—degenerate into a sort of big, savage rat.... You see, how I mean to live is underground. I've been thinking about the drains. Of course those who don't know drains think horrible things; but under this London are miles and miles—hundreds of miles—and a few days rain and London empty will leave them sweet and clean. The main drains are big enough and airy enough for anyone. Then there's cellars, vaults, stores, from which bolting passages may be made to the drains. And the railway tunnels and subways. Eh? You begin to see? And we form a band—able-bodied, clean-minded men. We're not going to pick up any rubbish that drifts in. Weaklings go out again."

"As you meant me to go?"

"Well—I parleyed, didn't I?"

"We won't quarrel about that. Go on."

"Those who stop obey orders. Able-bodied, clean-minded women we want also—mothers and teachers. No lackadaisical ladies—no blasted rolling eyes. We can't have any weak or silly. Life is real again, and the useless and cumbersome and mischievous have to die. They ought to die. They ought to be willing to die. It's a sort of disloyalty, after all, to live and taint the race. And they can't be happy. Moreover, dying's none so dreadful; it's the funking makes it bad. And in all those places we shall gather. Our district will be London. And we may even be able to keep a watch, and run about in the open when the Martians keep away. Play cricket, perhaps. That's how we shall save the race. Eh? It's a possible thing? But saving the race is nothing in itself. As I say, that's only being rats. It's saving our knowledge and adding to it is the thing. There men like you come in. There's books, there's models. We must make great safe places down deep, and get all the books we can; not novels and poetry swipes, but ideas, science books. That's where men like you come in. We must go to the British Museum and pick all those books through. Especially we must keep up our science—learn more. We must watch these Martians. Some of us must go as spies. When it's all working, perhaps I will. Get caught, I mean. And the great thing is, we must leave the Martians alone. We mustn't even steal. If we get in their way, we clear out. We must show them we mean no harm. Yes, I know. But they're intelligent things, and they won't hunt us down if they have all they want, and think we're just harmless vermin."

The artilleryman paused and laid a brown hand upon my arm.

"After all, it may not be so much we may have to learn before— Just imagine this: four or five of their fighting-machines suddenly starting off—Heat-Rays right and left, and not a Martian in 'em. Not a Martian in 'em, but men—men who have learned the way how. It may be in my time, even—those men. Fancy having one of them lovely things, with its Heat-Ray wide and free! Fancy having it in control! What would it matter if you smashed to smithereens at the end of the run, after a bust like that? I reckon the Martians'll open their beautiful eyes! Can't you see them, man? Can't you see them hurrying, hurrying—puffing and blowing and hooting to their other mechanical affairs? Something out of gear in every case. And swish, bang, rattle, swish! Just as they are fumbling over it, *swish* comes the Heat-Ray, and, behold! man has come back to his own."

For a while the imaginative daring of the artilleryman, and the tone of assurance and courage he assumed, completely dominated my mind. I believed unhesitatingly both in his forecast of human destiny and in the practicability of his astonishing scheme, and the reader who thinks me susceptible and foolish must contrast his position, reading steadily with all his thoughts about his subject, and mine, crouching fearfully in the bushes and listening, distracted by apprehension. We talked in this manner through the early morning time, and later crept out of the bushes, and, after scanning the sky for Martians, hurried precipitately to the house on Putney Hill where he had made his lair. It was the coal cellar of the place, and when I saw the work he had spent a week upon—it was a burrow scarcely ten yards long, which he designed to reach to the main drain on Putney Hill—I had my first inkling of the gulf between his dreams and his powers. Such a hole I could have dug in a day. But I believed in him sufficiently to work with him all that morning until past midday at his digging. We had a garden barrow and shot the earth we removed against the kitchen range. We refreshed ourselves with a tin of mock-turtle soup and wine from the neighbouring pantry. I found a curious relief from the aching strangeness of the world in this steady labour. As we worked, I turned his project over in my mind, and presently objections and doubts began to arise; but I worked there all the morning, so glad was I to find myself with a purpose again. After working an hour I began to speculate on the distance one had to go before the cloaca was reached, the chances we had of missing it altogether. My immediate trouble was why we should dig this long tunnel, when it was possible to get into the drain at once down one of the manholes, and work back to the house. It seemed to me, too, that the house was inconveniently chosen, and required a needless length of tunnel. And just as I was beginning to face these things, the artilleryman stopped digging, and looked at me.

"We're working well," he said. He put down his spade. "Let us knock off a bit," he said. "I think it's time we reconnoitred from the roof of the house."

I was for going on, and after a little hesitation he resumed his spade; and then suddenly I was struck by a thought. I stopped, and so did he at once.

"Why were you walking about the common," I said, "instead of being here?"

"Taking the air," he said. "I was coming back. It's safer by night."

"But the work?"

"Oh, one can't always work," he said, and in a flash I saw the man plain. He hesitated, holding his spade. "We ought to reconnoitre now," he said, "because if any come near they may hear the spades and drop upon us unawares."

I was no longer disposed to object. We went together to the roof and stood on a ladder peeping out of the roof door. No Martians were to be seen, and we ventured out on the tiles, and slipped down under shelter of the parapet.

From this position a shrubbery hid the greater portion of Putney, but we could see the river below, a bubbly mass of red weed, and the low parts of Lambeth flooded and red. The red creeper swarmed up the trees about the old palace, and their branches stretched gaunt and dead, and set with shrivelled leaves, from amid its clusters. It was strange how entirely dependent both these things were upon flowing water for their propagation. About us neither had gained a footing; laburnums, pink mays, snowballs, and trees of arbor-vitae, rose out of laurels and hydrangeas, green and brilliant into the sunlight. Beyond Kensington dense smoke was rising, and that and a blue haze hid the northward hills.

The artilleryman began to tell me of the sort of people who still remained in London.

"One night last week," he said, "some fools got the electric light in order, and there was all Regent Street and the Circus ablaze, crowded with painted and ragged drunkards, men and women, dancing and shouting till dawn. A man who was there told me. And as the day came they became aware of a fighting-machine standing near by the Langham and looking down at them. Heaven knows how long he had been there. It must have given some of them a nasty turn. He came down the road towards them, and picked up nearly a hundred too drunk or frightened to run away."

Grotesque gleam of a time no history will ever fully describe!

From that, in answer to my questions, he came round to his grandiose plans again. He grew enthusiastic. He talked so eloquently of the possibility of capturing a fighting-machine that I more than half believed in him again. But now that I was beginning to understand something of his quality, I could divine the stress he laid on doing nothing precipitately. And I noted that now there was no question that he personally was to capture and fight the great machine.

After a time we went down to the cellar. Neither of us seemed disposed to resume digging, and when he suggested a meal, I was nothing loath. He became suddenly very generous, and when we had eaten he went away and returned with some excellent cigars. We lit these, and his optimism glowed. He was inclined to regard my coming as a great occasion.

"There's some champagne in the cellar," he said.

"We can dig better on this Thames-side burgundy," said I.

"No," said he; "I am host today. Champagne! Great God! We've a heavy enough task before us! Let us take a rest and gather strength while we may. Look at these blistered hands!"

And pursuant to this idea of a holiday, he insisted upon playing cards after we had eaten. He taught me euchre, and after dividing London between us, I taking the northern side and he the southern, we played for parish points. Grotesque and foolish as this will seem to the sober reader, it is absolutely true, and what is more remarkable, I found the card game and several others we played extremely interesting.

Strange mind of man! that, with our species upon the edge of extermination or appalling degradation, with no clear prospect before us but the chance of a horrible death, we could sit following the chance of this painted pasteboard, and playing the "joker" with vivid delight. Afterwards he taught me poker, and I beat him at three tough chess games. When dark came we decided to take the risk, and lit a lamp.

After an interminable string of games, we supped, and the artilleryman finished the champagne. We went on smoking the cigars. He was no longer the energetic regenerator of his species I had encountered in the morning. He was still optimistic, but it was a less kinetic, a more thoughtful optimism. I remember he wound up with my health, proposed in a speech of small variety and considerable intermittence. I took a cigar, and went upstairs to look at the lights of which he had spoken that blazed so greenly along the Highgate hills.

At first I stared unintelligently across the London valley. The northern hills were shrouded in darkness; the fires near Kensington glowed redly, and now and then an orange-red tongue of flame flashed up and vanished in the deep blue night. All the rest of London was black. Then, nearer, I perceived a strange light, a pale, violet-purple fluorescent glow, quivering under the night breeze. For a space I could not understand it, and then I knew that it must be the red weed from which this faint irradiation proceeded. With that realisation my dormant sense of wonder, my sense of the proportion of things, awoke again. I glanced from that to Mars, red and clear, glowing high in the west, and then gazed long and earnestly at the darkness of Hampstead and Highgate.

I remained a very long time upon the roof, wondering at the grotesque changes of the day. I recalled my mental states from the midnight prayer to the foolish card-playing. I had a violent revulsion of feeling. I remember I flung away the cigar with a certain wasteful symbolism. My folly came to me with glaring exaggeration. I seemed a traitor to my wife and to my kind; I was filled with remorse. I resolved to leave this strange undisciplined dreamer of great things to his drink and gluttony, and to go on into London. There, it seemed to me, I had the best chance of learning what the Martians and my fellowmen were doing. I was still upon the roof when the late moon rose.

• • •

CHAPTER EIGHT
Dead London

AFTER I HAD PARTED FROM THE ARTILLERYMAN, I went down the hill, and by the High Street across the bridge to Fulham. The red weed was tumultuous at that time, and nearly choked the bridge roadway; but its fronds were already whitened in patches by the spreading disease that presently removed it so swiftly.

At the corner of the lane that runs to Putney Bridge station I found a man lying. He was as black as a sweep with the black dust, alive, but helplessly and speechlessly drunk. I could get nothing from him but curses and furious lunges at my head. I think I should have stayed by him but for the brutal expression of his face.

There was black dust along the roadway from the bridge onwards, and it grew thicker in Fulham. The streets were horribly quiet. I got food—sour, hard, and mouldy, but quite eatable—in a baker's shop here. Some way towards Walham Green the streets became clear of powder, and I passed a white terrace of houses on fire; the noise of the burning was an absolute relief. Going on towards Brompton, the streets were quiet again.

Here I came once more upon the black powder in the streets and upon dead bodies. I saw altogether about a dozen in the length of the Fulham Road. They had been dead many days, so that I hurried quickly past them. The black powder covered them over, and softened their outlines. One or two had been disturbed by dogs.

Where there was no black powder, it was curiously like a Sunday in the City, with the closed shops, the houses locked up and the blinds drawn, the desertion, and the stillness. In some places plunderers had been at work, but rarely at other than the provision and wine shops. A jeweller's window had been broken open in one place, but apparently the thief had been disturbed, and a number of gold chains and a watch lay scattered on the pavement. I did not trouble to touch them. Farther on was a tattered woman in a heap on a doorstep; the hand that hung over her knee was gashed and bled down her rusty brown dress, and a smashed magnum of champagne formed a pool across the pavement. She seemed asleep, but she was dead.

The farther I penetrated into London, the profounder grew the stillness. But it was not so much the stillness of death—it was the stillness of suspense, of expectation. At any time the destruction that had already singed the northwestern borders of the metropolis, and had annihilated Ealing and Kilburn, might strike among these houses and leave them smoking ruins. It was a city condemned and derelict....

In South Kensington the streets were clear of dead and of black powder. It was near South Kensington that I first heard the howling. It crept almost imperceptibly upon my senses. It was a sobbing alternation of two notes, "Ulla, ulla, ulla, ulla," keeping on perpetually. When I passed streets that ran northward it grew in volume, and houses and buildings seemed to deaden and cut it off again. It came in a full tide down Exhibition Road. I stopped, staring towards Kensington Gardens, wondering at this strange, remote wailing. It was as if that mighty desert of houses had found a voice for its fear and solitude.

"Ulla, ulla, ulla, ulla," wailed that superhuman note—great waves of sound sweeping down the broad, sunlit roadway, between the tall buildings on each side. I turned northwards, marvelling, towards the iron gates of Hyde Park. I had half a mind to break into the Natural History Museum and find my way up to the summits of the towers, in order to see across the park. But I decided to keep to the ground, where quick hiding was possible, and so went on up the Exhibition Road. All the large mansions on each side of the road were empty and still, and my footsteps echoed against the sides of the houses. At the top, near the park gate, I came upon a strange sight—a bus overturned, and the skeleton of a horse picked clean. I puzzled over this for a time, and then went on to the bridge over the Serpentine. The voice grew stronger and stronger, though I could see nothing above the housetops on the north side of the park, save a haze of smoke to the northwest.

"Ulla, ulla, ulla, ulla," cried the voice, coming, as it seemed to me, from the district about Regent's Park. The desolating cry worked upon my mind. The mood that had sustained me passed. The wailing took possession of me. I found I was intensely weary, footsore, and now again hungry and thirsty.

It was already past noon. Why was I wandering alone in this city of the dead? Why was I alone when all London was lying in state, and in its black shroud? I felt intolerably lonely. My mind ran on old friends that I had forgotten for years. I thought of the poisons in the chemists' shops, of the liquors the wine merchants stored; I recalled the two sodden creatures of despair, who so far as I knew, shared the city with myself....

I came into Oxford Street by the Marble Arch, and here again were black powder and several bodies, and an evil, ominous smell from the gratings of the cellars of some of the houses. I grew very thirsty after the heat of my long walk. With infinite trouble I managed to break into a public-house and get food and drink. I was weary after eating, and went into the parlour behind the bar, and slept on a black horsehair sofa I found there.

I awoke to find that dismal howling still in my ears, "Ulla, ulla, ulla, ulla." It was now dusk, and after I had routed out some biscuits and a cheese in the bar—there was a meat safe, but it contained nothing but maggots—I wandered on through the silent residential squares to Baker Street—Portman Square is the only one I can name—and so came out at last upon Regent's Park. And as I emerged from the top of Baker Street, I saw far away over the trees in the clearness of the sunset the hood of the Martian giant from which this howling proceeded. I was not terrified. I came upon him as if it were a matter of course. I watched him for some time, but he did not move. He appeared to be standing and yelling, for no reason that I could discover.

I tried to formulate a plan of action. That perpetual sound of "Ulla, ulla, ulla, ulla," confused my mind. Perhaps I was too tired to be very fearful. Certainly I was more curious to know the reason of this monotonous crying than afraid. I turned back away from the park and struck into Park Road, intending to skirt the park, went along under the shelter of the terraces, and got a view of this stationary, howling Martian from the direction of St. John's Wood. A couple of hundred yards out of Baker Street I heard a yelping chorus, and saw, first a dog with a piece of putrescent red meat in his jaws coming headlong towards me, and then a pack of starving mongrels in pursuit of him. He made a wide curve to avoid me, as though he feared I might prove a fresh competitor. As the yelping died away down the silent road, the wailing sound of "Ulla, ulla, ulla, ulla," reasserted itself.

I came upon the wrecked handling-machine halfway to St. John's Wood station. At first I thought a house had fallen across the road. It was only as I clambered among the ruins that I saw, with a start, this mechanical Samson lying, with its tentacles bent and smashed and twisted, among the ruins it had made. The forepart was shattered. It seemed as if it had driven blindly straight at the house, and had been overwhelmed in its overthrow. It seemed to me then that this might have happened by a handling-machine escaping from the guidance of its Martian. I could not clamber among the ruins to see it, and the twilight was now so far advanced that the blood with which its seat was smeared, and the gnawed gristle of the Martian that the dogs had left, were invisible to me.

Wondering still more at all that I had seen, I pushed on towards Primrose Hill. Far away, through a gap in the trees, I saw a second Martian, as motionless as the first, standing in the park towards the Zoological Gardens, and silent. A little beyond the ruins about the smashed handling-machine I came upon the red weed again, and found the Regent's Canal, a spongy mass of dark-red vegetation.

As I crossed the bridge, the sound of "Ulla, ulla, ulla, ulla," ceased. It was, as it were, cut off. The silence came like a thunderclap.

The dusky houses about me stood faint and tall and dim; the trees towards the park were growing black. All about me the red weed clambered among the ruins, writhing to get above me in the dimness. Night, the mother of fear and mystery, was coming upon me. But while that voice sounded the solitude, the desolation, had been endurable; by virtue of it London had still seemed alive, and the sense of life about me had upheld me. Then suddenly a change, the passing of something—I knew not what—and then a stillness that could be felt. Nothing but this gaunt quiet.

London about me gazed at me spectrally. The windows in the white houses were like the eye sockets of skulls. About me my imagination found a thousand noiseless enemies moving. Terror seized me, a horror of my temerity. In front of me the road became pitchy black as though it was tarred, and I saw a contorted shape lying across the pathway. I could not bring myself to go on. I turned down St. John's Wood Road, and ran headlong from this unendurable stillness towards Kilburn. I hid from the night and the silence, until long after midnight, in a cabmen's shelter in Harrow Road. But before the dawn my courage returned, and while the stars were still in the sky I turned once more towards Regent's Park. I missed my way among the streets, and presently saw down a long avenue, in the half-light of the early dawn, the curve of Primrose Hill. On the summit, towering up to the fading stars, was a third Martian, erect and motionless like the others.

An insane resolve possessed me. I would die and end it. And I would save myself even the trouble of killing myself. I marched on recklessly towards this Titan, and then, as I drew nearer and the light grew, I saw that a multitude of black birds was circling and clustering about the hood. At that my heart gave a bound, and I began running along the road.

I hurried through the red weed that choked St. Edmund's Terrace (I waded breast-high across a torrent of water that was rushing down from the waterworks towards the Albert Road), and emerged upon the grass before the rising of the sun. Great mounds had been heaped about the crest of the hill, making a huge redoubt of it—it was the final and largest place the Martians had made—and from behind these heaps there rose a thin smoke against the sky. Against the sky line an eager dog ran and disappeared. The thought that had flashed into my mind grew real, grew credible. I felt no fear, only a wild, trembling exultation, as I ran up the hill towards the motionless monster. Out of the hood hung lank shreds of brown, at which the hungry birds pecked and tore.

In another moment I had scrambled up the earthen rampart and stood upon its crest, and the interior of the redoubt was below me. A mighty space it was, with gigantic machines here and there within it, huge mounds of material and strange shelter places. And scattered about it, some in their overturned war-machines, some in the now rigid handling-machines, and a dozen of them stark and silent and laid in a row, were the Martians—*dead*!—slain by the putrefactive and disease bacteria against which their systems were unprepared; slain as the red weed was being slain; slain, after all man's devices had failed, by the humblest things that God, in his wisdom, has put upon this earth.

For so it had come about, as indeed I and many men might have fore-seen had not terror and disaster blinded our minds. These germs of disease have taken toll of humanity since the beginning of things—taken toll of our prehuman ancestors since life began here. But by virtue of this natural selection of our kind we have developed resisting power; to no germs do we succumb without a struggle, and to many—those that cause putrefaction in dead matter, for instance—our living frames are altogether immune. But there are no bacteria in Mars, and directly these invaders arrived, directly they drank and fed, our microscopic allies began to work their overthrow. Already when I watched them they were irrevocably doomed, dying and rotting even as they went to and fro. It was inevitable. By the toll of a billion deaths man has bought his birthright of the earth, and it is his against all comers; it would still be his were the Martians ten times as mighty as they are. For neither do men live nor die in vain.

Here and there they were scattered, nearly fifty altogether, in that great gulf they had made, overtaken by a death that must have seemed to them as incomprehensible as any death could be. To me also at that time this death was incomprehensible. All I knew was that these things that had been alive and so terrible to men were dead. For a moment I believed that the destruction of Sennacherib had been repeated, that God had repented, that the Angel of Death had slain them in the night.

I stood staring into the pit, and my heart lightened gloriously, even as the rising sun struck the world to fire about me with his rays. The pit was still in darkness; the mighty engines, so great and wonderful in their power and complexity, so unearthly in their tortuous forms, rose weird and vague and strange out of the shadows towards the light. A multitude of dogs, I could hear, fought over the bodies that lay darkly in the depth of the pit, far below me. Across the pit on its farther lip, flat and vast and strange, lay the great flying-machine with which they had been experimenting upon our denser atmosphere when decay and death arrested them. Death had come not a day too soon. At the sound of a cawing overhead I looked up at the huge fighting-machine that would fight no more for ever, at the tattered red shreds of flesh that dripped down upon the overturned seats on the summit of Primrose Hill.

I turned and looked down the slope of the hill to where, enhaloed now in birds, stood those other two Martians that I had seen overnight, just as death had overtaken them. The one had died, even as it had been crying to its companions; perhaps it was the last to die, and its voice had gone on perpetually until the force of its machinery was exhausted. They glittered now, harmless tripod towers of shining metal, in the brightness of the rising sun.

All about the pit, and saved as by a miracle from everlasting destruction, stretched the great Mother of Cities. Those who have only seen London veiled in her sombre robes of smoke can scarcely imagine the naked clearness and beauty of the silent wilderness of houses.

Eastward, over the blackened ruins of the Albert Terrace and the splintered spire of the church, the sun blazed dazzling in a clear sky, and here and there some facet in the great wilderness of roofs caught the light and glared with a white intensity.

Northward were Kilburn and Hampsted, blue and crowded with houses; westward the great city was dimmed; and southward, beyond the Martians, the green waves of Regent's Park, the Langham Hotel, the dome of the Albert Hall, the Imperial Institute, and the giant mansions of the Brompton Road came out clear and little in the sunrise, the jagged ruins of Westminster rising hazily beyond. Far away and blue were the Surrey hills, and the towers of the Crystal Palace glittered like two silver rods. The dome of St. Paul's was dark against the sunrise, and injured, I saw for the first time, by a huge gaping cavity on its western side.

And as I looked at this wide expanse of houses and factories and churches, silent and abandoned; as I thought of the multitudinous hopes and efforts, the innumerable hosts of lives that had gone to build this human reef, and of the swift and ruthless destruction that had hung over it all; when I realised that the shadow had been rolled back, and that men might still live in the streets, and this dear vast dead city of mine be once more alive and powerful, I felt a wave of emotion that was near akin to tears.

The torment was over. Even that day the healing would begin. The survivors of the people scattered over the country—leaderless, lawless, foodless, like sheep without a shepherd—the thousands who had fled by sea, would begin to return; the pulse of life, growing stronger and stronger, would beat again in the empty streets and pour across the vacant squares. Whatever destruction was done, the hand of the destroyer was stayed. All the gaunt wrecks, the blackened skeletons of houses that stared so dismally at the sunlit grass of the hill, would presently be echoing with the hammers of the restorers and ringing with the tapping of their trowels. At the thought I extended my hands towards the sky and began thanking God. In a year, thought I—in a year....

With overwhelming force came the thought of myself, of my wife, and the old life of hope and tender helpfulness that had ceased for ever.

* * *

CHAPTER NINE

Wreckage

AND NOW COMES THE STRANGEST THING in my story. Yet, perhaps, it is not altogether strange. I remember, clearly and coldly and vividly, all that I did that day until the time that I stood weeping and praising God upon the summit of Primrose Hill. And then I forget.

Of the next three days I know nothing. I have learned since that, so far from my being the first discoverer of the Martian overthrow, several such wanderers as myself had already discovered this on the previous night. One man—the first—had gone to St. Martin's-le-Grand, and, while I sheltered in the cabmen's hut, had contrived to telegraph to Paris. Thence the joyful news had flashed all over the world; a thousand cities, chilled by ghastly apprehensions, suddenly flashed into frantic illuminations; they knew of it in Dublin, Edinburgh, Manchester, Birmingham, at the time when I stood upon the verge of the pit. Already men, weeping with joy, as I have heard, shouting and staying their work to shake hands and shout, were making up trains, even as near as Crewe, to descend upon London. The church bells that had ceased a fortnight since suddenly caught the news, until all England was bell-ringing. Men on cycles, lean-faced, unkempt, scorched along every country lane shouting of unhoped deliverance, shouting to gaunt, staring figures of despair. And for the food! Across the Channel, across the Irish Sea, across the Atlantic, corn, bread, and meat were tearing to our relief. All the shipping in the world seemed going Londonward in those days. But of all this I have no memory. I drifted—a demented man. I found myself in a house of kindly people, who had found me on the third day wandering, weeping, and raving through the streets of St. John's Wood.

They have told me since that I was singing some insane doggerel about "The Last Man Left Alive! Hurrah! The Last Man Left Alive!" Troubled as they were with their own affairs, these people, whose name, much as I would like to express my gratitude to them, I may not even give here, nevertheless cumbered themselves with me, sheltered me, and protected me from myself. Apparently they had learned something of my story from me during the days of my lapse.

Very gently, when my mind was assured again, did they break to me what they had learned of the fate of Leatherhead. Two days after I was imprisoned it had been destroyed, with every soul in it, by a Martian. He had swept it out of existence, as it seemed, without any provocation, as a boy might crush an ant hill, in the mere wantonness of power.

I was a lonely man, and they were very kind to me. I was a lonely man and a sad one, and they bore with me. I remained with them four days after my recovery. All that time I felt a vague, a growing craving to look once more on whatever remained of the little life that seemed so happy and bright in my past. It was a mere hopeless desire to feast upon my misery. They dissuaded me. They did all they could to divert me from this morbidity. But at last I could resist the impulse no longer, and, promising faithfully to return to them, and parting, as I will confess, from these four-day friends with tears, I went out again into the streets that had lately been so dark and strange and empty.

Already they were busy with returning people; in places even there were shops open, and I saw a drinking fountain running water.

I remember how mockingly bright the day seemed as I went back on my melancholy pilgrimage to the little house at Woking, how busy the streets and vivid the moving life about me. So many people were abroad everywhere, busied in a thousand activities, that it seemed incredible that any great proportion of the population could have been slain. But then I noticed how yellow were the skins of the people I met, how shaggy the hair of the men, how large and bright their eyes, and that every other man still wore his dirty rags. Their faces seemed all with one of two expressions—a leaping exultation and energy or a grim resolution. Save for the expression of the faces, London seemed a city of tramps. The vestries were indiscriminately distributing bread sent us by the French government. The ribs of the few horses showed dismally. Haggard special constables with white badges stood at the corners of every street. I saw little of the mischief wrought by the Martians until I reached Wellington Street, and there I saw the red weed clambering over the buttresses of Waterloo Bridge.

At the corner of the bridge, too, I saw one of the common contrasts of that grotesque time—a sheet of paper flaunting against a thicket of the red weed, transfixed by a stick that kept it in place. It was the placard of the first newspaper to resume publication—the *Daily Mail*. I bought a copy for a blackened shilling I found in my pocket. Most of it was in blank, but the solitary compositor who did the thing had amused himself by making a grotesque scheme of advertisement stereo on the back page. The matter he printed was emotional; the news organisation had not as yet found its way back. I learned nothing fresh except that already in one week the examination of the Martian mechanisms had yielded astonishing results. Among other things, the article assured me what I did not believe at the time, that the "Secret of Flying" was discovered. At Waterloo I found the free trains that were taking people to their homes. The first rush was already over. There were few people in the train, and I was in no mood for casual conversation. I got a compartment to myself, and sat with folded arms, looking greyly at the sunlit devastation that flowed past the windows. And just outside the terminus the train jolted over temporary rails, and on either side of the railway the houses were blackened ruins. To Clapham Junction the face of London was grimy with powder of the Black Smoke, in spite of two days of thunderstorms and rain, and at Clapham Junction the line had been wrecked again; there were hundreds of out-of-work clerks and shopmen working side by side with the customary navvies, and we were jolted over a hasty relaying.

All down the line from there the aspect of the country was gaunt and unfamiliar; Wimbledon particularly had suffered. Walton, by virtue of its unburned pine woods, seemed the least hurt of any place along the line. The Wandle, the Mole, every little stream, was a heaped mass of red weed, in appearance between butcher's meat and pickled cabbage. The Surrey pine woods were too dry, however, for the festoons of the red climber. Beyond Wimbledon, within sight of the line, in certain nursery grounds, were the heaped masses of earth about the sixth cylinder. A number of people were standing about it, and some sappers were busy in the midst of it. Over it flaunted a Union Jack, flapping cheerfully in the morning breeze. The nursery grounds were everywhere crimson with the weed, a wide expanse of livid colour cut with purple shadows, and very painful to the eye. One's gaze went with infinite relief from the scorched greys and sullen reds of the foreground to the blue-green softness of the eastward hills.

The line on the London side of Woking station was still undergoing repair, so I descended at Byfleet station and took the road to Maybury, past the place where I and the artilleryman had talked to the hussars, and on by the spot where the Martian had appeared to me in the thunderstorm. Here, moved by curiosity, I turned aside to find, among a tangle of red fronds, the warped and broken dog cart with the whitened bones of the horse scattered and gnawed. For a time I stood regarding these vestiges. . . .

Then I returned through the pine wood, neck-high with red weed here and there, to find the landlord of the Spotted Dog had already found burial, and so came home past the College Arms. A man standing at an open cottage door greeted me by name as I passed.

I looked at my house with a quick flash of hope that faded immediately. The door had been forced; it was unfast and was opening slowly as I approached.

It slammed again. The curtains of my study fluttered out of the open window from which I and the artilleryman had watched the dawn. No one had closed it since. The smashed bushes were just as I had left them nearly four weeks ago. I stumbled into the hall, and the house felt empty. The stair carpet was ruffled and discoloured where I had crouched, soaked to the skin from the thunderstorm the night of the catastrophe. Our muddy footsteps I saw still went up the stairs.

I followed them to my study, and found lying on my writing-table still, with the selenite paper weight upon it, the sheet of work I had left on the afternoon of the opening of the cylinder. For a space I stood reading over my abandoned arguments. It was a paper on the probable development of Moral Ideas with the development of the civilising process; and the last sentence was the opening of a prophecy: "In about two hundred years," I had written, "we may expect—" The sentence ended abruptly. I remembered my inability to fix my mind that morning, scarcely a month gone by, and how I had broken off to get my *Daily Chronicle* from the newsboy. I remembered how I went down to the garden gate as he came along, and how I had listened to his odd story of "Men from Mars."

I came down and went into the dining room. There were the mutton and the bread, both far gone now in decay, and a beer bottle overturned, just as I and the artilleryman had left them. My home was desolate. I perceived the folly of the faint hope I had cherished so long. And then a strange thing occurred. "It is no use," said a voice. "The house is deserted. No one has been here these ten days. Do not stay here to torment yourself. No one escaped but you."

I was startled. Had I spoken my thought aloud? I turned, and the French window was open behind me. I made a step to it, and stood looking out.

And there, amazed and afraid, even as I stood amazed and afraid, were my cousin and my wife—my wife white and tearless. She gave a faint cry.

"I came," she said. "I knew—knew—"

She put her hand to her throat—swayed. I made a step forward, and caught her in my arms.

• • •

CHAPTER TEN

The Epilogue

I CANNOT BUT REGRET, now that I am concluding my story, how little I am able to contribute to the discussion of the many debatable questions which are still unsettled. In one respect I shall certainly provoke criticism. My particular province is speculative philosophy. My knowledge of comparative physiology is confined to a book or two, but it seems to me that Carver's suggestions as to the reason of the rapid he Martians is so probable as to be regarded almost as a proven conclusion. I have assumed that in the body of my narrative.

At any rate, in all the bodies of the Martians that were examined after the war, no bacteria except those already known as terrestrial species were found. That they did not bury any of their dead, and the reckless slaughter they perpetrated, point also to an entire ignorance of the putrefactive process. But probable as this seems, it is by no means a proven conclusion.

Neither is the composition of the Black Smoke known, which the Martians used with such deadly effect, and the generator of the Heat-Rays remains a puzzle. The terrible disasters at the Ealing and South Kensington laboratories have disinclined analysts for further investigations upon the latter. Spectrum analysis of the black powder points unmistakably to the presence of an unknown element with a brilliant group of three lines in the green, and it is possible that it combines with argon to form a compound which acts at once with deadly effect upon some constituent in the blood. But such unproven speculations will scarcely be of interest to the general reader, to whom this story is addressed. None of the brown scum that drifted down the Thames after the destruction of Shepperton was examined at the time, and now none is forthcoming.

The results of an anatomical examination of the Martians, so far as the prowling dogs had left such an examination possible, I have already given. But everyone is familiar with the magnificent and almost complete specimen in spirits at the Natural History Museum, and the countless drawings that have been made from it; and beyond that the interest of their physiology and structure is purely scientific.

A question of graver and universal interest is the possibility of another attack from the Martians. I do not think that nearly enough attention is being given to this aspect of the matter. At present the planet Mars is in conjunction, but with every return to opposition I, for one, anticipate a renewal of their adventure. In any case, we should be prepared. It seems to me that it should be possible to define the position of the gun from which the shots are discharged, to keep a sustained watch upon this part of the planet, and to anticipate the arrival of the next attack.

In that case the cylinder might be destroyed with dynamite or artillery before it was sufficiently cool for the Martians to emerge, or they might be butchered by means of guns so soon as the screw opened. It seems to me that they have lost a vast advantage in the failure of their first surprise. Possibly they see it in the same light.

Lessing has advanced excellent reasons for supposing that the Martians have actually succeeded in effecting a landing on the planet Venus. Seven months ago now, Venus and Mars were in alignment with the sun; that is to say, Mars was in opposition from the point of view of an observer on Venus. Subsequently a peculiar luminous and sinuous marking appeared on the unillumined half of the inner planet, and almost simultaneously a faint dark mark of a similar sinuous character was detected upon a photograph of the Martian disk. One needs to see the drawings of these appearances in order to appreciate fully their remarkable resemblance in character.

At any rate, whether we expect another invasion or not, our views of the human future must be greatly modified by these events. We have learned now that we cannot regard this planet as being fenced in and a secure abiding place for Man; we can never anticipate the unseen good or evil that may come upon us suddenly out of space. It may be that in the larger design of the universe this invasion from Mars is not without its ultimate benefit for men; it has robbed us of that serene confidence in the future which is the most fruitful source of decadence, the gifts to human science it has brought are enormous, and it has done much to promote the conception of the commonweal of mankind. It may be that across the immensity of space the Martians have watched the fate of these pioneers of theirs and learned their lesson, and that on the planet Venus they have found a securer settlement. Be that as it may, for many years yet there will certainly be no relaxation of the eager scrutiny of the Martian disk, and those fiery darts of the sky, the shooting stars, will bring with them as they fall an unavoidable apprehension to all the sons of men.

The broadening of men's views that has resulted can scarcely be exaggerated. Before the cylinder fell there was a general persuasion that through all the deep of space no life existed beyond the petty surface of our minute sphere. Now we see further. If the Martians can reach Venus, there is no reason to suppose that the thing is impossible for men, and when the slow cooling of the sun makes this earth uninhabitable, as at last it must do, it may be that the thread of life that has begun here will have streamed out and caught our sister planet within its toils.

Dim and wonderful is the vision I have conjured up in my mind of life spreading slowly from this little seed bed of the solar system throughout the inanimate vastness of sidereal space. But that is a remote dream. It may be, on the other hand, that the destruction of the Martians is only a reprieve. To them, and not to us, perhaps, is the future ordained.

I must confess the stress and danger of the time have left an abiding sense of doubt and insecurity in my mind. I sit in my study writing by lamplight, and suddenly I see again the healing valley below set with writhing flames, and feel the house behind and about me empty and desolate. I go out into the Byfleet Road, and vehicles pass me, a butcher boy in a cart, a cabful of visitors, a workman on a bicycle, children going to school, and suddenly they become vague and unreal, and I hurry again with the artilleryman through the hot, brooding silence. Of a night I see the black powder darkening the silent streets, and the contorted bodies shrouded in that layer; they rise upon me tattered and dog-bitten. They gibber and grow fiercer, paler, uglier, mad distortions of humanity at last, and I wake, cold and wretched, in the darkness of the night.

I go to London and see the busy multitudes in Fleet Street and the Strand, and it comes across my mind that they are but the ghosts of the past, haunting the streets that I have seen silent and wretched, going to and fro, phantasms in a dead city, the mockery of life in a galvanised body. And strange, too, it is to stand on Primrose Hill, as I did but a day before writing this last chapter, to see the great province of houses, dim and blue through the haze of the smoke and mist, vanishing at last into the vague lower sky, to see the people walking to and fro among the flower beds on the hill, to see the sight-seers about the Martian machine that stands there still, to hear the tumult of playing children, and to recall the time when I saw it all bright and clear-cut, hard and silent, under the dawn of that last great day....

And strangest of all is it to hold my wife's hand again, and to think that I have counted her, and that she has counted me, among the dead.

ROBERT CHARLES WILSON

The Night Wind and the Morning Star

IN JANUARY OF THE YEAR 2004, two spacecraft from Earth landed on the surface of the planet Mars. Unlike previous static landers, these robotic craft were mobile; they were equipped with sophisticated sampling and photographic equipment, and the images they broadcast to Earth were more spectacular than anything that had been seen before.

The second of the vehicles, named *Opportunity*, landed on a part of equatorial Mars called Meridiani Planum. According to a recent article in the science journal *Nature*, the area was once the site of an ancient ocean covering at least 127,000 square miles of the Martian surface, roughly the size of the Caspian Sea. Today Meridiani Planum is as desiccated as any other part of that small, nearly airless world. What remains of its watery past is recorded in its exposed bedrock, in its peculiar sulfate geochemistry and in the tiny spheres of hematite that litter the ancient seabed.

Because I'm a science fiction writer—or maybe just because my geekish impulses were fully engaged—I spent much of the spring and summer of 2004 poring over those panoramic photographs from Mars. I learned to appreciate, for instance, the color of the Martian sky, a delicate tangerine deepening at sunset to something almost like blue. The sun in a Martian afternoon is bright but distant; the shadows cast by sinuous drifts of Martian sand are stark and cold in the sub-frigid morning, melancholy as night approaches; and the tracks left by *Spirit* and *Opportunity* across their respective landscapes look eerily misplaced, a human intrusion on a world where nothing much moves except a few ethereal dust devils, faint clouds and winter frosts of frozen carbon dioxide. I learned from those photographs that Mars was not only a uniquely alien but a uniquely beautiful place.

And I learned something else. I learned that, when you've stared at a Martian landscape long enough, the Earth itself seems subtly altered. Suddenly it's not *the* world but *a* world: one among many, one variation on a whole palette of possibilities, water-rich and lively but also fragile, subject to the same slow erosions that dried the Martian seas and erased whatever may have begun of Martian life.

And this, above all else, is what H. G. Wells understood about the planet Mars: that it alters your perspective.

• • •

Jules Verne and H. G. Wells are both commonly cited as founders of modern science fiction. Verne, anticipating submarines and powered aircraft from the age of the gaslight, knew that technology changes with time. But Wells knew something infinitely more profound. He knew that *everything* changes.

Herbert George Wells came of age in a time of intellectual revolution, a war of worldviews in which he quickly became a frontline soldier. Born to an impoverished family in Bromley—his father was an unsuccessful shopkeeper and former gardener, his mother an occasional housekeeper who had once worked as a domestic servant—he attended the Normal School of Science on a scholarship. His first-semester zoology teacher was T. H. Huxley, the controversial exponent of evolutionary theory often caricatured as "Darwin's Bulldog."

The theory of natural selection espoused by Huxley was only one of the scientific heresies that were overturning the Victorian conception of man as the center of fixed moral universe, on a planet created by a benevolent God in historically recent time. This was the vision evoked by the poet Matthew Arnold in his elegiac "Dover Beach" (1867), of the Sea of Faith, "Retreating, to the breath / Of the night wind, down the vast edges drear / And naked shingles of the world." Many Victorians experienced it as a tragic loss.

But unlike Matthew Arnold, the young Wells wasn't dismayed by the scientific reconstruction of the universe. For Wells, the night wind was a freshening breeze. He gloried in it; he delighted in exploring both its bright, stern rationalism and its shadowy implications about human mortality and mutability.

And if Wells was ultimately an indifferent student—after passing Huxley's zoology class and a physics course he failed a geology exam and left the Normal School of Science for a job as an assistant schoolmaster—what he took from his studies was in the end a writer's perspective. Out of Huxley and Darwin he distilled a theme: if you remove mankind as the linchpin of the universe—if we're a product of the universe, not its purpose—then no point of view is privileged. Radical inversions of common sense and accepted wisdom become not only possible but essential. ("You must follow me carefully," says the Time Traveler in Wells' *The Time Machine*. "I shall have to controvert one or two ideas that are almost universally accepted.")

The eye that has seriously contemplated the depths of geological time and interplanetary space sees the present differently. It finds a desert at the bottom of an ocean, a forest in a lump of coal, an extinct monster in a slab of shale. It conceives of a time before man existed and a time when man will cease to exist. It sees humanity from a relativistic point of view: not large, but larger than some things and smaller than others; not wise, but wiser than it has been and less wise than it might be.

Wells forces this shift of perspective in *The War of the Worlds* repeatedly:

[A]s men busied themselves about their various concerns they were scrutinised and studied, perhaps almost as narrowly as a man with a microscope might scrutinise the transient creatures that swarm and multiply in a drop of water. With infinite complacency men went to and fro over this globe about their little affairs, serene in their assurance of their empire over matter. It is possible that the infusoria under the microscope do the same.

Or:

[L]ooking across space with instruments, and with intelligences such as we have scarcely dreamed of they see, at its nearest distance only

35,000,000 of miles sunward of them, a morning star of hope—our own warmer planet, green with vegetation and grey with water, with a cloudy atmosphere eloquent of fertility, with glimpses through drifting cloud-wisps of broad stretches of populous country and narrow navy-crowded seas.

Or more explicitly:

Perhaps I am a man of exceptional moods. I do not know how far my experience is common. At times I suffer from the strangest sense of detachment from myself and the world about me. I seem to watch it all from the outside, from somewhere inconceivably remote, out of time, out of space, out of the stress and tragedy of it all.

The narrator of *The War of the Worlds* describes himself as "a philosophical writer," and the text he takes for himself might as well be Heraclitus: *No single thing abides, but all things flow.*

• • •

Having established his Martian perspective—man as a contingent being in an ancient, evolving universe—Wells used it ruthlessly, in his life and in his art. Because he knew the economic system of imperial England was not ordained by God or nature, he was attracted to Fabianism and utopian socialism; because he knew social customs shift from continent to continent and century to century, he could espouse the doctrine of free love and eventually write *Ann Veronica*, a novel that incensed his contemporary audience.

But his deeper insight was not that the Victorian social order should be overthrown but that every social order everywhere is always being overthrown. Revolution is a state of nature, a fact of life. The trilobite in the shale is a fallen empire; London at its commercial and imperial apex, a ruin in waiting. When he began writing *The War of the Worlds*, Wells says in his autobiography, he often bicycled through Surrey, "marking down suitable places and people for destruction by my Martians." Not because he hated his neighbors, but because he knew they were not exempt from the universal processes of time, that neither guns nor clergy could protect Chobham or Weybridge from the forces that had driven the plesiosaur into the chalk at Lyme Regis.

And if there is a villain in *The War of the Worlds* it isn't entirely the

Martians, who, after all, are only obeying the strictures of their own harsh biology. The real enemy is what Wells calls "complacency," the inability to make that essential leap of perspective. Thus there is Mrs. Elphinstone, reluctantly fleeing before the invasion: "She had never been out of England before, she would rather die than trust herself friendless in a foreign country....She seemed, poor woman, to imagine that the French and the Martians might prove very similar....Her great idea was to return to Stanmore. Things had always been well and safe at Stanmore."

But complacency—the idea of a privileged place or point of view—isn't only a human vice. In the ultimate Wellsian irony, it's what defeats the Martians. Wells wrote long before the coining of the word "biosphere," but he understood the concept: Mars and Earth have different biospheres, and the two are incompatible. Earth's biosphere proves fatal to the Martian weed that chokes the Thames and equally to the Martians themselves: "But there are no bacteria in Mars, and directly these invaders arrived, directly they drank and fed, our microscopic allies began to work their overthrow." Despite their superior intelligence and technology, the Martians failed to make the leap to what they might have called the terrestrial perspective. "That they did not bury any of their dead, and the reckless slaughter they perpetrated among us points to an entire ignorance of the putrefactive process." They are overthrown, in other words, by their own complacency, by their serene assurance of their empire over matter, by their inability to think un-Martian thoughts.

· • ·

When H. G. Wells published *The War of the Worlds* in 1898 he could not have known that he had written a book that would remain in print throughout the twentieth century and into the twenty-first. Nor could he have understood that with this book and *The Time Machine* he had founded a genre.

Most early twentieth-century science fiction, especially as it was formulated in American pulp magazines like *Amazing Stories* and *Science Wonder Stories*, misunderstood Wells even as it tried to emulate him. His work was reconfigured as exotic window dressing for conventional adventure tales, westerns set on notionally alien planets. In his 1939 book *Plotting for Every Kind of Writing*, Depression-era how-to-write guru Jack Woodford describes the typical science fiction story of the day as one in which "[the] adventure to be undertaken by the hero takes him into unearthly realms. This may be in a space ship, to another planet or to a fourth or unknown dimension. . . . He may or may not take with him a girl. If he takes a girl her wardrobe need not be over replete. In the new and unknown world, he meets human beings in the form of animals, insects, reptiles, plants or reactionary Republicans. . . ."

But even Woodford acknowledged that there was another sort of science fiction. "When stories of this type contain no women with scanty wardrobes who are tortured, they are directed at a curious tribe of people whom the average author does not at all understand, and these people have to be addressed by the kind of author who does understand them."

People, in other words, who heard the Wellsian echo through the noise. In many of these stories Wellsian themes burn like a fire in a coal seam, hidden, underground. They are not explicit but *passim*, whispered in the annunciation of a date not yet arrived (1960, 2050) or in the mechanics of crude extrapolation (aircraft the size of New York City, weapons that destroy whole solar systems). Often in these stories the connection to "science" is approximate and hastily abandoned. Wells' Martians travel between planets in metal cylinders protected against vacuum and atmospheric friction, but in Edwin L. Arnold's 1905 *Lieutenant Gulliver Jones*, the title character arrives on Mars aboard a magic carpet; John Carter, in the 1917 Edgar Rice Burroughs novel *A Princess of Mars*, gets there essentially by wishful thinking.

But the Wellsian music beats on. Explicitly Wellsian stories surfaced throughout the 1920s and 1930s, in the work of writers like Stanley Weinbaum, Charles Tanner, Edmond Hamilton and the young John W. Campbell, who would go on to cultivate a fresh crop of Wellsians as editor of the postwar *Astounding Stories*. And just as literary science fiction was reconfiguring itself, *The War of the Worlds* surfaced in two new media, radio and the movies.

Amazingly, much of its power was preserved intact. The 1938 Orson Welles radio play succeeded in doing for New Jersey what H. G. Wells had done for Surrey, forcing the prosaic and the apocalyptic into intimate contact. But here the Martians seem to stand in for a less philosophical threat. The bulletin style of broadcast Welles mimicked—*We interrupt this program*—had become familiar to most Americans during the Czech crisis earlier that year, when Edward R. Murrow began to make pioneering live radio broadcasts from Europe. (At one point CBS offered to mail free "crisis maps" to listeners following the German invasion of Czechoslovakia. One imagines Orson Welles might have done something similar, had it been practical.) The drum beating in the background of Welles' radio play is the sound of war, not evolution, and the show's audience could be forgiven for imagining that the Germans and the Martians might prove very similar.

But the threat was authentic. The implied shift of perspective might have been less cosmic but was more urgent—*if the Sudetenland were Grover's Mills*—and paralleled the early scenes in another adaptation of Wells for the screen, William Cameron Menzies' 1936 *Things to Come*. The London debut of *Things to Come* was met with what H. G. Wells no doubt recognized as complacency or at least, in the modern sense, denial: audiences reacted to images of Piccadilly Square devastated by aerial bombardment with incredulity and laughter. The Orson Welles *War of the Worlds*, two years later, hit an exposed nerve among Americans and sent hundreds fleeing into the streets.

It was followed by war, the real thing, a war fought on the ground but also from the air and under the sea, Vernian in its technology, Wellsian in its scope and consequences, and by the time *The War of the Worlds* resurfaced in its George Pal incarnation, seven years after the death of H. G. Wells himself, the world had been changed almost beyond recognition.

• • •

What could this Victorian science fiction story possibly have to say to its own futurity, its children's children?

Plenty, as it turned out.

I was one of those children. I was born the year the George Pal movie was produced, and by the time it found its way onto some local TV station (probably KTLA) I was just old enough to understand it. It scared the bejeezus out of me, but more importantly, it changed the way I looked at things.

Because this time the Martians had landed in *my* neighborhood.

At least approximately. True, the small town depicted in the movie was nothing like the Orange County bedroom suburb where my family lived. Where I lived, nobody went to Saturday-night square dances, we didn't say "Goshdarn!" quite so often, and we didn't dress in what appeared to be surplus wardrobe from *The Howdy Doody Show*. But the gully where the Martian spaceship landed looked a lot like the scrubby chaparral I could see from my own back door, and anyway it *was* California: they said so! More importantly, the movie placed California in a context so large it threatened to swallow up everything familiar and reliable. It did this from the first reel, from the very first images of other worlds (Pluto, "its atmosphere frozen on its surface;" Mercury, "the temperature of molten lead"), represented by slightly animated versions of classic Chesley Bonestell astronomic paintings. And then the cloud-stippled Earth, as if we were traveling wrong-way down the telescope, and then California, and finally something in the sky—"a line of flame high in the atmosphere," stitching the worlds together.

I think I understood—though I couldn't have explained it—that the important thing about the movie wasn't the Martians *per se*. The Martians of the George Pal film, in their sleek jade-green killing machines (which looked superbly futuristic in their day and seem oddly contemporary even in 2004, like high-end bathroom scales from a Sharper Image catalog), were the "fiction" part of "science fiction." I knew better than to expect to see them floating down Hacienda Boulevard, ray-gunning used-car dealerships and pink stucco houses with barrel-tile roofs. But neither were the Martians purely fantasy, like Dumbo in the Disney movie. They were totems representing a truth: that the universe that contained my house, my family and myself also contained distant, unknowable, possibly inhabited planets; that the sun that rose on Whittier and La Puente also rose over the arid red plains of Mars.

Not for pretend. For real.

It was an idea so striking I couldn't stop thinking about it. It was the reason I began scouring the kids' section of the library for anything with the word "science" in the title. It was the reason I learned the names of the nine planets long before I learned the names of Major League ballplayers.

And it was the reason I made a prepubescent pilgrimage to the Barringer Meteor Crater in Arizona.

Not, of course, on my own hook. In those days (it must have been 1960 or 1961) my family made annual road trips from California to Pennsylvania to visit relatives. I had read about the Barringer crater at the library, and I pleaded (whined, groveled, begged) for a detour to see it, until my parents caved in.

The crater is a three-quarter-mile-wide impact basin created by a huge meteor that flared through the Earth's atmosphere almost 50,000 years ago and impacted our planet halfway between the present-day sites of Winslow and Winona, Arizona. The dry climate has preserved it against erosion. It looks strikingly like photographs of Martian impact craters, if you ignore the attendant restaurant, gift shop, visitor's center and so forth. The rilled walls of the crater are reddish-brown, a Martian color, and its rim is strewn with chunks of limestone blown out by the energy of the impact. The crater is situated in a plain of bleak red desert that looks similarly Martian, apart from the caps of snow on the distant San Francisco Peaks.

My parents snapped a photo of me on a sunbaked wooden platform at the brink of the 550-foot-deep bowl, surveying the scene with a degree of rapt attention that must have bewildered and dismayed them. My mother and father in those days belonged to a Protestant church called Disciples of Christ, and they may have detected in all this talk of time and evolution the faint sound of the retreating Sea of Faith. It controverted, I suspect, one or two ideas they would have preferred to be universally accepted.

But to me the Barringer crater wasn't about anything as abstract as religious faith. To me, it was evidence. Fifty thousand years ago a rock 150 feet in diameter and weighing, by modern estimates, some 300,000 tons had punched a hole in the desert—*this* hole, the one in front of my feet. It was evidence, hard courtroom evidence, Perry Mason–level evidence, that I didn't live only in La Puente, or California or even the United States. I lived in the universe. And the universe was terribly old and terribly strange, and by this time I knew who had said so most emphatically and dramatically: a man named H. G. Wells.

* * *

Forty-odd years later, I'm standing on the rim of another crater....

Well, no, not literally. The crater is called Endurance, and it's on Mars, and I'm sitting in front of my PC in Canada downloading another rack of NASA photos. But if I let my mind wander (and as a science fiction writer I'm paid to let my mind wander), here I am, surveying Endurance from its fractured rim in the thin Martian sunlight.

It's a spectacularly lonely place. The kind of place where you want company, someone to share the view. I've already shown these photos to friends and family, in fact pretty much anyone whose attention I could conscript. Right now, though, I want to show them to someone who can't be physically present.

I want to show them to H. G. Wells.

Not the aging, discouraged H. G. Wells of his later years. Not the disappointed utopian, not the man who flirted too long with Bolshevism. Not him, but the young author of *The Time Machine* and *The War of the Worlds*, the "philosophical writer" infatuated with what the best science of the nineteenth century had taught him about time and space and human destiny.

Of course, there is a lot to explain. What startles me is that I can explain most of it in his own words.

Here are images of *Spirit* and *Opportunity*, the mobile landers, being assembled in sterile labs prior to their launch. *Opportunity*, I tell him, successfully transited sidereal space and in January of 2004 descended through the Martian sky like a fiery meteorite, "a line of flame high in the atmosphere," until it had bled enough speed to safely open a parachute. Having landed, the machine extracted itself from its protective shell. Then it stood erect and after a few days began to travel across the Martian landscape, pausing to sample rocks and soil with tools attached to its telescoping arms, "a sort of metallic spider... with an extraordinary number of jointed levers, bars, and reaching and clutching tentacles about its body... a complicated system of sliding parts moving over small but beautifully curved friction bearings."

From the first moments of its arrival, *Opportunity* deployed its cameras and began to send home finely rendered images of Mars.

Here, for instance, is a panoramic view of Endurance crater and the frozen desert surrounding it, Meridiani Planum. "The secular cooling that must someday overtake our planet has already gone far indeed with our neighbour.... we know now that even in its equatorial region the midday temperature barely approaches that of our coldest winter. Its air is much more attenuated than ours...." Very much more. About as rarified as the air three miles above Mt. Everest. But it *is* an atmosphere, tenuous but substantial enough to support fierce winds, to lift fine particles of sand and deposit them in serpentine drifts half a planet away. One of the NASA photos even captures a wisp of cloud drifting through the sand-colored sky, an echo of ancient summers.

"That last stage of exhaustion, which to us is still incredibly remote, has become a present-day problem for the inhabitants of Mars."

There are no inhabitants of Mars, unless a few microbes survive somewhere deep beneath the crust. But the planet was once a warmer, wetter place. Some millions of years ago water covered this lifeless wasteland. That's one of the things we learned from *Opportunity*. But the sea at Meridiani Planum has retreated down the naked shingles of its world. "Its oceans have shrunk" to nothing. Their melancholy, long, withdrawing roar fell silent long before the Age of Reptiles.

"[Mars] must be, if the nebular hypothesis has any truth, older than our world; and long before this earth ceased to be molten, life upon its surface must have begun its course." Well, maybe. The possibility exists that life began on Mars when it was a young planet, as it did on Earth. Life may even have transited between the two worlds, carried by meteor impacts. The evidence is still ambiguous. We may share a common genesis with whatever Martians there ever were.

None of this comes as a surprise to Wells, who begins to take shape in my imagination, standing at the rim of Endurance crater in a stiff collar and a greatcoat, casting a Victorian shadow over the pebbles of hematite and gullies of fine red sand.

I ask him, *Is it what you imagined?*

And he smiles as if to say: *In everything but the particulars, yes.*

. • •

But there is one more image I want to show him. In some ways it's the most striking of all the 2004 Mars rover photographs. In this one the camera was aimed not at the horizon but higher, toward the Martian sunrise.

Look. A simple dot against the darkness. "But so little it was, so silvery warm—a pin's-head of light!" *Is that—?*

It is. "[A]t its nearest distance only 35,000,000 of miles sunward...a morning star...our own warmer planet...with a cloudy atmosphere eloquent of fertility...." Earth, as seen from the surface of another world, scrutinized by intelligences which are not merely mortal but, in an irony Wells would have relished, our own.

The image of Earth from Mars is a technological triumph, and for a moment it seems as if we're actually peering up from the edge of Endurance, two ghosts, simultaneously Martians and Earthlings, mutually triumphant and a little in awe of ourselves, serene in our assurance of our empire over matter.

Then the frost settles, a few grains of sand scurry down the slope of the crater, our complacency evaporates into the frigid air, and the night wind rises and carries us away.

Robert Charles Wilson's works include the Hugo Award nominees *Darwinia* and *Blind Lake*. His *The Chronoliths* received the John W. Campbell Memorial Award, and he has also won the Philip K. Dick Award and Canada's Aurora Award; several of his novels have been *New York Times* Notable Books. His latest novel is *Spin*, in which the Earth itself is projected four billion years into the future.

LAWRENCE WATT-EVANS

Just Who Were Those Martians, Anyway?

"NO ONE WOULD HAVE BELIEVED in the last years of the nineteenth century that this world was being watched keenly and closely by intelligences greater than man's...minds that are to our minds as ours are to those of the beasts that perish, intellects vast and cool and unsympathetic...."

So says Wells' narrator—but can we really believe him? How does he know? His own epilogue tells us just how little is really known of the Martians after the war, and he gives us no evidence at all to support his melodramatic introduction.

He knows that the Martians have a technology vastly superior to that of his own land and time, but does that really imply greater intelligence? Were the English of 1898 greater intelligences than their less fortunate neighbors in Africa and Asia, or their own ancestors of a thousand years before, or were Wells' countrymen merely the beneficiaries of historical chance? I think any citizen of the twenty-first century will concede that our cell phones and computers do not mean we are ourselves superior in intelligence to our grandparents; technology is not, in itself, proof of superior intellect. And given that the narrator himself emphasizes that Mars is older than Earth—well, he interprets this as indicating that the Martians have presumably evolved further along our own supposed path, and are therefore our mental superiors, just as we are the superiors of our nearest cousin, the chimpanzee. But could it not just as well be true that Martian evolution did not follow that same path any farther than we have, and that the Martians are of roughly human-level intelligence? Evolution, we now know, is not linear, but a matter of fitting inherited traits to the available ecological niches, and it may well be that intelligence greater than our own has no real survival value.

In that case, the Martians' advanced weapons would be merely the result of a more mature technology. If a few centuries could take humanity from stone castles and wooden plows to skyscrapers and John Deere, then surely a few thousand years of Martian history are adequate to explain Heat-Rays and Black Smoke, without postulating greater-than-human intellect.

Perhaps the narrator thinks that the Martians' oversize brains indicate greater intelligence; this may be a better indicator than their technology, but it is still unreliable—elephants and whales are bright enough, but well short of human levels. And who knows what effects the Martian environment may have had? Perhaps all that additional brain tissue is required to be effective in the cold, thin air of Mars.

Really, the only way to judge intelligence is from a creature's behavior—and were the Martians' actions indicative of high intelligence, signs of "intellects vast and cool"?

Consider: Ten cylinders, sent at one-day intervals, with no means of retrieving them should the invasion fail. The first arrivals more or less start blasting every Earthling in sight, ignoring attempts at communication. This is usually interpreted as sublime confidence on the Martians' part, the result of their absolute certainty of their own superiority, but isn't it just as easily interpreted as reckless, bloodthirsty stupidity?

Consider also that soul-searing moment in chapter four when the Martians first emerge from their cylinder. Our narrator stares in horror at their hideous, alien, unprotected faces, and then... "[s]uddenly the monster vanished. It had toppled over the brim of the cylinder and fallen into the pit, with a thud like the fall of a great mass of leather."

Superior intelligences, as far above us as we are above cattle, that don't bother with space suits, armor, weapons, scanning equipment, signaling devices or even a *ladder* before taking a pratfall out of their ship? Superior intelligences that don't seem to have given any thought to the higher gravity, the thicker air, the possibility that some panicky farmer will put a load of buckshot into them at the first glimpse of alien life? Not worrying about microorganisms when their native environment apparently has none I can accept, but they hadn't taken even the most basic precautions against environmental toxins!

I'm sorry, but these creatures are clearly not the vanguard of a carefully planned attack by an ancient civilization of vast, cool intelligences.

Unsympathetic, yes—that description we can agree with. Otherwise, though, they seem no brighter than *Star Trek*'s Federation, with its mysterious inability to equip starships with seat belts or circuit breakers.

Are these really the best Mars can send against us?

In fact, I think it's safe to conclude that they are *not* a civilization that can survive in the cold and hostile Martian environment, that can launch unpowered craft across interplanetary distances in such a way that the passengers survive impact. These spacecraft surely could not have been built and maintained by fumble-tentacled doofuses.

But in that case, if these aren't the elite leaders of a carefully planned invasion by an advanced civilization, who *are* these guys?

Well, let us consider the evidence. A mere ten cylinders, sent on a one-way trip across the void—this isn't much of an invasion at all. It's generally assumed, with some sound reasons, that a technological civilization can't exist without a population in the millions; automation and artificial intelligence might provide a way around that, but we see no evidence that these Martians have much in the way of robotics—the tripods are piloted, not autonomous. There must, then, be millions of Martians back on Mars. Therefore, if they were serious about conquering and occupying a planet with roughly the land surface area of their own, they would have sent thousands or millions of troops, rather than a couple of hundred. If it were a scouting expedition, they would have provided a method of retrieving their forces. They did not. In fact, all the evidence indicates that they *did not want these people back.*

Why else use unpowered cylinders? Surely, the technology that created the fighting tripods could have built true spaceships, rather than suicide craft—but they didn't, *by choice.*

In short, these were not an invasion fleet. My theory, which I think obvious in retrospect, is that they were exiles, sent to Earth (and later Venus) to get them off Mars. Whether they were fleeing of their own free will or being sent into exile by their enemies we cannot immediately say—the evidence, though suggestive in ways I will describe shortly, is inconclusive. That they were indeed exiles, though, seems the only explanation for the manner of their arrival.

And really, given the evidence of their behavior on Earth, these Martians were a bunch of trigger-happy idiots; assuming that their native culture on Mars is a reasonably peaceful and civilized one, who can blame the authorities for wanting this group removed?

But wait, you say—why am I assuming that their native culture was peaceful?

Well, human scientists have been studying Mars for some time now, closely enough to observe the launching of the ten cylinders; have there been any observations of anything that might indicate large-scale warfare on the fourth planet? I've certainly never heard of any, nor does Wells mention any. Furthermore, Mars is an old world, with an advanced technology but a harsh environment and limited resources; war and conflict waste resources, while cooperation conserves them. If the Martians are as intelligent as humans, let alone possessed of minds "vast and cool," they must surely have figured this out long ago. Ironically, it seems unlikely that the planet named for the god of war would be home to any wars.

The Martians we saw on Earth were anything but peaceful, of course—but the very fact that they *were* on Earth would seem to indicate that they're the exception. If they were merely a losing faction on a war-torn and barbaric world, they would not have been exiled to Earth and Venus; they would have been exterminated. The fact that they were allowed to live, and precious resources devoted to sending them to another planet rather than just turning them into food or fertilizer, indicates that their opponents were humane and civilized—unlike the exiles themselves—or at any rate preferred to *appear* humane.

This would explain the exiles' behavior nicely. These were the losing side in some internecine Martian brouhaha, exiled to another planet, allowed to take along some weapons to protect themselves from the native wildlife on the assumption that there's no sentient life on Earth for them to harm. These were the Martians too stubborn to realize they were on the losing side, too stupid to talk their way out of being shot into space, bitter and angry and scared when they landed—of course they lashed out at the natives!

And once they had secured a position they linked up, tried to establish a defensible position and exploit the available resources. That's sensible enough, from a military point of view.

The refusal to make any attempt to communicate with humans, though—that's really a bit dumb. Humans are clearly intelligent, if perhaps not up to Martian levels; humans have cities and machinery, and as the *Thunder Child* demonstrates, they can pose a genuine threat. Wouldn't it have made sense to even the meanest intelligence to try to open communications, perhaps offer terms for England's surrender to the Martians? The exiles' overwhelming technological advantage meant they would win all the early encounters, but in the long run the sheer numbers of humans, the preexisting industrial base in human hands, might turn the tide; wouldn't it be obvious that a negotiated settlement would work to the Martians' benefit? They could easily break the treaty later, if their position justified it.

But these are the Martians who fell on their faces climbing out of their own spacecraft, not the cream of the Martian intelligentsia. Apparently it wasn't obvious to *them*.

I think we must conclude that not only were the exiles the losing side in some mysterious Martian dispute, but that they were stupid, arrogant and bloody-minded, probably just as much so by Martian standards as by our own.

And perhaps we can guess just what sort of dispute got them exiled. Might they, perhaps, have been plotting a *coup d'etat* against the enlightened (they would undoubtedly say weak) and peaceful (they would surely say passive) government of Mars? Was their intent, perhaps, to use Earth as a base where they could regroup, rebuild and launch a fresh attack?

That would explain why they showed interest in neither communicating with humans nor exterminating them—they weren't planning to stay. Humans were just a temporary inconvenience.

One wonders when it would have occurred to them to use the human *Untermenschen* as slave labor in building the gun that would launch them back to Mars.

And one also wonders whether the government that exiled them had any concerns about an eventual return. Might it be that the Martian high command knew perfectly well that Earth's environment would be lethal in the end? Might it be that the apparently humane exile was, in fact, a death sentence, disguised to appease the soft-hearted Martian masses, and to avoid martyring the troublemakers? After all, according to Wells' epilogue the Martians also launch cylinders to Venus, and how could any native of cold, thin-aired Mars hope to survive in the superheated pressure cooker of the Venusian atmosphere? If our own species is used as a model, it probably wouldn't be hard to sell the idea to the Martian man-in-the-street—or octopoid-in-the-tunnel—that the exiles would have a fighting chance. The educated elite, though, would know perfectly well that the plotters would be fried the instant they unscrewed the cylinder's hatch.

And I think that pretty much eliminates any possibility that the exiles fled voluntarily; even a stupid Martian would surely stop and ask, "Can we survive there?" before agreeing to be launched to an alien planet. No, they must have been dispatched hither by the Martian overlords, whoever and whatever they may be.

It may well be that the worst exiles, the smartest of the plotters, were sent to Venus, to die quickly in the searing blackness there, while the less dangerous underlings, the mere thuggish minions, were sent to Earth. That would explain nicely just how they could be stupid enough to fall naked from their craft, there on Horsell Common—these were Martians chosen by their leaders for loyalty, aggressiveness and brutality, not for brains. Their Lenin, their Hitler, their bin Laden would have been sent to a fast end on Venus, while their street fighters and bully-boys were permitted to strut about on Earth for a few days before succumbing to the subtler menaces of our ecology. When the Martian powers staged their version of Nuremberg, Venus served as the hangman's noose, Earth as their Spandau.

All this is mere speculation on my part, of course, but in all modesty, I think it fits the known facts far better than the narrator's unexamined assumptions. I do not mean to fault Mr. Wells, of course; I have the advantage of an additional century's perspective—and a very busy century it was, at that, one which taught its survivors a great deal about what humans are capable of, and thereby gave us a better insight into the Martians. We also know now that no second wave of invaders ever arrived, a circumstance that the narrator had just cause to doubt, which supports the supposition that the "invasion" was nothing of the sort, but merely the convenient disposition of a few troublemakers.

Still, it may be that I am completely wrong, that Martians, having evolved on a planet so unlike our own, think and act in ways so alien that we cannot begin to guess them. That would render all speculation, by Wells, the narrator or myself, meaningless—but it would also run counter to all past human experience. All known life seems to share the same basic drives, though they may be expressed in a myriad of unlikely ways, and there is no reason to believe that would not be just as true on Mars as on Earth.

So let us now consider the significance of my theories, should they prove correct. What do they tell us about what we might find when we at last repay the unfortunate visit of a century past, and set foot upon the Red Planet?

Obviously, to state the most basic fact, we know that there were Martians on Mars as of 1898, though we have seen no evidence of their presence in any of the reports sent by our various robot probes in the past half-century. Either the entire Martian civilization vanished sometime in the twentieth century—an event that would, I concede, fit better with Wells' speculation about the last survivors fleeing a dying planet than with my own supposition that our attackers were cast out by the outraged rulers of a thriving nation—or it remains hidden, presumably underground. We can draw no conclusions from any evidence visible on the surface; we will know nothing for sure until we can explore whatever may lie below the red sands.

We may find nothing but empty ruins, or the starving remnants of a dying race—that would fit Wells' expectations.

My own belief, though, is that we will find a complex living society, one that pays lip service to mercy and benevolence—they did exile their enemies, rather than slaughtering them on the spot—but which is, beneath the kindly surface, as ruthless as its rulers deem necessary. They had no compunctions about sending those exiles to certain death, after all, and spared no thought for what the exiles might do to our own great-grandparents. These beings might in truth be the vast, cool and unsympathetic intellects Wells assumed.

We will want to approach them cautiously, negotiate with them, make whatever treaties seem appropriate—but never trust them.

And I would think it wise to equip every expedition to Mars with a sealed container of Antarctic bacteria—microscopic creatures that can live in the Martian climate, that our own immune systems can easily handle, but that could, if necessary, be unleashed upon the defenseless Martian masses.

If that seems cruel—well, reread Wells' novel, and consider that these are the heirs of the creatures that unleashed that dreadful chaos upon Earth. We cannot allow them an opportunity to finish what their exiles began!

Lawrence Watt-Evans is the author of some three dozen novels and over a hundred short stories, mostly in the fields of fantasy, science fiction and horror. He won the Hugo Award for short story in 1988 for "Why I Left Harry's All-Night Hamburgers," served as president of the Horror Writers Association from 1994 to 1996 and treasurer of SFWA from 2003 to 2004, and lives in Maryland. He has two kids in college, a pet snake named Billy-Bob, and the obligatory writer's cat.

PAMELA SARGENT

The Martians Among Us

"...minds that are to our minds as ours are to those of the beasts that perish, intellects vast and cool and unsympathetic, regarded this earth with envious eyes, and slowly and surely drew their plans against us...."

—H. G. WELLS, *The War of the Worlds* (1898)

I FIRST READ H. G. WELLS' *The War of the Worlds* when I was around eleven years old, which has its disadvantages. For example, I don't recall being able to appreciate the irony Wells employed in various scenes, and I lacked the knowledge of history, military history in particular, that would have enabled me to admire his foresight into the future of warfare. The name of "H. G. Wells" carried no particular attraction for me, either; I had only the vaguest notion of who H. G. Wells was, although I quickly learned to seek out books that had his name attached to them. The late nineteenth- and early twentieth-century England in which *The*

War of the Worlds is set was a place I had glimpsed only through the reading of historical novels, a genre I devoured, not much caring which era provided the setting for such stories as long as it wasn't the tedious America of the late 1950s and early 1960s in which I was doomed to exist. I began reading with an unconscious expectation of nothing more than an enthralling adventure set in another time.

But reading *The War of the Worlds* at that naïve and unformed stage of my life also had its advantages, one of them being that the central idea of an alien invasion was probably as fresh and thrilling to me as it was to Wells' contemporaries. Another was that Wells had hit upon an ideal way of telling his story that could appeal to both children and adults, which may help account for this novel's continuing popularity. His narrator, even while going through the worst of his experiences, remains curious about what's going on around him, and continues struggling to understand it, in the way children do before those around them train them out of such behavior. Adults can reflect upon the narrator's more philosophical musings, while kids—those who are still curious and full of wonderment, anyway—can easily identify with the protagonist while picking up on his more somber and reflective notions at least unconsciously. The novel is also a great adventure for a child, scary and suspenseful, but with the reassurance that the narrator has survived—after all, he's telling you the story—and that you'll make it through safely, too.

At that point in my life, science fiction was pretty much unknown territory to me, except for the occasional volume taken out of the library or borrowed from a neighbor. I had managed to escape exposure to the more lurid science fiction movies being made at the time, partly because I was a squeamish and overly suggestible child easily prone to nightmares; my parents discouraged me from going to such movies, but the fact is that I was too fearful to watch even the televised promos for them, and my avid reading of Edgar Allan Poe stories had already given me plenty of material for nightmares. But Poe's visions, however frightening and spooky, could be kept at some psychological distance, at least as long as I was awake on a sunlit day.

The War of the Worlds, however, was different. I understood that almost instinctively. My relatively cozy world (even the ever-present threat of a nuclear war in those days seemed to offer to my child's imagination only a possible opportunity to eventually throw off all social constraints and run wild) was abruptly enlarged. Something *completely alien* might cross the vast distances of space and change everything!

Yet even through this haze of childish wonderment, I somehow sensed that there was a lot more to this novel, something much deeper and more profound than simply opening my mind to the possibility of alien civilizations or invaders from another world. There was an underlying plausibility to Wells' vision that went beyond that. I felt, without knowing why, that I had glimpsed some deeply disturbing truth about the universe, something that perhaps the adults around me would have preferred to keep hidden.

• • •

"When a French steamship was sighted off the shores of Vietnam in the early nineteenth century (or so the story goes) the local mandarin-governor, instead of going to see it, researched the phenomenon in his texts, concluded it was a dragon, and dismissed the matter."

—Frances FitzGerald, *Fire in the Lake* (1972)

As a child with little mechanical aptitude, I found much of technology as mysterious as magic, so didn't fully appreciate the efforts Wells had put into imagining a suitably alien yet workable technology for his Martians. His Mars was consistent enough with my hazy images of the planet (ancient, reddish sand, maybe even canals or waterways of some kind) that I could easily accept it as real. It was only later, upon rereading *The War of the Worlds* and learning more about the world in which Wells lived, that I came to admire his ingenuity and his realism. But if that had been all there was to his novel—a well-told tale with respect for the facts as they were known during his time—*The War of the Worlds* might seem as dated now as many other works of science fiction, stories you're better off recalling fondly rather than actually trying to revisit.

This novel has never dated; it seems as immediate now as when I first picked it up, as compelling as it must have been for its first readers. There's an unfortunate tendency of some people, many of them in the entertainment industry, many of them Americans, to believe that one must be able to "identify" with the central characters in a story, especially in a movie, and that transplanting a story from its original time and place to contemporary times will make it far more appealing to a mass audience, as well as save money on set design and costumes. Maybe doing so does, and fortunately *The War of the Worlds* has survived such transplants. Orson Welles' radio broadcast in 1938 did justice to the story and lent the kind of immediacy to t⟨…⟩at readers of the novel in 1898 might have felt; listening to this ⟨…⟩y, it's easy to understand how so many people could have mist⟨…⟩ broadcast for news of an actual invasion and been thrown int⟨…⟩. Whether the Martians were attacking New Jersey and New Y⟨…⟩or London and the English countryside, the underlying plausibility and believability of Wells' story remained intact. The 1953 motion picture based on *The War of the Worlds* (another scary film I didn't get to see until I was an adult), by setting the tale in the California of that time instead of in H. G. Wells' England, was probably a good deal more frightening to most of its audience than a meticulous recreation of the novel would have been; no doubt some would have viewed such a movie more as a costume drama, at a safe remove in another time.

Yet even though *The War of the Worlds* might readily be retold in any number of ways, there are still particular pleasures to be found in the details of the author's own time and place. The flight of the narrator's brother through threatened London and the countryside toward the English Channel is just one such sequence, and perhaps an even more poignant one now, because reading these passages inevitably brings up too many images of countless refugees fleeing from the wars and violence of the twentieth and early twenty-first centuries.

I also have to confess that, as a child, such scenes didn't lose any of their terror for me by being set in a different time and place. Wells' narrator seemed so convincingly to be telling me of actual events that it was fairly easy for me to make the leap to imagining that what I was reading had actually happened, that I was reading a kind of personal history, and that the threat of a Martian invasion might still lie in our future.

· ● ·

"The most extraordinary thing to my mind, of all the strange and wonderful things that happened…was the dovetailing of the commonplace habits of our social order with the first beginnings of the series of events that was to topple that social order headlong….for the most part the daily routine of working, eating, drinking, sleeping, went on as it had done for countless years—as though no planet Mars existed in the sky."

—H. G. WELLS, *The War of the Worlds*

It may seem as though the time when people could continue going about their business as such a deadly invasion was taking place is long past. After all, we have TV now, and the Internet, along with cell phones and other such devices; if the Martians were to attack now, many of us would probably feel immediately as though we were directly threatened no matter how far away we were from their first onslaught. All we would have to do is turn on our TVs, log on to the Internet or answer our phones. Certainly we wouldn't be able to go about our daily lives as heedlessly as Wells' characters do in the passage above.

And we didn't on 9/11, a day that bears at least a superficial resemblance to the mood of the people in the earliest passages of *The War of the Worlds*. Thanks to modern communications, many of us could feel as though we were under direct assault even if we didn't live or work in downtown Manhattan or in Washington, D.C. People hundreds and thousands of miles away could imagine that their normal routines might be severely disrupted for some time to come.

But Wells, as usual, was insightful about how human beings might behave in such circumstances. Even before we were advised to go about our usual pursuits, to go on as we would have if nothing had changed, and even though contradictorily we were also inclined to think and were encouraged to believe that everything had changed, the more mundane aspects of our lives were reasserting themselves. Except for a blossoming of patriotic symbols and displays, some often annoying or ludicrous security measures and a steady erosion of civil liberties that seems oddly invisible to a lot of people, it's remarkable how little has changed in early twenty-first-century America, even if we are assured that our enemies, like Wells' Martians, still have us in their sights. It's almost as if we were mimicking the Londoners in the early sections of *The War of the Worlds* in slow motion, with years instead of days passing before the next, more devastating attack. Even the greatly changed lives of those serving in the armed forces and their families don't seem to have affected the lives of many of their neighbors. Modern communications can do as good a job of concealing realities as revealing them.

Or maybe we more closely resemble the people of the novel's conclusion, the "busy multitudes in Fleet Street and the Strand . . . the sightseers about the Martian machine that stands there still," those Wells' narrator sees as "the ghosts of the past . . . the mockery of life in a galvanised body." The narrator may be haunted by what has happened, and worrying about the possibility that the Martians may return, but there's little evidence that those around him are so preoccupied. Wells saw how readily people can dismiss any number of horrors, to fall back into our earlier and more comforting states of mind. Wells' narrator muses on the knowledge that space will no longer protect Earth, just as Americans have been forcefully reminded that oceans won't protect us, and the more reflective among us have had their outlook changed forever, yet the careless habits of the past persist.

*   *   *

"I met my first Falloojeh refugee last week. . . . As I sat staring at the woman, the horror of the war came back to me—the days upon days of bombing and shooting—the tanks blasting away down the streets, and helicopters hovering above menacingly. I wondered how she would spend the next couple of agonizing days, waiting for word from her son and husband. The worst part of it is being separated from the people you care about and wondering about their fates. It's a feeling of restlessness that gnaws away inside of you, leaving you feeling exhausted and agitated all at once. It's a thousand pessimistic voices whispering stories of death and destruction in your head. It's a terrible feeling in the face of such powerful devastation."

—"Riverbend," a pseudonymous female Iraqi Weblogger,
at the Web site "Baghdad Burning"
(http://riverbendblog.blogspot.com/), 2004

Wells' portrayal of the Martians, if not exactly sympathetic, also isn't unthinkingly condemnatory of the aliens. There is no malice in their decision to invade, only a need to survive and to seize the resources the Earth has to offer. Presumably they entertain no thoughts of glory, of proving their heroism in battle or of bringing a better way of life to Earth's inhabitants; they are simply abandoning a dying world for a living one. Perhaps the Martians, lacking our emotions, can be more honest about their motives, and as Wells acknowledges, humankind has had plenty of experience in dehumanizing fellow human beings in order to justify war against them. The preemptive strike is a notion his Martians might well have had.

The Martians in *The War of the Worlds* have worn out their own planet, and it's not hard to believe, given the accumulating evidence, that we are well on the way to exhausting our own. Behind the events of our own day, and the violence and disruption being endured by the contemporary equivalents of Wells' infantryman, curate, the Elphinstone women, the fearful but observant narrator and the nameless multitudes fleeing destruction, it isn't particularly difficult to imagine minds that are "vast and cool and unsympathetic" looking out at a world of diminished resources and "drawing their plans" to seize what is left. Whether they overlay such underlying convictions with ideas about securing an empire, conducting a holy war, fighting against terror or battling imperialism may be only for the benefit of the less insightful and less ruthless, those of us who would prefer to believe that those who rule us have only our best interests at heart.

It may be our misfortune, and our tragedy, that *The War of the Worlds* will always be a novel that will speak to humankind, and that we will continue to see ourselves not only in its human characters, but in Wells' Martians as well.

Pamela Sargent has won the Nebula Award and the Locus Award and has been a finalist for the Hugo Award. Her books include the historical novel *Ruler of the Sky*, the alternate history *Climb the Wind* and the science fiction novels *The Shore of Women, Venus of Dreams, Venus of Shadows* and *Child of Venus*. She has also edited several anthologies, among them *Women of Wonder, The Classic Years* and *Women of Wonder, The Contemporary Years*. Her most recent collection of short fiction is *Thumbprints*. She lives in Albany, New York.

STEPHEN BAXTER

H. G. Wells' Enduring Mythos of Mars

IN THE MORE THAN A CENTURY that has passed since the first publication of H. G. Wells' *The War of the Worlds*, the reality of Mars, exposed by remote observations and spacecraft visits, has shaped and reshaped the imaginatively constructed Mars of science fiction. But certain key tropes which Wells established right at the beginning of Martian science fiction have endured to the present day, ideas which even have echoes in the latest science. These tropes are: the notion of Mars as an old, dying world; Mars as the site of a superior civilization capable of great wisdom and tremendous feats of engineering; and Mars as a source of invaders.

Wells' book deserves its survival just on its merits as a great piece of literature. But the ideas captured and shaped by Wells exert influence far beyond readers of his fiction.

* * *

Wells' Mars was based on the understanding of his scientific contemporaries. And that understanding was best expressed in the marvelous visions of Percival Lowell.

Wells was writing after three centuries of detailed observations of Mars. Galileo had observed Mars through his early, crude telescope in 1610, but saw little more than the planet's phases. The first useful drawing of Mars was made by Christiaan Huygens in 1659. In 1666, Giovanni Cassini spotted white polar caps. In 1837, Wilhelm Beer and Johann von Madler spotted a "wave of darkening": a seasonal variation of albedo near the north polar cap. Mars' two moons were discovered by Asaph Hall in 1877. And Secchi, in the 1860s, and Schiaparelli, in 1877, observed, in the moments of apparent clarity allowed by Earth's turbulent atmosphere, what seemed to be linear features on the tiny, blurred Martian disc. Schiaparelli called these lines channels—in Italian, "canali."

The time was ripe, with these partial and dubious observations, for a most fantastic and wonderful hypothesis to be drawn.

Percival Lowell was a good American astronomer who ingeniously observed, among other things, dust storms in the Martian atmosphere. But he let Schiaparelli's language of "canali" overwhelm him. In 1895 Lowell published a book called *Mars* in which he spun a story of a cool, arid, dying world; he later followed it with several similar works.

On Lowell's antique Mars there were great red deserts and shrinking tracts of arable land. An intelligent race of Martians had unified politically to build irrigation canals thousands of miles long, in order to transport meltwater from the polar caps to their desiccating fields. This great civilization had mown down any awkward mountains in the way, so Mars' surface was flat—as Lowell believed he had observed. And Beer and von Madler's "wave of darkening" must be vegetation, which bloomed across the dusty plains every Martian spring.

As you might expect, this terrific paradigm evoked an immediate response from science fiction writers. Edgar Rice Burroughs' Barsoom series, begun in 1912, would extend to eleven volumes over thirty years. Burroughs' books are gorgeous, entertaining and completely daft—but their scenario is not all that far, give or take a few egg-laying princesses, from Lowell's "scientific" narrative.

And, of course, another strand of the Lowellian tapestry was woven by H. G. Wells: the impact of the Martians on *us*. In *The War of the Worlds* Wells' Martians, those "intellects vast and cool and unsympathetic [who] regarded this world with envious eyes," sprang directly from the canal-irrigated soil of Lowell's Mars. It is a small step from a titanic struggle to save one dying world to a vaster ambition to seize another, younger globe.

Wells had his Martians raining down in then-contemporary Surrey, using techniques of what we would now call "faction" to generate a powerful sense of fear and paranoia. Wells' tale derives authority from the contemporary paradigm of Mars as a failing abode for life, and draws its power from allegory: Wells was pricking the complacency of the late Victorian English by giving them a taste of being on the receiving end of a hostile colonization. The paranoiac impact of Wells' story would survive several updatings, on radio, in the movies and on TV, though the allegorical allusions would change: George Pal's 1953 film version set in Los Angeles, for instance, taps into Cold War fears.

Once Wells had opened the floodgates, the Martian invaders kept on coming. The Martians of *Two Planets* by Kurd Lasswitz come to Earth to create a utopia, but most invaders were less benign. In William Cameron Menzies' movie *Invaders from Mars* (1953), the big-brained alien leader has curiously Wellsian echoes. In *Red Planet Mars* (1952), directed by Harry Horner, a message apparently received from Mars is actually faked by an ex-Nazi who hopes to panic the Western world: Martian invaders are always the embodiment of our contemporary fears and anxieties.

While all this was going on, the astronomers made slow but steady progress in unveiling the Mars of science.

• • •

In the first decades of the twentieth century the atmosphere and surface of Mars were measured with thermocouples and spectrometers. Soon it emerged that Mars was too cold to sustain liquid water. Lowell's grandiose network of canals could have no purpose: Burroughs' Barsoom slowly crumbled. Still, Mars was believed to be a home away from home, basically Earthlike, with an atmospheric pressure maybe a tenth of Earth's and at least some water around. Probably Mars held life, but it would be rather feeble: dour, unthreatening stuff, perhaps plants with tough, leathery skin to retain water.

Mars was now a place to explore. In Arthur C. Clarke's *The Sands of Mars* (1951), you can walk around on Mars with nothing but a breathing mask ("Make sure the sponge rubber fits snugly around your neck!"), and the heroes find primitive, constrained life.

This vision of Mars became something of an obsession with the great space engineers of the mid-twentieth century. The planet was seen as the first great stepping stone to the stars and the beginning of an infinite future for humankind. In 1953, in *The Mars Project*, Wernher von Braun, who in the 1960s would build the Apollo program that reached the Moon, proposed a Mars mission on a heroic scale, with ten four-thousand-ton spacecraft; the astronauts would have glided down to the surface in shuttles buoyed up by the thick atmosphere. During the 1960s, under von Braun's leadership, NASA continued to push for a Mars mission, and in 1969 came desperately close to receiving approval to carry on after *Apollo* and fly to Mars by 1986, using *Saturn V* and nuclear rocket technology.

But in this period, though the scientific view of Mars had changed utterly since Lowell's day, the notion of Mars as a dying world, a trope Wells had crystallized from Lowell's musings, still lingered in the imagination. In Ray Bradbury's *The Martian Chronicles* (1950) the planet is strewn with canals and crystal cities, and haunted by the ghosts of a vanished civilization. Earthmen who arrive are equally haunted by the ghosts and their own guilt. In a way Bradbury's work is an exercise in nostalgia for the vanished dream of Barsoom.

Elsewhere another Wellsian trope, Mars as the home of an ancient and powerful civilization, endured. Robert Heinlein's *Stranger in a Strange Land* (1961) features a human raised by all-wise Martians, who returns to Earth to build a religious philosophy from the alien cultural heritage and uses Martian psi-powers to become a messiah figure. More holier-than-us Martians are encountered in C. S. Lewis' *Out of the Silent Planet* (1938), a religious allegory in which wise spiritual Martians inform the hero that Earth (the eponymous silent planet) is fallen.

The news from Mars itself, however, was about to get worse.

• • •

In 1964, the space probe *Mariner 4* made a close flyby of the planet. In the words of the U.S. Information Service's booklet on the mission, "Where astronomers had expected to find features similar to those on Earth, *Mariner 4*'s pictures clearly showed a terrain resembling that of the Moon. Huge craters pocked the surface...." *Craters,* despite the fact that *Mariner 4* had been directed over an area where, even in 1964, canals (if no longer believed to be built by intelligence) had been expected. A million dreams died with a single, grainy snapshot.

Space insiders believe that the disappointment of *Mariner 4* killed off the post-Apollo space program; von Braun died in 1977 without seeing his final dream of a Mars mission come true.

As more probes followed *Mariner 4*, the early images of Mars were further dismantled. The "wave of darkening" was nothing to do with vegetation, just clouds and evaporation around the polar caps. The air of Mars, which had been thought to be equivalent to Earth's at an altitude of maybe twice the height of Everest, was actually more like the edge of space. In the 1970s the Viking landers carried experiments to look for Earthlike life. They found some odd chemistry, but the Martian soil appeared to be not just dead but actually sterilized—blasted free of organic molecules, presumably by the sun's ultraviolet light. It was all a shattering disappointment.

But, remarkably, Wells' tropes continued to echo in the thinking of the scientists as they picked through the new data. In 1973, to account for the dried-up riverbeds the spacecraft had observed, Carl Sagan proposed that Mars oscillates between phases when the atmosphere is dense and "Long Winters," such as now, when most of the atmosphere is frozen as carbon dioxide ice at the north pole. In 25,000 years the tipping of Mars' axis will reverse the situation, with all the atmosphere frozen in the south; but between those extremes, as the air washes from one pole to the other, there will be a huge excursion in atmospheric pressure, sufficient to allow a warm, moist surface environment. So Mars is not dying, only sleeping.

And we continue to dream of powerful Wellsian civilizations on Mars—not in the past, but in the future.

The first serious fictional attempt to terraform Mars, to make it like the Earth, seems to have been Arthur C. Clarke's *The Sands of Mars,* in which Phobos becomes a miniature sun—although Edgar Rice Burroughs' Barsoom stories featured an air-making machine, and a similar machine is used to terraform the planet in a matter of minutes in the 1990 movie *Total Recall.*

Sagan's Long Winter model of Mars' climate led to the first scientific terraforming suggestions, from Sagan himself, among others. If the poles locked up an atmosphere's worth of carbon dioxide, as was believed, Martian spring might be advanced if the polar caps were destabilized, for instance by reducing their albedo with a layer of dust or plants. More speculatively, the planet's precessional cycle might be adjusted with an artificial moon.

Sagan's model did not last long, however. The Viking probes of 1976 determined that the permanent northern cap was predominantly water ice; even if they melted completely the polar caps could not raise the atmospheric pressure by the orders of magnitude required for Sagan's model.

Further, the apparently water-carved features were much more than a few thousand years old. Mars' winter is much longer than Sagan feared.

However, terraforming schemes have continued to be drawn up. All these schemes have echoes of Lowell and Wells, for they are all based on the idea that Mars is a failing world in need of the touch of intelligence to keep it alive—but now we are the planetary engineers, not the Martians.

Sometimes, even the details of the terraformers' dreams echo Lowell. In Lowell's scheme the Martian polar ice caps, as the source of water for the canals, were crucial: "Both polar caps would be pressed into service in order to utilise the whole available [water] supply and also to accommodate most easily the inhabitants of each hemisphere" (from *Mars as the Abode of Life*, 1908). In modern schemes, water and carbon dioxide are also expected to be found in aquifers and the Martian soil, but melting the polar caps' exposed ice is often a vital first step. James Lovelock (of the Gaia hypothesis) described a (fictional) scheme to "green Mars" by using CFC greenhouse gases to melt the poles and kick-start a runaway greenhouse effect.

The greatest fictional evocation of terraforming is the trilogy by Kim Stanley Robinson, *Red Mars* (1992), *Green Mars* (1993) and *Blue Mars* (1996), a grand saga about the colonization and ultimate terraforming of Mars. However, the ethical dilemma of terraforming, as explored by Robinson, is that if Mars were made like Earth, Mars as it exists today, with its volcanoes and canyons and deep, silent history, would be turned to slush and mud.

Meanwhile the image of Mars changed again.

· ● ·

In 1996, a remarkable new message about life on Mars emerged from a nondescript bit of rock in a Houston lab. NASA engineers boldly announced that they believed a meteorite from Mars contained traces of ancient, fossilized life. A new Mars was born in our minds—and yet, once more, the new world retained an inheritance from Wells' original.

Once, we now believe, in its very earliest days, Mars was warm and wet. Perhaps life self-started there, just as on Earth, and perhaps it briefly flourished—but Mars, too small, too far from the sun, quickly settled into a permanent Ice Age. Life could only have survived by huddling deep underground, sustained by Mars' inner heat. Works envisioning this new Mars include *The Secret of Life* by Paul McAuley (2001), Geoffrey A. Landis' *Mars Crossing* (2000), Gregory Benford's *The Martian*

Race (1999) and *White Mars* (1999) by Brian Aldiss and Roger Penrose. Even Hollywood has discovered the new Mars. In the movie *Mission to Mars* (2000), ancient life on Mars seeded Earth—but this time the Martians were not meteorite-riding bugs but humanoids, wiped out by a comet.

But still the Wellsian paradigms endure. The story of NASA's archaic microbe-world is just like Lowell's, except the dying of Mars is set not in our present day, but aeons in the past—and the Martians are not canal-builders, but humble bugs who never got a chance.

McAuley's *The Secret of Life* concerns yet another invasion of Earth by Mars. But in a series of inversions of the Wellsian paradigm, this time we bring the Martians here, as bugs which readily attack us and devastate our ecology. (It is ironic: in Wells' novel the invading Martians were killed off by earthly bugs; in McAuley's book the invaders *are* bugs.) However, the deeper meaning of the fiction has moved on. In Wells' prototype the Martians were allegories of imperial invaders, thus speaking to Victorian-age fear and guilt; McAuley's Martians, imagined in our new century, embody modern fears of out-of-control biology and ecological collapse.

But there is a new development. If meteorites like NASA's famous Mars rock sail regularly between our worlds, perhaps they can transport not just traces of life, but life itself. It is possible that those putative Mars bugs in NASA's meteorite are actually Earthlings—or maybe the transfer worked the other way; maybe we're all Martians. What a wonderful twist to this ancient tale!

* • *

Our modern view of Mars, in fiction and science, clearly draws on the tropes H. G. Wells extracted from Percival Lowell's visions, expertly mythologized and cemented into our racial awareness. Mars is still a dying world, though now we have pushed its brief youth much deeper into the past than Wells imagined. Martians continue to invade, though now they are bugs rather than complex multicelled beings (and they may be our own lost cousins). And a mighty canal-building civilization may exist on Mars—but in the future, not the past, and the Martians will be us.

The science moves on; the detail changes. But perhaps there is, after all, only one story to be told of Mars—the one H. G. Wells told us so brilliantly in 1898.

Further Reading

Patrick Moore, *Patrick Moore on Mars*, London, 1998. The history of
    Martian observations.
Martyn Fogg, *Terraforming: Engineering Planetary Environments*,
    Warrendale, PA, 1995. Ideas on the terraforming of Mars.
Stephen Baxter, *The Hunters of Pangaea*, Boston, 2004. Contains an
    essay on changing images of Mars in science fiction and science.

Stephen Baxter was born in Liverpool, England, in 1957. He is a chartered
engineer. He applied to become a cosmonaut in 1991—aiming for the guest
slot on *Mir* eventually taken by Helen Sharman—but fell at an early hurdle.
His first professionally published short story appeared in 1987, and his science
fiction novels have been published in the U.K., the U.S. and many other countries. His most recent books include *Exultant* (Del Rey, 2005), part of a series
called Destiny's Children; and *Time's Eye* (Del Rey, 2004), the first of a new
collaborative series with Sir Arthur C. Clarke called *A Time Odyssey.*

JACK WILLIAMSON

The Evolution
of the Martians

DARWIN'S *ORIGIN OF SPECIES* was published in 1859. Victorian England met the idea of evolution with angry skepticism. Outraged churchmen assaulted it. Darwin himself was too shy to speak for it; the stress of having guests for dinner could put him to bed for a couple of days. His great defender was the biologist Thomas Henry Huxley, "Darwin's bulldog," who bested Bishop Samuel Wilberforce in a famous debate in 1866, the year H. G. Wells was born. Wells learned evolution as a student of Huxley himself.

Describing the class in his autobiography, he writes of the "excitement of continual discoveries...filling up new patches in the great jigsaw puzzle...[a] sweepingly magnificent series of exercises.... It was a grammar of form and a criticism of fact. That year I spent in Huxley's class was beyond all question the most educational year of my life." He was nineteen then. When the time came, it created his Martians.

Victoria's long reign (1837–1901) was an age of change. Wells' own life was shaped by its impact. The knowledge of evolution he got from Huxley made him a major voice of change, first in the science fiction he wrote in the final years of her reign, then in four decades of effort to warn and educate the world to survive the future change he feared.

He was born into a sharply stratified society. His parents were upper servants, above lower servants but below those at better levels of wealth, education and social rank. His father, Joseph Wells, was a head gardener who couldn't hold a job. His mother, Sarah, was a lady's maid, but made of sterner stuff and more important in his life.

Piously religious, she taught him the fundamentalist faith that gave him nightmares of hellfire. Trying to fit him for a better social level, she apprenticed him to a chemist (a druggist) and then a draper (a dry goods dealer). He lacked the Latin for the first. After two years of the twelve-hour days of tedious toil, he rebelled against the other.

Making his own way in life became a bitter struggle against poverty, ignorance and the whole social system. His mother sent scraped shillings to pay his fees at a little private school instead of sending him to the free national school, because that had a lower social rating. He read when he could, and his mind kept growing. He summed up his early personal and literary career in 1895 in a letter to an editor.

> I was born at a place called Bromley in Kent, suburb of the damnest, in 1866, educated at a beastly little private school there until I was thirteen, apprenticed to all sorts of trades...became a kind of teaching scholar to him, got a scholarship at the Royal College of Science, S. Kinsington (1884), worked there three years...failed my last year's examination (geology), wandered in the wilderness of private school teaching, had a lung haemorrhage, got a London degree B.Sc. (1889) with first and second class honors, private coaching...article in the *Fortnightly* (1890)...had haemorrhage for the second time (1893), chucked coaching and went for journalism.... Found *Saturday Review* when Harris bought the paper. *Review of Reviews* first paper to make a fuss over *Time Machine*—for which I shall never cease to be grateful.

The lung hemorrhages were due to tuberculosis. Overworked and poorly fed, Wells was a natural victim. The disease forced him to stop teaching. Living a Darwinian drama of competition and survival, he tried journalism and finally found his fitness as a writer. The letter is a summary of his strenuous climb out of his social class, out of poverty, sickness and failure, to the sudden literary success that came in 1895 with his short stories and *The Time Machine*. *The Invisible Man* followed in 1897 and *The War of the Worlds* in 1898. All his great science fiction was done by 1901, the year he published *The First Men in the Moon*, and the year of Victoria's death.

In his private life he was also escaping the Victorian mold. Sex had been an unspeakable word, women a subject class, roles of gender strictly fixed. He found the enterprise to break the mold, first at age fourteen, with a curious and experimental cousin a few years older. He says he didn't enjoy it, but he did better with another cousin, Isabel, who became his first wife.

That marriage began happily enough. He says their love was mutual, but her mind was no match for his. "In spite of differences, marriage and divorce, [we remained] friendly and confident of one another to the end of her days, but I think we should have been brother and sister."

A small man with a cockney voice, he had a charisma that led to liaisons with women more nearly his intellectual equals. While still a teacher, he fell in love with an able student, Amy Catherine Robbins, ran away with her and married her when he could. That union did better than the first. He writes that "I could talk of ideas and ambitions more freely than I had ever done before." The marriage lasted. She typed and criticized his manuscripts and managed his investments till the end of her life.

She tolerated his search for an ideal lover that never ended. He had affairs with other brilliant and beautiful women, most notably Rebecca West, with whom he had a son. That search for an ideal companion led him to grapple with Victorian standards of gender and sex. With such novels as *Ann Veronica*, he campaigned for sexual freedom and rights for women.

The whole of his early life mirrors the seismic changes of the age, a revolt against the dogmas that had ruled religion and every field of life. The theory of evolution was the driving engine, though myriad other forces were at work. When Victoria was crowned in 1837, the British Empire ruled half the world. The nation was stable, times prosperous, orthodox religion solidly established. As Bishop Ussher had calculated the date, God created the universe in the year 4004 B.C. The future was determined, the world a sort of clock set to run forever with no more divine attention. The doctrine of predestination made the future as unchangeable as the past.

Slowly but surely as a glacier flowing, the old order gave way to the new. The last vestiges of the feudal system were fading into private capitalism. Steam power, replacing muscle power, was ushering in the Industrial Age, altering every avenue of life and history. Charles Lyell's *Principles of Geology* (1830), with his convincing evidence that creation must have required long ages rather than only seven days, challenged Ussher's chronology. The Boer War (1899–1902) signed the coming collapse of Victoria's empire.

The greatest single shock to frozen thought and habit was certainly Darwin's *Origin of Species*. The theory of evolution shattered past certainties beneath the impacts of an uncertain future. It made the universe a natural thing, not a miraculous divine creation. The world was no longer ruled by divine fiat, but by comprehensible natural law. Man became part of nature, no longer a hapless puppet, damned or saved at the whim of an angry God. We were set free to think for ourselves.

Churchmen fought a stubborn resistance, a long war that creationists still wage today. Accepted as fact and no longer debatable theory, evolution opened the mind of the world to kinder realms of religion, to new directions in science and philosophy, to advances in everything from art and literature to zoology to politics. It paved the way for Freud's psychology, Einstein's relativity and Heisenberg's principle of uncertainty. Human history became process, continued change inevitable.

Wells had taught biology and written a little schoolbook on it, but it was that year as Huxley's student that shaped his whole career and made him first of all the chief creator of modern science fiction. Before him, Verne and Poe and Mary Shelley had pioneered the path, but they lacked the future vision, the sense of the world as flow, that Wells got from his classes with Huxley.

Evolution taught him that change is not always upward. Huxley had never taught evolution as the natural path to human perfection. He wrote, "The theory of evolution encourages no millennial anticipations. If, for millions of years, our globe has taken the upward road, the summit will be reached and the downward route will be commenced. The most daring imagination will hardly venture the suggestion that the power and intelligence of men can ever arrest the procession of the great year."

Wells was no more optimistic. One of his early essays had been titled "The Extinction of Mankind." The "round black things" flopping about the beach under the dying sun at the end of *The Time Machine* display his vision of the final men. Discussing that story in *Evolution and Ethics*, Huxley writes, "[T]he survival of the fittest might bring about, in the vegetable kingdom, a population of more and more stunted and humbler organisms, until the 'fittest' that survived might be nothing but lichens, diatoms, and such microscopic organisms as those which give snow its red color."

In my book, *H. G. Wells: Critic of Progress*, I read his science fiction as framed by the limits he saw. In *The Time Machine* he follows our future evolution to the end. The rise of civilization leads to its fall. The Eloi, descended from the old upper class, are no longer able to care for themselves. The gray Morlocks, children of the working class, live underground and work underground machines and raise the Eloi for food.

My own little book considers the way Wells used the limits to progress as dramatic themes. The limits are cosmic, as when the sun dies in *The Time Machine* or when the Martians cross space to invade the Earth. They are human, as when Dr. Moreau's humanlike creations revert to the animals they had been. Ironically, progress can limit itself, as in *The War of the Worlds*.

Except perhaps for *The Time Machine*, *The War of the Worlds* is no doubt Wells' greatest work. Not yet writing to teach, persuade or reform, he was still discovering the power of the literary art that carried him out of his long struggle to escape poverty and illness. He had two households to support, his first wife's and his own, but he wrote for more than money. He was exhilarated with his newly developed gifts and rejoicing in their command. He says, "I continued to write with excitement and industry, I found that ideas came to hand more and more readily." The short stories came to him easily, sometimes two or three a week. The novels are still exciting entertainment, but they were inspired by the sense of the world he had gained from the theory of evolution.

Though *The War of the Worlds* was certainly not written to make any conscious point, it may be seen as a sermon on evolution and the survival of the fittest. Invading Earth, the Martians were fighting for their lives.

The secular cooling that must some day overtake our planet has already gone far.... That last stage of exhaustion, which is still for us incredibly remote, has become a present-day problem for the inhabitants of Mars. The immediate pressure of necessity has brightened their intellects, enlarged their powers, and hardened their hearts. And looking across space with their instruments, and intelligences such as we have scarcely dreamed of, they see ... our own warmer planet, green with vegetation and grey with water.

And we men, the creatures who inhabit this earth, must be to them as alien as the monkeys and lemurs to us. The intellectual side of man already admits that life is an incessant struggle for existence, and it would seem that this too is the belief of the minds upon Mars. Their world is far gone in its cooling and this world is still crowded with life, but crowded only with what they must regard as inferior animals. To carry warfare sunward is, indeed, their only escape from the destruction that generation after generation creeps upon them.

One night our astronomers see a flare of light on the face of Mars and another on the next night, until there are ten. These are the muzzle flashes of a gigantic cannon that sends the Martian invaders to Earth in ten huge cylinders. Night by night, they fall in and around London.

Wells discussed the art of his fantasies, a skill he might have borrowed from Daniel Defoe. It is "the method of bringing some fantastically possible or impossible thing into a commonplace group of people and working out their reactions with the greatest gravity and reasonableness."

"As soon as the magic trick has been done," he writes in the preface to *Seven Famous Novels*, "the whole business of the fantasy writer is to keep everything else human and real. Touches of prosaic detail are imperative, and a rigorous adherence to the hypothesis. Any *extra* fantasy outside the cardinal assumption immediately gives the whole thing a touch of irresponsible silliness to the invention. So soon as the hypothesis is launched the whole interest becomes the interest of human feelings and human ways, from the new angle that has been acquired. One must keep the whole story within the bounds of a few human experiences."

To do that, he has the events of the story reported in a documentary style by a thoughtful journalist patterned after himself. Historian rather than hero, the narrator is caught in the center of the action. He relates his own experiences and speculates on wider implications. To present a broader picture, he includes the story of a brother who was outside of London. When the first cylinder falls, the narrator is "alone at that hour and writing in my study."

His friend Ogilvy was among the first to reach the cylinder in the pit its impact had made.

The heather was on fire eastward, and a thin blue smoke rose against the dawn. The Thing itself lay almost entirely buried in the sand.... The uncovered part [was] caked over and its outline softened by a thick scaly dun-coloured incrustation.... [H]e noticed that some of the grey clinker that covered the meteorite was falling off the circular edge of the end.... A large piece came off and fell with a sharp noise that brought his heart into his mouth....

And then he perceived that, very slowly, the circular top of the cylinder was rotating.... Then the thing came upon him in a flash. The cylinder was artificial—hollow—with an end that screwed out! And something in the cylinder was unscrewing the top!

Notice the careful introduction of the Martians and the reason for their migration, the deliberate use of convincing descriptive details to build reality and suspense, Ogilvy's shock of horror, the air of accurate precision. A whole chapter intervenes before the narrator himself sees Martians.

I looked again at the cylinder and ungovernable terror gripped me. I stood petrified and staring.

A big greyish rounded bulk, perhaps the size of a bear, was rising slowly and painfully out of the cylinder. As it bulged up and caught the light, it glistened like wet leather.

Two large dark-coloured eyes were regarding me steadfastly. The mass that framed them, the head of the thing, it was rounded, and had, one might say, a face. There was a mouth under the eyes, the lipless brim of which quivered and panted, and dropped saliva. The whole creature heaved and pulsed convulsively. A lank tentacular appendage gripped the edge of the cylinder, another swayed in the air.

Those who have never seen a Martian can scarcely imagine the strange horror of its appearance. The peculiar V-shaped mouth with its pointed upper lip, the absence of brow ridges, the absence of a chin beneath the wedge-like lower lip, the incessant quivering of this mouth, the Gorgon groups of tentacles... above all the extraordinary intensity of the immense eyes—were at once vital, intense, inhuman, crippled, and monstrous.... I was overcome with disgust and dread.

Yet monstrous as they are, the Martians have their roots in the evolution of mankind. In 1885, back when Wells was Huxley's student, he had written a paper on "The Past and Present of the Human Race." He went further in a later essay, "The Man of the Year Million" (1893). The narrator of *The War of the Worlds* refers to it.

It is worthy of remark that a certain speculative writer of quasi-scientific repute, writing long before the Martian invasion, did forecast for man a final structure not unlike the Martians....He pointed out...that the perfection of mechanical appliances must ultimately supersede limbs; the perfection of chemical devices, digestion; that such organs as hair, external nose, teeth, ears, and chin are no longer essential parts of the human being, and that the natural selection would lie in the diminution through coming ages. The brain alone remained a cardinal necessity. Only one other part of the body had a strong case for survival, and that was the hand, 'teacher and agent of the brain.' While the rest of the body dwindled, the brain would grow larger....

To me it is quite credible that the Martians may be descended from beings not unlike ourselves, by a gradual development of brain and hands (the latter giving way to delicate tentacles at last)....Without the body the brain, of course, would become a mere selfish intelligence, without any of the emotional substratum of the human being.

In *The Time Machine*, he follows the future evolution of mankind to the end.

At the vividly imagined conclusion of that story, at the end of human time, the traveler sees a black thing flopping about a desolate beach below a dying sun.

A horror of this great darkness came upon me. The cold, that smote my marrow, and the pain I felt in breathing overcame me. I shivered, and a deadly nausea seized me....As I stood sick and confused I saw again the moving thing upon the shoal....It was a round thing, the size of a football, perhaps...and tentacles trailed down from it; it seemed black against the weltering blood-red water, and it was hopping fitfully about.

This image of the last man finds shape in the round black things hopping about that desolate beach as the world ends in *The Time Machine*, but also in the vast brain of the Grand Lunar in *The First Men in the Moon*. With no digestive systems, the Martians don't eat. They are vampires, living on injected blood. They come not to kill us but to milk us for our blood.

And they come well-equipped. Raising a periscope out of the pit where the cylinder fell, a tall pole with a mirror at the top, they turn it to survey the space around them. When people approach, waving a flag, trying to reach some friendly understanding, they incinerate the "deputation" with a deadly Heat-Ray. This sweeps the space around the pit, burning trees and houses. They leave the pit in a war machine that stalks the landscape on three long stilt-like legs, spreading destruction. Defense is useless. Another cylinder falls every twenty-four hours, landing more Martians to build more machines. Armed with "Black Smoke," as well as the Heat-Rays, they march against London. The Heat-Ray explodes guns and slaughters men. The Black Smoke forms deadly black dust. The human defenders are quickly overrun.

The narrator's brother describes the exodus from London.

Before dawn the black vapor was pouring through the streets....

So you understand the roaring wave of fear that swept through the greatest city in the world just as Monday was dawning—the stream of flight rising swiftly to a torrent, lashing in a foaming tumult round the railway stations, banked up into a horrible struggle about the shipping in the Thames, and hurrying by every available channel northward and eastward. By ten o'clock the police organization, and even the railway organisations, were losing coherence, losing shape and efficiency, guttering, softening, running at last in that swift liquefaction of the social body....

Never before in the history of the world had such a mass of human beings moved and suffered together. The legendary hosts of Goths and Huns, the hugest armies Asia has ever seen, would have been but a drop in that current. And this was no disciplined march, it was a stampede—a stampede gigantic and terrible—without order and without a goal, six million people, unarmed and unprovisioned, driving headlong. It was the beginning of the rout of civilisation, of the massacre of mankind.

Toward the end of the novel, the homeless narrator penetrates the silent streets of dead London. He comes upon dead bodies and the black powder that killed them. He hears a strange remote wailing, "a voice for [the] fear and solitude. Ulla, ulla, ulla, ulla." He breaks into a public house and finds biscuits and cheese, though the meat-safe holds nothing but maggots. Wandering on, he finds Martians dead in their fallen machines, dogs and birds feeding upon them. The "ullas" were the cries of a dying Martian. Invincible to human weapons, they were vulnerable to our bacteria.

Those germs of disease have taken toll of humanity—taken toll of our

prehuman ancestors since life began here. But by virtue of this natural
selection of our kind we have developed resisting power; to no germ
do we succumb without a struggle....But there are no bacteria on
Mars, and directly those invaders arrived, directly they drank and fed,
our microscopic allies began their overthrow.

At first glance, this might be seen as an easy way out for the hurried
writer in search of an ending. The critic might take it as a defect in story
structure, a violation of the principle that the conclusion of a drama
must result from the character and action of the protagonist. Looking
at it as a tragedy with the Londoners as heroes, it fails to fit the classic pattern. They do nothing to cause their downfall. But of course the
protagonists are the Martians. Sanitizing Mars, wiping out the native
bacteria, they display their hubris, the fatal flaw, the arrogant pride that
goes before the fall. Looking at it through the eyes of the evolutionist, it
is a grand panorama of the struggle for existence and the survival of the
fittest. Though our own astronauts have found no Martians, *The War of
the Worlds* remains a great novel, the work by which Wells will be best
remembered.

Jack Williamson was born in Arizona Territory in 1908. He moved to New
Mexico by covered wagon in 1915, and still lives there. A retired professor
of English at Eastern New Mexico University in Portales, he still teaches a
course there every spring semester. He has been publishing science fiction
since 1929, with an output of fifty-five novels and many shorter works. His
new novel, *The Stonehenge Gate*, is out this year. One section of it, "The
Ultimate Earth," won the Hugo and Nebula Awards. He has published *H.
G. Wells: Critic of Progress*, an academic study of Wells' early science fiction.

DAVID GERROLD

Wars
of the Worlds

NO ONE WOULD HAVE BELIEVED in the last years of the nineteenth century that this world was being watched keenly and closely by a very human and very insightful intelligence. Well, no, that's not quite true. Lots of people would have believed that. They just might not have recognized it. But no one would have believed in the last years of the nineteenth century that a "scientific romance" (what they used to call science fiction in the last years of the nineteenth century) would have such an extraordinary literary impact.

With infinite complacency men went to and fro over the globe about their little affairs, serene in their assurance of their empire over matter. No one gave a thought to the older worlds of space as sources of human danger, or thought of them only to dismiss the idea of life upon them as impossible or improbable—except possibly a fellow named Herbert George Wells.

At most terrestrial men fancied there might be other men upon Mars, perhaps inferior to themselves and ready to welcome a missionary enterprise. Yet across the gulf of space, Wells postulated minds that are to our minds as ours are to those of the beasts that perish, intellects vast and cool and unsympathetic, regarding this earth with envious eyes, slowly and surely drawing their plans against us.

The planet Mars, Wells reminded the reader, revolves about the sun at a mean distance of 140,000,000 miles, and the light and heat it receives from the sun is barely half of that received by this world. It must be, if the nebular hypothesis has any truth, older than our world; and long before this earth ceased to be molten, life upon its surface must have begun its course. The fact that it is scarcely one seventh of the volume of the earth must have accelerated its cooling to the temperature at which life could begin. It has, Wells accurately postulated, air and water and all that is necessary for the support of animated existence.

Yet so vain is man, and so blinded by his vanity, that no writer, up to the very end of the nineteenth century, expressed any idea that intelligent life might have developed there far, or indeed at all, beyond its earthly level. Nor was it generally understood that since Mars is older than our Earth, with scarcely a quarter of the superficial area and remoter from the sun, it necessarily follows that it is not only more distant from time's beginning but nearer its end.

Today, scarcely more than a hundred years later, we are still vain. We know more, but we're still vain. *Opportunity* and *Spirit* have roved the surface of the Red Planet for a year, sending back startling images, opening the way to new challenges, new puzzles, new possibilities, creating more questions than they've answered. We know now for sure that there is water on Mars. There are hematites and sulfates and salt structures embedded in the rocks. We know the composition of the Martian atmosphere and the volcanic nature of its dirt. Vicariously, we've tasted and touched and smelled the surface. We've looked and listened and marveled. We've wondered at the fabled past of our closest neighbor. But for all of this magnificent machinery—and make no mistake, the effort has been truly heroic—most of what we have done has confirmed more than challenged Wells' original description of Mars. Bitterly cold, small, distant and very, very old. He wrote:

> The secular cooling that must someday overtake our planet has already gone far indeed with our neighbour. Its physical condition is still largely a mystery, but we know now that even in its equatorial region the midday temperature barely approaches that of our cold-

est winter. Its air is much more attenuated than ours, its oceans have shrunk until they cover but a third of its surface, and as its slow seasons change huge snowcaps gather and melt about either pole and periodically inundate its temperate zones. That last stage of exhaustion, which to us is still incredibly remote, has become a present-day problem for the inhabitants of Mars—

Well, maybe. If Mars is currently barren, it's no problem. If there's no one there to experience the situation as a problem, there's no problem. But it would be a problem if there were Martians. And it will be a problem again, when we send human beings to live permanently on Mars, very likely within our own lifetimes.

Wells wrote that the immediate pressure of necessity brightened the intellects of his fictional Martians, enlarged their powers and hardened their hearts. Yes, necessity can do that to humans as well. Looking across space with instruments, and intelligences such as we have scarcely dreamed of—orbiting lenses, interferometry, digital enhancement, etc.; okay, we're starting to dream of such things and build them ourselves—the fictional Martians looked 35,000,000 miles sunward of and saw a morning star of hope, our own warmer planet, green with vegetation and grey with water, with a cloudy atmosphere eloquent of fertility, with glimpses through its drifting cloud wisps of broad stretches of populous country and narrow, navy-crowded seas.

Well, no—but Wells couldn't possibly have known what the Earth really looked like from space. Not green, but blue. Mostly blue. The big blue marble. Some green, but a lot more brown. And a lot of white, a surface streaked with airborne moisture, the slurry of clouds that circulate our abundant wetness back and forth, to and fro, about its daily business of evaporation and erosion. We are not simply a planet where water is abundant; we are a water world. We are bags of water, spreading water, sharing water, mixing water, transforming water, moving water from place to place, using water, abusing water. We are vehicles for water.

Life is water. Life is the way that water transcends its own condition. Where water exists, life follows inevitably. That there is water on Mars today is the most significant finding in the history of sentience—it means that *we are not alone in the universe*. Even if it is only microbial, life is inevitable. Life will always find a way.

In the coming decades, the big surprise will *not* be the discovery of life on Mars—the biggest surprise will be the *absence* of life on Mars. Because that would imply that life is not as vigorous and fecund and determined as we believe. It would suggest that life is far more fragile than we want to admit.

Nevertheless, the presence of water on Mars still tells us that life is possible elsewhere. No matter what form that life may take—"It's life, Jim, but not as we know it"—no matter how it occurs or how we chance upon it, we are not alone in the universe.

That was the immediate impact of Wells' short novel. That was the awakening slap to the consciousness of the world. We are not alone. And we are not necessarily the highest possible form of sentient being in the universe.

Wells detailed the invasion of the Earth, from the first sporadic landings of cylinders here and there across the English countryside, and later across the entire planet. He postulated deadly clouds of black billowing gas (precursor of the deadly mustard gas unleashed in WWI), Heat-Rays (precursor to laser, X-ray and particle beam weapons now in development), and the ecological infestation of the deadly red weeds (the same way that European, Asian and African plants and animals have had enormous impact in North and South America, and Australia—think prickly pears and rabbits and kudzu and tumbleweeds and Africanized honeybees[1]). Wells' descriptions of death and destruction rivaled the battlefield reports from the Spanish-American War in their immediacy and horror.

By telling the story through the eyes of a fictitious narrator, seemingly identical to his own real-world identity, Wells personalized the terror, made it immediate and credible. He made his readers doubt the evidence of their own senses. Wells' account was so believable that it created its own horrific reality.

The War of the Worlds was published in 1897 as a serial in *Cosmopolitan* magazine. (No, not the same *Cosmopolitan* magazine you can buy today for fashion and beauty tips. We're talking about another *Cosmopolitan* magazine, one more in league with *Punch* or *Colliers* or the *New Yorker*.) In those days, magazines often published longer works as serials. Many English and American novels were first published in serial form, Charles Dickens' *A Tale of Two Cities* and Harriet Beecher Stowe's *Uncle Tom's Cabin*, for instance.[2] Cliffhanger endings kept the readers in suspense from one issue to the next and pushed sales up.

---

[1] Look it up. I'm not going to do all the work.

[2] Harriet Beecher Stowe only wrote one novel in her entire life, *Uncle Tom's Cabin*. The book is credited with triggering the American Civil War. This is the measure of success that every writer since then has aspired to.

One hundred and eight years later, Wells' novel still has the power to disturb us. That two separate movie versions have been scheduled for release this year—one contemporary, the other accurate to the time period of the original story—is not a coincidence. Humanity's fascination with Mars extends all the way back to the moment the first man or woman looked up at the sky and wondered about that bright red star that moved across the sky. The Romans called it Mars, the God of War. Astrologists consider it one of the most powerful of all the stellar influences. ("Mars might be in retrograde, but Mercury is still in stupid.") Wells' story tapped into the mystique of the Red Planet, but what he wrote had an impact that extended far beyond the literary realm. His story transcended itself and became a cultural icon—like *King Kong* and *The Wizard of Oz* and *Star Wars*.

Why? Because it tapped into both the cultural and the emotional roots of fear. The Martians represented an implacable, dispassionate, uncaring force. The Martians represented a troubling uncertainty, a reflection of some deeper concern about the uneasy nature of the larger universe. The story, what it suggested about the scale of destiny, evoked the growing unspoken awareness that great events could overwhelm the carefully structured order of the (so-called) civilized world.

Science fiction—as we know it today—began in the middle of the nineteenth century, with the "scientific romances" of Jules Verne. Those stories also represented the first tentative groping toward a global consciousness, an awareness of Earth as a planet. The shape of the continents was now known. Most of the world's coastlines had been mapped. Faraway lands were distant, but no longer out of reach; the world could be traversed in eighty days. Newspapers and magazines carried regular reports from distant places, exotic and alluring—from the windswept Tibetan wastelands to the wet green furnace of the Amazon. The unknown was rapidly becoming the known, and although it seemed as if the world was shrinking, the truth was that human consciousness was expanding. People were now aware that they lived on a large, but very finite globe.

But the grandiose vision is equally balanced by the extravagant nightmare, the counterweight fear. So, if the closing days of the nineteenth century promised a better future, it also threatened an equally terrifying one as well. *The War of the Worlds* was the emotional foreshadowing of that possibility. In the same way that a towering black wall of clouds on the horizon warns of a coming storm, so did Wells' novella evoke the possibility of incomprehensible horror just over the next horizon.

Wells had to be aware that the industrialization was changing the world; England, Germany, France and America were all at the forefront of the technological revolutions in manufacturing, transportation, communication and, inevitably, weaponry. It was becoming easily apparent, at least to those who were actually looking forward, that the future was going to be different from the past—*vastly* different. Wells had to have sensed that the next war, however it occurred, would bring about a scale of death and destruction hitherto unknown.

A story that predicted a human war on that scale would not have been believable, because it was too far beyond human experience. Ironically, by making the otherworldly Martians the architects of that war, Wells made the scale of the devastation frighteningly credible. It was only later—after Europe had actually experienced World War I—that Wells was able to predict a great civilization-toppling conflagration; but then again, in the days presaging WWII, *The Shape of Things to Come* wasn't a fantastic speculation—it was a much more mordant probability.

Unknown to most contemporary readers, *The War of the Worlds* spawned an immediate (and unauthorized) "sequel." Six weeks after *The War of the Worlds* was published, *Edison's Conquest of Mars* appeared as a serial in a New York newspaper. The story portrayed the famous inventor Thomas Alva Edison as the leader of an expeditionary force to counterattack the Martians.

Edison's Conquest of Mars was commissioned by the publisher of the *New York Evening Journal*, Arthur Brisbane. Inspired by the phenomenal sales figures of the Wells novel, as well as the cultural impact, he hired Garrett P. Serviss to write his own circulation-boosting science fiction adventure.[3]

Serviss is almost completely unknown in the history of science fiction. At the time, he was a forty-seven-year-old journalist, as well as a lecturer in astronomy. When Brisbane approached him to write a "sequel" to *The War of the Worlds*, Serviss went to Edison for help. Edison was too busy inventing lightbulbs, phonograph records, motion pictures, dynamos, electric motors, adhesive tape, alkaline batteries, concrete molds, electric motors, etc., etc., so he turned Serviss down; but he did agree to be featured as the hero of the story.

Unfortunately, when the newspaper published an announcement and a photograph of Edison with Serviss, the inventor objected. He felt that the newspaper was portraying him as a collaborator. Edison wrote to

---

[3] See http://members.aol.com/taedisonjr/conquest.htm for more details.

Serviss, "I am not literary with a 200 horsepower imagination like your-self, so I don't want a reputation for things I can't do." Despite Edison's polite protests, some historians suspect he was privately pleased with the attention.

Edison's Conquest of Mars began in the January 12, 1898, issue of the *Evening Journal* and ran until February 10. The story was more evoca-tive of Edgar Rice Burroughs than Herbert George Wells, but although it was well-received at the time, it did not have the same lasting literary impact. It was easily recognized as an attempt to cash in on the larger impact of the Wells story and quickly faded into obscurity.

In 1947, four dedicated science fiction fans rediscovered the original story; they obtained copies of each installment from the Library of Con-gress and formed their own publishing house. They reprinted *Edison's Conquest of Mars* in a very limited (1500 copies) edition. Unfortunately, it was also very unsuccessful, and it was the only book that the short-lived Carcosa House ever published.

An abridged version appeared in *The Treasury of Science Fiction Clas-sics*, a large hardcover anthology, published in 1954. (Most of the stories in that anthology were from the early years of the twentieth century and many were already in public domain.) In 1969, Forrest J. Ackerman edited the original story and republished it as *Invasion of Mars*, but this version was no more successful than any of the previous editions.

In his May 1999 article (*In the Groove* magazine) on *Edison's Con-quest of Mars,* Rene Rondeau observed: "It is, however, a shame that the story has not had more recognition. Aside from its historic interest as an homage to the great Edison, as well as a reflection of its times (hot on the heels of the patriotic fervor of the Spanish-American war), it is im-portant in science fiction as the first story to describe space suits (to al-low the travellers to space-walk and repair their ship), the first instance of a "ray-gun" and the first description of a battle in outer space."

There's another way to look at the story, as well. It represents an at-tempt at literary closure, an antidote to the bad news, very likely be-cause Wells' story was such an unsettling wake-up call. Wells wrote:

> At any rate, whether we expect another invasion or not, our views of
> the human future must be greatly modified by these events. We have
> learned now that we cannot regard this planet as being fenced in and
> a secure abiding place for Man; we can never anticipate the unseen
> good or evil that may come upon us suddenly out of space. It may
> be that in the larger design of the universe this invasion from Mars

is not without its ultimate benefit for men; it has robbed us of that serene confidence in the future which is the most fruitful source of decadence, the gifts to human science it has brought are enormous, and it has done much to promote the conception of the commonweal of mankind. It may be that across the immensity of space the Martians have watched the fate of these pioneers of theirs and learned their lesson, and that on the planet Venus they have found a securer settlement. Be that as it may, for many years yet there will certainly be no relaxation of the eager scrutiny of the Martian disk, and those fiery darts of the sky, the shooting stars, will bring with them as they fall an unavoidable apprehension to all the sons of men.

The broadening of men's views that has resulted can scarcely be exaggerated. Before the cylinder fell there was a general persuasion that through all the deep of space no life existed beyond the petty surface of our minute sphere. Now we see further. . . .

Considering the history of the nineteenth and twentieth centuries, it is enormously ironic for human beings to expect morality or compassion or even wisdom from any other species. And that may very well have been H. G. Wells' intention. He left his readers unsettled. And he wasn't subtle about it either. There might not be a human victory in this universe. We might not be alone, and if there are others out there, we have no reason to expect goodwill from them.

Wells did not give his readers the satisfying thud of a door slamming shut on an ugly possibility. He left it uncomfortably ajar. Humanity escaped the Martians not by our own wisdom, but by the Martians' shortsightedness. Wells was prescient enough to recognize that life exists on many different scales:

. . . stark and silent and laid in a row, were the Martians—*dead!*—slain by the putrefactive and disease bacteria against which their systems were unprepared; slain as the red weed was being slain; slain, after all man's devices had failed, by the humblest things that God, in his wisdom, has put upon this earth.

For so it had come about, as indeed I and many men might have foreseen had not terror and disaster blinded our minds. These germs of disease have taken toll of humanity since the beginning of things— taken toll of our prehuman ancestors since life began here. But by virtue of this natural selection of our kind we have developed resisting power; to no germs do we succumb without a struggle, and to

many—those that cause putrefaction in dead matter, for instance—
our living frames are altogether immune. But there are no bacteria in
Mars, and directly these invaders arrived, directly they drank and fed,
our microscopic allies began to work their overthrow. Already when I
watched them they were irrevocably doomed, dying and rotting even
as they went to and fro. It was inevitable. By the toll of a billion deaths
man has bought his birthright of the earth, and it is his against all
comers; it would still be his were the Martians ten times as mighty as
they are. For neither do men live nor die in vain.

Perhaps in the aftermath of World War I, Wells' story lost some of
its immediacy. After the Roaring Twenties and the Great Depression of
the thirties, it had slipped from public consciousness. During the thirties, much of the "civilized"[4] world had its attention directed elsewhere.
The world economy had plunged into a lasting depression; stock markets
had collapsed as hollow dollars evaporated. Fascist political parties took
advantage of the situation to seize power in Spain, Italy, and Germany.
As the decade wore on, Germany's growing military strength became a
source of world concern, and as early as 1936, it was apparent that Hitler's
territorial appetites would lead to another global conflagration.

The movies made it possible for people to see images of faraway
places and events. In 1937, the zeppelin *Hindenburg* exploded at Lakehurst, New Jersey. (It is now believed that a charge of static electricity
ignited the aluminum powder-infused fabric covering the airship.) Film
of the airship's destruction, as it fell to the ground in a flaming mass,
was shown all over the world in a matter of days. Herb Morrison's live
broadcast, describing the falling airship, is remembered as one of the
great moments in radio history. It was a forewarning of things to come,
because it allowed a whole nation to experience the emotional impact
of an event as it happened.

Perhaps, in an intellectual way, people understood that a radio broadcast could create simultaneity of experience; but they hadn't yet *experienced* the fact. On October 30, 1938, that changed when Orson Welles'
The Mercury Theatre on the Air presented H. G. Wells' *The War of the
Worlds* as a Halloween broadcast. Welles had already achieved critical
acclaim for the radio plays he directed and often starred in. With his
compelling "voice of God" presentation, Welles infused every play with

---

[4] The quotation marks are appropriate. Could you really call the behavior of the Western
nations in the thirties civilized?

importance. *The Mercury Theatre* also included such luminaries as Joseph Cotton and Agnes Moorehead.

But in his youthful exuberance (he was only twenty-three at the time), Welles made a crucial mistake. He forgot that sometimes people tune in to shows in the middle. Those who did missed the disclaimer that this was just a Halloween prank. So *The War of the Worlds* was presented as a live radio broadcast to a nation already nervous and unsettled by world events, already emotionally prepared for the now seemingly inevitable global conflagration.

Herb Morrison's frantic description of the death of the *Hindenburg* had to have been part of the inspiration for the form of the play—as it began, a program of dance music was interrupted by frantic news bulletins that a large flaming object had fallen onto a farm in Grovers Mill, New Jersey. Actors playing reporters and officials described the scene as the Martian war machines emerged and advanced toward New York City, firing Heat-Rays, destroying everything in their path. An imaginative sound effects team created the background noises of people and machines, and the even more frightening sounds of the Martian tripods:

> Good heavens, something's wriggling out of the shadow like a gray snake. Now it's another one, and another. They look like tentacles to me. There, I can see the thing's body. It's large as a bear and it glistens like wet leather. But that face. It...it's indescribable. I can hardly force myself to keep looking at it. The eyes are black and gleam like a serpent. The mouth is V-shaped with saliva dripping from its rimless lips that seem to quiver and pulsate.... The thing is raising up. The crowd falls back. They've seen enough. This is the most extraordinary experience. I can't find words. I'm pulling this microphone with me as I talk. I'll have to stop the description until I've taken a new position. Hold on, will you please, I'll be back in a minute.[5]

Some of the people listening to this simulation thought they were hearing an actual news account. People who had not heard the disclaimer had no way of knowing that this was not real. It was unlikely that they would check another station. In those days, channel surfing was an uncommon behavior; the remote control had not yet been invented. People sat in their living rooms, knitting, working puzzles, reading books, while listening to programs. In those days, people could

---

[5] See http://www.transparencynow.com/welles.htm for more information.

focus on a program for longer than fourteen minutes at a time; thus the effect of the program was compelling.

Although Grovers Mill was an entirely fictitious location, some people believed they knew where it was. They packed their belongings in cars and fled. They hid in cellars, they loaded their guns, and some even wrapped their heads in wet towels as protection from Martian poison gas. The irony is that they were becoming the panic-stricken public portrayed in the radio play. Welles and his cast did not know of the growing panic until *after* the broadcast concluded. And despite his quick apology, a national outrage grew up around the event. Welles had played a terrible trick on America. But one of the more insightful observers, Dorothy Thompson, writing in the *New York Tribune*, suggested that the broadcast revealed how demagogues could use the power of mass communications to manipulate the public. (On the other side of the Atlantic, a fellow named Joseph Goebbels was already demonstrating just that.)

Thompson wrote:

All unwittingly, Mr. Orson Welles and the Mercury Theatre on the Air have made one of the most fascinating and important demonstrations of all time. They have proved that a few effective voices, accompanied by sound effects, can convince masses of people of a totally unreasonable, completely fantastic proposition as to create a nation-wide panic.

They have demonstrated more potently than any argument, demonstrated beyond a question of a doubt, the appalling dangers and enormous effectiveness of popular and theatrical demagoguery....

Hitler managed to scare all of Europe to its knees a month ago, but he at least had an army and an air force to back up his shrieking words.

But Mr. Welles scared thousands into demoralization with nothing at all.

Other radio broadcasts produced similar panics. On November 12, 1944, in Santiago, Chile, a radio station broadcast its own version of the play—and another panic was triggered. In one province, troops and artillery were briefly mobilized. The broadcast even used an actor to impersonate the interior minister.

On February 12, 1949, in Quito, Ecuador, another Spanish-language broadcast sent tens of thousands of people running into the streets. The event was reported around the world, even on the front page of the February 14 edition of the *New York Times*. That broadcast had Martians landing in and destroying the community of Latacunga, twenty miles south of Quito, then advancing on the larger city. The program included realistic impersonations of local politicians and journalists. An actor portraying the mayor made a public announcement that the men of Quito must defend the city against the invaders. An announcer, ostensibly positioned atop Quito's tallest building, reported that he could see a giant monster advancing in the distance. That was when people fled their homes and ran through the streets, many dressed only in nightclothes. When it became known that the broadcast had been a hoax, a riot broke out. An enraged mob burned down the radio station, killing fifteen people.[6]

There have been other radio adaptations of *The War of the Worlds*. Providence, Rhode Island, on October 31, 1974, and northern Portugal, in 1988; while both of these broadcasts did produce some frightened listeners, neither triggered widespread panic.

In 1953, legendary film producer George Pal produced what some fans feel is his best film ever, *The War of the Worlds* starring Gene Barry and Ann Robinson. The film rights had been purchased in 1925 by Paramount Pictures for Cecil B. DeMille. Despite several attempts to develop a script, the DeMille film never happened. At one point in the thirties, Alfred Hitchcock also tried to secure an opportunity to make a film version. Later, after the 1938 broadcast, RKO wanted Orson Welles to make a *War of the Worlds* movie, but he decided to make *Citizen Kane* instead.

It wasn't until 1951, while finishing up *When Worlds Collide*, that George Pal decided to take on *The War of the Worlds* as his next challenge. Barre Lyndon wrote the script, Byron Haskin directed. Art director Al Nozaki designed Martian war machines to evoke both manta rays and flying saucers. The time frame of the film was moved to the present, and the first Martian cylinder comes down just north of Los Angeles, in the hills above a small town. The local residents are on hand to see the first Martians emerge, and the three men who approach the meteor waving a white flag are instantly burned to a crisp by the Martian Heat-Ray.

Very quickly, the army is brought in to dispatch the Martians, and in a direct reference to Welles' earlier broadcast, a radio announcer feverishly describes the scene to his unseen listeners until the Martian war machines advance and his radio connection is abruptly incinerated. None

---

[6] See http://www.csicop.org/si/9811/martian.html.

of the best weapons developed during World War II and the postwar era are sufficient to stop the Martians. The Martians have Heat-Rays and green disintegration plasmas, and they are immune to attack because their war machines are shielded by protective energy blisters. Even an atomic bomb, dropped from a flying wing, is insufficient to stop them.

Gene Barry, as stoic scientist Clayton Forrester, is fascinated by the Martians. He tries to get as close as possible so he can collect tangible evidence to study. Although the actual Martians are seen only briefly in the film—effectively leaving much to the viewers' imaginations—one of the most suspenseful moments has become a cinematic icon. As Gene Barry works to clear the wreckage away from the door of a broken farmhouse so that he and Ann Robinson can escape, Ann Robinson watches him from behind—and as she does so, a dark clawlike hand reaches into the frame and comes down on her shoulder. She screams. Gene Barry turns the flashlight on the Martian and the audience finally sees a ghastly hunched thing with three bright-colored eyes in a posture that is uninterpretable but appears to be curious, abject and threatening all in the same instant. But the Martians can't be trusted—they've already killed hundreds of soldiers. Gene Barry throws a board at the Martian, it flees, and so do he and Ann Robinson. (That iconic moment, the hand reaching into the frame and down onto Robinson's shoulder, has been referenced in more science fiction and horror films than I can remember or care to research. But literate film fans always recognize it.)

Eventually, the Martians advance on the city of Los Angeles. The residents flee in panic while the war machines start burning and blasting major landmarks, including one towering oil storage tank (still in existence) and the Los Angeles city hall (apparently now rebuilt).

The War of the Worlds was produced for less than one million dollars and was one of Paramount Pictures' most successful films of the year. It won an Academy Award for best special effects.[7] Even today, more than half a century later, the film remains convincing. Although some of its moments might seem quaint to a contemporary viewer ("That's funny, my watch has stopped.") the film retains a strong feeling of credibility. A remastered edition is now available on DVD.

In 1975, a made-for-television movie, *The Night That Panicked America*, portrayed how Welles and his troupe created the radio drama, and

---

[7] It's worth mentioning that in those days, there were no computer-generated effects. Everything had to be done with miniatures and traveling mattes. Because the film was shot in three-strip Technicolor, where each primary color requires its own negative, some of the effects shots required nine separate strips of film for each negative, twenty-seven in all.

how listeners reacted. Although somewhat dramatized in its presentation, the movie is a fairly accurate recreation of Welles' original broadcast and the panic that began in New Jersey. Especially interesting, it
reveals how many of the special sound effects were created.

Other movies since then have also referred to the Welles broadcast.
The 1984 cult classic *The Adventures of Buckaroo Banzai Across the Eighth
Dimension!*[8] suggests that the 1938 Martian invasion was real—actually it
was an incursion by Red Lectroids from the Eighth Dimension. The government covered up the real invasion by portraying it as a radio hoax.

Woody Allen's marvelous evocation of the thirties, *Radio Days* (1988),
also includes an episode based on the Welles broadcast. Mr. Manulis has
invited Aunt Bea on a date. Ostensibly he runs out of petrol on a dark
and foggy night. It is the night of the radio broadcast. They turn on the
radio and hear about Martians landing in New Jersey. Mr. Manulis (An-
drew Clark) runs away in fear, leaving Aunt Bea (Dianne Wiest) to walk
home alone. Or be a victim of the marauding aliens. Whatever.

In 1986, Paramount Pictures planned to create a new *Star Trek* series,
with Greg Strangis producing. But Gene Roddenberry, who had always
objected to anyone else producing *Star Trek* in any incarnation, raised
even stronger objections to a new TV series occurring without his par-
ticipation. Strangis was moved sideways, off the show, and given the job
of developing *The War of the Worlds* as a TV series. Paramount planned
to use it as a follow-up to the success of *Star Trek: The Next Generation*.

Although Strangis made a valiant effort to tie the TV series in to George
Pal's 1953 film, using the same design for his Martians and Martian war
machines, it very quickly became a labored effort; and quite frankly, the less
said about it, the better. The whole dismal mess is better left forgotten.[9]

In 1976, rock impresario Jeff Wayne created a rock opera version
of *The War of the Worlds*, released by Columbia Records. With Richard
Burton's mellifluous narration, drawn from the original novel, the music creates an eerie audio portrait of the invasion; the Martians have
their own musical motifs—distant echoing screeches evoke the terrifying cries of the invading war machines. Justin Hayward's song from this
album, "Forever Autumn," eventually became his biggest solo hit. The
album's original release on vinyl was remarkable for its audio quality as

---

[8] If you have never seen this movie, stop reading this book and go buy the DVD right now.

[9] Okay, I'll say this much. The series began with the idea that the 1953 invasion had simply been
forgotten. Um...let's see now, whole cities had been destroyed, major landmarks were gone, millions were dead—and human beings had forgotten the invasion as if it hadn't occurred...? No. I
don't think so. I only look stupid.

well as its inventiveness. The latest CD release has four bonus tracks, and the sound is now spectacular. The album has developed an enormous cult following and is well worth seeking out.

When he wrote *The War of the Worlds*, it was unlikely that Wells intended to create a whole subgenre of fiction, but in the past century, invasion stories have become a mainstay of science fiction, especially in the movies. Robert Anson Heinlein tackled the subject in his Hugo-winning novel *The Puppet Masters* and again in *Starship Troopers*, also a Hugo winner. The movie version of *The Puppet Masters* (1994) is a much better film than the movie version of *Starship Troopers* (1997); although the latter film substitutes special effects for brains, it was successful enough to spawn a direct-to-DVD sequel and a CGI animated series.

Jack Finney's *Invasion of the Body Snatchers* spawned three film versions, the first in 1956, the second in 1978, the third in 1994. Ray Harryhausen provided the special effects for *Earth vs. the Flying Saucers*, a lower-budget effort from Columbia Pictures, also released in 1956.

Independence Day (1996) is a thinly disguised retelling of *The War of the Worlds*, except in this one, human beings are able to decode the aliens' communications network and plant a nuclear bomb in the coordinating vessel, allowing contemporary weapons to penetrate the alien force fields and make satisfyingly big explosions in the theater. Translation: we're not going to wait for the bacteria to do their job. We can do it ourselves. Notice the philosophical shift from humility to self-righteousness.

Lesser films in this genre include *Spaced Invaders, Invasion of the Saucer Men,* and *Santa Claus Versus the Martians* (don't ask).

On the literary side, many science fiction authors have brought their own perspectives to the idea of invasion from space. In John Varley's novels, the aliens have simply chased human beings off the Earth and humanity exists on the Moon, Mars, the moons of Jupiter and Saturn and places even farther out. Larry Niven and Jerry Pournelle wrote *Footfall*, in which elephant-like aliens bombard the Earth with asteroids as weapons. And Christopher Priest wrote *The Space Machine* as a deliberate homage to Wells, set in the Victorian era and using *The War of the Worlds* and *The Time Machine* as starting points for a whole other adventure. (A man and a woman are shot off into space and arrive on Mars before the invasion.)[10]

---

[10] And yes, my own series of novels, The War Against The Chtorr, is also a modern-day retelling of *The War of the Worlds*—except my invasion isn't a technological one, it's an ecological infestation. Never mind, this essay is about Wells, and I will avoid all further excesses of shameless self-promotion.

Perhaps, after we step past the simple telling of the adventure, we can look at Wells' story as a metaphor for the twentieth century. A peaceful, almost idyllic era is suddenly invaded by destructive technology, shattered and broken; great masses of people are thrown into turmoil—and even though the Martians fail, the Earth can never be the same again. In Wells' own words:

> The torment was over. Even that day the healing would begin. The survivors of the people scattered over the country—leaderless, lawless, foodless, like sheep without a shepherd—the thousands who had fled by sea, would begin to return; the pulse of life, growing stronger and stronger, would beat again in the empty streets and pour across the vacant squares. Whatever destruction was done, the hand of the destroyer was stayed. All the gaunt wrecks, the blackened skeletons of houses that stared so dismally at the sunlit grass of the hill, would presently be echoing with the hammers of the restorers and ringing with the tapping of their trowels. At the thought I extended my hands towards the sky and began thanking God. In a year, thought I—in a year....

> With overwhelming force came the thought of myself, of my wife, and the old life of hope and tender helpfulness that had ceased for ever.

David Gerrold is an expert on Martians, having raised one for thirteen years.

MERCEDES LACKEY

In Woking's Image

"No one would have believed in the last years of the nineteenth century that this world was being watched keenly and closely by intelligences greater than man's and yet as mortal as his own; that as men busied themselves about their various concerns they were scrutinised and studied, perhaps almost as narrowly as a man with a microscope might scrutinise the transient creatures that swarm and multiply in a drop of water."

SO BEGINS H. G. WELLS' *The War of the Worlds*, with words which have been quoted at the beginning of virtually every treatment of this work that has ever been produced. There could be no better way to begin the story, after all; this paragraph sets the tone for the entire book—or radio play—or televised version—or movie. There is a terrible poetry in those words, an ominous tone that sets the hair up on the back of one's head, and makes one turn uneasily to look over the shoulder to see if something, after all, *is* watching....

What follows is a step-by-step description of the wreck of civilization, as mimicked in miniature by the wreck of a single "civilized" man. But what many people reading the work today don't realize is how faithfully Wells portrays that civilization; his Woking and the suburbs of London are exactly the Woking and suburbs of London at the end of the 1890s; his protagonist is very much drawn from Wells himself. Attitudes that modern readers may find incomprehensible in the work now (a hundred years removed) were things that Wells' readers took absolutely for granted. In the very largest sense, in *The War of the Worlds*, Wells was following that hoary old chestnut of advice given to all writers and would-be writers, "Write what you know."

In fact, Wells himself lived in Woking during the period in which he wrote not only *The War of the Worlds* but *The Island of Dr. Moreau, When the Sleeper Wakes, The Invisible Man* and *The First Men in the Moon.* The complacent, sleepy, self-satisfied people he describes were his neighbors. When he describes their lack of curiosity about the strange goings-on just over the hill on Horsell Common, he does so because this is how the majority of his neighbors would have reacted.

It seems incredible to us; when a large meteorite flashes across the sky these days, there are at least half a dozen videotapes of it on the news in the next couple of hours, even if the tapes are of nothing more than the reflection of its passing in the hood of a car on a security tape. If an actual object the size of one of the Martian cylinders came to Earth, there would be fifty news trucks around it within three hours. But having been reading period literature extensively for the last several years as I have done research for Edwardian "retro-urban fantasy," I found nothing surprising in the attitude at all. The average Englishman really didn't think much about anything outside his own backyard, his office and his personal concerns. So for the astronomer Ogilvy to find even Henderson, the journalist, quietly manuring the roses when the cylinder has fallen within walking distance of his house strikes my nineteenth-century sensibilities as perfectly reasonable behavior.

> . . . when he saw Henderson, the London journalist, in his garden, he called over the palings and made himself understood.
>
> "Henderson," he called, "you saw that shooting star last night?"
>
> "Well?" said Henderson.
>
> "It's out on Horsell Common now."
>
> "Good Lord!" said Henderson. "Fallen meteorite! That's good."
>
> "But it's something more than a meteorite. It's a cylinder—an artificial cylinder, man! And there's something inside."

Henderson stood up with his spade in his hand.

"What's that?" he said. He was deaf in one ear.

Ogilvy told him all that he had seen. Henderson was a minute or so taking it in. Then he dropped his spade, snatched up his jacket, and came out into the road.

Even when my twenty-first-century mind is asking, "Why isn't there a mob out there within five minutes of the fall?"

Even when a crowd does gather, it is comprised of people who simply haven't anything better to do than to gawk.

By eight o'clock a number of boys and unemployed men had already started for the common to see the "dead men from Mars." That was the form the story took.

There were four or five boys sitting on the edge of the pit, with their feet dangling, and amusing themselves—until I stopped them—by throwing stones at the giant mass. After I had spoken to them about it, they began playing at "touch" in and out of the group of bystanders.

Among these were a couple of cyclists, a jobbing gardener I employed sometimes, a girl carrying a baby, Gregg the butcher and his little boy, and two or three loafers and golf caddies who were accustomed to hang about the railway station.

Allow me, reader, to introduce you to the life of the middle-class English reader of Wells' fiction. Let me put you inside his mind. It's the mind of H. G. Wells himself, in fact—though probably a mind with less imagination. Despite having titled his work *The War of the Worlds*, Wells has to ease his audience into the notion that the civilization they know so well and are so certain will stand forever is as fragile as a soap bubble.

To begin with, you, the late-Victorian reader of H. G. Wells' "scientific romances," are probably male, and when I say "probably," I mean the likelihood that you are female is less than five percent. These were not the sort of books that women read. Even at the turn of the century, "good girls" and "proper women" weren't to trouble their minds with such wild speculations. Oxford was not to award degrees to women—though they did have a Women's College—until after the end of the First World War.

So, reader, you are male. You are probably middle-class; the working class, while not entirely illiterate, was still too busy laboring at twelve-to sixteen-hour days, seven days a week (half the day off on Sunday, perhaps, to attend church or chapel), to have time to read. This was assuming they could afford a book in the first place.

So you are male, and middle-class. You are probably a clerk of some sort, the Victorian equivalent of a white-collar worker, or a student. Your mind is more open than most of your contemporaries, who content themselves with the morning and evening papers, and the occasional volume of *Punch*. You can actually imagine that another *country* might one day invade England—and there is, at this time, some speculation that Germany might do just that, to the point where H. H. Munro ("Saki") wrote a novel on the subject. Not only that, but you can encompass the notion that another *planet* might do the same.

Middle-class, male and possessed of an imagination. But it is your surroundings that place you dramatically apart from your counterpart in 2004.

You probably live in a small house in the suburbs of a large city, a place virtually identical to Woking. You have a wife, and perhaps a child under the age of three. You have one or two servants—either a maid-of-all-work, or a maid and a cook.

You do *not* own a motorcar or a horse, and you probably do not have electric lighting, gas or water under pressure from water mains. You cannot afford a motorcar, even if there was a place in your village to get fuel for it. There is no room in your little suburban "villa" for a horse. Electric lighting, only now coming into wide use in the big cities, might be used for street lighting but will not penetrate to the houses of your suburb for another twenty years, and gas lighting will probably not be installed in your little home, nor can you yet afford to put it in. There are no water mains, although there is a sewage system. Your water has to be pumped up to cistern at the top of the house several times a day; this is one of the jobs of the maid. Your heat—fireplaces only, there is no "central" heating in houses like yours—comes from coal. Your food is cooked over the latest in coal-fired "patent" stoves, and your hot water is heated in a boiler at the back of it, to be pumped up into the bathroom. This is reckoned a vast improvement over water heated in "cans" on top of the stove and hand carried upstairs. You probably do not own more than four good suits of ascending levels of quality, some bits of old clothing that you use to work in your garden, two pairs of shoes and a pair of rubber "Wellies." You ride into the city every day on the train to work (or if you are in the city, you take the bus or the new Underground) and come home again at or after sunset.

Your wife—well, the labors of your wife, without mechanical cleaning devices or the plethora of household cleaners we know to help her—will be invisible to you, and she will labor to keep it that way. Nevertheless, there was a reason why all those dark colors were so popular to the Victorians. They didn't show the dirt and stains.

Not that you would notice such things anyway, since you will rise to go to work by candlelight or lamplight, and return home to the same lighting.

You get your news by the morning and evening papers, or in extreme cases by the "special editions." The papers get *their* news via telegraph and messages sent via the railway trains. Detailed news takes three to five days to arrive from the Continent or from the more remote parts of England. For the most part, there are no photographs in the newspapers; instead, you will see "artist's sketches" of how a scene was imagined to play out. Most of the music you are likely to hear regularly will be played by your wife on the family piano, plus the choir and organ in church on Sunday. You will be Christian—Anglican (or as we know it, Episcopalian), although if you are Scottish, you might be Presbyterian. Only the lower orders were likely to be members of unorthodox sects like Baptists, Lutherans or other dubious aberrations. You will occasionally go to lectures or concerts in the village hall. There is no cinema in your village. You will not go to a music hall unless you happen to be staying overnight in London and there is no chance that anyone will recognize you there—music halls are risqué at best, and someone of your stature, socially or intellectually, does not attend them except clandestinely.

You may, however, belong (as Wells himself did) to some free-thinking organization like the Fabian Society, who were Socialists in all but name, and you will attend their meetings and debates regularly.

You will probably never travel farther than twenty miles from your home in all your life. You married the first girl who took your fancy. You have very little interest in what is happening in the next village or suburb; their doings cannot really affect you, so why should you be curious? Anything important enough will come to you in the papers in a day or two. While you might take an academic interest in the affairs of the wider world, in reality, they do not have much effect on you, and without photographic evidence to give them much substance, they are as emotionally remote to you as the Arabian Nights, and in some cases, seem just as fanciful.

England and the British Empire are the center of your world. You take it for granted that the British Army and Navy are supreme in the world, that nothing can defeat either for long. This, even if you are a member of the Fabian Society or some other progressive organization; it is something you were raised to believe was true from the time you were a small child.

And this is why you will have no trouble in believing that the good people of Woking would not go running off after rocks fallen from the sky.

"The right sort of people" didn't go traipsing across the commons on the chance of seeing a "sight." These fine, upstanding, middle-class people had things to do, even on a Sunday afternoon. One didn't idle about. Ogilvy the astronomer, Henderson the journalist and our unnamed narrator, of course, have "business" being there—Ogilvy because of his profession, Henderson to collect the news and the narrator because of his friendship with Ogilvy and his own standing as a "philosophical writer."

Indeed, the narrator himself is drawn from life—Wells' own life. Certainly Wells described himself as a "philosophical writer" more than once, and the narrator, like Wells, lives in a modest middle-class home in Woking, with "many little luxuries," makes his living at writing and is married. Although it is clear from the narrative that the narrator supports himself and his family (wife, one servant) on essays rather than fiction, in all else he is a thinly disguised version of Wells.

And this may be why Wells makes him a passive observer through the entire book, rather than an active participant in the story. Bad enough that it is in first person—worse that an astute reader would certainly note the similarities between Wells and his subject, but to make the narrator an active hero would have been too much. Wells was too good a writer to fall into the trap of creating his own wish-fulfillment as fiction. But the narrator strikes the modern reader, unaware of this connection, as weak and ineffectual. We expect the sort of hero for the novel that the later adaptations for radio and screen gave us, someone who actively pursues the means to rid the world of this hideous invasion, not someone who passively wanders a blighted landscape, hiding and watching, but watching to no purpose.

Yet precisely that sort of lower-case hero is what is appropriate here, and not only because the narrator is a kind of shadow-Wells. Wells did not intend to write a tale of how mankind overcame the monsters. Wells wanted to show how easily civilization can be made to fall—and what happens to people when it does.

And for that to become real to his readers, they must identify with the narrator. So put your mind into the mindset of that petty little clerk who is reading Wells' novel for the first time. He knows the narrator. He *is* the narrator. He prides himself on being a man of intellect. And confronted with the horror of the Things in the cylinder and the worse horror of the effect of the Heat-Ray, he knows what he would do.

He would do exactly what the narrator does. He would run. *He* is not a soldier or a policeman. Fighting is what soldiers and policemen do; it is their job, not his. That the narrator runs is not cowardice, it is prudence. After all, what could one unarmed man do against the Heat-Ray?

But the Army! Now there neither he, nor the narrator, has any doubt. The Army has modern weapons, and plenty of them; the Martians, so the experts have assured both the reader and the narrator in the context of the story, are weak in the greater gravity of the Earth. The Army will swiftly deal with the Martians, their Heat-Rays and all.

So the narrator goes quietly, if not altogether calmly, back to Woking and his wife, and the reader thinks nothing the worse of him.

> With wine and food, the confidence of my own table, and the neces-sity of reassuring my wife, I grew by insensible degrees courageous and secure.
>
> "They have done a foolish thing," said I, fingering my wineglass. "They are dangerous because, no doubt, they are mad with terror. Per-haps they expected to find no living things—certainly no intelligent living things.
>
> "A shell in the pit," said I, "if the worst comes to the worst will kill them all." ...
>
> So some respectable dodo in the Mauritius might have lorded it in his nest, and discussed the arrival of that shipful of pitiless sailors in want of animal food. "We will peck them to death tomorrow, my dear."

So Wells warns his reader of what is to come.

Now Wells give us a very clear picture of how very insular the setting of the tragedy to come is.

> In London that night poor Henderson's telegram describing the grad-ual unscrewing of the shot was judged to be a canard, and his evening paper, after wiring for authentication from him and receiving no re-ply—the man was killed—decided not to print a special edition.
>
> Even within the five-mile circle the great majority of people were

inert. I have already described the behaviour of the men and women to whom I spoke. All over the district people were dining and supping; working men were gardening after the labours of the day, children were being put to bed, young people were wandering through the lanes love-making, students sat over their books.

The narrator knows—and the reader knows—that the Army has been summoned. The narrator knows that the greater number of people he tries to warn will not believe him, and there is a reticence on his part to make a laughingstock of himself for nothing—and this, too, is very typical of his class. There is nothing more that the narrator believes he can, or needs, to do.

The military arrives, with their guns and about two hundred men; the narrator believes that all is well. And perhaps the original readers of this piece believe it too, and expect that the rest of the book will contain a narrative of the capture of the creatures and their study—Wells continues to lull them with a description of a typical sleepy, yet suspenseful, suburban Saturday. The peace of the afternoon is finally broken by the sound of guns.

My imagination became belligerent, and defeated the invaders in a dozen striking ways; something of my schoolboy dreams of battle and heroism came back. It hardly seemed a fair fight to me at that time. They seemed very helpless in that pit of theirs.

And then—the narrator's world falls to pieces as the Heat-Ray sweeps across the sky and torches the tops of buildings in his own town.

But even now, he does not, as the readers of that time and place would not, think of fighting himself. Nor does he through the rest of the book. He remains a passive observer from beginning to end. But he hasn't the skills even to survive outside of looting increasingly moldy and dubious food from deserted shops and homes, and in this, he is the reflection of the readers of the time. Dependant on what came from shops in a way that his own immediate ancestors were not, unskilled in the most humdrum of chores, such as the lighting of fires, Wells' middle-class narrator is the same helpless and passive creature that he and his readers are, and unconsciously his readers knew this and continued to identify with the narrator as civilization crumbles within the zone of Martian occupation.

The only active person in this story is the narrator's brother—a student, younger, fitter and presumably less steeped in the inertia of respectability. He helps a pair of women to escape the slaughter, resorting to fighting to protect them. He, too, is mostly a witness rather than an active part in resisting the invasion, but Wells probably decided that the use of his fists was enough action. It is through the brother's eyes that the reader sees the complete defeat of the forces of the British Empire.

And this, after all, is the purpose of the narrator and his brother. Humans are not to be the heroes here. Wells has two purposes: to do to "modern civilization" what modern civilization had done to the natives of Tasmania not fifty years earlier, and to prove to his readers just how easily it could be done. He does not need or want a Fighting Prime Minister (in the image of the Fighting President of the movie *Independence Day*) manning the cockpit of the *Thunder Child*. He wants death and defeat to be certain in the minds of the narrator and the readers. And by the last quarter of the book, though the modern readers, steeped in the traditions and expectations of hundreds of movies and books featuring the lone hero conquering the conquerors against all odds, might be impatient of this, Wells' *fin de siècle* contemporaries are entrapped in the narrative and left despairing of a "happy" ending.

It certainly does not seem as if one is going to come. The only other "active" person in the narrative, the artilleryman who has survived and meets the narrator near the end of the book, has grand plans for the survival of the human race, but is clearly not capable of bringing those plans to fruition. After the spreading of the poison gas, those humans still left alive are too demoralized, too dazed, too shocked by Martian superiority, to even think of resisting. Their veneer has peeled away, and there is nothing beneath it to sustain them. Those who have not fled or been killed are now hiding like mice. All seems to be lost.

And then, in what must have been a true shock of a surprise ending, salvation comes (as we, familiar with a number of versions of this novel, are well aware) at the agency of the bacteria, "the humblest things that God, in his wisdom, has put upon this earth."

This is Wells' final blow to his original readers' sense of pride of place. It is a brilliant piece of theatrics, the narrative plot twist to end all twists. It could be viewed today as a plea for environmental diversity, but in fact, it was meant as a humiliating topple to late Victorian hubris. "The Empire you live in may have conquered half the Earth," Wells says to the subconscious of his readers, "but humans are small fish in a very large sea. Larger fish can come to eat us up, and if that comes to pass it may be the things we most despise that, in the end, save us."

He could not have gotten to that point for those readers without making his narrator exactly what he was—an ordinary middle-class man. Not good, not bad, not particularly competent nor incompetent, surviving more by accident than by wits, and exactly like the reader was most likely to be. He strikes Victorian hubris to its knees by degrees, so that when it comes, the fall is the more profound, and the realization of just how hollow that hubris was, is the more penetrating.

It is a lesson that the modern world could afford to take to heart.

Mercedes Lackey is a xenoanthropologist, who spends her free time operating a private-detective agency specializing in the investigation of extra-planar kidnappings and psychic invasions, and she thinks that if you believe any of that, you need to stop buying your newspapers at the grocery checkout counter.

She lives in Oklahoma with her husband, artist and author Larry Dixon, in the second-weirdest house in the state. They share their house with their flock of parrots, many of which attempt to help her type with varying levels of success, or lack thereof. She has written, alone or in collaboration, over sixty books, including the Elemental Masters series for DAW, the Bedlam Bardz series for Baen and the Obsidian Mountain series for Tor. She has never juggled knives, though she often juggles deadlines, which are just as lethal.

FRED SABERHAGEN

Wells, Welles, Well!, or Who Called the Martians Down?

I MISSED THE SHOW. Whatever my eight-year-old self was doing in our Chicago suburb on that last night before Halloween of 1938, a good decade before we or other common folks had television, neither I nor my parents were tuned to *The Mercury Theatre on the Air*. The radio play of the night was *The War of the Worlds*, produced for the CBS network by John Houseman and Orson Welles.

Not until the following day did I learn how my Aunt Mabel, dwelling a hundred miles to the west, had run out of her house into the small-town night, searching the sky for a glimpse of the next incoming Martian spacecraft. She had been a young lady when the Wright brothers first took off, and was never a fan of science fiction; the threat of invaders from another planet must have come as something of a shock.

The drama of the show depended heavily on fake "news bulletins," and in taking them seriously Aunt Mabel was not alone. Far from it.

Only by sheer chance, or perhaps by the grace of God (who is thought to have a sense of humor), were there no deaths or serious injuries. One woman in Pennsylvania was on the point of drinking poison, telling her husband she preferred that death to the black clouds of Martian gas. Police stations and radio studios were flooded with telephone calls, the switchboards choked useless at CBS and elsewhere. (Anxious caller: "Is the world coming to an end?" CBS operator: "I'm sorry, we haven't that information here.")

Religious services were interrupted, wedding receptions abandoned, roads in New Jersey and eastern Pennsylvania jammed with traffic as people threw an assortment of possessions into automobiles and tried their best to flee for their lives. Folk demented by fear drove wildly to escape, or to reach loved ones, ignoring cops and traffic signals.

All this despite the fact that the play had been advertised ahead of time, and the fictional nature of the program was made quite clear at its beginning and several times during its course. ("You are listening to a CBS presentation...of an original dramatization...the performance will continue after a brief intermission.")

Next day I heard something of the story, the broadcast and the major tumult it had caused. I learned that a man called Orson Welles was somehow responsible for it all. Or was it H. G. Wells? And couldn't the man decide whether he wanted that extra 'e' in his name or not?

The man with the extra 'e' was a dazzlingly talented and successful actor less than a generation older than I was. At twenty-three, Orson Welles was well launched on his life's work, already commanding his own theatrical company, many of whose actors would appear with him three years later in his landmark movie *Citizen Kane*. To say that the radio production of *The War of the Worlds* accelerated his career, which would be long and tempestuous, is understating the case, even though the immediate reaction of outrage seemed to threaten ruin.

The outrage erupted incredibly, astonishing everyone involved in the production, even before the broadcast was over. The police came. As producer John Houseman described it, "...we are now off the air and the studio door bursts open. The following hours are a nightmare. The building is suddenly full of people and dark blue uniforms. We are hurried out of the studio...into a back office. Here we sit, incommunicado, while network employees are busy collecting, destroying or locking up all records of the broadcast....Hours later, instead of arresting us, they let us out a back way...like hunted animals to their holes. It is surprising to see life going on as usual in the midnight streets."

Trouble peaked the morning after. Across the nation, there were many who took more drastic action than Aunt Mabel. Rumors abounded, though all soon proved false, of deaths and serious injuries caused by panic. Over the next few days, potential lawsuits against Orson and CBS loomed in swiftly increasing numbers, though all were eventually dropped.

A study done subsequently at Princeton University (this time I mean the real Princeton—but see below) estimated that of more than six million people who heard the play, more than a million accepted the described invasion as a fact, the supposed news bulletins quite genuine.

Some saw in the Martian onslaught the hand of God, meting out punishment to a sinful nation. Others believed the true attackers were Hitler's Germans, while a Nazi newspaper later blamed the "war scare" on some kind of Jewish plot. Still other frightened Americans preferred to hold the crafty Japanese accountable.

Panic had spread from casual CBS listeners to people who had not bothered to turn on a radio that night, and to those who had been part of the audience for another network's *The Chase and Sanborn Hour,* featuring the very popular ventriloquist Edgar Bergen and his star dummy Charlie McCarthy. (Ventriloquism on the radio? You bet. The sound of Fred Astaire tap-dancing was also a hit, though Fred's act never became a regular program. Everyone knew, from seeing these characters in glorious movie black and white, just what they looked like, and imagination drew in the face or dancing figure.)

When the Bergen-McCarthy act broke for a musical interlude a few minutes into their program, many thousands of their audience began to do what we now call channel surfing. Large numbers happened to tune in to the middle of an authentic-sounding news bulletin describing an attack on the United States by alien monsters. Perhaps understandably, a high percentage of these never tuned back.

Thousands of Americans, their numbers concentrated mostly in New Jersey and adjoining states but scattered all the way to California, were goaded into strenuous action by H. G.'s original story line, Howard Koch's quasi-realistic script and the performances on mike of Orson and his crew. Either absorbing snatches of dramatic dialogue and sound effects as factual information, or else catching the fever from those who had already fallen into delirium, the victims made frantic efforts to save themselves, their loved ones and their pets from interplanetary conquest. But sooner or later truth dawned on everyone, and many cried out for vengeance.

Very early in the approximately forty-five minutes of imaginary doom, listeners heard reports relayed from "the Mount Jennings observatory in Chicago" of explosions on the planet Mars ("like a jet of blue flame shot from a gun") followed quickly by the impact in the eastern United States of several spacecraft that resembled enormous artillery shells or bullets. (No one in the play remarked what sturdy folk those Martians were, that they seemed to have been propelled at nearly the speed of light, and survived the crushing jolts at both blastoff and impact.)

News of the aliens' arrival quickly gave way to description of crowds gathering at impact sites, where they were almost immediately slaughtered by Martian Heat-Rays. Urgent voices on sober commercial radio, just where real news stories came, told how police and soldiers, in escalating numbers, were being mobilized with incredible speed to battle the invaders. But over the next few minutes the warriors in uniform fared very little better than helpless civilians ("seven thousand men armed with rifles and machine guns pitted against a single fighting machine.... One hundred and twenty known survivors").

Of course the grim realities of the late thirties had done much to prepare the soil for panic. Less than a month before the broadcast, Hitler's Reich had in effect swallowed Czechoslovakia, affording the Chancellor a nearly bloodless triumph and encouraging him in the mistaken belief that he might soon be able to get away with gobbling Poland. In the Soviet Union, Stalin continued his bloody rule. The Japanese invasion of China had been monotonously producing atrocities for years. We in the United States were just emerging from our Great Depression. We were also plagued by an uneasy feeling, which turned out to be absolutely justified, that our part in the Great War of 1914–18 might have been only the first chapter of a prolonged involvement in deadly conflict.

More than thirty human lives, along with the future of lighter-than-air transportation, had gone up in flames on a May evening in 1937, when the great dirigible *Hindenburg* accidentally crashed and burned while attempting to land in New Jersey, the same state where Martians first arrived—or rather did not arrive—in 1938.

A radio announcer had been sent to cover the *Hindenburg's* arrival—a transatlantic flight by the most luxurious airship in the world was still something of an event. The recorded voice of the announcer, as he struggled almost incoherently to report the disaster, was heard by millions. And perhaps New Jersey was identified, in the collective American subconscious, as a locale where incredible horror could actually come true. Less than a year and a half later, in rehearsal for *The War of the Worlds*, actors of *The Mercury Theatre* listened to the recording over and over, striving to emulate the authentic tones of astonishment, terror and pity.

By way of a sidelight, it is intriguing to speculate whether the exploding dirigible, the roaring flash of seven million cubic feet of hydrogen gas going up in flames in less than a minute, might have been visible to a properly equipped observer on Mars, even though that 1937 evening at the landing site was wet and cloudy. Were the fabricators of the Martian Heat-Rays, those beings described in both book and play as "intellects vast and cool and unsympathetic," also skilled in long-range infrared detection?

Playing along with fiction, there is also room for conjecture as to whether the Martians, shocked by what their instruments were telling them about our savage intramural slaughters, felt compelled to invade our planet to set our benighted people free. Perhaps they came only to destroy the terrorists among us with whom we evidently could not cope unaided (and who might be planning an attack on Mars) and to shower us with the blessings of improved government—in whatever form it was favored on the Red Planet at that moment.

Of course, had they postponed the invasion for only a few decades, we would not have had to depend on bacteria to defend our lives, homes and political systems. The invaders' slow-to-focus Heat-Rays, their tall cumbersome fighting machines, even their devices that might enable them to take advantage of our thick air and learn to fly (H. G. tended to see that as a mind-blowing advantage), would have been badly overmatched against cruise missiles, smart bombs and Abrams battle tanks. Probably it would not be worth polluting our precious, watery atmosphere, the envy of the solar system, to obliterate the intruding monsters with a small nuke.

I hope Aunt Mabel enjoyed decent weather on that October night when she ran out to search the skies. But whatever the local conditions might have been, one object she could *not* have seen was Mars. Nor could "Professor Pierson," the famous astronomer (his rich voice sounding remarkably like Orson Welles'), have gazed at the Red Planet from his Princeton (this time not the real one) observatory in New Jersey. He must have been staging a performance for the reporter who came in act one to interview him there.

Solemnly gazing through his fictional telescope, Pierson told the reporter he observed "a red disk swimming in a blue sea," and could give no explanation for the flashes recently observed upon it. But we, armed with the electronic gadgetry of the early twenty-first century, can easily determine that Mars, around the date of Halloween in 1938, did not rise over New Jersey until about 4:30 in the morning, thereafter conducting the bulk of its daily transit across the heavens invisible in broad day-light. Far from being nearby in opposition, as Pierson claimed, and less than forty million miles from Earth, the Red Planet was actually well around toward the far side of the sun, a difficult target for observation at much more than two hundred million miles away.

At broadcast time, a half moon would have been the most promi-nent object in the professor's (and Aunt Mabel's) sky. Jupiter was big and bright and high—my aunt, and a legion of other non-astronomers across the country, could very well have mistaken it for Mars. Professor Pierson's telescope could have picked out Uranus. I hate to think he might have confused that small, dim planet with the one the reporter asked about—but is it possible?

Writer Howard Koch, after listening to the broadcast in his New York apartment, fell into an exhausted sleep and knew nothing of any un-usual result until late the next day. His script gained him immediate fame in the narrow circles of those who care about such things, and he went on to success in Hollywood, a few years later winning an Academy Award as one of the contributors to *Casablanca*.

Koch had certainly earned some kind of a reward. Welles had al-lowed him only six days to adapt the long novella for radio, a daunting task further complicated by Orson's tendency to keep inserting his own changes in the script, up to the very last minute. The job would have been complex enough even without such tinkering; to tell the story in the time available it was necessary to compress the events of H. G.'s text, which spread over approximately a month, into forty-five minutes of dramatization and narration. This jarring discrepancy in real time was disguised, to some extent, by brief intervals of bland music ("Ramon Raquello and his orchestra, playing for you in the Meridian Room of the Park Plaza Hotel...") between nerve-rattling bulletins detailing horror, massacre and despair. It seems that no one foresaw the extent to which many listeners would fail even to notice the warped chronology.

Time was not all that needed changing. Everything in the book, pub-lished 1898, had to be translated forty years into the future and across an ocean not only geographical but cultural. Koch had to reroute the Martians from end-of-nineteenth-century England—the heart of a pow-erful empire still largely horse-drawn but long accustomed to launch-ing invasions of its own—to an America where radios and automobiles abounded. Where flying machines, far from being an awesome Martian monopoly, were more than a generation old and on the verge of becom-ing commonplace. Where a people who had not sent sons and husbands off to war for twenty years, and who were protected from invasion by vast oceans, were growing very edgy about both possibilities.

In England H. G.'s first reaction on hearing of the program was unfavorable. When he gave permission for the story's use, his understanding had been that it would simply be read on radio, not changed in important ways or dramatized, certainly not broadcast in the form of news. But the resultant great jump in the sales of his book soon soothed his feelings, and when he and Orson had their only face-to-face meeting, on the broadcast's second anniversary, they engaged in a cordial joint interview on radio.

Koch's script in its final form contains some very nice, evocative touches not in the book: for example the bombing planes, launched in pursuit of long-legged Martian walking machines, but able to fly only fast enough to "keep the speeding enemy in sight." There are also occasional blunders, jolts sharp enough to get the attention of any listener fully awake and in his right mind. In one scene an officer of the "22nd Field Artillery," getting ready to shell some landed Martians, solemnly intones: "Range, thirty-two meters." (*Boom of heavy gun…pause.*) But after missing the target, which the officer has just described as only about a hundred feet away, his "observer" chides him: "One hundred and forty yards to the right, sir."

With the 22nd aiming that poorly, small wonder this report was followed in a minute or two by even grimmer news: "Our army wiped out…artillery, air force, everything wiped out."

The unnamed "Secretary of the Interior"—in real life it would have been Harold Ickes—was allotted about a minute of broadcast time to appeal for calm, and express his hope for "preservation of human supremacy on this earth." Actor Kenny Delmar's speech was so good an imitation—not of Ickes, whose voice few would have recognized—but of President Roosevelt's famous and distinctive tones, that it alone ought to have given the game away to any American adult who was listening with brain turned on. Later, conflicting explanations were given for the mimicry, which was not called for in the script. But it seems certain that it was a grace note ordered by Orson.

The people who fled their homes in panic could hardly have been the same individuals who sat down at the beginning of the broadcast to enjoy a play. Besides the bald repeated announcements that yes, you are listening to a play, and an afterword in the script from Orson speaking "out of character to assure you that *The War of the Worlds* has no further significance than as the holiday offering it was intended to be. *The Mer-*

cury *Theatre's* own version of dressing up in sheet and jumping out of a bush and saying Boo!" there were subtle sins against reality. To note a few: Chicago, its low and smoky air glaring with a million lights, must have seemed a very unlikely site for a serious observatory, especially with no mountain, called "Jennings" or otherwise, within hundreds of miles. The fictional reporters of the broadcast's early minutes, racing by auto from one catastrophe to another, fly across the landscape at very nearly Martian speed. One military unit after another is mobilized, sent into action and destroyed, in less time than many sergeants would need to get a squad out of the barracks and call the roll.

In a matter of only a few days almost all of the outrage had died away, to a great extent crowded out of people's minds by growing amusement. There was no war in America after all, no one had been killed, and most folks could appreciate a joke. Cartoons, editorials, comedians and parodies poked fun at the recently panic-stricken. More soberly, pundits urged that a serious retuning of the national psyche was in order, along with a reform of our educational system.

Koch had selected the town of Grovers Mill for the first landing by closing his eyes and stabbing a pencil at a highway map. There was no one in the area called "Wilmuth," the name he'd chosen randomly for the affected landowner—but there was a Wilson nearby, and reporters and other enthusiasts quickly decided that was close enough. The farmer profited handsomely by charging admission for visitors to come and park their cars and stroll around his fields, feasting their eyes on the site made special by the fact that Martians, as far as anybody could prove, had never landed on it. Hundreds came and paid in the next few days, and most seem to have gone away satisfied.

A person sitting in a theater knows that he or she is in a theater, but one who listens to voices on the radio may have some real grounds for doubt as to just what sort of a reality the voices are trying to convey, and why.

Words, cleverly chosen and cleverly spoken words, aided only by a few odd sound effects, transported the Martians more swiftly than light across interplanetary space, landed their slimy bodies, their tentacles, their V-shaped mouths and ruthless purpose right in our minds. Mere words succeeded in creating an imagery more ferocious, far more convincing, than any twenty-first-century motion picture has yet been able to do, even when fortified with a hundred million dollars' worth of software, hardware, high-priced talent and advertising. The mental pictures evoked were tailor-made on site by each individual psyche, crafted by what is still the most advanced and capable computer in the known universe.

Fred Saberhagen's stories of fantasy and science fiction, including the popular Berserker series, have been appearing in books and magazines for more than forty years. An Air Force veteran and former writer and editor at *Encyclopedia Britannica*, he lives in New Mexico with his wife, Joan Spicci.

GEORGE ZEBROWSKI

The Fear
of the Worlds

THE WAR OF THE WORLDS teems with ideas and confronts complex implications beyond its time. The novel juggles ideas about first contact with alien intelligence along with forays into religion, history, social disorder, evolution and biology, the personal side of violence—all to assemble a larger, more uncertain picture of man's place in the universe. Although the story can be read as a thriller, it rewards later returns to its pages, in which readers are challenged to play out ideas along with the author. Fail to do so and you miss too much; nothing presented is irrelevant as Wells also sets *the* artful example for a thinking science fiction.

"Now and then, though I rarely admit it," H. G. Wells wrote in his 1934 preface to his *Seven Famous Novels*, "the universe projects itself toward me in a hideous grimace." It did so in *The Island of Dr. Moreau* (1896), as "a youthful blasphemy," by his own description; in *The Time Machine* (1895), *The Invisible Man* (1897), and in *The War of the Worlds* (1898), which he came to regard as yet "another assault on human self-satisfaction." He adds:

All three books are consciously grim, under the influence of Swift's tradition. But I am neither a pessimist nor an optimist at bottom. This is an entirely indifferent world in which willful wisdom has a perfectly fair chance. It is after all rather cheap to get force of presentation by loading the scales on the sinister side. Horror stories are easier to write than gay and exalting stories.

Wells was understandably hard on his younger self. The Second World War was fast approaching, and too many pages from his works continued to be ripped out and pasted into the real world. Atomic bombs and a nuclear arms race waited at the end of the coming war, both of which he lived to see. "Atomic bomb" was a Wells-coined term, and the arms race was predicted by him in his novel *The World Set Free*, in 1914, which was later credited by physicist Leo Szilard for suggesting to him how nuclear fission would work. Szilard hurried to Princeton from a darkening, now twice-failing Europe, to convince another exile, Albert Einstein, who in the mid-1930s had scoffed at the practical use of nuclear energy. Einstein then alerted President Roosevelt to the danger in the now famous letter that launched the Manhattan Project. The clear line from Wells to Hiroshima is only one instance among many in which science-fictional imaginings changed the world.

The blood-red "reality" of *The War of the Worlds* had emerged in the new weapons of World War I, and in how the colonial powers continued to treat Third World peoples as "slopes," "gooks," "ragheads" and "hajjis"— demote them and you can kill them with little or no concern, which is how the Martians exterminated human beings, as one steps into a nest of ants.

The recent renewed interest in Wells' novel through two new movies with differing adaptations suggests that our fascination with a possible contact with an alien culture goes far beyond a xenophobic fear of strangers, to an emerging recognition of the momentous possible event that would irreversibly change how we view our own origins and future destiny. In the midst of destruction, the panicky curate asks Wells' narrator, "What are these Martians?" And the narrator answers with a profound question that is the very heart of the novel: "What are we?" And this is amplified later as the narrator writes, "The broadening of men's views that has resulted can scarcely be exaggerated."

World War I brought us modern warfare, as if casting its shadow back into Wells' novel. *The War in the Air* (1908), an eye-popping vision of aerial battle, showed us a very vulnerable New York City. Writing in *The Wellsian* in 2003, Patrick Parrinder comments that

...in the aftermath of 11 September 2001, it is interesting to note that the 'Dead London' chapter of *The War of the Worlds* is replaced in the radio version [the 1938 radio hoax by Orson Welles] by a series of reports from an abandoned and dying New York, in which the Martian tripods rise 'like a line of new towers' over the city's West Side. The New Yorkers [of 1938] who mistook this drama for reality included one man who climbed to the roof of his Manhattan building and claimed that he could see the 'flames of battle.' He and other victims of Welles' Halloween prank were among the first to realise the terrors of a surprise attack on the world's wealthiest and most powerful country. That is why the curious events of an autumn night in 1938 remain relevant today.

But this is only one instance in which Wells' vision continued to update itself.

The story of alien invasion has grown into a myth beyond stories that only reflect the fears of powerful nations bubbling up through the fictional arts (where we whisper guilty truths too terrible to speak plainly), from the violent understuff of our survivalist inheritance from nature. As we look out into the universe, contact with alien civilizations has become a common idea, a possible reality, and the two views that continue to trouble us are that the aliens might be benevolent or hostile; either reality would change us irrevocably.

There are many variations on these two categories, with degrees of alien indifference to the human life of our planet belonging to both possibilities. For many years the idea of a peaceful first contact was influential, popularized by Carl Sagan in his *Cosmos* television series of 1980, and in the movies *Close Encounters of the Third Kind* (1977) and *E.T.* (1982). Peaceful scenarios warred with hostile ones in print sf, but few SETI scientific papers have dealt with hostile ETI encounters, following instead what has been called the Sagan Doctrine. Hope for peaceful contacts with alien cultures, perhaps through long-term radio exchanges (see James Gunn's 1972 novel *The Listeners*), reached a quasi-religious fervor, secularly prayerful in the idea that such cultures might help us solve our earthly problems.

But let us, with Wells, consider the other extreme, while keeping in mind that the hostile possibility may very well be an anthropocentric prejudice; it may be that and still become a reality, and it may be that disastrous contact is common on the interstellar scale. Given our violent origins, this fear of hostile strangers from the stars may be present in aliens as much as it lives in us. In his last years Isaac Asimov warned of attracting attention to ourselves on the interstellar stage, lest we be "drawn into a game we do not want to play." The paranoia of Wells' famous opening page, with its foreboding about our being "scrutinised and studied" speaks most clearly to the kind of Darwinian creature that we are. Do advancing cultures reach this level of discussion, then wait cowering before the implications in their sunspaces, hoping to find a way to make contact without calling destruction down upon their histories? Do they reach out, as we may well do one day, from the ruins of their worlds, from no other motive than survival?

There is a logic of outcomes to the process of "first contact" that is very disquieting. In the mid-1990s I wrote a provocative novel with scientist-author Charles Pellegrino entitled *The Killing Star*, which develops the ideas of Asimov and others about what revealing ourselves on the interstellar horizon might trigger. Reviewers noted that the book pushes the Wellsian alien invasion idea to its logical conclusions and amounts to a reinvention of the theme; our aliens conduct a preemptive total war of extermination. Wells had pulled on a thread of thinking about contact with extraterrestrial life, thus beginning a discussion that continues in both science and science fiction. And Wells did so in terms of Darwinian biology, speculating not only on exobiology, but on exopsychology, and on what we now call sociobiology.

Wells' Martians make a heroic, well-organized attempt to conquer and colonize the Earth, and do so in what seems devoid of any animosity: nothing can outweigh their survival. Human pride and arrogance are reduced to mere pretensions before the modern weapons of the invaders. This not only suggested a critical look at how the imperial powers subdued the poorer peoples of the world for economic gains, but also prefigured the inhuman mechanization of wholesale slaughter in World War I. The American Civil War, which some called the first modern war, had been a mere foreboding. And Wells lived to see World War II, and his atomic bomb; his despair was great in this second go-around.

The outcome of Wells' Martian invasion affirms the integrity of our ecological, survivalist niche, forged in the cauldron of natural selection, against which the defenses of the Martian technology collapse. Earthly biology breaches their isolation within their war machines. The care needed to prevent infection was a failure which we might ascribe to the decline of the Martian civilization; or it may have been carelessness, perhaps as a result of Martian panic during their desperate effort. Wells did not know about ubiquitous viruses, but plague bacilli serve as well as these "humblest things" that got the Martians. It is not by our efforts that they die. They fall before the defenses from lower down in the hierarchy of our planet's life.

It is revealing to consider Garrett P. Serviss' *Edison's Conquest of Mars*, which tells us that the first Martian attack had been only the beginning. Hurriedly serialized as an unofficial sequel in 1898, the novel affirms human arrogance by carrying the fight back to Mars, in a preemptive fashion that nearly destroys what is left of the Martian species, thus ensuring "a peaceful state of affairs between the two planets." A vague riposte to Wells' novel is the movie *Independence Day* (1996), an enjoyable wish-fulfillment tribute to American pride, sharing with Wells only that in both cases human salvation is achieved by an unstoppable virus, bacteria for Wells and an impossible use of a laptop-sent computer virus for *Independence Day*.

Yet the reality of encountering an alien civilization stands as a genuinely possible event. The thinking in *The Killing Star* builds on Wells' novel and a century of dialogue about alien contact, and answers the question first posed by the Russian space scientist Konstantin Tsiolkovsky in 1933 and asked again by atomic scientist Enrico Fermi in 1950, who could not imagine that a universe full of life would wish to ignore us. One answer to Fermi's "Where are they?" may be that we pose them no danger or are simply uninteresting at this stage, having as yet not exhibited any capacity for interstellar travel, which would be signaled by the ability to accelerate objects to relativistic speeds (any significant portion of the speed of light), which would also bring with it the capacity for preemptive weapons of frightening proportions.

My coauthor on *The Killing Star* calculated that

a golf ball mass hitting the Earth at ninety-two percent of lightspeed would detonate with a kinetic force of several thirty-three megaton hydrogen bombs, plus an equal conversion of mass from the Earth's compressed atmosphere ahead of and through the ball. The heat and blast would vaporize and flatten all of Manhattan, Staten Island, the Bronx, Brooklyn and Newark. But heat and blast would spend only a fraction of the relativistic onslaught. At the cemetery near Big Brook Creek, New Jersey, the top layer millimeter of the city-facing sides of the granite tombstones, sixty kilometers away, would glow a ghostly cherry red, as would the remains of shark's teeth from the Cretaceous period in Big Brook's cliff face. This microwave glow would reach deeply into buildings as far away as Philadelphia, and most people inside those buildings would receive lethal neurological doses of radiation and would die anywhere between three minutes and three days after exposure. An entire case of golf balls, striking our atmosphere at ninety-two per cent of lightspeed, would turn the entire United States into an instant microwave grill. Ten Toyota Celica masses would create a fearful picture of ripped atmosphere, steaming oceans and cooked humanity, sparing only bacteria inside deep ocean hydrothermal vents.

There would be no way to know what a relativistic object is, or plot its course, as it approaches—a friendly visitor or a weapon? As soon as two cultures capable of relativistic flight learned of each other, nothing would outweigh even the smallest chance of destruction of one by the other. Neither could risk it, if they truly examined the problem. One might destroy the other with relativistic objects as soon as possible, because even the remotest chance of being hit first could not be risked. No hatred, no animosity, no struggle for resources—only the need to be certain of survival would count. No one would dare risk waiting to find out whether the enemy was peaceful or hostile, and the irony might well be that utterly "civilized" intelligences would destroy each other, or one the other, without an ounce of hatred being involved, without ever knowing the facts, without ever being able to "afford" knowing the truth. Once this paranoia begins, cultures might be drawn, in Isaac Asimov's words, into "a game they do not want to play," but must play.

The answer to Fermi's question, or paradox, might be that since the danger of relativistic bombs is known to all the advanced cultures, a great silence reigns between them; no one wants to be the first to say hello and risk losing their entire history.

What is our history worth to us?

Everything.

That is the ultimate implication of Wells' novel today, as we continue a discussion in which everything is still debated as reality bears down on our history. We do not hear from alien cultures because we show no development that might either interest or threaten them enough to provoke a response.

But light up the "gamma burn" of a matter-antimatter propulsion system, or some as yet unknown advanced form of propulsion that would become visible on the galactic scale, and the game might begin, delayed only by the speed of light's signaling of the fact, and maybe not even by that limit. Time would slow the response, as would the probability that, given the extent of the universe in space and time, cultures might mercifully miss each other throughout all the ages of their existence. Or maybe not. Klaatu's warning in the movie *The Day the Earth Stood Still* (1951) takes on new meaning when he warns of our application of nuclear power to space travel, and omits telling us exactly where he has come from.

Perhaps both interstellar travel and contact with alien cultures may not be as difficult as we think today. Developments in the last year have made it possible to produce antihydrogen—the key enabling technology needed to achieve relativistic spaceflight, and by the same relativistic weapons—some twenty thousand times more efficiently than was possible only five years ago. "It's a disturbing thought," my coauthor points out, "when we consider that all this is *not* science fiction."

It may be difficult for many readers today to grasp how *new* the idea of alien invasion was in the nineteenth century. Wells gave it a chilling familiarity by grounding his presentation in the human imperial experience as seen from the victim's view, and in the unapologetic attitude of the British Empire's right to rule, while at the same time speculating on the notion of a genuine "other" who is not just another kind of human being (although he speculated that the Martians may be a highly evolved form of humankind—mostly brain). The entire invasion was both new and familiar, then and today.

A century of science fiction writers since have either carried the debate forward or debased it. The George Pal film of 1953 is a provocative and impressive movie, dramatically sound despite what it leaves out or alters, but it lacks Wells' critical view of human history; the Martians are not here to convert us, but to survive, yet the minister of the screenplay sees them "as closer to God" because of their advanced abilities. He goes out to make "contact" and is promptly reduced to ashes, suggesting a Godless evil come to Earth. But the film finds the minister's effort admirable, and seeks to frighten us, and only vaguely suggests that a pious response is useless, since the Martians do not answer to reason or faith. One might vaguely conclude, although even this much was not intended by the screenwriter, that the minister is deluded rather than praiseworthy in his attempt to negotiate with the invaders. In Wells' novel the minister has lost his mind and is about to endanger his own life and that of the narrator by revealing himself to the Martians, in order to "bear witness." The narrator attempts to stop him, grabs a meat chopper, then with "one last touch of humanity" overcoming his own fear, he turns it to the handle side and strikes the curate down, killing him, as it turns out. It is inconceivable that a screenwriter of the 1950s would have included this complex scene, or a director been permitted to put it on America's screens without turning the narrator into a villain. Wells shows us a shaken man, nearly broken by what he has had to do to survive.

We are meant to conclude in the 1950 movie that the bacterial life, "our microscopic allies" who kill the invaders, were put here by God to protect us. Wells' curate, desperate to deny the collapse of his theology, might well have proclaimed a miracle wrought by the personal god of his faith; while Garrett P. Serviss, echoing Wells' narrator's idea of humanity's biological right to the Earth, announced that the fight would be "the evolution of earth against the evolution of Mars," a declining ecology against a vital one. "It never was a war," says Wells' artilleryman, "any more than there's war between man and ants." The real war was between the plague bacilli, "our microscopic allies," and the Martians.

Wells' narrator notes that our survival through natural selection, our resistance to native forms of life competing with us for the planet, has given us the right of survivors who have paid their dues to be here, through the billions of deaths necessary to evolution. He speaks only figuratively when he mentions "God's wisdom" in placing the microbiota on the Earth to defend us, and gives equal time to the idea that "It may be that the destruction of the Martians is only a reprieve. To them, and not to us, perhaps, is the future ordained." In the 1953 film, American scientists conclude that a biological weapon is needed to defeat the Martians, thus giving a nod to the novel and foreshadowing the end of the movie; but even as human panic destroys any chance for a biological weapon, as humanity descends into social chaos and fails to mount any effective defense, the Earth itself has already been on the job. The "massacre of humanity" cannot help but remind us that we have done a good job of that on ourselves quite regularly, fighting war after war and failing to defeat ourselves. For once, the movie trailer is absolutely correct: "The biggest story that could ever happen to our world." But the movie only gives us a few California snapshots of a story unfolded with greater insight in Wells' novel, in which the visuals are as striking as any film viewer would wish.

Interestingly, the idea of our paid-up *right to be here* found a secular expression a half-century after Wells' novel in his contribution to the "Universal Declaration of Human Rights" approved by the UN in 1948. Keep that in mind as the invading human globalizers seek to privatize water and other basic resources for the benefit of the few. Our right to the planet, our place in nature and in the universe, which is Wells' over-arching theme, finds a religious expression in our professed relationship to a God, and also finds expression in an evolutionary, even a legal, context. First contact with another intelligent species might very well throw into contest our lordship of the planet, a right which we have denied, by degrees, to various less powerful regional peoples.

In *The Thing* (1951), the film of John W. Campbell's much more subtle 1938 story "Who Goes There?" the secular scientist who goes out to make contact is seen as naïve, even a traitor, as he makes an admirable, even moving, last effort to communicate, survives with a broken collarbone, then is given only a guilty patronizing praise for his effort on behalf of his enlightened views. In *This Island Earth* (1955), when humankind's place in the universe is belittled, Dr. Meacham replies to the alien, in a startling, clearly tacked-on fit of jingoistic belligerence for a scientist, that "our true size is the size of our God," when nothing earlier had suggested that he was religious. In *The Day the Earth Stood Still*, Klaatu is asked whether his robot policeman, who has just revived him from death, has the power of life and death. Klaatu responds that only the Almighty has that power but that this technique of resuscitation restores life for "brief" periods ("brief" presumably making it less blasphemous to the audience). Today's audiences laugh at this added bit of sugarcoating, since we restart hearts routinely. George Pal's other fine film of this period, *When Worlds Collide* (1951), is also full of religious sentiment. Clear commercial needs made these inserts seem necessary to the producers.

Over the years, viewers have paid less attention to the religious propaganda in the 1953 movie of Wells' novel and in the other films of this period, when the filmmakers felt obligated to stand with religion in fear of alienating audiences. But current surveys sadly suggest that most Americans still feel the need to at least say that an atheist or even an agnostic "cannot be a moral person." George Bush senior has said in a published interview that "I don't know that atheists should be considered as citizens, nor patriots." And the scientist-egghead of Pal's film had to be cast against imagined type—the handsome Gene Barry—to be acceptable to an anti-intellectual audience. Wells' narrator is a congenial, thoughtful philosopher, who does more than tell the story, but stops and *thinks* whenever he can and offers insights, some unflattering to himself and humankind, along the way, without which the novel would have been poorer. "Perhaps I am a man of exceptional moods," writes Wells' narrator. "I do not know how far my experience is common. At times I suffer from the strangest sense of detachment from myself and the world about me; I seem to watch it all from the outside, from somewhere inconceivably remote, out of time, out of space, out of the stress and tragedy of it all." *This* is Wells shaping the very method of sf as a way of thought about change. His narrator observes, he acts on evidence and need, and turns away from arrogance, megalomania and delusion when he sees them in the curate and in the artilleryman. And he prays, in well-understood desperation, after his accidental killing of the maddened curate.

Was H. G. Wells a religious man? He explored a form of theism in *God the Invisible King* (1917), but soon retreated to skepticism, agnosticism and a robust atheism, as World War I receded and he came to see his dalliance with theistic faith as "a falling back...under the stress of dismay and anxiety," and perhaps, he admitted in later years, as a use of theocratic ideas to widen his readership and effect the betterment of the world. Religion as social engineering recalls "The Grand Inquisitor" in Dostoevsky's *The Brothers Karamazov*. But Wells recovered, and found the godliness of the universe in humanity's responsibilities to itself, and in each of us to one another, in what even to an atheist is Christ's core ethical teaching.

Wells certainly would not have accepted the religious protective coloration that was added to his story in the movie, which tries to have it both ways; if anything the defeat of the Martians confirms Darwin's theory of evolution through natural selection, much in the same way that vaccination proves the truth of evolution by strengthening our immune response to invading life. Vaccination would not work to stimulate our immune defenses if Darwin's idea of natural selection by the environment was wrong; also, the bugs would not evolve immunity to our antibiotics through natural selection of the strongest, and we would not have to seek ever more effective antibiotics. But the truth of evolution does not leave us with moral anarchy and a meaningless universe, as many mistakenly believe. Where religious people speak of God, Wells spoke of a real natural ethics and our personal responsibility to each other—a profoundly moral position. The buck stops with us, whether we believe in or deny a cosmic Father or Mother.

Wells' novel, in depicting collective madness, seems today to have been written as if the future that would shatter the world's certainties was in fact casting a shadow back into 1898. The terror of the *Titanic* sinking still lay ahead—a catastrophe that pointed up the bitter irony of "how certain" the builders were to decide it was unnecessary to have enough lifeboats for all the passengers. That certainty, motivated \ defense of their profits before people, was lethal. World War I was coming, with its dead-end battles resulting in death by the tens of thousands. The Great Influenza of 1918–1919 killed millions worldwide, and the politics of its denial in the United States has been a horror that is only now making its way back into our critical thinking. And once again, even as we comprehend past failures, new collective delusions, masking real dangers, are rushing toward us.

Wells' narrator comes to understand that we can no longer "regard the planet as being fenced in and a secure abiding place for Man; we can never anticipate the unseen good or evil that may come upon us suddenly out of space. It may be that in the larger design of the universe this invasion from Mars is not without its ultimate benefit for men; it has robbed us of that serene confidence in the future which is the most fruitful source of decadence...."

If you feel uneasy reading this novel, that is because Wells was engaged in presenting serious implications well beyond his pages. Not all violent invasions come from outside; they also wait to be loosed from within us upon the world.

Wells' evolutionary conception teaches that only a growing power born of self-knowledge and of nature's universe can help us, if we can also control the empowerment of our dark side by that same increase. As the twentieth century ran its course, the dangers to the planet also grew, but they had always been there, and it was only our awareness that grew: new diseases, eco-catastrophe, asteroid collision (see Wells' 1897 short story, "The Star" for a pioneering vision of this possibility), and nuclear war by accident or design. Today, a civilization-ending asteroid strike, coming in at a mere 30,000 miles an hour, has about a 1-in-20,000 chance of hitting us, each and every day—about the odds of an airplane crash. Weathering has not hidden the evidence on the Moon as it has on Earth. And we are overdue to be struck, and doing little to prevent it.

Few would deny that our existence is precarious and growing more so as we also delay countermeasures against lethal possibilities created by our own hands. And contact with an alien culture (although it has moved out of fictional solar systems to an as yet fictional but more plausible interstellar stage of our galaxy) still looms as one of the great waiting developments of human history, taxing our reason and imagination to work more clearly. How will we see ourselves in the mirror of the "other"? Will the contact be peaceful or catastrophic, or just baffling?

What questions are we failing to ask, as we remind ourselves how recent is the very conception of a nonhuman "other" as more than "funny-looking but intelligent" beings "not of this Earth"? Has this imaginative vaccination been a good thing? Sir Arthur C. Clarke has written that if we do not find other intelligent life in the universe, then the consequences for us may be catastrophic; better to have neighbors we don't like, even enemies, in place of no one at all to measure ourselves and our history against. Satirists, humorists and misanthropes have struggled to make us step back and look at ourselves, to get a better view; but their efforts lack plausible conviction when we consider "who" or "what" is speaking to us. Even in the greatest of science fictions lurks a self-serving element that insists we are a "breakout species" and not a failure waiting to happen. We are both the accused and the judge, trapped in a logical absurdity which cannot reach a conclusion.

The possibility does exist that advanced cultures may come and go, missing each other more often than not in the vastness of space-time, and only advanced forms of interstellar travel would break this quarantine. But perhaps such forms of travel are not quickly possible, or ever possible, and the interstellar quarantine is a good thing until laborious slow travel makes rational contact possible; but will the fear of the worlds ever be overcome? Is there a way to make contact without mutual annihilation? Will anyone ever take such a chance, given the risks, real or not? Would easy interstellar travel in the hands of intelligent life only magnify its flaws of origin? When we see how power has magnified our own flaws, we see that technology helps us lose control of ourselves. A drunk in a car is a simple example.

Contact with an alien culture cannot be conceived with certainty; only when it happens, if it ever does, will we learn whether it happens benignly or not. Perhaps its "slowness," as imposed by the speed of light, will ease the dangers. The doing will tell, and by then it may be too late. That is the lesson of the evolutionary cauldron of biology that we call a planet, in which life is vampiric on other life. Darwin found it appalling and wondered why it had to be this way, this endless agriculture of death that nevertheless has brought forth such a wondrous variety of life.

Today, we see that built upon biology are what we call our cultures, our series of rising and falling civilizations which have not escaped the struggle of nature's wars, despite our dreams of reason and peace. The *cooperative* element in evolutionary biology is still neglected, but it exists in our efforts at civil order, slowly, imperfectly growing, even as we continue to idolize the rogue. The megalomaniacal artilleryman is admired by Wells' narrator for his spirit of resistance and his projected view of a heroic human life under the rule of the Martians. John Christopher's Tripod Trilogy (1967–1968), also a striking television series, carries out this scenario with hopeful insight; while Thomas M. Disch's 1965 novel *The Genocides* takes the idea to its bitter end. William Tenn's *Of Men and Monsters* (1968) delivers the artilleryman's vision of humanity living as rats under an alien occupation, and doing quite well, thank you.

In *The War of the Worlds*, Darwin's natural world blindly allows humanity to survive through defenses older than our conscious efforts; but sometimes, as in death by pneumonia in the individual, these defenses suddenly fail. Wells spent his life warning us to make better use of our survival when things are going well in our "piling up" of a civilization that we hold precariously on the knife-edge foundation of our biology, before our luck runs out.

Reading *The War of the Worlds* today, we should try to imagine the helplessness of those who come under superior firepower and the bravery of resistance to such slaughter which we saw during the twentieth and now in the early twenty-first century. Keep in mind that Wells' story has been surpassed by our own ingenuity in the arts of death. Recall the witness of those warriors and victims of war who suddenly realized, in the horror of a moment, that *nothing* is worth tearing human bodies apart. I knew a soldier who was living a wounded life. Tough and resentful, not unlike Wells' artilleryman in his pride and ignorance, he rarely spoke of his experiences and his physical injuries, but one day he said to me, "They take you when you're young and don't know better, and teach you to do terrible things to people." Then he fell quiet into his trauma, and never spoke of it again. I saw him involuntarily hit the ground like a puppet when a car backfired, and he slept with a guard dog under his bed.

Why read *The War of the Worlds* today? Why read about all those period settings in which the science fiction never happened? The answer is to gain perspectives that cannot be had in any other way. Are not readers, and readers of science fiction in particular, all time travelers who can see beyond the styles of history to the heart of the matter? If we are not such questioning travelers, then we are hopeless temporal provincials, unworthy of the imaginative liberation offered by the best science fiction, which grows out of the freedom bestowed by knowledge wedded to literary insight.

Writing, fiction and nonfiction, even when it fails, is a miraculous act, because it stops time and presents experience and thought in lasting form. Our imaginings are also experiences—of ourselves—and as such are "additions to life," in C. S. Lewis' words. The worth of writing, among many worths, is best exemplified by the fact that, today, we would desire to have even the lowliest writings from ancient Greece and Rome to add to the few surviving texts. I think of what lies buried in today's landfills, in the cultural landfills of our collective memory, in the packed rot of our willful ignorance, and do not wonder why we often fail to see the worth of the contemporary. Today flashes by our blindered minds into the abyss. Gift boxes from our talented are seen as empty, waiting for later times to value treasures that will one day open in the papery solidity between the covers of books, as we struggle to see the past, lose the present, and not just long for but invade the future.

I did not expect, in rereading *The War of the Worlds*, to find it so full of inspired greatness, not only in its language, but in its ideas to the right, left, above and below the main idea of the title. To read this book afresh is to feel the world around you fade away before *implications*. The boy who once read this story for the invasion, for the action, could not see what I now see. Where once I cheered at the bloodied flesh of a Martian hemorrhaging in the shiny metal of its war machine as it was struck by a human artillery shell, I now applaud and feel relief from the "broadening of men's views" described by the Wellsian narrator.

Finally, any discussion of *The War of the Worlds* must come to grips with the importance of its author to the literature that took its inspiration from his work. It was not enough to present startling possibilities, or even fantastic impossibilities that open up new dramatic avenues; true artfulness needed to give us the meanings, the thinking behind the plausible imaginings. And that is what Wells gave us in addition to thrills and good writing, which are in fact inseparable from his accomplishment, because otherwise it would play as so much less in the reader's mind.

When Wells' narrator speaks of the "broadening of men's views" that follows the failure of the Martian invasion, the author is suggesting much more than a consequence of the story's outcome. Wells is also talking about the kind of writing he has undertaken in this and later works, based on a growing body of knowledge about humanity's place in nature. Wells did not see himself as an sf writer in today's sense, but as a writer and thinker whose subject was the shifting future of humankind. The fantastic direction of fictional imaginings had preceded him, but he gave them the enrichment of the growing sciences, from which he took much more than a catalog of factual knowledge, but also the critical, self-correcting, exploratory method of science. It is when so much of today's science fiction forgets this heritage of the Scientific Revolution and the Enlightenment that it trivializes its efforts, loses its cogency and seems little more than arbitrary extravagance.

More than a century of ideas first stated as print science fiction have passed into science and technology, the social sciences and the humanities—and even diluted by movies and adventure fiction, through the ulterior motives of commerce, into what we call entertainment (where, recall, we can often whisper what we fear to say out loud). These ideas have set us to live for the future and to hope that we might shape it.

There is an interest in Wells' work that has been growing ever since his death at the dawn of the atomic age in 1946 (the two differing Martian movies of his novel are only one sign), a rediscovery and reassessment not only of his early science fiction but also of his nonfiction and contemporary novels—a hundred or more books which show the same eloquence found in *The War of the Worlds*, by the writer who invaded our possible futurities when the very idea of thinking about them seemed an impossible extravagance. He made us all into time travelers through thought and imagination, without which there is no science fiction worthy of the name.

∗ ● ∘

This is in memory of W. Warren Wagar (1932–2004), historian, science fiction writer and friend, with whom I shared a scholarly interest in H. G. Wells, and whose last book, *H. G. Wells: Traversing Time* (Wesleyan, 2004) is both a lucid page-turning education in world history and the personal guide like no other to Wells' work.

George Zebrowski's more than forty books include the Campbell Award winner for best novel of the year, *Brute Orbits*; the classic *Macrolife* and its companion *Cave of Stars*; various anthologies edited with Isaac Asimov, Gregory Benford, Jack Dann and Thomas N. Scortia; and the five volumes of the legendary Synergy series. His award-nominated short fiction has been collected in the Publishers Weekly-starred *Swift Thoughts*, in *In the Distance*, and *Ahead in Time*, and in *Black Pockets* (Golden Gryphon). A new edition of *Macrolife* (with an introduction by Ian Watson and an afterword by the author) will be published by Pyr, a division of Prometheus Books.

DAVID ZINDELL

Martian Compassion

MANY PEOPLE, THANKS TO H. G. WELLS and other developers of science fiction, do believe in the first years of the twenty-first century that this world is being watched by intelligences greater than man's. Few, though, suspect the identity and true nature of these beings. Across the gulf of space, minds that are to our minds as ours are to those of the beasts that perish, intellects vast and cool and yet strangely sympathetic, are still regarding this Earth with envious eyes and drawing their plans against us.

We know now that the Martian threat is real—as real as the Martians themselves. Remarkable new information about these aliens and their ancient civilization has come forth in various forms from virtually every corner of the Earth.

In London, upon the recent death of Lord Richard Herbert, his son Keith discovered a packet of musty, yellowed letters in a locked drawer of his father's study. Their handwriting has been authenticated as that of H. G. Wells, who wrote them to Lord Richard's grandmother, Claire Truesdale, over a period of six years around the beginning of the twentieth century. The letters are, mostly, love letters. There no longer can be any doubt that Claire Truesdale conducted a long affair with H. G. Wells, both before her marriage to Lord Anthony Herbert and after, and that Wells fathered Truesdale's son, David Herbert, and perhaps two of her four daughters as well. Biographers will cite this as yet another instance of Wells' promiscuity in his lifelong quest for the perfect sexual union. But the letters reveal his deeper motives for having children with the numerous women he took to his bed, both in and out of marriage: he wanted to leave numerous progeny scattered about the world, for he understood better than anyone else of his generation what fate likely awaited the Earth.

In a letter dated March 23, 1904, Wells admits to Truesdale his long association with the psychic Wilfred MacAndrews, perhaps Madame Blavatsky's greatest if least-known disciple. MacAndrews, while hiking around Stonehenge in1893, received the first of a series of communications concerning the Martians. At first he had difficulty making sense of his terrifying visions. MacAndrews clearly "saw" the Martian invasion of England, from the impact of their first cylinder in the sandpits of Horsell Commons to its logical conclusion. But none of the papers made mention of this invasion or the Martian assault upon London. After MacAndrews completed his holiday exploring the countryside around Horsell, Ottershaw and Woking, he concluded that his vision must have been that of another world. A dream world, he initially called this, although he felt in his heart that the world revealed in his visions was very real. Likewise he abandoned the terminology of an astral world, for he felt as well that the Martian destruction of England must have occurred on the material plane of existence. Finally, he settled on naming it the "counter-Earth." This was perhaps the first conception of what we now usually refer to as a parallel Earth.

The great New Age physicist, Vijay Mohan, has determined that this parallel Earth belongs to a universe very close to ours, separated by only a few billion quantum events. He has classified it as PU3593074091. In respect for empiricism, of course, he has refused to speculate as to the nature of the parallel Mars or the parallel Earth belonging to it. But he did confirm that the information channeled by Wilfred MacAndrews had its source in that universe. Considering the mentality of the late Victorian era, it can be no wonder that H. G. Wells chose to reveal his knowledge of the parallel Earth as a fictional jeremiad taking place in our own.

If *The War of the Worlds* happened to be our only account of that invasion, we would not know important details about the Martians and their invasion, for Wells had good reason to withhold them from us. Of other matters concerning the Martians he was ignorant, while in a few critical things he felt compelled to deceive his readers altogether. Fortunately, though, we are now in possession of a growing body of channeled literature concerning Mars. Only a year ago, in Poona, India, Devora Sakti Ananda (born as Shirley Judd in Texas and possibly one of Wells' great-great-granddaughters) delivered the famous Red Planet Prophecies. In the Brazilian Amazon, the shaman Don Vincente Alvarez "spoke" with the ayahuasca spirits, who informed him that his sacred plant had its origins in the spoors that had drifted across space from Mars—and explained much about the ecology of that planet as well. Even in my own backyard, so to speak, here in Boulder, Colorado, one of my acquaintances has told me of numerous past lives that she lived as a Martian. From these sources, and many others, it is possible to assemble a much clearer picture of the Martians than the one that Wells painted for his readers.

Who can blame Wells, for instance, for lying outright concerning the nature of Martian sex? True, the Martians form their progeny, as do hydras, through a budding process much as Wells told. But asexual this process is not. Wells, as revealed to Claire Truesdale in a letter dated August 3, 1903, describes in detail the exterior Martian sexual organ, much resembling the pipettes that the Martians use to transfuse the blood of their prey into their own veins. That this organ extruded from and worked in conjunction with the tentacles around the Martian mouth he feared would disgust Truesdale, and perhaps excite her, too. Wells had more trouble explaining the Martians' sexual biology. In 1903, of course, Watson's and Crick's discovery of DNA lay a half-century in the future. Wells had only the vaguest conception of how the single-sexed Martians passed back and forth to each other their germ plasm, which circulated through their greenish blood and came to reside in a small organ connected to their massive brains. Through the conscious control of this organ (Hans Friedrich Fadenrecht calls it the Götterborn), the Martians engineered the DNA of their multiple mates sequence by sequence, here creating new codons, there snipping out old ones, much as artists might add or subtract pigments to a collaborative painting. Finally, the DNA was passed on to its final recipient, who used the DNA to make RNA and form up tissues and organs in budding off a piece of itself as a new Martian.

If Wells understood only poorly the technical aspects of Martian procreation, he had a much better grasp of their complex copulation. Wilfred MacAndrews described to him in exquisite detail what can only be called an orgy. The Martians, according to MacAndrews, most often conjoined in groups of three, though unions of six, nine or more, up to as many as twenty-seven, were common, too. To our eyes, the sight of the naked Martians en masse—with their oily brown skin, their quivering and tentacled mouths dripping saliva and their reddened, stabbing sexual organs—would be a horror. Add to that the image of a great clump of their huge bodies, heaving and pulsating convulsively over a period lasting up to ten days and their unearthly howls, shrieks and ululating calls to each other, and we have a nightmarish vision that most men of Wells' times could dispel only with several glasses of good whiskey, while those of our age would require years of counseling. We should applaud Wells for being able to contemplate Martian sex so coolly and rationally. He could not, of course, reveal his ultimate conclusions in this matter through any of his public speeches or writings. How could he even hint at the truth of things to the prim Victorians, who sometimes covered their tables' legs with cloths because the sight of bare legs, even wooden ones, was thought to be indecent? To Claire Truesdale, though, and perhaps to other intimates, he revealed the astonishing actuality of Martian sex: that far from being an abomination both hideous and sinful, it engendered an ecstasy almost too great for human beings to imagine.

To understand why this should be so—and to understand as well the causes and course of the Martian invasion—it is necessary to delve far back, tens of millions of years into the ancient past of these mysterious aliens. At some point in their long history, the Martians were much like us. Jared Rice, a fan of the great science fiction writer Ray Bradbury, tells of this species' genesis and evolution in *The True Martian Chronicles*. It seems that this species did not originate on Mars; rather they evolved on our solar system's fifth planet, which they called, simply, OurHome.

The Martians—their name for themselves translates best as "the People"—faced problems and asked themselves questions that have always vexed human beings: What is the meaning of life? What it is the best way to live it? How should they treat the other people, animals and plant life with which they shared OurHome?

The Martians for a long time were riven into many tribes and polities. Like us, they waged terrible wars upon each other and enslaved the defeated and the weak. They tortured their enemies, to extract information or for pure sport. They drank their blood.

As they evolved things became ever worse. The wars grew in fury, and entire populations were annihilated. The People of the various polities found it necessary to bind in hard labor ever greater parts of their *own* populations. They no longer called them slaves, but workers, and they put them to tending machines in the People's factories instead. In a story that must have been repeated countless times on countless worlds across the stars, the rich grew ever richer while the poor grew so poor they were forced to sell their very blood. Most of the stronger and more fortunate Martians would have shrugged their shoulders at this (if they had possessed shoulders), and they would have said: "That is just life. The fittest survive and thrive. Over time, our riches of energy, material and ideas provide a greater life for all, even the poorest of the poor Bloodsellers."

This is an easy philosophy for those at the top of a society to believe; for some millennia, on OurHome, it even seemed to be true. But inexorably, the People expanded into every niche and corner of their world and tore out of the ground almost every mineral capable of being shaped into a machine or consumed by them. They despoiled their forests and oceans; they filled the air with a poisonous smoke and made their watercourses into sewers.

And still the wars grew more terrible. The coolest and most rational of the Martians clearly saw that a great deal of the People's energy, material and ideas was being used to dominate or kill each other. Toward the ideal of equality, peace and a better way of living, in a few polities the Martians tried to change their economic and social systems to something resembling communism. As on Earth, however, this new way of life failed, and for much the same reason. H. G. Wells, in one thing at least, was right about the Martians: they were not by nature a compassionate people. Outside of their mating triads—and sextuples, nonuples and so on—they cared little about other Martians. Certainly they were not willing to sacrifice any of their hard-won wealth to the poorest of their kind, who would only be tempted to ease their labor at their machines or quit it altogether. And if they had searched their hearts (if they had possessed true hearts), they would have admitted that they took much of their wealth and their good life from the labor of the poorest Martians, even as they took their blood.

And so their revolutionaries had to impose communism upon them, and they tried to change Martian nature in a longer and more brutal totalitarianism than anything we human beings ever suffered. In the end, these communistic experiments all decayed or were destroyed by the more traditional Martian polities. And so life on OurHome continued on its logical course.

Very late in the evolution of the People on the fifth planet—but still very long ago, when our human ancestors stood only a few feet high and were being eaten by leopards—life on OurHome grew dire. The Martians had invented many massively destructive weapons: the poisonous Black Smoke, the Heat-Ray, the nuclear bomb. Over time, a few of these weapons came under the control of rogue polities and fell into the hands (if the Martians could be said to have possessed hands) of rebels who called themselves "WeWhoLiveFreeOrDie." The wealthy Martians, of course, who controlled the vast bulk of OurHome's arsenals, called the rebels the "EvilWorldDestroyers." Most human beings of our time, here on our Earth in the early twenty-first century, would think of them, simply, as terrorists.

The Martians of the fifth planet did all they could to defeat or destroy the terrorists: they set whole populations to spying on each other; they implanted microchips beneath the oily skin of their millions and tracked their movements through their global positioning satellites; they hunted down anyone suspected of terrorist sympathies in a pitiless campaign that degenerated into a massacre. All to no avail. The terrorists began blowing up the Martian cities, one by one, in an even more murderous devastation. To the most enlightened Martians, one thing became clear: there could be no defense against nuclear weapons. A single bomb, in the "hands" of a determined terrorist, could and did incinerate millions. And for every thousand terrorists and bombs that the ruling Martians found out and destroyed, at least one terrorist and one bomb survived. No threat of torture or death could deter these most dedicated of terrorists. And so the Martian cities began vanishing into a rubble of glowing, radioactive waste, and OurHome began to die.

Around this time, one of the greatest Martians in history was born—or rather, budded off from one of the Martian rulers. DreamsImpossibleDreams can be seen as a sort of Einstein, Moses and Gandhi (or Madame Curie, Joan of Arc and Mother Teresa) composed into one brilliant being. Even before reaching maturity, Dreams saw that Martian society must be utterly transformed. Dreams was the most logical of a very logical race, and reasoned like this: since the terrorists could not be completely destroyed, they must be completely redeemed. The only way to do this would be to eradicate the causes that drove them to terrorism. The Martians, as Dreams argued before the ruling council of OurHome's greatest polity, must all be made happy and sane, down to the lowest of the Bloodsellers. If they were not, if even one Martian fell to envying the freedom and riches of the other Martians and determined on revenge, then this single malcontent might blow up all of OurHome with the long-theorized UWMD: the Ultimate Weapon of Mass Destruction. In the words of Dreams, as translated by Jared Rice: "We must make the lives of all Martians better, not because it is right—not just because it is right—but because if we don't, they will make our lives worse or end them altogether."

The ruling Martians reminded Dreams that communism had already been tried, and had failed. Actually, Dreams was proposing something much more radical and profound than communism: the very evolution of Martian consciousness. The ruling council understood this. They labeled Dreams' ideals as utopian, and therefore dismissed them as impossible. Dreams asked the Martian rulers a question that later became famous: "How is it possible that the impossible is not only possible but inevitable?" Dreams then prophesied that the Martians would create for themselves only one of two futures: either a society that very much resembled a utopia, or utter destruction.

The rulers did not listen. In truth, they *could* not listen. Although only slightly less logical than Dreams, they could not accept this logic's conclusion. Therefore they despaired and fell a little mad. They fell upon the terrorists with even greater frenzy. One of them, Exterminates-DisloyalPeople, castigated Dreams' ideas as terroristic and Dreams as a terrorist. Dreams was forced to flee into a neighboring rogue polity, along with the two others of his mating triad. There, they began work on Dreams' greatest conception: an advance in biology and consciousness that would forever transform the Martians.

After many failures, Dreams' triad managed to engineer with a cold rationality a wholly new organ, whose purpose was anything but rational or cold. Vijay Mohan calls it the *tatvam asi*. These three idealists implanted the tatvam asi in themselves, just beneath their massive brains. They mated with a furious bliss over several years, and began budding dozens of offspring, each of which bore the tatvam asi conjoined to its brain by right of genetic inheritance.

How is it possible for us, people of Earth locked within the lonely bone prisons of our heads, to understand this greatest advance in all the evolutionary history of our solar system? Perhaps like this: as a transmitter of nerve signals. The tatvam asi, quite simply, functioned as a sort of cell phone that interconnected the Martians' brains to each other.

At first the powers of the tatvam asi had strict limits. Its signal fell off as with the square of the distance of any two Martians from each other, therefore weakening quickly and practically vanishing at a hundred yards. It didn't matter. Dreams' triad—and the nonuple of nonuples now descended from it—remained always close to each other, physically, and mentally, too, for they found themselves able to communicate in silence with a rudimentary, though effective, telepathy. H. G. Wells, in *The War of the Worlds*, remarks upon this astonishing ability. He makes no mention, however, of the tatvam asi's more profound property, the true purpose toward which Dreams had designed it: the tatvam asi functioned even more perfectly as an organ of empathy. That which any bearer of the tatvam asi experienced, either pleasure or pain, any other bearer experienced in equal or even greater measure.

The evolution of the tatvam asi effected an immediate, deep and lasting change in Dreams' people. They found it nearly impossible to harm each other. Jesus might have been channeling Dreams' ideal when he formulated the Golden Rule: "Do unto others as you would have them do unto you." Many human beings accept this as the fundamental moral principle. For the Martians associated with Dreams, however, it became a vital necessity. If one Martian injured another, the hurt of it could return to the Martian's own brain ninefold or more through the amplification of many other brains. Torture became impossible. The very thought of drinking of another's blood was loathed as an abomination. To kill another was, literally, to kill oneself.

After some years, Dreams' people grew to number hundreds and then thousands. Within the violent society of OurHome, they created their own society: peaceful, harmonious, compassionate and just. The Martian rulers, and even the rebels of the rogue polity that had given them shelter, reviled them as communists and deluded utopians. But their way of life soon evolved far beyond any of the primitive Martian notions about communism, for Dreams' people found themselves *wanting* to share their energy, material and ideas with each other, and more, their very lives. In them lived the human ideal of the family, and with great gladness they sacrificed for each other and strove to make each other happy, as a mother might with her child.

At last, Dreams' society became too great a threat to the ruling Martians, who planned its obliteration in a series of nuclear strikes. Upon learning this, Dreams' people said farewell to OurHome. Dreams gathered everyone into metal cylinders; great explosions shot them out into space toward the fourth planet, which we call Mars. Upon setting foot on their new world (if Dreams' people could be said to have possessed feet), Dreams named it OurNewHome. They found Mars to be too cold and dry and with too little gravity to support the kind of life they had known. And so they built domed cities half buried in the sand; they shot communication satellites into the sky, not to track each other's movements, but to amplify the range and power of the tatvam asi. They found time at last to eradicate the bacteria and viruses that had plagued the Martians' bodies from time immemorial, and so overcame even disease. For long millennia they dwelt with each other in peace, and lived as one.

Soon after their colonization of Mars, they looked out through their telescopes to witness the fate of the world they had fled. As Dreams had feared, one of their kind—perhaps the dreaded terrorist called Madly-AnnihilatesAll—succeeded in employing the Ultimate Weapon of Mass Destruction. Madly had long ranted that either all Martians should enjoy the bounty of OurHome equally, or no one would. *Someone*, certainly, succeeded in using the powerful Martian mind to touch directly upon the infons composing the deepest level of matter of the molten core of OurHome. Through pure consciousness, a sort of perfect understanding of the onstreaming mindstuff that underlies all matter, its omega-point energy was released in a cataclysmic blast of pure energy. The explosion blew OurHome to smithereens. Great chunks of dead rock, all that was left of the planet, cooled slowly and orbited the sun between Jupiter and Mars as asteroids. Although none of the exterminated race possessed the tatvam asi to channel this racial death anguish, Dreams and his people grieved nearly to the point of dying themselves. Dreams thought long and hard about the UWMD, this utter understanding of a thing that could bring about its destruction. He called it *grokking*, and he foresaw that the future of life through the solar system, and perhaps the whole universe, might depend upon who grokked what and why they chose to grok it.

After that, life on Mars went on. Dreams grew old and died, as did generation after generation of Dreams' descendants. The People spread very slowly across OurNewHome. It took a million years, and more, for them fill up every niche capable of supporting their way of life and to begin exhausting Mars' resources. At last, they turned their telescopes sunward to study the third planet, which we call Earth and the more visionary Martians named as OurFutureHome. They discussed the Earth's invasion, and began making their plans.

How, we might wonder, could a race as compassionate as the Martians had become so coolly contemplate the horrors they intended to visit upon humanity? According to Wilfred MacAndrews, the answer to that question is simple, though hard to accept: the Martians regarded us as animals. Over more than a million years of their evolution, they had come to define the very essence of Martianness according to the tatvam asi and its powers. Only the People possessed this miraculous organ; and only those who possessed it could be considered true people.

And so, yes, the Martians were and are highly compassionate beings— but only toward other Martians. Lower creatures, such as us, through whose veins streams a rich if primitive life, they regarded, mainly, as food. We can protest that it should not be so. We can argue that we are rational and highly evolved beings, even possessed of a divine spark. What greater crime could there be than to waste such a noble work in enslavement, murder or even predation?

H. G. Wells understood otherwise. Near the beginning of *The War of the Worlds*, he takes pains to mention the European extermination of the Tasmanians, whom he denigrates as an inferior race. He might have cited, as well, the Maori slaughter and cannibalization of their cousins, the Moriori, or the Aztecs' ripping out of their captive's hearts—to say nothing of the Nazi's gassing of millions of Jews and making their skin into lampshades. If we can wreak such atrocities upon each other, why should the Martians feel at all squeamish about exploiting what truly *is* a lower race?

The truth is, they didn't and don't. At least most of them, the orthodox, don't. On the Red Planet, over thousands of years as the Martians watched the Earth's peoples master fire and the growing of plants for food, and more advanced technology, the hungry many waited as our numbers grew from a couple of scattered millions toward the hundreds of millions and then a billion. And all the while, the pitying few argued that the People should leave human beings alone. The orthodox Martians, if they had possessed such organs and terminology, might have called these few "bleeding hearts." We might best think of them by another name, suggested by Nina Martinelli, a psychic and a founding member of PETA. Nina, who was once arrested for throwing blood on a famous actress walking down Aspen's streets flaunting a fur coat, usually refers to this practically angelic alien minority as the Martians for the Ethical Treatment of Animals. Or, more simply, the METANS.

As with human beings and PETA, most orthodox Martians consider those belonging to META to be a little nuts. *Not* because the METANS lack logic, but because they push logic to absurd ends. The METANS have long argued that the ancient Martians had extended basic rights to the slaves and the Bloodsellers, and had ultimately tried to abolish both supporting institutions. If even the lowest of Martians had the right to life, why didn't animals? And the orthodox Martians responded: Why didn't plants, such as the red weed they had brought with them from OurHome, have rights? Why didn't the bacteria that had once infested the Martians' bodies deserve to exist? For surely the most fundamental right was the right to life. But if all things possessed that right, then nothing could consume anything, and the entire biosphere would fail. And then *nothing* would live at all.

Some of the METANS declared that a line must be drawn: animals, particularly higher ones such as human beings, could feel pain and existential anxiety whereas plants could not, and therefore should be spared. Did the Martian *might* give them the *right* to make complex beings suffer and die? Upon what fundament should the Martians base their ethics?

The orthodox Martians responded that the way of nature was that almost anything killed anything if it was to their advantage and they could get away with it. Animals certainly didn't treat animals ethically. From where do rights come, they asked? Does the lowly urquark, the Martians' primary prey, have a right not to be killed and consumed? Or only not to be consumed by the *sapient* Martians, who should know better? The orthodox finally eschewed impossible philosophical debates in favor of pragmatism: animals were only animals, whether complex or not, and in any case, Martians required the fresh, living blood of animals to survive. Should the Martians, out of misplaced compassion, simply refuse to eat and die?

Many METANS, in their horror of life's monstrous nature, argued that they should. Other METANS preached that the Martians should evolve complex digestive tracks and even huger bodies that would enable them to consume the red weed and other plant matter. A few hypothesized that the Martians might implant chlorophyll beneath their skin, and so utilize light as do plants. The most extreme dreamed of using the power of grokking in reverse: they would gather light to themselves and transform it into the matter of their bodies. Nina Martinelli calls them the Live On Lighters, or the LOL.

For a long time, both on the parallel Mars and our own solar system's fourth planet, the debate raged on. At last, ProtectorOfAnimals defected from the METANS to the orthodox camp. Protector observed that the Martian psychohistorians had predicted the Earth's nuclear and environmental devastation. Protector declared that the Martians should mount a crusade to *save* the Earth's animals: the many mammals, birds, fishes and other species that human beings were destroying in the millions. Three kinds of Earth life the Martians esteemed above all others: the dog, for its amazing empathy; the bonobo chimpanzee for the way these creatures sexualized every aspect of their society and managed to live in a joyous harmony with nature; and the cetaceans in almost all ways. Man, as even the METANS agreed, should be ranked well below these kinds. (It should be stressed that all the Martians had become as used to technology as the fish are to water, and did not regard humans' ability to manipulate and fabricate *things* as any great accomplishment. And, of course, human language, philosophy and apprehension of life's deepest mystery seemed primitive in comparison with that of the great whales.) ProtectorOfAnimals' crowning argument was that human beings, while unworthy of being ranked with the highest animals, still had value. They too must be saved: above all, saved from themselves.

And so Protector won the orthodox and even many of the METANS to this point of view. The plans for Earth's invasion proceeded and reached their final stage. Great metal cylinders were fabricated, along with the Black Smoke and terrible weapons that radiated heat. The Martians waited for Earth's orbit and that of Mars to bring our two planets to their closest conjunction.

We know much of what happened on the parallel Earth, for Wells describes this with fair accuracy in *The War of the Worlds*. The Martians' cylinders came to ground outside of London. Within a short period, their Heat-Ray destroyed many buildings and trees across the English countryside and burnt many people to a black crisp. Many more the Martians scooped up into metal baskets as we might gather raspberries.

We know as well what fate the Martians intended for these poor people, and for every human being who survived the invasion. Wells gives a hint of this near the end of his book, in his narrator's encounter with the artilleryman. Through the artilleryman's speech, Wells reveals not only his own vicious, racist Darwinism but his appreciation of man's essentially low estate. The Earth is to become a sort of prison planet incarcerating human beings, or more accurately, a farm. As the Masai do with their cattle in Kenya, the Martians will keep us in a herdlike docility for the purpose of drinking our blood. And worst of all—this is perhaps Wells' deepest anxiety and the source of his deepest loathing for his own kind—we will keep ourselves in a slavish debasement. Wells sees most of the overly civilized people of his times as like rabbits, with "no proud dreams and no proud lusts." As Wells puts it:

The Martians will be just a godsend to these. Nice roomy cages, fattening food, careful breeding, no worry. After a week or so of chasing about the fields and lands on empty stomachs, they'll come and be caught cheerful. They'll be quite glad after a bit. They'll wonder what people did before there were Martians to take care of them.

Wells, of course, through many conversations with Wilfred MacAndrews, must have known that this is almost exactly the way the invading Martians saw human beings. They characterized most people as Bloodsellers, not literally, but in the way the rich and powerful took from them their life energies. What the Martians planned for us was only what we were used to anyway. If anything, the Martians argued, most people's lives would be better than they were before the invasion. In a very real sense, the Martians would be doing us a favor.

A few Martians, however, still opposed the invasion. The most fanatic of the fanatical LOL gathered near the invasion fleet. They doused their leader, DreamsTrulyImpossibleDreams (one of the famous Dreams' descendants), with rocket fuel and stood watching while DreamsTruly gripped with trembling tentacles an unlighted match. On the parallel Mars, DreamsTruly could not quite find the will to light it. On our Mars, however, within DreamsTruly's great and compassionate brain, there occurred the 3,593,074,091 quantum events that caused our two universes to diverge: DreamsTruly saw the light of the possible and found the courage to strike the match. DreamsTruly's flesh burst into fire, and this great being died in a crackling, writhing agony.

Almost instantaneously, ten million Martians across the Red Planet suffered DreamsTruly's death anguish, and nearly died with him. Other members of the LOL were inspired to threaten such self-immolation if the invasion wasn't called off. This proved too much for the orthodox Martians, especially those leading the invasion. They could not bring themselves to enter the assembled metal cylinders. They waited and watched as Mars and the Earth neared each other, reached conjunction and then drifted apart through space.

And so the Earth, *our* Earth and that of H. G. Wells, was saved. Wells often discussed this miracle with Wilfred MacAndrews in private. In public, in *The War of the Worlds*, he writes of the deliverance of the parallel Earth: by the germs to which human beings have long since developed immunity but which killed the defenseless Martians down to the last monstrous, merciless one. This, aside from being a most unsatisfactory *deus ex machina*, in the literary sense, was sheer nonsense:

an obvious lie. Wells knew with a sickening certainty what had really occurred on the parallel Earth.

Even in his famous novel, he betrays his illogic and duplicity in the way the novel's very beginning undercuts the ending: how could the Martians possibly have studied us as if we were "infusoria under the microscope" and not known about the plagues and diseases that have ravaged every human population on every continent throughout history? No, Wells' fiction was a sop to his readers' fears and vanities. Who, living in the late Victorian era, could accept the horrible truth: that the Martians of the parallel universe easily reduced England to a factory farm with men, women and children as its primary food product? The invaders had even less difficulty in subduing the Eurasian continent— and North America, Africa and every other land on Earth.

True, as Wells' artilleryman prophesied, a few brave souls lived like animals within the filth-cleansed sewers of London and other unlikely places, from which they tried to mount a resistance. Wells clearly hoped that the invasion would unite those few human beings who kept their proud hopes and proud lusts alive. (Even as in our own times, in the movie *Independence Day*, which might have been a channeled account of yet another parallel universe, human beings successfully—and ridiculously—came together to defeat a vastly superior extermination force.) In truth, these ragtag survivalists had about as much hope of usurping the Martians' machines and weapons and turning them against the Martians as a few wild hunter-gatherers might of prevailing against an army of tanks and airplanes with blowguns. The Martians paid them even less attention than we do to rats.

Wells did not live to "witness" the regreening of the parallel Earth or the saving of its whales and other creatures, for the fruit of the Martians' great crusade took many years to ripen. The Martians, while keeping human beings on their farms, left the rest of our world to return to its wild and natural ways. Even the METANS, who ventured to Earth in the invasion's thirty-third wave, had to admit that the invasion had been a success. Upon dipping their feeding parts into our veins and tasting the incredibly rich, sweet human blood that so quickened their own lives, they allowed that perhaps it *was* best to protect human beings from each other, so long as they were well-treated. Their monstrous mouths would have turned up in a smile, if they had been able to smile. After all, the human beings of the parallel Earth did indeed seem happy.

As for *our* Earth, after DreamsTruly's noble sacrifice, life continued on its logical course. The Martians had put off their invasion until human beings reached a critical point in Earth's history: long enough for our population to swell sufficiently to provide the Martians with nearly unlimited food, but not so long that we could develop nuclear weapons mounted on rockets and so defend ourselves. It shocked the Martians that human beings fabricated the first fission devices so quickly, barely fifty years after the aborted invasion, for it seemed that the Martian psychohistorians had badly miscalculated our technological capabilities. *All* Martians, both the orthodox and the METANS, watched in alarm as the first nuclear bomb exploded near Alamogordo in the desert of North America. The destruction of two cities in Japan in nuclear blasts a couple of months later only deepened their horror. For a few years, after the ending of what human beings called the Cold War, the Martians found themselves hoping that human beings might make a planetary peace, and perhaps abolish nuclear weapons altogether. But when the Earth's greatest nuclear power fell to the religious and economic fundamentalists and began waging war so wantonly, the orthodox Martians decided that intervention would be necessary. They began planning another invasion, despite the threats of the suicidal LOL. Events, however, had finally convinced most of these most compassionate Martians that human beings had become too dangerous to be left alone. They added their voices to the chorus of siren-like howls calling for invasion. But as the rational Martians came to realize, it was already too late.

They watched as on Earth, ironically, humans' strongest polity invaded one of the weakest under the pretext that it was concealing Weapons of Mass Destruction. This, of course, was nonsense. If the weak polity had actually possessed WMDs, the rulers of the strong polity never would have risked invasion for the very good reason that they didn't wish, in retaliation, to be massively destroyed. So it was with the Martians and Earth. Due to the potentially nerve-shattering powers of the tatvam asi, which could cause a spreading wave of empathic death, they could not risk the destruction of even one of their cylinders, let alone a hundred or a thousand. And so the rational Martians convinced the most reckless and desperate to put off the invasion yet again.

And so the Martians continue to watch us. The most optimistic—and these are mostly of META and the LOL—would like to regard human beings as children who will some day grow up, similar to the ancient Martians on OurHome before the evolution of the tatvam asi: children with hydrogen bombs. But other Martians are more cynical. Their warnings echo the words of one of Earth's greatest philosophers, Homer Simpson: "Children are our future—unless we stop them now."

These militant Martians, as Devora Sakti Ananda tells us, will do what they must to stop us from making the Earth a radioactive wasteland, and even more so with Mars. Perhaps, despite the ancient Martians' despair, they *will* find a defense against nuclear weapons. Perhaps they will employ the UWMD to melt the triggers of every nuclear weapon on Earth and render them useless, all in the flash of a thought, in a single moment. Then an invasion would become possible, again. Or perhaps they will simply grok that human beings must be utterly destroyed—and along with them the whole Earth, in a fiery end like that of OurHome. The Martians would be sad beyond telling to destroy as well the dogs, bonobos and whales, and all our world's other myriad species, but if necessity determines such a fate for the Earth, can we believe that they will hesitate?

H. G. Wells, despite his natural pessimism, labored all his life to avoid the worst for his planet and his people. As he often said: "Human history becomes more and more a race between education and catastrophe." He realized better than almost anyone just how great a catastrophe human beings might suffer. And he worked very hard, through his writings, lectures and personal meetings, to educate and uplift the people of his times, and even those of future generations.

We know from historical accounts that Wells wanted to awaken humankind to the instability of the world order—with good reason. After the Great War, he argued with passion in support of the League of Nations. Some years later, he met with Stalin and Roosevelt, the rulers of our world's greatest polities, in order to reconcile pseudo-communism with the more traditional monopolizing by the rich of energy, material and ideas that Roosevelt's people practiced. Almost by force of will, he made himself into a utopian, looking always for ways to better humankind. According to the *Encyclopaedia Britannica*: "He everywhere and continuously urged upon the world the necessity of what he called an open conspiracy to defeat the forces that were leading mankind to its own destruction."

He tried to organize a secret conspiracy as well. Although he more or less publicly exhorted the utopian Fabian Society to adopt his daring recommendations for sexual freedom, we know of the full extent of his ideals only through his very private letters to Claire Truesdale. It is perhaps sad that Truesdale finally had to break with Wells over this matter. Wells, as he admitted to Truesdale, envied the Martians their omnivorous sexuality, and he argued that human beings would do well to emulate them. He believed that the pleasure of sexual communion might increase, at the very least, according to the cube of the number of people so communing. Possibly it might even shoot off toward infinity. He tried to persuade Truesdale to include her cousin, Poppy Truesdale, in what Wells conceived as the first true human mating triad. But this demand proved too much for Claire, who feared and envied her famously beautiful cousin much more than she did the Martians.

After this, of course, Wells did not give up. No one knows the identity or even the number of all the women he charmed. He had affairs with very young women twenty-five or forty years his junior, and with a Boston Brahmin, a French countess who later married Ernest Hemmingway, as well as an enigmatic Russian baroness, who was probably a spy. Did he try to form triads with all or even most of these women? We do not know. We *can* be certain, however, that he spent much of his life in trying to realize what most people would call an impossible dream. Just before Claire Truesdale asked him never to contact her again, he admitted his desire that Claire, Poppy and he should form the central triad in what can only be described as a sort of world orgy. In his last letter to her, dated July 9, 1905, there is little of the lascivious. Clearly, Wells wanted to prove to himself—and more importantly, to the Martians—that human beings, through education and rational application of his principles, could come together in peace and harmony. And in sexual ecstasy. He hoped, simply, that the mass, worldwide sharing of great joy might dissolve much of the enmity that human beings had held for each other for so long. In truth, he hoped for a miracle. For he thought that we might somehow, through the uplifting of the human spirit that he fought so hard to bring about, through the genius of our kind, come into a true empathy for each other without the need to evolve an organ like the tatvam asi. Then the Martians would see that we were indeed worthy of joining them as brothers and sisters in the great crusade to spread sentient life throughout the universe—or at least worthy of being spared.

Wells died in on August 13, 1946, just a year after the explosion of the first nuclear bombs. Everywhere, people mourned the passing of a great human being, and called him by many names: novelist, philosopher, historian, superman, seer. But we might remember him best by the name he chose for himself in honor of one of the greatest of Martians, for he saw himself as this being's distant descendent, in spirit at least. As far as we know, Wells confided this name to only one person, Claire Truesdale, who in the end forgave him his peccadilloes and in her own journals always referred him as: "My Dear One, DreamsInevitableDreams."

After majoring in, at various times, philosophy, anthropology, linguistics and physics, David Zindell graduated in 1984 from the University of Colorado with a degree in mathematics. All this proved helpful in his turn toward writing science fiction, a literature which he had always read and loved. An early story, "Shanidar," won first prize in the Writers of the Future contest. *Neverness,* a novel set in the same universe, was nominated for the Arthur C. Clarke Award for best novel published in England and also nominated for the Campbell Award. A successor trilogy, A Requiem for Homo Sapiens, came next. He is presently working on the fourth book of Ea Cycle, a Grail quest to end all Grail quests. It is an exploration of good and evil, as well as a statement as to the possibilities open to humankind.

MIKE RESNICK

The Tiniest Assassins

OKAY, BOILED DOWN, it comes to this: the Martians come here, do a little serious devastation, scare the hell out of us and then catch colds and die.

Never gonna happen. For one thing, given the weaponry H. G. Wells and the movie outfit the Martians with, they won't even have to emerge from their ships until they've destroyed every last one of us and the battle is over—and as long as they stay in their ships, they're immune to the one indefensible weapon we have: our peculiarly human viruses.

And there's something else to consider. Let's not forget that Wells lived before the era of modern medicine. I think it's only logical to assume that any creatures, benevolent or hostile, that can traverse the void and reach planet Earth have doubtless developed their science—and especially their medical science—to the point where they can pinpoint and identify any dangerous germs in our atmosphere, and either develop some form of immunization to them or create some way to annihilate them at the source, which is to say Earth, before invading us.

It's just common sense. You wouldn't invade the waters off the coast of Australia unless you had some protection against the great white shark. You wouldn't wander through a pride of hungry lions without protection. Hell, we don't send our soldiers into battle these days without protection against bullets, chemical agents, biological agents—everything we can think of.

So I think it's fair to say that our germs are not going to kill any extraterrestrial invaders once they get here.

Nope. We're going to kill them long *before* they get here. And by the very same means that we (or Earth, if you prefer) used to kill Wells' Martian invaders.

How?

Well, as likely as not, it'll be by accident.

You see, in recent years NASA has been examining ships, rovers, orbiters—just about everything we send into space.

And guess what?

Neither the cold of space nor the heat of reentry nor the direct gamma radiation from the sun kills every living thing on those objects.

Oh, there's nothing there that'll bother *us*—at least not so far. But that doesn't mean an alien race with an alien physiology isn't looking down a barrel loaded with newly identified microbes from good old planet Earth.

We've even got names for them.

For example, there's *Bacillus odysseyi*, which has been found on the Mars *Odyssey* orbiter. Why is this noteworthy? Because the damned stuff has been orbiting Mars for close to four years. It survived the forty-million-mile trip, it survived three years in orbit, it survived gamma radiation, and it's doing just fine, thank you.

Now, no humans have ever been killed by *B. odysseyi*, and probably none ever will be. But that's not to say that it couldn't wipe out a squad of Wells' Martians or Edgar Rice Burroughs' green Tharks in an afternoon, depending on what particular germs they're vulnerable to.

Then there's *Bacillus safensis*. This baby is not only found in the Jet Propulsion Lab's Spacecraft Assembly Facility (known as SAF, which gave it its name), but it is alive and well today on *Spirit* and *Opportunity*, the current Mars rovers.

So what do these—and a dozen other microbes that have survived the heat and cold and radiation of spaceflight—actually do?

Nothing much. They tend to go forth and multiply, like every other living thing, but they're not harmful to us. Hell, they've even been found in the water supply of the *Mir* space station. Astronauts drank it. They all survived.

But they're human astronauts, not Martian or Centaurian or Antarean astronauts. Or citizens.

Right. Citizens. Don't forget: we've sent out a few deep-space probes, and we'll send out more. A couple have already left the solar system. They're not traveling fast, not by galactic standards, and it could take them a hundred thousand or even a million years to make planetfall somewhere out there—but they're going to arrive with a zillionth generation of perfectly healthy microbes and bacilli ready to find new homes.

Maybe the planet they touch down on won't have any life on it at all. (Which is okay by the microscopic hitchhikers; they can wait a billion years until some comes along.) Maybe it'll have life that's as unbothered by exposure to them as we are.

And maybe it will have life that finds them to be pure poison—life that, unlike the hypothetical invaders discussed above, is totally unprepared for a visit by microscopic creatures than can wipe them out, that will never know what hit them, that might indeed have been the friendliest folk in the galaxy.

All right. That's the nonfiction side of it. Those bacilli are out there, some of them aren't coming back, and sooner or later they're going to make contact with *something*.

Now let's look at the possibilities, science-fictional today, but perhaps less so in the future.

We've got a million dedicated computer hackers, plus some truly powerful equipment in the hands of experts, searching the heavens every night for signals from other worlds—SETI, the Search for Extraterrestrial Intelligence. They're probably not going to discover any in my lifetime or yours, but sooner or later they're going to latch on to some signals, because we're finding out that just about every star in the galaxy has planets, and with tens of millions of G-type stars out there, the odds are that an awful lot of them have, or once had, or someday will have, life. And some of it will be sentient. And some of that will be searching the skies for signs of life just the way we are.

So eventually we're going to make contact with them. If we like what they have to say, fine. If we don't...well, if we can trace their signals back to their source, we can send them a little present. Not the microbes that are living on the Mars rovers today, but rather some of the most powerful stuff we can whip up (after we lie to them about our physiology and hope they're telling us the truth about theirs).

And even if we don't know what their motives are, if meeting them at a neutral point in space is kind of like a blind date on a grand scale, it doesn't mean we won't go armed. Not with guns or lasers or any of that movie garbage; they'll be able to detect it from a light-year away. But with the most subtle weapons imaginable—men, each carrying germs and viruses that we are immune to, each ready to transmit them by the simple act of breathing in and out.

Sounds pretty crude and heartless, I realize, and hopefully it will never come to that—but if the Earth is at risk, a visionary named Wells showed that there is a far more efficient way of attacking the enemy than with a new generation of weapons, which history teaches us will be obsolete in a few years' time.

Much better to use a weapon neither time nor heat nor cold nor radiation has been able to kill. There are going to be some alien immune systems that can't kill it either.

So how do we avoid killing off a friendly alien population?

We're working on it right now. NASA is aware that if enough of the bacilli I mentioned take root on Mars (or Venus, or Io, or any other world or moon in the solar system), we might one day discover life there, and if the bacilli have evolved or mutated enough, we may never realize that it came from Earth in the late twentieth and early twenty-first centuries. So some of the NASA scientists have been given the task of learning how to terminate these microscopic agents that space can't kill.

They already know that if they hit them with a few million degrees of heat they can't survive—but neither can the equipment they live on, and it's slightly counterproductive to melt a spaceship before it ever takes off just to make sure that it doesn't take any microscopic travelers with it.

But they're learning, and before long they'll find a method. And that's absolutely vital, because although Wells didn't realize the practical implications of his story, we already have the ability to destroy the bad aliens. Now we have to make sure we don't kill the good ones by accident.

Mike Resnick is the winner of four Hugo Awards, a Nebula and numerous other major awards in the USA, France, Japan, Spain, Croatia and Poland. He is the author of forty-five science fiction novels, nine books of nonfiction, twelve collections, 175 short stories and two screenplays, and has edited more than forty anthologies. His work has been translated into twenty-two languages.

H. G. WELLS,

AS CHANNELLED THROUGH

IAN WATSON

Of Warfare and
The War of the Worlds

WAR, OH DEAR ME, WAR: the perennial curse of mankind! And the fascination of mankind as well. Perhaps war is less fascinating to womankind, since so many women are innocent victims of war. Various famous female warriors do spring to mind, yet often bellicosity was forced upon them by ill-treatment at the hand of men, as upon Queen Boadicea by the Romans.

The very word *War* in the title of a novel seems to serve as a magnet for extensive sales—how much more so, then, a war *of the worlds*? Evidently I happened upon a title of great moment, so I am unsurprised at how that early flight of fancy of mine endures, even if this is a cause of regret to me in some respects.

Why a cause of regret, you may ask?

Mr Glenn Yeffeth of BenBella Books, a rather beautiful name for a publishing house, in my opinion (I was once acquainted briefly with a delightful young lady named Bella, whose varied charms included considerable intelligence), put this question to me recently, and I shall endeavour to answer this now.

I should explain that in recent years (if I may phrase it thus) I have been travelling in time, and in the process I have encountered readers of my books who live in the early twenty-first century. In any event, Mr Yeffeth informed me that not merely one, but two, extremely costly kinetoscopic adaptations of my *War of the Worlds* were shortly to appear, one of these directed by a Mr Steven Spielberg and starring a popular "action-hero," Mr Tom Cruise, the other film made by a company called (if I recall aright) Pendragon Pictures. Mr Yeffeth was preparing a book of essays to appear synchronously with Mr Spielberg's visual drama— and serendipitously as regards the other visual drama, which I gather was made in secret, so as to surprise the world.

I was given to understand that Pendragon Pictures aimed at utter authenticity in conjuring up the last years of the nineteenth century in England and the exact narrative of my novel; so I may perhaps be moderately hopeful of the result in that case. The contrary was definitely so with the radio adaptation by Mr Orson Welles, who took totally unwarranted liberties with my book by relocating its events to New Jersey in order to astonish Americans—in which aim at least he succeeded! Consequently I harbour profound qualms about Mr Spielberg's adaptation. Already, in the year 1897, the American newspaper the *Boston Post* serialised a stolen version of my book, the action relocated to America. I protested strongly back then, just as I later protested at Mr Welles' radio show. Maybe Mr Spielberg is unaware that, due to my time machine, I am still able to object to violations of my work if need be.

Such vulgarizations are one reason for regret. As regards vulgarity in its literal meaning, I always wrote in the language of the common man, as opposed to the meandering gilded oratory of Mr Henry James, which only connoisseurs can understand; but my hope was always to make my readers *think* while I entertained them. I fear that the principal aim of Mr Spielberg's visual drama may simply be to astonish its spectators rather than to cause any intellectual reflection—to astound them, and also to make them feel patriotic, a sentiment which I have always regarded with some suspicion as it is often allied to xenophobia (a dislike of the alien, the stranger) and consequently is a cause of war.

As regards patriotism in the sense of excessively vaunting one's country, my own "war of the worlds" is a singularly one-sided campaign. Confronted by its Martian enemy, Great Britain—so proud of its army and navy—is not so great. In fact, it is almost impotent.

Ahem. On the subject of potency, if I may put it so—which is itself something of a *double entendre*—Mr Yeffeth suggests that "womanist" readers might take offence at my casual reference to Bella, finding such a comment patronising to their sex. Well, one aspect of my novel upon which certain "womanist" commentators of the early twenty-first century certainly commented to me somewhat scathingly is the fact that my narrator's wife has no name, and is simply referred to throughout as "my wife." "As if she is *a thing* you have mislaid!" one redoubtable young lady with red hair expostulated to me. However, I was not writing a romance in which the narrator will rescue his beloved from peril. Would it appease that young lady with red hair if I had named the narrator's wife Isabel or Gwendolin? Would this mere piece of nomenclature add any more to her identity or importance? I do hope that the impertinent kinetoscopic adaptation of my novel to twenty-first-century America does not inflict a spurious "love interest" upon my story, for this would be to miss the point of what I undertook, namely a salutary humbling of our smugness.

Yes, our devastating defeat. In this regard I must plead guilty to evincing considerable relish at the process of destruction, a sentiment distinctly at odds with my hopes for peace on Earth. There is in the violence of war and the demolition of cities a kind of fascination which we must surely lose as a species if we are to survive. War, slaughter, destruction and a relish in the instruments of war must become not merely outlawed but unthinkable.

And yet in my novel I destroyed, to use a cogent phrase, *with a vengeance*. I must admit that I personally am a mixture of contraries, and my imagination can often be belligerent. Indeed, belligerence is a part of our evolutionary heritage—one which has now ceased to play any useful role in the survival of our species. Maybe it is not too surprising that my interplanetary mayhem has captured the popular imagination; yet I now see it as cause for regret if I have contributed to an appetite for destruction on a grand scale as popular entertainment. And I understand that a great deal of destruction exists in films today, often at a great cost and in lieu of a sensible or logical story.

I may of course be wrong in my anxieties about Mr Spielberg's adaptation. Yet I have been told of another film, entitled *Independence Day*, in which the president of the United States himself engages successfully in combat against alien invaders, like some medieval chieftain. Nothing in my own *War of the Worlds* sounds such a triumphant and jingoistic note as finale.

At this point I must drift a bit from my primary subject to sound a note of amazement, not only at what my *War of the Worlds* seems to have begotten, but also what itself and the other fantasies of my youth have brought forth in their wake. I refer to the enormous number of novels and stories, produced since approximately the middle of the twentieth century, which bear the name of *science fiction*. Apparently I am the "father" of this form of popular entertainment.

Recently I attended (or rather, I *will* attend) a "World Science Fiction Convention" in the city of Glasgow. In the Dealers' Room at this extremely extensive event I was astonished to see the sheer number of such books, many of them concerned with conflicts in outer space, either set in our own solar system or in the far reaches of the Milky Way galaxy. *Stars Wars, Forever Wars*. . . .

Books concerned, too, with time travel and with journeys to other worlds and with the creation of new breeds of men and with the "uplifting" of animals to sentience, which are all the themes of my early books.

I appear to be responsible for such proliferation, and this too I must regret.

The myriad tales of latter-day "science fiction"—with their matter transmitters and time-travel portals and warp-travel and hyperspace travel and antigravity machines, and their aliens who might be giant ants or heaven knows what, and their ansibles for communicating instantly from star to star, namely all the paraphernalia of marvels without which such stories could not exist at all—these derive from what is frankly the least important part of my work, and furthermore they have nothing scientific about them!

When I penned *The War of the Worlds* and *The Time Machine* and *The First Men in the Moon*, for example, I was doing what a conjuror does with his quick-witted patter to fool an audience. (Should I say "spiel," rather than patter? This may seem appropriate in view of the name of my latest kinetoscopic interpreter!) Frankly, I was substituting words of science for bits of magic or sorcery as the basis for those novels. An invasion from Mars? A society of insects dwelling within the Moon? Or, to take another instance, an Invisible Man? Those were sheer flights of fancy! Such tales were certainly fiction. But *science?* Not at all!—not in my scientifically trained opinion. Pray recall that I was scientifically trained, rigorously so, by Thomas Huxley in the tradition of Charles Darwin as an evolutionary biologist. Above all I pride myself on possessing a scientific mind. The works of modern "science fiction" are simply not scientific. Adding the word "fiction" to the word "science" does not redeem such productions.

But I must not dwell on these minor annoyances any longer, and allow war to rear its head once more. For in that Dealers' Room in Glasgow, in addition to literally thousands of novels purporting to be "science fiction," I saw numerous examples of *war games*. Leaving aside the paternity of science fiction, which I disavow, I can most certainly claim that I, and none other, am the father of war-gaming. I refer to war-gaming practised as a hobby, evidently pursued in fantasy and futuristic settings by many visitors to that World Science Fiction Convention.

Back in 1913, you see, I published an illustrated book entitled *Little Wars* and subtitled "A Game for boys from twelve years of age to one hundred and fifty and for that more intelligent sort of girl who likes boys' games and books, with an appendix on Kriegspiel."

Thus I invented war-gaming with rules and models, to be played on a table or a carpet or even a lawn, summarising in that book what I had developed after numerous years' study. That I have been influential in the field was made clear to me somewhat gallingly when I picked up a highly priced volume entitled *Warhammer 40,000: Rogue Trader* (produced by a company called Games Workshop) and discovered therein a battle between "Space Marines" and ugly green-skinned aliens called "Orks" entitled "The Battle at the Farm." *Warhammer* was illustrated with photographs almost identical to my own photographs illustrating my own chapter in *Little Wars* entitled "The Battle of Hook's Farm"! No credit was allocated to me, naturally, but I most certainly perceived the source of Games Workshop's tableau and rules.

"In the grim darkness of the far future there is only war"—that is one of the mottos of this Games Workshop, and part of their appeal. My own motive in inventing war games was quite different—namely, to demonstrate that real war is too big a thing for our heads. Professional military men have played my own war game, the rules of which are fairly elementary, and not one has avoided getting into difficulties and confusions. War is a blundering insanity, and self-declared patriots who favour war ought to be shut up in a room to play my game and thus satisfy themselves, out of the way of the rest of the mass of mankind upon whom they must not be allowed to inflict such suffering and monstrous inconvenience as real war entails. What we should seek is ample living for mankind, open ways, magnificent cities, more liberatory power and knowledge. In place of war I suggest nothing less than utopia.

There is a kind of war in me too, a perpetual inner conflict—a tension in myself between the man of science and the creative artist. You might say that I am a man of science by training and a creative artist by intuition.

Personally I have never confused these two categories. Nor has England as a nation confused them because, most unfortunately, the English ruling class has paid scant attention to science. This is because the ruling class, educated at our great universities, is fundamentally illiterate in science. Consequently the mandarins of culture are men of letters who possess little understanding of what a star in the night sky is, or of how evolution operates. My much underestimated colleague Ford Madox Ford rightly commented that "no one bothered his head about Science. It seemed to be an agreeable parlour-game—like stamp-collecting."

Thus it is that artistic gentlemen tend to have written books and essays about me, and their considerations are literary considerations. By and large, as a consequence, my books as a whole have been assessed disgracefully. Many deeply thought-out books—which impinge upon our very survival—have been virtually ignored, and in this disdain I must also include my ambitious novels of contemporary life, disregarded by critics because they were not "experimental" in the manner of Mr James Joyce or Mrs Virginia Woolf. What do those artists of the word know about *scientific* experiments and deductions, eh? What do they know about humanity in the grand blind scheme of nature, which grants human beings no privileged status whatever? Mr Joyce, or Mr Henry James previously, are like hippopotami picking up, with great skill, a pea.

Not that I myself lacked a trick or two when it came to experimenting with narrative. To me, indeed, everything has been an experiment—including my *Experiment in Autobiography*, and my very life. But artistic gentlemen focus their attentions upon my fantasies as though nothing else matters, and then as like as not they declare that with a few early exceptions I tossed off my books in haste and wrote far too many, whereas the truth is that I took great pains with the writing and rewriting—but I happened to write for the common reader in a popular, not an aesthetic, style.

As I say, it is one of my early "successes" that Mr Yeffeth has asked me to comment upon, rather than any of my neglected books that I might rate more highly, and I suppose as an evolutionary biologist I should accept the fact that *The War of the Worlds* has survived, while other fine novels by me have become virtually extinct.

Not merely survived—but engendered many hybrid offspring, often of rather strange appearance, and several akin to massive dinosaurs, at least as regards the financial aspects.

I might mention in passing one offspring of my fantasies which came to my attention, an ingenious variation entitled *The Space Machine*, penned by a Mr Christopher Priest, who perceived that logically my "time machine" must be a machine which traverses not only time but also space, since of course the Earth and its sun do not remain in one single fixed location in the universe but move constantly. If we travel ahead one million years to the very same place which our Earth occupies now, we will find ourselves isolated in the interstellar void. Consequently my time machine must also move through space and thus can be used to visit Mars in an attempt to thwart the Martian invaders of Earth. It is not that this implication did not occur to me, but that my time machine serves as the equivalent to a magical lamp empowered by a genie.

I think that the authors of "science fiction"—if such was what those authors truly intended to produce—ought perhaps to have taken less heed of my own works and to have paid more attention to the productions of my younger French counterpart, Monsieur Jules Verne. Monsieur Verne appreciated the range of my imagination—yet he wished to know how precisely my Martians produced their Heat-Ray. How indeed?

My literary "descendants" did not so take heed. My genial magical lamps mesmerised them, and thus begot fantasies dressed as science (although, curiously, I understand that an organisation called the Pentagon has devoted much money to trying to make my Heat-Ray a practical device).

The principal origin of *The War of the Worlds* was twofold. Firstly, as my Time Traveller in *The Time Machine* plunges towards far futurity, he is moved to speculate that with the passage of 800,000 years mankind may have developed by the process of evolution "into something inhuman, unsympathetic, and overwhelmingly powerful," to whom the Traveller must surely seem to be "some old-world savage animal...a foul creature to be incontinently slain." And secondly, when I was out walking one evening along a rural lane with my brother Frank, Frank suddenly observed to me, "Suppose some beings from another planet were to drop out of the sky suddenly, and began laying about them here?" I took heed of Frank's remark. Oh, how I took heed. As I have observed elsewhere, the human animal is not constituted to anticipate anything at all; it is constituted to accept the state of affairs about it, as a stable state of affairs, *whatever its intelligence may tell it to the contrary.*

And yet I pause. Despite such terrible events as the Lisbon Earthquake, which still horrified all civilised nations a century later, when I was writing, the final years of the nineteenth century found most people, especially in the British Isles, feeling very secure, often to the point of complacency. We could have no inkling of the horrors and chaos of the era awaiting us subsequent to the fatal year 1914, an era during which it came to seem that all life on Earth might easily be extinguished because of atomic warfare, not to mention the mass psychosis of the German nation, with its programme bent on exterminating entire races of human beings. And following the suppression of the German nation as the result of a second world war, a hundred lesser but lethal and bloody wars have erupted in all parts of the world.

Wars, wars, wars, as if the name we give ourselves, *Homo sapiens*, might more appropriately be *Homo bellicosus!* Does any other creature, except for the army ant, *Eciton burchelli*, collectively practise war to the same degree and as regularly as *Homo bellicosus?* The army ant is a creature dominated by instinct, but with no concept of improving its weapons. How dangerous are the ways our own pugnacious instincts dominate us when allied to intelligence!

I understand that we are acquiring a growing awareness of other dangers, too—namely the sheer frailty of our life upon a planet subject to catastrophic climate change, asteroid impact from outer space, mutating pathogenic super-viruses and imminent scarcity of essential resources. This awareness is honed by an instantaneity in comprehensive news of calamities scarce imaginable in the age of communication by mere telegraph, and exacerbated further by the fact that a whole range of possible calamities is the stuff of vivid films shown worldwide, presenting new ice ages or floods or plagues as all too possible in the near future.

People of the early twenty-first century assuredly ought to be more conscious of *instability* than people of the late nineteenth century. Nevertheless are they really, in a truly radical way? Ultimately the human animal does not believe it will die, nor that its race will inevitably die, too. Arguments that the intervention of science has altered, or potentially altered, this fate—and that science now commands the process of blind evolution—ignore the fact that *if* the human race does survive into futurity then its thoughts and interests will bear as little resemblance to those of us alive now as the thoughts of the Martians bear to our own human thoughts in my novel. A million years from now Homer and Shakespeare, Leonardo and Beethoven will signify nothing—therefore *we* will have passed away as surely as if a plague had extinguished us. That plague will be the progress of *time itself*, sheer geological time.

My Martians were also, despite their scientific powers, complacent. Having apparently eradicated bacteria from their world in the distant past, they utterly neglected to take the bacteria of our own world into account. Would this negligence apply also to their attempts to invade the planet Venus, to which I allude in the closing pages of my novel? Indeed, would those mighty minds on Mars have learned at all of the reason for their failure to conquer the Earth?

One further speculation in which perhaps I may indulge is the nature of the food creatures, some of whom my Martians took on their voyage in order to transfuse their blood for sustenance, and whom they must have bred and farmed rather as we breed and farm cattle or sheep.

"These creatures," I wrote, "to judge from the shrivelled remains that have fallen into human hands, were bipeds with flimsy, silicious skeletons…and feeble musculature, standing about six feet high and having round, erect heads, and large eyes in flinty sockets."

In other words, they somewhat resemble human beings whom the lesser gravity of Mars—together with millennia of husbandry—have enfeebled and attenuated. Would these bipeds have arisen naturally upon the Red Planet, as a case of parallel evolution—parallel to our own evolution, I mean? Why should this be so, when the dominant species on Mars is as I describe it to be—more like an octopus (or duopus) with a huge head. Admittedly, I suggested in my novel that the dominant Martians may once have resembled ourselves, and that subsequently bodily organs had atrophied. Thus the food animals may be relatives of the Martians—ones who retain a primeval appearance.

Yet may it not be that in the very distant past, while the various breeds of *Homo* were evolving, and before the eradication of bacteria, the Martians had mounted an earlier expedition to Earth and had carried off specimens of *Homo* of breeding age as captives?

The aim of the Martians, at the time, may have been to ensure a food supply in view of the progressive changes to their own anatomy—which they may have *planned consciously* by manipulating their own genetic material in order to free mental cerebration from the troubling influences of hormones, glandular secretions and such. (I am aware that by the dawn of the twenty-first century such genetic intervention is becoming a very real possibility.) Only when the Martians' own planet was becoming uninhabitable would they have elected to quit Mars for the greater, impeding gravity of Earth.

As regards the technical achievements and inventions of the Martians I made no assumption of similarity to those of human beings. Most notably, the wheel is unknown on Mars. Instead, complicated systems of sliding parts moving over small frictionless bearings replace the fixed pivot. Why, then, should I assume that at any stage Martian evolution resembled terrestrial evolution in giving rise to bipeds? The more I think about it, the less likely this seems. Abduction from Earth during prehistory seems more plausible.

How would the Martians return to their home world with their captives (including enough surplus captives to be drained of blood for nourishment *en route*)? How would they escape from the greater gravity of Earth? I think that within a reasonable time their handling-machines would be capable of constructing more powerful projectiles than were used to cross the void from Mars to the Earth.

However, here I fear I am veering into the realms of "science fiction," with its addiction to sequels and what I understand are called prequels. Mr Priest appears to have made a very honest stab at creating an alternative novel in parallel with my own, yet I understand that he shares with me in his own work a disdain for repeating himself. Of my early fantasies—*The Time Machine, The War of the Worlds, The Island of Dr. Moreau, The First Men in the Moon*—all were markedly different from one another and addressed different themes. A man of vigorous imagination and originality can scarce behave otherwise. The many examples such as I saw at the book room in Glasgow of sheer repetition of an idea which was once original—either because of authors plagiarising earlier authors such as myself, or else plagiarising themselves ten times over in so-called sagas and epics, or both crimes at once—that is most regrettable. I am tempted to say that I declare war upon the imitative trend.

A final thought occurs to me—how this matter niggles! It may be that the enemy "world" in Mr Spielberg's *War of the Worlds* will not even be Mars. Just as Mr Welles, almost my namesake, exchanged an English setting for New Jersey, maybe in his efforts to be *science-fictional* Mr Spielberg will exchange Mars for some fantastical world of his imagination orbiting some distant star, whose denizens could in reality no more visit us across the vast gulfs of interstellar space, nor wage war upon us, than we could ever visit them.

Dear me, it may even be that Mr Spielberg has simply usurped the title of my book and that little, *if any*, connexion whatever exists between my novel and his film! I think I must soon depart in my time machine, before further irritating possibilities occur to me. There are so many times and places that I wish to visit—so many intelligent and personable young ladies to meet. I hear tell that a "summer of love" occurred in California during the 1960s....

Now what if I were to invite a celebrant of that event to accompany me forward in time to a showing of the Pendragon Pictures version of my novel? That experience might impress her favourably.

Ian Watson has written sf full time for the past thirty years, from *The Embedding* (1973) to *Mockymen* (2003), in which aliens adopt human guises. Sometimes he himself adopts the guise of H. G. Wells at sf conventions, which exonerates him from any naughty conduct—see www.ianwatson.info. A year's work with Stanley Kubrick in 1990 led to screen credit for screen story for *A.I. Artificial Intelligence*, subsequently directed by Steven Spielberg. Ian lives with a black cat in a tiny village in rural England. His tenth story collection, *The Butterflies of Memory*, is due in the fall 2005 from PS Publishing.

CONNIE WILLIS

"The Soul Selects Her Own Society"

Invasion and Repulsion: A Chronological Reinterpretation of Two of Emily Dickinson's Poems: A Wellsian Perspective

UNTIL RECENTLY it was thought that Emily Dickinson's poetic output ended in 1886, the year she died. Poems 186B and 272?, however, suggest that not only did she write poems at a later date, but that she was involved in the "great and terrible events"[1] at the turn of the century.

The poems in question originally came to light in 1991,[2] while Nathan Fleece was working on his doctorate. Fleece, who found the poems[3] under a hedge in the Dickinsons' backyard, classified the poems as belonging to Dickinson's Early or Only Slightly Eccentric Period, but recent examination of the works[4] has yielded up an entirely different interpretation of the circumstances under which the poems were written.

---

[1] For a full account, see H. G. Wells, *The War of the Worlds*, Oxford University Press, 1898.

[2] The details of the discovery are recounted in *Desperation and Discovery: The Unusual Number of Lost Manuscripts Located by Doctoral Candidates,* by J. Marple, Reading Railway Press, 1993.

[3] Actually a poem and a poem fragment consisting of a four-line stanza and a single word fragment* from the middle of the second stanza.

*Or word. See later on in this paper.

[4] While I was working on *my* dissertation.

The sheets of paper on which the poems were written are charred around the edges, and that on Number 272? has a large round hole burnt in it. Martha Hodge-Banks claims that said charring and hole were caused by "a pathetic attempt to age the paper and forgetting to watch the oven,"[5] but the large number of dashes makes it clear they were written by Dickinson, as well as the fact that the poems are almost totally indecipherable. Dickinson's unreadable handwriting has been authenticated by any number of scholars, including Elmo Spencer in *Emily Dickinson: Handwriting or Hieroglyphics?*, and M. P. Cursive, who wrote, "Her a's look like c's, her e's look like 2's and the whole thing looks like chicken scratches."[6]

The charring seemed to indicate either that the poems had been written while smoking[7] or in the midst of some catastrophe, and I began examining the text for clues.

Fleece had deciphered Number 272? as beginning, "I never saw a friend— / I never saw a moom—," which made no sense at all,[8] and on closer examination I saw that the stanza actually read:

I never saw a fiend—
I never saw a bomb—
And yet of both of them I dreamed—
While in the—dreamless tomb—

A much more authentic translation, particularly in regard to the rhyme scheme. "Moom" and "tomb" actually rhyme, which is something Dickinson hardly ever did, preferring near-rhymes such as "mat/gate," "tune/sun" and "balm/hermaphrodite."

The second stanza was more difficult, as it occupied the area of the round hole, and the only readable portion was a group of four letters farther down that read "ulla."[9]

---

[5] Dr. Banks' assertion that "the paper was manufactured in 1990 and the ink was from a Flair tip pen" is merely airy speculation.*

*See "Carbon Dating Doesn't Prove Anything," by Jeremiah Habakkuk, in *Creation Science for Fun and Profit,* Golden Slippers Press, 1974.

[6] The pathetic nature of her handwriting is also addressed in *Impetus to Reform: Emily Dickinson's Effect on the Palmer Method* and in "Depth, Dolts and Teeth: An Alternate Translation of Emily Dickinson's Death Poems," in which it is argued that Number 712 actually begins, "Because I could not stoop for darts," and recounts an arthritic evening at the local pub.

[7] Dickinson is not known to have smoked, except during her Late or Downright Peculiar Period.

[8] Of course, neither does, "How pomp surpassing ermine." Or, "A dew sufficed itself."

[9] Or possibly "ciee." Or "vole."

This was assumed by Fleece to be part of a longer word such as "bul-lary" (a convocation of popes),[10] or possibly "dullard" or "hullaba-loo."[11]

I, however, immediately recognized "ulla" as the word H. G. Wells had reported hearing the dying Martians utter, a sound he described as "a sobbing alternation of two notes[12] . . . a desolating cry."

"Ulla" was a clear reference to the 1900 invasion by the Martians, previously thought to have been confined to England, Missouri and the University of Paris.[13] The poem fragment, along with 186B, clearly in-dicated that the Martians had landed in Amherst and that they had met Emily Dickinson.

At first glance, this seems an improbable scenario due to both the Martians' and Emily Dickinson's dispositions. Dickinson was a recluse who didn't meet anybody, preferring to hide upstairs when neighbors came to call and to float notes down on them.[14] Various theories have been advanced for her self-imposed hermitude, including Bright's Dis-ease, an unhappy love affair, eye trouble and bad skin. T. L. Mensa sug-gests the simpler theory that all the rest of the Amherstonians were morons.[15]

None of these explanations would have made it likely that she would like Martians any better than Amherstates, and there is the added dif-ficulty that, having died in 1886, she would also have been badly de-composed.

The Martians present additional difficulties. The opposite of reclus-es, they were in the habit of arriving noisily, attracting reporters and blasting at everybody in the vicinity. There is no record of their hav-ing landed in Amherst, though several inhabitants mention unusually loud thunderstorms in their diaries,[16] and Louisa May Alcott, in nearby

---

[10] Unlikely, considering her Calvinist upbringing.

[11] Or the Australian city, Ulladulla. Dickinson's poems are full of references to Australia. W. G. Mathilda has theorized from this that "the great love of Dickinson's life was neither Higginson nor Judge Lord, but Mel Gibson." See *Emily Dickinson: The Billabong Connection,* by C. Dundee, Outback Press, 1985.

[12] See Rod McKuen.

[13] Where Jules Verne was working on *his* doctorate.

[14] The notes contained charming, often enigmatic sentiments such as, "Which shall it be—Gerani-ums or Tulips?" and "Go away—and Shut the door When—you Leave."

[15] See *Halfwits and Imbeciles: Poetic Evidence of Emily Dickinson's Opinion of Her Neighbors.*

[16] Virtually everyone in Amherst kept a diary, containing entries such as "Always knew she'd turn out to be a great poet," and "Full moon last night. Caught a glimpse of her out in her garden plant-ing peas. Completely deranged."

Concord, wrote in her journal, "Wakened suddenly last night by a loud noise to the west. Couldn't get back to sleep for worrying. Should have made Jo marry Laurie. To Do: Write sequel in which Amy dies. Serves her right for burning manuscript."

There is also indirect evidence for the landing. Amherst, frequently confused for Lakehurst, was obviously the inspiration for Orson Welles' setting the radio version of *The War of the Worlds* in New Jersey.[17] In addition, a number of the tombstones in West Cemetery are tilted at an angle and in some cases have been knocked down, making it clear that the Martians landed not only in Amherst, but in West Cemetery, very near Dickinson's grave.

Wells describes the impact of the shell[18] as producing "a blinding glare of vivid green light" followed by "such a concussion as I have never heard before or since." He reports that the surrounding dirt "splashed," creating a deep pit and exposing drainpipes and house foundations. Such an impact in West Cemetery would have uprooted the surrounding coffins and broken them open, and the resultant light and noise clearly would have been enough to "wake the dead," including the slumbering Dickinson.

That she was thus awakened, and that she considered the event an invasion of her privacy, is made clear in the longer poem, Number 186B, of which the first stanza reads: "I scarce was settled in the grave— / When came—unwelcome guests— / Who pounded on my coffin lid— / Intruders—in the dust—"[19]

Why the "unwelcome guests" did not hurt her,[20] in light of their usual behavior, and how she was able to vanquish them, are less apparent, and we must turn to H. G. Wells' account of the Martians for answers.

On landing, Wells tells us, the Martians were completely helpless due to Earth's greater gravity, and remained so until they were able to build

---

[17] The inability of people to tell Orson Welles and H. G. Wells apart lends credence to Dickinson's opinion of humanity. (See footnote 15.)

[18] Not the one at the beginning of the story, which everybody knows about, the one that practically landed on him in the middle of the book, which everybody missed because they'd already turned off the radio and were running up and down the streets screaming, "The end is here! The Martians are coming!"*

*Thus proving Emily was right in her assessment of the populace.

[19] See "Sound, Fury, and Frogs: Emily Dickinson's Seminal Influence on William Faulkner," by W. Snopes, Yoknapatawpha Press, 1955.

[20] She was, of course, already dead, which meant the damage they could inflict was probably minimal.

their fighting machines. During this period they would have posed no threat to Dickinson except that of company.[21]

Secondly, they were basically big heads. Wells describes them as having eyes, a beak, some tentacles and "a single large tympanic drum" at the back of the head which functioned as an ear. Wells theorized that the Martians were "descended from beings not unlike ourselves, by gradual development of brains and hands...at the expense of the body." He concluded that, without the body's vulnerability and senses, the brain would become "selfish and cruel" and take up mathematics,[22] but Dickinson's effect on them suggests that the overenhanced development of their neocortexes had turned them instead into poets.

The fact that they picked off people with their heat-rays, sucked human blood and spewed poisonous black smoke over entire countries would seem to contraindicate poetic sensibility, but look how poets act. Take Shelley, for instance, who went off and left his first wife to drown herself in the Serpentine so he could marry a woman who wrote monster movies. Or Byron. The only people who had a kind word to say about him were his dogs.[23] Take Robert Frost.[24]

The Martians' identity as poets is corroborated by the fact that they landed seven shells in Great Britain, three in the Lake District[25] and none at all in Liverpool. It may have determined their decision to land in Amherst.

But they had reckoned without Dickinson's determination and literary technique, as Number 186B makes clear.[26] Stanza Two reads:

I wrote a letter—to the fiends—
And bade them all be—gone—
In simple words—writ plain and clear—
'I vant to be alone'

---

[21] Which she considered a considerable threat. "If the butcher boy should come now, I would jump into the flour barrel,"* she wrote in 1873.

*If she was in the habit of doing this, it may account for her always appearing in white.

[22] Particularly nonlinear differential equations.

[23] See "Lord Byron's *Don Juan*: The Mastiff as Muse," by C. Harold.

[24] He didn't like people either. See "Mending Wall," *The Complete Works*, Random House. Frost preferred barbed wire fences with spikes on top to walls.

[25] See "Semiotic Subterfuge in Wordsworth's 'I Wandered Lonely as a Cloud': A Dialectic Approach," by N. Compos Mentis, Postmodern Press, 1984.

[26] Sort of.

"Writ plain and clear" is obviously an exaggeration, but it is manifest that Dickinson wrote a note and delivered it to the Martians, as the next line makes even more evident: "They [indecipherable][27] it with an awed dismay—"

Dickinson may have read it aloud or floated the note down to them in their landing pit in her usual fashion, or she may have unscrewed the shell and tossed it in, like a gentle hand grenade.

Whatever the method of delivery, however, the result was "awed dismay" and then retreat, as the next line indicates: "They—promptly took—their leave—"

It has been argued that Dickinson would have had no access to writing implements in the graveyard, but this fails to take into consideration the Victorian lifestyle. Dickinson's burial attire was a white dress, and all Victorian dresses had pockets.[28]

During the funeral Emily's sister Lavinia placed two heliotropes in her sister's hand, whispering that they were for her to take to the Lord. She may have slipped a pencil and some Post-its into the coffin, or Dickinson, in the habit of writing and distributing notes, may simply have planned ahead.[29]

In addition, grave poems[30] are a well-known part of literary tradition. Dante Gabriel Rossetti, in the throes of grief after the death of his beloved Elizabeth Siddell, entwined poems in her auburn hair as she lay in her coffin.[31]

However the writing implements came to be there, Dickinson obviously made prompt and effective use of them. She scribbled down several stanzas and sent them to the Martians, who were so distressed at them that they decided to abort their mission and return to Mars.

The exact cause of this deadly effect has been much debated, with several theories being advanced. Wells was convinced that microbes killed the Martians who landed in England, who had no defense against

---

[27] The word is either "read" or "heard" or possibly "pacemaker."

[28] Also pleats, tucks, ruching, flounces, frills, ruffles and passementerie.*

*See "Pockets as Political Statement: The Role of Clothing in Early Victorian Feminism," by E. and C. Pankhurst, Angry Women's Press, 1978.

[29] A good writer is never without pencil and paper.*

*Or laptop.

[30] See "Posthumous Poems" in *Literary Theories that Don't Hold Water,* by H. Houdini.

[31] Two years later, no longer quite so grief-stricken and thinking of all that lovely money, he dug her up and got them back.*

*I told you poets behaved badly.

Earth's bacteria, but such bacteria would have taken several weeks to infect the Martians, and it was obviously Dickinson's poems which caused them to leave, not dysentery.

Spencer suggests that her illegible handwriting led the Martians to misread her message and take it as some sort of ultimatum. A. Huyfen argues that the advanced Martians, being good at punctuation, were appalled by her profligate use of dashes and random capitalizing of letters. S. W. Lubbock proposes the theory that they were unnerved by the fact that all of her poems can be sung to the tune of "The Yellow Rose of Texas."[32]

It seems obvious, however, that the most logical theory is that the Martians were wounded to the heart by Dickinson's use of near-rhymes, which all advanced civilizations rightly abhor. Number 186B contains two particularly egregious examples: "gone/alone" and "guests/dust," and the burnt hole in 272? may indicate something worse.

The near-rhyme theory is corroborated by H. G. Wells' account of the damage done to London, a city in which Tennyson ruled supreme, and by an account of a near-landing in Ong, Nebraska, recorded by Muriel Addleson:

> We were having our weekly meeting of the Ong Ladies Literary Society when there was a dreadful noise outside, a rushing sound, like something falling off the Grange Hall. Henrietta Muddie was reading Emily Dickinson's "I Taste a Liquor Never Brewed," out loud, and we all raced to the window but couldn't see anything except a lot of dust,[33] so Henrietta started reading again and there was a big whoosh, and a big round metal thing like a cigar[34] rose straight up in the air and disappeared.

It is significant that the poem in question is Number 214, which rhymes[35] "pearl" and "alcohol."[36] Dickinson saved Amherst from Mar-

---

[32] Try it. No, really. "Be-e-e-e-cause I could not stop for Death, He kindly stopped for me-e-e." See?*

*Not all of Dickinson's poems can be sung to "The Yellow Rose of Texas."**

**Numbers 2, 18 and 1411 can be sung to "The Itsy-Bitsy Spider." Could her choice of tunes be a coded reference to the unfortunate Martian landing in Texas? See "Night of the Cooters," by Howard Waldrop, p. 120, this volume.

[33] Normal to Ong, Nebraska.

[34] See Freud.

[35] Sort of.

[36] The near-rhyme theory also explains why Dickinson responded with such fierceness when Thomas Wentworth Higginson changed "pearl" to "jewel." She knew, as he could not, that the fate of the world might someday rest on her inability to rhyme.

tian invasion and then, as she says in the final two lines of 186B, "rear-ranged" her "grassy bed— / And Turned—and went To sleep."

She does not explain how the poems got from the cemetery to the hedge, and why we may never know for sure,[37] as we may never know whether she was being indomitably brave or merely crabby.

What we do know is that these poems, along with a number of her other poems,[38] document a heretofore unguessed-at Martian invasion. Poems 186B and 272?, therefore, should be reassigned to the Very Late or Deconstructionist Period, not only to give them their proper place as Dickinson's last and most significant poems, but also so that the full symbolism intended by Dickinson can be seen in their titles. The properly placed poems will be Numbers 1775 and 1776, respectively, a clear Dickinsonian reference to the Fourth of July[39] and to the second Independence Day she brought about by banishing[40] the Martians from Amherst.

NOTE: It is unfortunate that Wells didn't know about the deadly effect of near-rhymes. He could have grabbed a copy of the *Poems*, taken it to the landing pit, read a few choice lines of "The Bustle in a House," and saved everybody a lot of trouble.

Connie Willis has won six Nebula and Six Hugo Awards (more than any other science fiction writer) and the John W. Campbell Memorial Award for her first novel, *Lincoln's Dreams*. Her novel *Doomsday Book* won both the Nebula and Hugo Awards, and her first short-story collection, *Fire Watch*, was a *New York Times* Notable Book. Connie was born on December 31, 1945, in Denver, Colorado. She married physicist Courtney Willis in 1967, and has one daughter, Cordelia. They live in Greeley, Colorado.

---

[37] For an intriguing possibility, see "The Literary Litterbug: Emily Dickinson's Note-Dropping as a Response to Thoreau's Environmentalism," P. Walden, *Transcendentalist Review*, 1990.

[38] Number 187's "awful rivet" is clearly a reference to the Martian cylinder. Number 258's "There's a certain slant of light" echoes Wells' "blinding glare of green light," and its "affliction / Sent us of the air" obviously refers to the landing. Such allusions indicate that as many as fifty-five* of the poems were written at a later date than originally supposed, that and the entire chronology and numbering system of the poems needs to be considered.

*Significantly enough, the age Emily Dickinson was when she died.

[39] A holiday Dickinson did not celebrate because of its social nature, although she was spotted in 1881 lighting a cherry bomb on Mabel Dodd's porch and running away.*

*Which may be why the Martians' landing attracted so little attention. The Amherstodes may have assumed it was Em up to her old tricks again.

[40] There is compelling evidence that the Martians, thwarted in New England, went to Long Island. This theory will be the subject of my next paper,* "Green Light at the End of Daisy's Dock: Evidence of Martian Invasion in F. Scott Fitzgerald's *The Great Gatsby*."

*I'm up for tenure.